OLD SCHOOL INDIAN

OLD SCHOOL INDIAN

A NOVEL

AARON JOHN CURTIS

HILLMAN GRAD BOOKS

A zando IMPRINT

Copyright © 2025 by Aaron John Curtis

Zando supports the right to free expression and the value of copyright. The purpose of copyright is to encourage writers and artists to produce the creative works that enrich our culture. Thank you for buying an authorized edition of this book and for complying with copyright laws by not reproducing, scanning, uploading, or distributing this book or any part of it without permission. If you would like permission to use material from the book (other than for brief quotations embodied in reviews), please contact connect@zandoprojects.com.

Hillman Grad Books is an imprint of Zando.
zandoprojects.com

First Edition: May 2025

Text design by Neuwirth & Associates, Inc.
Cover design by Emily Mahon

Layli Long Soldier, excerpt from "38" from *WHEREAS*. Copyright © 2017 by Layli Long Soldier. Reprinted with the permission of The Permissions Company LLC on behalf of Graywolf Press, Minneapolis, Minnesota, graywolfpress.org.

Quote from Hanif Abdurraqib's *They Can't Kill Us Until They Kill Us* reprinted by kind permission of Eric Obenauf and Two Dollar Radio.

Anthony Gary Dworkin and Rosalind J. Dworkin's *The Minority Report: An Introduction to Racial, Ethnic, and Gender Relations* quoted by permission of Cengage Learning.

The publisher does not have control over and is not responsible for author or other third-party websites (or their content).

Library of Congress Control Number: 2024949496

978-1-63893-145-4 (Hardcover)
978-1-63893-146-1 (ebook)

10   9   8   7   6   5   4   3   2   1
Manufactured in the United States of America

FOR MY FAMILY

The achievement levels of American Indians are among the lowest of all racial groups in the United States.

—Anthony Gary Dworkin and Rosalind J. Dworkin,
*The Minority Report: An Introduction to Racial,
Ethnic, and Gender Relations*

If we don't write our own stories, there is someone else waiting to do it for us.

—Hanif Abdurraqib,
They Can't Kill Us Until They Kill Us

Everything is in the language we use.

—Layli Long Soldier, "38"

A NOTE FROM
DOMINICK DEER WOODS

Coming up, you're gonna see the word "Tóta" a bunch of times. When you do, please know it's not some cutism like Nana or Gammy or Pop-Pop; it's the Mohawk word—or rather, the Kanien'kéha word—for "grandparent." No particular gender because we're all evolved and shit, innit. Kanien'kéha won't be italicized because it's not a foreign language (although I hear we're calling that practice linguistic gatekeeping nowadays, which feels right to me); it's one of this land's many original languages.

I don't much care how you read the Kanien'kéha words you encounter here (I'm sure my own butchering of the language amuses my ancestors to no end), but I've included this note because I want you to get Tóta right. I've got my reasons. Foremost—while I'm snuggled up in bed trying to dream, your mispronunciation will sound in my skull like a woodpecker drumming. So let's learn one word in Mohawk, hey? It'll bring us closer together, I promise.

First off, the t's in Tóta are like the one in Tao; they sound like d's. Think Taoism (Daoism) when you read Tóta (Doda) and you're off to a great start. Next, the first syllable sounds like French for "two"—deux, and the second sounds like German for "yes"—da. Put them together with the emphasis on the first syllable and you have

DEUX-da, or Tóta. Great job! And you thought learning Mohawk would be hard.

If you want to go next level and sound Native, then don't get too en français with that "deux." You're not on the trip of a lifetime to Paris trying to blend in, you're in high school French and you don't want your classmates to mock you for trying too hard. I'm saying, use a lazy deux, not Édith Piaf's deux.

If all this is too much, then rent the movie *Frozen River*, skip to seventy-seven minutes in, and listen to Lila Littlewolf speak the line, "Say goodbye to your Tóta." Or I don't know, find the clip on YouTube if you're in such a damn hurry.

While I'm chinning, I'd like to point out you'll see the word "Indian" in this text about as often as you'll find Native, Mohawk, Kanien'kehá:ka, First Nations, NDN, or Indigenous. If you find "Indian" jarring the first time you come across it, please keep going. I promise we'll gut that particular fish later.

When the Turtle collapses, the world ends.

OLD SCHOOL INDIAN

One

be stands on the shaggy living room rug of his great uncle's trailer, shoes off, stripped to the waist. The coffee table has been pushed aside to make room, but Abe still feels like he could reach out and touch both wood-paneled walls. There's a record player on top of an audio cabinet in one corner with extra records leaning against the side. A tall bookcase to the left of the hallway, which leads back to the bathroom and bedroom, overflows with mass-market thrillers. Books which Abe, after years as a bookseller, thinks of as "dreaming-up-new-and-interesting-ways-to-kill-people" lit on a generous day, or "dick lit" when he's feeling especially judgy (which hasn't stopped him from enjoying the genre himself from time to time). With the curtains drawn, the only light comes from the cloudy fluorescent drop ceiling in Budge's kitchen. A small wood-burning stove sits in the middle of the fading linoleum, propped up on loose bricks. Abe assumes it was lit the night before, because it's still putting off warmth.

"Here, get comfy." Uncle Budge pulls two of the cushions from the seat of his couch. He passes one to Abe before dropping the second one on the floor by his own feet. Abe's heart starts beating fast. It's what he's here for after all, some sort of massage, but now that it's about to happen, he finds the idea of an Elder touching him a little creepy. Abe sees a dusty outline of crumbs and stray hairs where the cushions were, a scattering of coins in the empty space. Beneath the pleasant smell of the wood stove, Abe can make out artificial lemon and, even more faintly, bleach, so he knows parts of the trailer are clean. But it's likely been a good long while since his great uncle has plugged in a vacuum. Abe is probably standing on chip crumbles, half-moons of toenails, and who the hell knows what else. He drops the couch cushion down and sits on it, crossing his legs to keep his feet off the rug. His Great Uncle Budge eases into a kneeling position on his own cushion, releasing a fart in the process.

"Oop, barking spider," Budge says, chuckling to himself. Budge is supposed to be what, the Rez holy man? It's 2016; Mohawks are more interested in tourist dollars than spirituality. But don't worry, here comes leathery-skinned, barrel-chested, big-bellied Budge Billings to smite colonialism with his healing hands.

His hair is right—iron-gray streaked with black, twirling down his chest in twin braids—but let's talk about his outfit. Heavy white socks that have quit on him and balled around his ankles, jeans worn to the colorlessness of an overcast sky, and a faded black t-shirt depicting four pot-bellied naked dudes standing in profile. "The Butthole Surfers: brown reason to live," the shirt reads. While Abe is not familiar with the Butthole Surfers' oeuvre, he's fairly sure a Mohawk healer shouldn't be wearing one of their album covers. But even if you put him in buckskin leggings and a three-feather headband, Budge would be too cheerful. He should look put-upon, desolated by all the pain he encounters, reserved and stoic.

Looking at the picture of four flaccid penises stretched over Budge Billings's belly, Abe wishes he had never come back to Ahkwesáhsne. If Rheumatologist Weisberg hadn't canceled his appointment the day before he was supposed to finally get a diagnosis, Abe would probably still be in Miami, trying to decide which Halloween parties to attend. He'd spent months watching the flesh on his shins and calves rot. First red dots appeared that became clusters of purple-black holes, then the holes had widened, bled together, and become jagged divots the size of quarters, filled with black-red muck that never heals—"lesions" in medical jargon. Pale, waxy flesh edges the lesions, and the surrounding skin is rashy and marked with maroon streaks. The antibiotic ointments and pills he's been taking since summer have affected the shape of the wounds, but nothing has closed them or stopped them from multiplying. His eyes burn, too, and exhaustion takes him at odd times of the day. Pain randomly shoots through his limbs, digs into his torso, and grinds inside his joints. Doctors can't distinguish between side effects of the heavy antibiotics and whatever else is wrong. He's had dozens of blood tests, several biopsies, and contrast imaging of his internal organs. Just last week, a neurologist electrocuted Abe's hands in an attempt to map numb spots in his fingers and knuckles, the most recent symptom. All these tests, and doctors still can't tell Abe what's chewing holes in his skin, where the pain is coming from, nor what infection or disease he might have. He'll panic if he gives all these questions too much thought, so Abe doesn't. Instead, he locks the panic and anxiety away from his conscious mind and barrels through his days. But the physical symptoms are undeniable, impossible to escape or ignore.

As he's sitting cross-legged on Uncle Budge's couch cushion, Abe's knees bounce. His jaw clenches and unclenches. He can hear his own breathing, shallow puffs coming from his nose that make him sound like a bull. Night sweats have come for him during the day. Abe thinks the doctors should know whether his overheating is a side effect or a symptom, but they don't.

Uncle Budge rests a hand on Abe's shoulder, the other over Abe's knee. Gently, the old man begins to probe.

"What is that?" Abe asks slowly, because Budge's touch feels strange. Not like an electric charge, not a mother's comfort or a lover's caress, but somewhere the three feelings intersect. You know the face a baby makes the first time she eats cake? Budge's touch makes Abe want to make that face.

"Some people say touchin' me is like leanin' against a transformer." Budge isn't bragging. His voice is flat, matter-of-fact.

"Is that so?"

"Jus' what I heard." Budge's fingers explore Abe's back, shoulder, and thigh, manipulating his skin more than massaging the muscle beneath. "Also been told bein' near me is like bein' next to a stream."

"Bullshit." In Abe's head it sounded okay, the answer he'd give if Budge said, *I can do a backflip*. Laughing it off, waiting for the punchline. Aloud in the quiet trailer, the two syllables sound like he's spitting poison. "I'm sorry, Uncle Budge."

"S'okay, kid."

At forty-three years old, Abe relishes being called "kid." Like he has all the time in the world. But Abe's been through four rounds of testing, and that's if you don't count the two sets of biopsies and the mini cattle prod; he feels the decades ahead dwindling to months.

"We're close," Dermatologist Unger had promised. Apparently if your insurance is shit, then your pathologist is shit. The one covered by Abe's indie bookstore had repeatedly called his biopsies "inconclusive," so Unger had decided to cut Abe again and use the lab at the University of Miami. "When you get the bill, bring it to my office," she'd said. Part of Abe was flattered that a doctor was interested enough in him to pay for his care. A larger part of him found the implications terrifying.

After what would hopefully be his final biopsy, Unger had prescribed a megadose of steroids and reiterated the command she'd given him the first time they'd met: stay off the internet. Abe had never listened. After each appointment, he'd googled everything he could recall: idiopathic and putrefacient flesh and necrotic tissue and great pretender. Searches that keyed off more terms he'd filed away and forgotten: maculopapular rash, pyoderma, vasculitis, gangrenosum. Taken together, the internet promised Abe any number of grim, painful deaths. Speculating turned his thoughts into rodents skittering inside his skull.

When Rheumatologist Weisberg's office called to confirm Abe's appointment—the day before the torment of not knowing was due to end—it turned out they'd scheduled him to come in on Yom Kippur.

"Obviously, the doctor can't see you tomorrow." The secretary's tone was brusque. Abe wanted it to be conciliatory; he didn't choose the date, after all. "The next available appointment is October thirty-first."

"That's three weeks from now." His vision turned red and his heart pounded in his ears. Dr. Unger had warned him such a high dose of steroids would make him "crazy," but the phone call with the rheumatologist's office was his first experience. *Three weeks*, he thought, *three goddamn weeks*. The anger didn't build, it boomed. "I realize being Jewish doesn't automatically mean Dr. Weisberg observes Yom Kippur, but shouldn't you have known one way or the other when you scheduled the appointment? They took the biopsy two weeks ago. You could have called me at any point. I've been waiting months for an answer. Any kind of answer. I was ready for a diagnosis tomorrow. Do you even care? Are you even sorry at all?" Abe's not sure how much stayed in his head and how much he unloaded on the poor receptionist.

"Would you like me to rebook the appointment, sir?"

After decades in retail, Abe recognized the don't-make-your-shitty-mood-my-problem tone, reserved for customers who inflicted their bad day on service workers just because they could. Hearing the secretary's condescendingly patient tone, Abe felt like his pulse would rip through his throat, burst from his temples.

"I'll take the appointment," he said through gritted teeth, "thank you so much, you've been very helpful." As soon as he hung up, Abe grabbed the closest thing at hand—a bullet thermos of coffee he'd just brewed—and threw it across the living room. Abe heard it shatter inside, becoming a slurry of coffee and bits of ceramic. Thankfully, his wife had already left for work.

When he arrived at his job, Abe had tried to run a sales report four times, messed it up four times, and finally clocked out in disgust. He'd left and called his boss, who wasn't surprised when he asked for time off. Despite the heat, Abe had taken to wearing long pants to cover his bandages, but the doctor visits had been impossible to hide.

"Take all the time you need, kiddo," his boss said, his low-key, basso profundo voice soothing. Abe flew from Miami to Ahkwesáhsne shortly afterward, for reasons we'll get into later. For now, I don't want to lose sight of Budge.

Abe had first met his great uncle a decade ago, at Tóta's funeral. The front room of the Jacobs' family home had become a makeshift funeral parlor, cleared out and crammed with folding chairs, every horizontal surface covered with framed photographs and vases of flowers. Where the couch should have been, Tóta's body lay in a plain pine coffin. The lid was open, her body covered by one of her award-winning quilts.

The crowd of family and community grew and shrank over the nine days of ceremonial grieving. At one point Abe's sister had nodded her chin across the kitchen, toward a small group of men standing in a cheery cluster, their flannels and denim crisply ironed. Abe's sister said the one in the green flannel was Tóta's younger brother, "the healer."

The other men were bent with laughter as the man in green flannel held forth, collar digging into his bull neck, looking like it cost him oxygen to keep buttoned all the way up.

Abe had given his sister a dubious look. "How come I've never heard of him?"

"He's a Billings," Sis answered. "You know."

Abe grunted. He did know. Now the difference between Catholic and Methodist is roughly equivalent to the difference between

Mocha Fudge Chunk and Rocky Road, but in 1933, the Billings, Tóta's Methodist family, disowned her for marrying a Catholic. What can I say? Missionaries worked hard to assimilate us; we took white folk's religion seriously. On first glance, Abe didn't appreciate Budge joking around with his sister's dead body a couple rooms over. He'd shaken the man's hand but couldn't recall speaking with him.

Summertime Abe would've scoffed at the idea of a healing from his great uncle. When Abe's mom suggested it upon his return, Autumn Abe was desperate enough to acquiesce.

"Breathe, kid. Not from here." Budge puts a calloused hand on Abe's chest, then moves it to his stomach. "From here. You get me?"

Budge's clinical tone makes his touch less uncomfortable. At first, Abe doesn't know what Budge means. His breath still comes too fast. His face is flushed. He feels like he might burst into tears, or hyperventilate and pass out.

"Don' do that," Budge says.

"Do what?"

Budge's eyes go wide, and his lips turn down; he scrunches his shoulders together and pulls his head back, looking like a frightened turtle. Abe snorts a laugh.

"Better." Budge pushes against Abe's stomach. "You feel where that came from?"

Abe nods. He makes an effort to breathe into Budge's palm.

"That's more like it."

Abe's heartbeat slows. Sweat stops rolling down his face. As his breathing calms, it becomes almost mediative.

"Shit, Uncle Budge, maybe you are a stream."

Budge smiles wide enough to show the gaps on either side of his mouth. He sits back on his haunches and moves the couch cushion in front of Abe, then scoots over and kneels on it.

"Ain' gonna say I toldja so." When Budge Billings was born, Kanien'kéha was the main language on the Rez, but putting his accent on the page exactly as it sounds looks ridiculous—does for those, den for then. Hopefully you're getting just enough to remind you these are not the words Budge's tongue was made to speak.

His great uncle's hands cover Abe's own, then move up his arms to his shoulders and neck. His fingers play up and down the base of Abe's skull, making his head bob.

"Whad'ya wanna get outta this?"

Abe frowns. Is he supposed to say, *Cure me*, right out loud like that? *Take those calloused palms and rub them down my shins and calves. Stop the oozing and itching. Wipe the rotting flesh away like we rubbed glue from our fingers when we were kids in art class. Smooth the holes over like wet clay. Reach into my joints and muscles and stop their throbbing. Hold my hands and bring the dead nerve endings back to life, and while you're at it, pull out my internal organs and give them a good once over, make sure the rot hasn't traveled.*

"Abe, stay with me. What d'you want?"

"I . . . I want to live."

"In my expert opinion"—Budge gently rests a thumb on the pulse at Abe's throat—"you're alive right now."

Abe sighs. He has an uncle on his father's side who lost an arm working construction and had been called Lefty ever since. Abe's dad loved to ask Lefty how relearning to jerk off with the wrong hand was going. If Lefty was an asshole, we would have figured he had it coming. Since Lefty was a good guy, we figured he'd lost one arm so he wouldn't lose both, or lose his son, or lose his life.

"Uncle Budge, what's the Mohawk word for 'pity'?" Abe regrets the question immediately. Budge was born speaking Kanien'kéha, but Abe knows plenty of old folks who never recovered the language after teachers beat it out of them in grade school, including his own parents. If Budge doesn't speak Kanien'kéha then Abe's question might make him feel like he's not Indian enough, even though he's more Indian than Abe will ever be.

■   ■   ■

said I'd gut that fish later—the fish being the word "Indian"—so I guess later is now. Abe is Mohawk Indian. You could argue Indian is a misnomer and you'd be right. I could argue no one asked us when they decided we should be called Native American and I'd be right. Somewhere in the eighties, non-rez folks decided "Indians" was wrong at best and offensive at worst, so they let everyone— including us—know we should be called "Native Americans." Maybe call Abe that. You shouldn't call him Indian. Sorry, but you don't know Abe like that. It sounds weird coming from your lips, dismissive in some way. In fact, I'm not sorry. And don't call him Native American, either. It's a bullshit PC phrase no matter who's using it, just a way of saying you don't know any Native people. How about you call him Abraham Jacobs, since that's his name? Abraham Jacobs might not sound like an "Indian" name, but you've got the hardcore Catholic first name and the surname of what used to be the biggest landowners on Ahkwesáhsne. So if you're in the know, then you know the name Abraham Jacobs is rez as hell, cuz.

Shit, you want to talk misnomers, then let's talk Mohawk. In the sixteenth century, bridging a language gap didn't happen one-to-one. A translator somewhere spoke a common tongue with another translator somewhere else. So translator number one (let's call him Burt) translated the first language (let's say Kanien'kéha) into the shared language (usually French). Then translator number two (we'll say Ernie) translated the translation into the second shared language. So Burt did Kanien'kéha into French, then Ernie did French into English. And that's if you were lucky. More often, you had to mix and match between three and four translators like a half-assed game of Rummikub (or keeping the bridge metaphor, a bunch of stepping stones that had to fit together just right). In the Indigenous understanding of life, this is a wonderful opportunity to spend time getting to know one another. To the settler's mind, this is an incredible waste of time, which could be better spent gaining wealth and status. Is it any wonder settlers stopped talking and started shooting?

Anyway, "Mohawk" is the garbled French version of an Algonquin word. Whether you're talking to the Narragansetts of Rhode Island who called us Mohowawogs ("man-eaters") or the Lenape of the Unami Delaware who called us Muhuweyck ("cannibal monsters"), they're telling you we ate people. We called ourselves Kanien'kehá:ka, "People of the Flint." Flint might be brittle but it's also a thousand times sharper than surgical steel and never loses its edge. Being experts in that weaponry made us fierce indeed—we did most of the fighting for the Six Nations—so perhaps Mohawk is a metaphor. Or maybe Mohawks really did rip the beating hearts from their enemies' chests on the battlefield and eat them raw, like a book Abe pulled from the school library in third grade claimed. Seems like a practical thing to do, innit? Particularly for a people so bad at war, that, in the words of Benjamin Franklin (enslaver, abolitionist, and hypocritical intellectual), we might "labor at it for seven years and only take seven lives." Stupid, primitive us, not trying to obliterate everyone we met.

But doesn't "man-eating cannibal monsters" sound like sour grapes from a rival nation? The Algonquin and the Hotinonshón:ni hated each other, is what I'm saying. Although "hate" might be a strong term from a settler perspective. "Rivalry" is probably closer. If we killed someone during a skirmish over our shared borders, the accident brought the Nations closer together through atonement ceremonies. Just ask Ben Franklin.

If you go by maps, and English, or if you ask a white dude, then Abe is a Mohawk Indian from the Saint Regis Tribe, part of the Six Nations Iroquois Confederacy. Ask a traditional dude, she'll say Abe is Kanien'kehá:ka from Ahkwesáhsne, of the Hotinonshón:ni.

That's People of the Flint, from Where the Partridge Drums, of the People Who Build, if you're keeping score. I've got just enough Kanien'kéha to define the names for you but not enough to string them into a sentence.

For some reason, I don't think we're establishing anything other than a lot of confusion around Native identity. Which is the point, so we're cool. Now you can call Abe "Indian" because we both know it's a shorthand for something neither of us has time to get into. You can call Abe Indian because you know it's not him.

If I told you our names for the Narragansetts and the Lenape, you could never unhear them. Thinking of those words while you ate would make every morsel taste rotten. Those words would desiccate your laughter. You'd be having sex and the words would flash through your mind, scaring off your orgasm. I can't do that to you, so I'll keep those names to myself. That's a joke. Truth is, I can't tell you the Kanien'kéha words for the Nations who shared this portion of Turtle Island with us. Like I said, Catholic schools beat the language from us decades ago. Unless you're actively involved in language preservation, most of us could barely say hello if the situation called for it . . . but everyone speaks English on the Rez these days, so what situation might that be? Probably two folks Budge's age, catching up in their childhood tongue, turning time into poetry.

Asking Budge the Mohawk word for "pity" felt like asking Tóta; it popped out of Abe's mouth before he considered his great uncle was likely a victim of state-sponsored violence. Budge may be a charlatan, but Abe still doesn't want to hurt the man.

"Ratihnará:ken," Budge says without missing a beat, surprising another laugh out of Abe. This is one of the few Mohawk words he actually knows. It means "people of the place where their skin is white," one of our terms for a white person.

"Keep laughin', kid. That's good Medicine." Budge asks Abe to straighten his legs. He moves his hands to Abe's feet, digging his fingers deep. It's the first time he's actually massaged Abe, and it feels amazing. Squares of stained gauze peek out from the bottom of Abe's pants. "Seeing those, it's weird how little pain is in your feet."

Abe nods, blowing frustrated air from his lips. It would be so much easier to dismiss him if Budge's tone wasn't so dry. Abe wants his uncle to proclaim, Abe wants him to chant, Abe wants to hear a healing song so he can do a mental eye roll, wait for the time to be up, then go home and give his family shit for dropping him off at this old trailer in the first place.

Not a healer, just observant, Abe thinks. Abe's knuckles are red, swollen. Obviously inflamed somehow, but numb instead of painful. His feet, on the other hand, look normal.

"What is it you want, Abe?"

No amount of shifting his body can make him comfortable, but Abe shifts anyway. He runs his thumbs over his fingertips, brushing the edges of the numb areas. "Mild neuropathy," the neurologist called it. Those little patches he can't feel on his fingers and hands, like parts of him have been scooped away, negate the appellation "mild." Consulting Dr. Google gave him more symptoms to look forward to. How long before the seizures and strokes? When could he expect vascular dementia to begin?

Abe swallows the lump that's formed in his throat.

"I don't want to lose my mind," he whispers.

Budge's hands go still.

"That's a strong answer."

Again, Budge enfolds one of Abe's hands in both of his own. Budge's hands are amber gold to Abe's sun-kissed walnut. Budge's hands tell the story of catch-as-can labor and poor skincare on a reservation that straddles the border between New York and Canada. Abe's have lifted stacks of books and punched keypads at Miami's largest independent bookstore, moisturized by monoï oil. Budge's hands are thick, creased with age and scarred. Abe's are lithe, and— apart from his red knuckles—handsome. Abe feels like his great uncle is somehow reading everything he's done since leaving the reservation, the good and the bad, tracing his path in wrinkles of skin. He might also be probing the numb spots, but that's likely Abe's imagination.

"I was a drunk, you know," Budge says.

Abe nods. He's heard.

Budge nods as well. Teierihwenhawíhtha is big on the Rez. It means, more or less, "This is what people are saying, but is it really so?" Gossip, if you have to nail it down like that. But gossip is a toad-like creature slinking herky-jerky through muck, while Teierihwenhawíhtha is a singsong wind rustling through tree limbs. Now doesn't Teierihwenhawíhtha sound nicer than gossip?

"When I was in seventh grade, my dad died," Budge says. "Your Tóta was already outta th'house by then, with family of her own. Priscilla was away at college. Only me, Maggie, an' my mom livin' there. You remember Priscilla an' Maggie, right? From your Tóta's funeral?"

Abe nods.

"Sure you do. Anyway, before a year goes by, this man Roger, he's our stepdad. Roger, he . . . touched Maggie you know? He'd come for her at night, two, three times a week. My sister an' I slept in the same room. I had to lie in the dark an' listen while he took little pieces of her soul. Before he left the room, he'd come sit on my bed. 'Hey, Budgie—you awake?'"

Abe has never met Roger, never heard his voice, but when Budge whispers, every hair on Abe's body stands at attention.

"'Listen to me, Budgie. You ever tell anyone, ever, and I'll fucking kill you. But I'll kill that little bitch first. I'll kill her and make you watch.'" Budge wipes tears from his eyes, then speaks to himself in a low voice, "I'm tellin', Roger. How about that, you son of a bitch?" He stops speaking for a few long moments. When he resumes exploring Abe's hand, Budge's fingers are rubbery with moisture. "I guess I should be glad Roger didn't like little boys, too," he finally says in his matter-of-fact tone. "When he left the room, Maggie came over to my bed, an' I'd hold her. Sometime, if she din't come to me first, I'd go to her. I'd hold her while her tears soaked my pajamas. I rocked her to sleep."

Budge is still for a moment. He clears his throat, prodding Abe's fingers, palm, and wrist. "Maggie drinks maybe more'n she should but she seems to be ridin' it okay. She's got a husband, sons, grandsons. She's okay. But when she wa'n't, she had me. She told me the only reason she survived growin' up in that house was because a me. She even forgave me for doin' nothin'. But I couldn't forgive myself. Sober hurt, so I stopped doin' it. Musta been oh . . . fourteen or thereabouts."

Abe's throat feels thick with the story. He doesn't want to speak but feels he has to. "You were just a kid, Uncle Budge," he manages to say.

"Sure." By Budge's tone, he might be agreeing the earth is flat—not because he believes it, but because it's not worth arguing with someone who'd believe something so foolish. He lowers the hand he's massaging to the rug, then lifts Abe's other one.

"I think because of what happened with Roger, I got more leeway than some others. People thought I jus' needed time. That cost me, what? Forty years? Then your Tóta pulled me aside n' asked how long I was gonna hide."

"Tóta?"

"Akhtsí:a." My older sister, Budge agrees. More than anything, this offhand lapse into Kanien'kéha makes Abe think Budge might really be one of the last fluent speakers alive, living history sitting right in front of him, wearing a be-penised band t-shirt. Every time Abe heard the language in conversation, Tóta had been one of the speakers. She'd taught him most of the phrases he knew, she'd given him a name when he was born, as the eldest woman in the Turtle Clan has named every Mohawk child since the first Nine Clan Mothers returned from the forest, stood before the Creator, and . . .

Look, I'm uncomfortable with how Native that came out. Even though it's true, it feels like a performance of Indigenousness. If sociologists want to know what it feels like to be Native in America, that about sums it up.

"Your Tóta was old enough to be my mother, so her words hit me hard. She told me I had somethin' inside that other people needed. Said even though I kept tryin' to drown it, she could hear it callin'. She told me there wa'n't a lot of what I had left in the world, and there was a special place waitin' for me in hell if I din't start honoring it.

"It's not like I poured all my liquor out that day and never bought another bottle. But your Tóta, she started me down the path."

Path to what? Abe wonders. *Being a Rez stray, grubbing odd jobs for money?*

"Fuckin' healer, my ass," Budge mutters, as if reading Abe's mind. The old man's tears are back, but he doesn't drop Abe's hand this time. He twists his head side to side, using his shoulders to wipe the tears away, leaving dark spots on the faded fabric. "I couldn't heal Maggie's pain. Couldn't heal mine. You sure you're into this, kid?"

Abe doesn't know how to answer.

Tóta's exact age was a mystery. Her birth certificate from the Mohawk Council of Chiefs lists 1911 as the year she was born, while her Saint Regis Tribal Council birth certificate says 1912 and her New York State birth certificate says 1913. Whether she was ninety-three, ninety-four, or ninety-five when she died, Abe's Tóta enjoyed a nice span of years. She lived well. She died loved. She danced her last at Thanksgiving, two laps around a bonfire surrounded by family. Five months later, she died. I can't leave Tóta lying in a box of unfinished pine in Abe's childhood home, so to honor her strength, here's a Tóta story.

It was 1955. Forty-something Tóta had three teenage girls, two infants who died before their first birthdays, three boys under the age of ten, and an ironworker husband who lived most of the year on the road. On a shopping excursion with the whole brood, Tóta stopped to speak with a woman we'll call Helen Finley.

The full story is lost because the children cared little for grown-up talk. We have the woman's name because the siblings agree that before Tóta walked away from the encounter, she said, "Never talk about my family again, Helen Finley." But whatever the specific offense against the Jacobs name may have been, they can't say. They just remember the grown-up talk stopping. In the silence, Tóta gathered her children behind her, folded her right hand into a fist, and delivered a single blow that sent Helen Finley flying.

From this story a family joke was born: "How did the lady cross the room? Tóta punched her there." More than a joke, it also became a family rallying cry. Abe's first year of college, he was one of twelve students in an accelerated program which allowed them to take extra credits without paying extra money. In addition to the heavy course load, he worked four jobs to pay for everything scholarships didn't cover. Eating once a day, sleeping three hours a night, twenty pounds lighter, with no idea how much longer he could keep up the pace, Abe had called home and vented. Mom made conciliatory noises in all the right places. When Abe fell silent, Mom said, "Tóta Punch."

Almost two decades after Helen Finley felt the might of the Tóta Punch, Abe was born and Tóta gave him an Indian name. Don't get the idea everyone you meet from one of the thousand First Nations in the US has an "Indian name" different from the postcolonial name they offer you. The Jacobs are Mohawks of the Turtle Clan. Tóta was the oldest woman in the Turtle Clan. The naming ceremony is one of our traditions.

Aunt Maisy is the oldest of the three Jacobs sisters. Tóta's death made Aunt Maisy—the tallest sister, as befits corn, and the loudest, as befits a Mohawk woman—the new matriarch. The nuns at the Saint Lawrence Catholic School had taken Kanien'kéha from Maisy when she was eight years old. At Tóta's funeral, Abe realized future generations of his family might not have Indian names. His nephew Rowi—Sis's younger son—took classes and spoke more Mohawk than any of them. Maybe the naming ceremony would fall to the youngest male. It could happen. There's no written history of Mohawk spiritual tradition; you live it, rather than follow it.

Had he been born in a different time, Abe might have earned many names. Talking too fast when he got excited might have garnered him the name Tehawenná:sere', "his words are on top of each other." Leaving for college might have led to his family calling him Aronhiakeh:te, "he is carrying the sky on his back." But he only has the one he was given as a baby, which traditionally should've been a placeholder until he started becoming himself. I can't tell you Abe's one Indian name. Even though it's a placeholder, he keeps it in his heart.

POINTS DEDUCTED FOR GENOCIDE

by Dominick Deer Woods

In third grade Teacher
encouraged us to unearth
rare words for extra credit.

Teacher vetted the vocabulary.
Teacher presented worthy words
to the class.

I pulled the Mohawk dictionary
off my parents' bookshelf
and searched for the longest word ever written.
Ionterahkwawehrhohstáhkhwa means umbrella.
I asked Tóta to repeat it
until she tired of my pestering.
Armed with pronunciation
I brought the Mohawk word for umbrella
to third grade.

"Umbrella is not a rare word," Teacher said.
"Ionterahkwawehrhohstáhkhwa is," I said.
"Foreign languages aren't allowed," Teacher said.
"On this land English is the foreign language," I said.
Teacher's lips quirked.
"Kanien'kéha

Mohawk
was here first," I said.
Teacher frowned.
"What does it mean?" Teacher asked.
"It means umbrella," I said.
"Yes, but what is the literal meaning?"
"It means umbrella," I said, setting my jaw.

Teacher let me write
the Mohawk work for umbrella
on the board
where it loomed for a week.

Next test
the Mohawk word for umbrella
had become chalk dust
extra credit for any eight-year-old.

I spelled Ionterahkwawehrhohstáhkhwa precisely
down to the acute accent over the third a.

Teacher slashed
a red line
through my answer.

"The definition of Ionterahkwawehrhohstáhkhwa is
'open and stand underneath to keep dry,'" Teacher said.
We memorized and forgot
while Teacher learned.

Teacher smirked.
What Teacher's smirk taught me
I cannot say.

I showed Teacher
the mask I wore
to school.
You can't hurt me
     you can't hurt me
          you can't hurt me
the mask said.

Two

be's massage—or whatever you'd call it—is done. His black
t-shirt and navy-blue Tommy Hilfiger button-down are
back on, along with his thick up-North socks and black Doc
Martens. As Budge ushers him out the trailer door, Abe wonders if
his uncle is on a schedule, if there are more "clients" coming today.

The three steps from Budge's door to the lawn have no handrail.
The metal steps are studded for a better grip, but Budge takes them
carefully, in deference to his age. Budge has at least twenty-five,
maybe as many as thirty years on him, but Abe follows in kind.
Lately, his thighs have felt weak. Side effects of the medication? A
sign his mystery illness is attacking his nerves, his muscles?

Dermatologist Unger, a zaftig Teutonic femme fatale from some
old black-and-white movie, and Rheumatologist Weisberg, who is
small, loud, and whippet-thin, live in the same high-rise on Key
Biscayne. They've bonded over Abe's case. They'll get together for
dinner, then call Abe around nine, ten o'clock at night to pepper him
with questions about his symptoms—Unger on the phone, sounding like she was a few glasses of wine deep, Weisberg yelling in the
background. Didn't matter that much of it was redundant to his

biweekly visits; they had a mystery to solve. The nightly calls made Abe feel like part of the team.

Once Weisberg canceled the appointment where Abe was supposed to get his diagnosis, both doctors went radio silent. Abe presumes the pathologist at the University of Miami had gotten an answer and shared the diagnosis with them. Abe? He's just the guy with the rotting skin who panicked and fled his wife, friends, and job in Miami. Why should he need to know what's going on? It's just his sanity. A different person might have called their cell phones and offices nonstop, demanding answers. However, I mentioned Abe's steroid-induced blowup at the secretary because it was so out of character; it didn't even occur to him to advocate for himself. Abe thinks he's too introverted to muster the gumption for those calls, but I'd say he's a poster child for generational trauma leading to "impaired life skills."

"Shit, it's freezing out here." Abe rubs his hands up and down his arms for warmth.

"It's October," Budge snorts. With his hands in the pockets of his jeans, he looks comfortable in his t-shirt. "What'd they do to you down there in Miami?"

"I guess the sun boiled most of me off," Abe says, hooking a thumb into his belt to show how loose it's gotten.

"There's still a lotta good stuff left," Budge says. He grabs Abe's shoulders, pulling them face-to-face. Abe wonders if his great uncle has shrunk with age; at five ten, he's likely the shortest man in the family. Budge's tone turns serious. "Abe, I think you can be helped." Budge's eyes are as dark as truck stop coffee. A goose walks over the younger man's grave, causing a shiver that has nothing to do with the autumn air.

"Okay," Abe tells his great uncle, keeping his voice as noncommittal as possible. At last, the Elder drops his hands. They turn toward the road, waiting on Budge's daughter, Sharon Oaks, who will drive Abe back to his family home.

■   ■   ■

Abe first met Sharon Oaks a decade ago, another Billings who came to Tóta's funeral ceremony. When Abe left the coffin and made it to the kitchen, he saw Mom, Dad, the aunts, and the uncles sitting at the old Formica table. Sis, who wasn't allowed to smoke in the house, was on the porch out back. A woman he didn't recognize—nearly six feet tall and built like a linebacker—stood monitoring the Corn Soup as it gently burbled in a huge pot. Abe wondered why a stranger was handling such an important task. He also wondered why the pot rested on a plug-in warmer instead of the stove.

Before he could ask, Mom came over to draw him into a hug. They held each other longer than usual but besides that she didn't seem overly upset. Tóta had left palliative hospice six months prior so everyone had been preparing for the end.

"Where's Adam?" Abe asked. His brother lived downstate in Syracuse, working construction and landscaping.

"You beat him here," Dad said. "He's driving."

"Did you say hi to Priscilla and Maggie?" Mom asked.

Hearing their names, Abe remembered the vaguely familiar pair he'd seen in the living room, two great aunts on the Billings side he met for the first time when Tóta was in hospice. Tóta'd had a minor heart episode and walking pneumonia. Testing determined none of her internal systems were functioning correctly. Since she wouldn't survive surgery, doctors had told the family to make arrangements. While she was still in hospice care, Abe had taken a long weekend off work to say goodbye.

The hospice had looked like any other hospital, except Tóta had her own room. She'd been losing her hearing for some time. By age ninety-two (or thereabouts, innit) her hearing had degenerated to the point where she couldn't hear any low-pitched sounds, including the majority of men's voices. Whenever a man wanted to communicate with Tóta, he needed a woman to speak for him. Abe's is a matriarchal family from a traditionally equal society. Tóta had to watch toxic Western patriarchal values infect Ahkwesáhsne over the course of nine decades, but she died deaf to men's words. I dig that so much.

Knowing she wouldn't be able to hear him, Abe brought his laptop. Even with the thick glasses, her eyes weren't so great. Abe wrote how happy he was to see her, setting the font so the scant message filled the screen. She read the words and nodded. Abe wrote other things that weekend, and she read them, and the family laughed at her reactions. Before his flight home Monday afternoon, Abe wrote, "I love you." Tóta looked him in the eye and nodded as though she expected nothing less.

Tóta never once used the word "love" with her children. Whenever this fact pained them, the Jacobs liked to remind each other, *There's no Mohawk word for "love."* It's true there's no word for "love" in Kanien'kéha. You'd have to express those feelings your own way, different for each person—maybe even differently every time—to show your family, friends, and partners how special they are. *Time without you scatters my mind over the ground. The blood that flows belongs to you. Speaking with you is cold water on a summer day.* But English gave us "love," so nowadays people rarely make the effort.

Besides Abe, a constant stream of family from across the country came through hospice. The parade of visitors was not lost on Tóta. She waited to ask about her condition until she found herself alone with one of her daughters: Abe's mother, as it happened.

Tóta sat in a chair beside her hospital bed, arm hooked up to fluids spiked with heparin to help blood flow to her heart. She burned through five true-crime paperbacks a week, but she left her current selection over the arm of her chair and tugged on the newspaper Abe's mom was reading.

Mom folded her newspaper down and saw Tóta's gaze, still powerful and lucid.

"Hari," the old woman asked, "am I dying?"

The Jacobs hadn't discussed how they'd tell Tóta her prognosis. If they had, then I'm sure they would have wanted to do it together. But Mom wasn't about to make Tóta wait for an answer.

"Yes," Mom said.

Tóta nodded. She looked down and sighed. Then she gathered herself, sat up, and made three requests. First, she described the dress she wanted to be buried in. Not a problem, as Mom knew the 1940s periwinkle party dress with the little flowers; the one dress Tóta never let any of her daughters borrow (true to form, Tóta refused to explain why).

Second, Tóta said she wanted a plot set aside behind Grace United, the Methodist Church on the Rez. Tóta's husband had died eight years after the Tóta Punch, nine years before Abe was born. As I said, Tóta was a Methodist and Skahiónhati (Abe's grandfather) had been Catholic. Since both churches overlooked the Saint Lawrence River, Skahiónhati had hatched a plan when they married. "They can bury me at Saint Regis and you at Grace United," he'd told Tóta. "After we're dead, I'll meet you at the river."

After forty-five years without her man, the thought of returning to him must have given Tóta renewed energy. Once the plot had been arranged and she'd returned from hospice, Tóta asked Abe's mom to bundle her up and help her out to the bonfire for her last Thanksgiving. Tóta used a walker-chair combo, and she sat beside the flames covered in blankets while the Jacobs sang Christmas carols. They ran through all the obvious suspects, then scoured the recesses of their minds for the lyrics to more, mostly humming to keep the sing-along going.

Then, Mom heard Tóta mutter, "Try it and see." A moment later her voice rang out loudly, singing a song without words. The youngest children laughed, thinking these strange sounds must have been a joke; parents quickly shushed them. When the last note died out, a reverent silence filled the night air. Then the Jacobs began talking over one another: *Did she just—I can't believe she—Tóta sang, can you—?* On the heels of that wonder came another: Tóta stood, threw her blankets onto her walker-chair, and began to dance around the bonfire, singing the entire time. The family joined in. Tóta managed two laps before she collapsed back into her chair and gestured for the family to go on without her. The Jacobs turned it into Indian sprints, going for as long as they could before the feeling of reverence faded. Tóta called it her "parting gift."

The third request Tóta made of Abe's mom in hospice was for a traditional funeral ceremony, one that would finally unite the Billings with the Jacobs. She had often talked about inviting her estranged family for Thanksgiving or a summer barbecue, but it took her death to finally make it happen. One night in April, Tóta insisted on a salt pork dinner. Salt was a big no-no, both for her kidneys and heart. Abe's mom and aunts told her as much.

"You girls listen to me," Tóta had said. "This was my house before youse come along, and it's still my home. I am having salt pork for dinner tonight. You are going to make it for me, and I am going to eat it."

The phantom scent of oranges had been filling Aunt Abby's nose; she quietly told Aunt Maisy to let it go. Aunt Maisy set her jaw, but one look at Aunt Abby's watery gaze softened her.

"Orange peels?" Aunt Maisy's normally shrill voice was subdued. Since they were children, the youngest Jacobs sister had smelled orange peels when someone was going to die.

"All week," Aunt Abby confirmed.

So Tóta, Mom, Aunt Abby, Aunt Maisy, an uncle or two, and a few of Abe's cousins sat down for a salt pork dinner with sides of mashed potatoes and succotash. Comparing notes later, the family realized they'd all noticed Tóta looking around the table, but beyond them. "The house must've been full of shadows," Mom said. Shadows might gather in the edges of your vision when death is near, if you have eyes to see them. Normally, if you look directly at them, then the shadows disappear. The fact that Tóta could look around the dinner table at them like they were simply more guests? No surprise she fell asleep in her favorite chair in front of the TV that night and didn't wake up.

In the Longhouse, when someone dies, the remaining family can't light a fire during the burial ceremony. They have to rely on other families for warmth and nourishment, which ensures they won't grieve alone. During the nine days of Tóta's burial ceremony, this meant the Billings—the family she hadn't seen in years, and whom some of Abe's side had never met—made food at home and brought the dishes to keep the Jacobs and their visitors fed.

Abe didn't know any of this when he saw Sharon Oaks stirring Corn Soup in his family's kitchen (the plug-in hot plate a modern work-around for the prohibition on fire), but he learned as the days went on. Once he made his hellos to his aunts and uncles— who looked red-eyed but stout—Mom gestured to the woman at the stove sporting a thick brush cut. "This is Sharon Oaks. Uncle Budge's daughter."

The large woman gripped Abe's hand solidly. He leaned in and kissed her cheek, as he would a Latin woman. Sharon stiffened in surprise. Abe realized he had to get the Miami out of his system while he was back home, or else risk getting his ass kicked. Stepping back, Abe went through some mental gymnastics, trying to figure how he was related to Sharon Oaks. "What's up, cuz?" she said, making it simple.

"Thanks for taking care of us," Abe said.

Sharon handed him a bowl of Corn Soup with a fried roll on top. "Try it first, thank me later. I made the scones myself."

Abe brought his bowl to the kitchen table. Sharon's scone was something like a fried comma-shaped biscuit, unlike the fry bread at the Cornwall Island Powwow, Ahkwesáhsne's yearly festival, which was either thin and used for tacos, or thick, puffy rounds halved and stuffed for sandwiches. Abe dunked the scone into his first Corn Soup that hadn't been made either by Tóta or using her recipe, and took a huge bite.

"Good, innit?" Sharon asked.

"My mouth just died and went to heaven," Abe replied, making his new cousin grin. Since leaving the Rez, Abe only ate Corn Soup when he visited once a year. He could have made it himself, but it wouldn't have been the same. Sharon's recipe was not the Jacobs', but it still tasted like home.

"You have to be ready next time," Budge tells Abe now, as they wait for Sharon in front of his trailer. Sis drove Abe over. When Sharon picks him up, it will be the first time he's seen her this visit. He's a little nervous. Not only does Sharon still live on the Rez, which makes her Indian-er than Abe, but her side of the family practices Longhouse tradition, so she's doubly Indian-er. Abe hopes to impress Sharon, or at least not embarrass himself.

"Next time, you'll bring a tribute." Budge leans down and pulls an ashtray and a pack of smokes from beneath his bottom stair. "We'll do real work. If you're up for it."

"*Tribute*" huh, Uncle Budge? Abe thinks. *You want that in small denominations, or do you accept personal checks? Then there's the "if you're up for it." Read between the lines and you get, "You have to believe in order for this to work," the motto of faith healers and char-latans the world over.* Abe nods to show he's heard but shrugs at the same time. He slowly exhales through his nose. He scrunches his shoulders into a half cup, trying to contain his warm exhalations of air. He's a kid again, waiting on bus stops in the morning cold. Back then, they'd stand in circles with their heads bowed to keep warm.

Using breath for warmth doesn't work any better now than it did when he was a kid.

"We can wait inside, if you want," Budge says, popping the top of his cigarette pack. There's a paper matchbook from the Bingo Palace tucked into the plastic wrapper around the box. Budge opens it, revealing a row of charred paper sticks, and a fresh row in back.

"Nah. It's nice being outside and not feeling like you're stuck inside someone's sweaty armpit."

"Gee, can't wait to visit." Budge puts a cigarette between his lips, going through a complex folding process with the matchbook so he doesn't have to tear the one he's using off. It's easy for Abe to imagine Budge leaning against a coffee counter, looking out on Eighth Street, joking with the old men in their guayaberas over cafécitos.

"Would you visit, Uncle Budge?"

"Sure," Budge says, in a tone Abe can't read. Is he worried about money? Does he hate airplanes? Is he blowing sunshine up Abe's ass? Or maybe Budge thinks Abe will be dead before there's time to plan any visits.

His great uncle takes a drag, scanning the road for his daughter.

"You don't smell like a smoker," Abe tells him.

"I smoke two a day," Budge says. "One with my mornin' coffee, an' another one after dinner." It's just past three.

"Which one does this count as?" Abe asks with a grin in his voice.

"I'll call it . . . enhancin' a rare pleasure, enjoyin' the fall air with my great nephew."

"Aw, man." His great uncle might be teasing, but Abe is still touched.

"Listen." Budge points at Abe, using the fingers clamped around the filter of his cigarette. "People say smokin' is bad for you. I say bullshit. It's smokin' like a white man that's bad for you. The same way drinkin' like an Indian is bad for you.

"Our ancestors thought tobacco would solve the White Man problem. White men smoked so much tobacco we thought they'd smoke themselves into the ground, innit. Well, we gave 'em tobacco and they gave us booze, so you tell me who got the shit end a that stick."

Abe grunts deep in his throat to agree with Budge—a legitimate Kanien'kéha expression Abe can't remember the last time he used. Off the reservation, people don't usually pay close enough attention that you can pass off a grunt as agreement (disagreement is two grunts, with different inflections). The Mohawk language really doesn't have words for "yes" or "no," a fact Abe had verified with Tóta on more than one occasion. Supposedly, this means fewer miscommunications because you have to repeat what someone is asking in order to agree or disagree with them.

Mother: Have you gathered water?

Daughter: I have gathered water.

Turtle Clan Member: Will you fish with us tomorrow?

Wolf Clan Member: Tomorrow I will hunt. We will fish another day, friend.

Young Buck: Should we run up this mountain and fuck one of those does?

Old Buck: We should walk up this mountain and fuck all of those does.

If you're familiar with the language, I suppose you could make an argument for "hen" as yes. But hen isn't really yes, it's a word you throw into an answer to let someone know you agree with them (the way you throw "ken" into any sentence to make it a question). You start looking for the English "equivalent" and you'll end up using Mohawk words to express English thoughts. Like, now we use nia:wen for "thank you" when nia:wen is really giving thanks to the Creator. Look at me, talking about how we're always evolving while simultaneously offering absolutes. Just keeping you on your toes, hey.

"What do you think of e-cigarettes, Budge?" Knowing no chemical mist can bring anyone's prayers anywhere (as opposed to smoke from the tobacco plant), Abe passionately hates vapes. He assumes

Budge must as well; he's dying to hear what Budge sounds like worked into a rant.

"What's that, an app? Help you quit or somethin'?"

Sharon Oaks's Subaru—a two-tone maroon and gray wagon from the nineties—appears up the road. Budge smiles and waves.

"No, it's an electronic cigarette."

"I don't know what you mean, kid."

"They make these little cartridges filled with nicotine. You plug them into a battery-powered pen. Then steam comes out, and you puff on it, and you get your fix. Supposedly it's all the buzz of nicotine without any of the health problems."

"An' that's smokin'?"

"Yeah. Well, vaping."

Budge eyes Abe. *I was born at night but it wasn't last night*, the look says.

Abe gives him a wide-eyed shrug. *I don't make the news, I just report it.*

Sharon Oaks's wagon pulls into the driveway, gravel crunching beneath the tires.

"Now that I've told you about them, I bet you'll see them everywhere."

"Reminds me of that test they did on lab rats to see if nicotine was addictive." Budge snorts. "They could either press a food button or a nicotine button. The rats all pressed the nicotine button 'til they starved t'death."

Sharon Oaks steps out of her car. She looks the same as Abe remembers—thick brush cut, broad face framed by a pair of large beaded earrings. She's wearing blocky supermarket jeans, a long-sleeve tie-dye t-shirt, and Frye boots.

"Who starved to death?" she asks.

"Me," Abe says, "waiting for you on your dad's front lawn."

"You look it, with your skinny ass. What're they feedin' you down in Miami, Toots?"

Toots is what they call Abe on the Rez. To hear his family tell it, toddler Abe would yell, "Tootashay! Tootashay!" whenever this old cartoon called *Touché Turtle* came on. So Abe was Tootashay as a child, and then Toota as a teen. The first time he came home from college, it had morphed into Toots, which is what's stuck whenever he comes back. Maybe he doesn't need more Indian names, come to think of it.

Abe knows how his brother or his half-Irish cousins would answer Sharon: *Pussy and beer, what do you think?* As a child, he used to try to emulate them, but it always felt like performing in an ill-fitting suit. Somewhere before his teens, Abe made quiet his default setting. "How's it going, Sharon?"

"It's goin'." She gives Budge an upward nod. "Toots comin' back or what, Dad?"

"Up to him. I think we can work together, but he's got some thinkin' t'do." He pats Abe's shoulder. "You wanna see me again, you give my daughter a call."

"You're not coming over for dinner?" Abe asks.

"Gotta get back t'my memoirs." Budge grins, then an *oh, shit* look covers his face. He pats Abe's shoulder again. "Hang on a second."

Budge stubs his cigarette out, sets the ashtray and cigarettes down, and goes back into his trailer. Abe looks a question at Sharon—*What's he up to?* She shrugs in response—*Your guess is as good as mine.* They stand there in silence, Abe chilled by air he bets his cousin finds crisp and refreshing, like he once did. He shifts from foot to foot while she stands with her weight on one hip, hands in her pockets, looking at him calmly. Maybe he's being paranoid, but Abe could swear it's the gentle condescension he used to wear when he pumped gas for tourists on Route 37; he's been away too long.

"How's Rez life treating you, Sharon?"

"You know me, cuz," she says with a grin.

Except Abe knows very little. Sharon was a late-in-life baby for Budge and is younger than Abe by several years. She's got a daughter, a husband, and—like a lot of rez women Abe knows—her demeanor is no-bullshit-but-really-everything-is-bullshit.

"Are *you* coming over for dinner, at least?" he asks.

Her grin widens. "You know me, cuz."

"Nice."

Budge emerges from his trailer with a leather notebook curled against his chest. He hands it down to Abe.

"Almost forgot," Budge says. "Maybe you wanna write some while you're up here."

THIS ONE GOES OUT TO ALL THE COLONIZERS

by Dominick Deer Woods

"The roots of education are bitter,
but the fruit is sweet."

—Aristotle

Our word for grandmother is Tóta.
Our word for grandfather is Tóta.

In another world you learned.
Here you claimed
what you wanted,
named it yours,
and mulched the rest
to Manifest your Destiny.

The word for mother is istá.
The word for aunt is istá.

In a parallel universe
you are a capillary,
we are a bronchiole,
dogs are follicles,
trees are a mucus membrane,
the earth is marrow,

laughter is a white blood cell,
music is a synapse,
love is a breath.

Our word for father is raké:ni.
Our word for uncle is raké:ni
The word for husband is takení:teron.
The word for wife is takení:teron.

I dreamed another world
where your soul cracked
open
when we embraced.

In this world you put a bounty of $60 on Kanien'kehá:ka
    scalps.
$3,876.25 in purchasing power today.
The scalps of Kanien'kehá:ka children were small,
a mere $20.
Still
not bad for quick, wet work.

We don't have words for rape
or massacre
or genocide
so we use the fruit
you fed us.

Three

lthough built to resemble a colonial-style home, the Fort Covington Border Inspection Station looks like a gas station. Only the pump island is a booth for customs agents, and the garage bays are there in case inspectors want to give your car a good once-over. With only two lanes, it can take a solid half hour to get through if you arrive at the wrong time. Which Abe has—Monday morning, right when everyone is commuting to work. He has a FaceTime call with his rheumatologist at nine, and the Jacobs home doesn't have Wi-Fi or good cell service, which didn't leave Abe with many choices.

The first couple of nights back in Ahkwesáhsne, he'd tried calling his wife in Miami. The first call he couldn't hear her, the second she couldn't hear him, and the third cut out so often nothing they said made sense. The steroids had robbed Abe of any patience he might have once had for the effort, so they'd switched to texting, though even that could be spotty and sending pictures was out of the question.

The Jacobs are world-class at shooting the shit all day, with occasional breaks for food and drinks, but the conversations have been white noise, unable to penetrate Abe's low-grade panic. He'd spent the last three weeks climbing the walls. The day before the call with the rheumatologist, anxiety over what he might learn turned Abe's blood to batter dancing on a hot skillet. He finally cracked and texted his dermatologist (even though he was meeting with Weisberg, Unger had been the approachable one). The doctor always called him, never the other way around. Still, Abe couldn't contain himself. "I need to know if I'm getting an answer tomorrow," he wrote.

It took hours for Unger's response to come through. "Been thinking of you. Yes, you'll know tomorrow. Stay off the internet!"

Feeling like he might claw off his own skin, Abe left the house and walked toward the copse of trees behind it. As a teenager, Abe's therapist had wanted him to beat a pillow with a wiffle bat to get in touch with his anger in a clinical setting. Abe had tried it; it hadn't been nearly enough.

Abe put maples, pines, and beech between himself and prying eyes until he stood in front of a tall, smooth birch. He felt foolish. He was a grown man and this was a boy's errand. The steroids in his blood tipped the scales. *Garnett's disease*, he thought. He wound up and drove his clenched fist into the birch.

The trick was not to punch the way you'd punch a person, by aiming through the back of his skull. Instead, Abe delivered a surface jab that would hurt enough to chip away at the anger, while keeping his bones from breaking. Shock vibrated through his hand. *Night sweats*. Greeting the pain like an old friend, Abe smacked his fists against the tree. *Necrosis*. Smack. *Burning*. Smack. *Tingling, numbness*. Smack, smack. *Prognosis: terminal*. The blow sent a shockwave to his elbow, cutting something loose inside of him.

Putrefactive Nodosa—weakness, lesions, pain, fatigue, fevers… *Prognosis: terminal*. Flecks of red dotted the white skin of the birch tree. Abe was tired, but he kept punching. *Kobayashi's arteritis*. *Graveolent Periarteritis*. *Balcan's disease*. Dots of blood became two patches, one for each clenched fist. *Terminal. Terminal. Terminal*. At last his rage began to ebb, the void it left flooded by shame. Not for how he'd expressed his anger, but for the anger itself. Years removed from that raging teenager, only to end up in the same place again. In high school, his mother had grown tired of the elaborate stories Abe used to excuse the swelling and bruising, the missing skin.

"You know," she'd said casually over breakfast one morning, "when your father was an angry young man, he used to punch the telephone pole across from his house." She didn't say anything about the bandages on Abe's hands. Dad had stared over his plate, saying nothing.

"Why?" Abe asked.

"Angry," Dad answered, the corner of his mouth dented into a bitter smile.

Abe had felt seen by them in that moment. He'd also felt fresh rage, like for the first time he could see the bars of a cage surrounding him, one he hadn't known existed.

As he stood in front of the birch, tears stung Abe's eyes. He looked dully at his hands, at the wet pink where the skin of his knuckles used to be. One thing had changed from when he was a kid—Abe had forgotten to bring first aid supplies. He snuck in the back door, cleaned and bandaged his hands, and covered them with mittens, blaming the cold.

That night, Abe lay jittering in bed, tucked beneath the slanted ceiling of the attic bedroom he'd shared with his brother growing up. After months of multiplying lesions, of test after test, of relentless pain, of ongoing cluelessness from doctors, panic and fear were woven into the meat of his body. Instead of sleeping, he listened to his youngest uncle snoring softly from Adam's old bed across the room. When Abe was growing up, his uncle had drifted in and out of living with them between relationships—an occurrence so common they'd taken to calling him Uncle Ghost. As morning approached, Uncle Ghost's snoring seemed to get louder, mocking Abe's inability to find the same satisfaction. The last time Abe glanced at his bedside clock, the glowing digits showed it was just after six.

When his alarm went off at eight, Abe bolted awake, heart thud-ding. The lack of sleep kicked his pain into overdrive. Unlike the shooting pains he'd come to expect, his entire torso ached like a boxer had used it as a heavy bag for training. The sensation traveled down to clench his testicles, making them throb until his stomach was queasy. As he sat up, his hips and knees pounded. When he walked, his leg muscles felt like sludge. So far, he didn't think much of Budge's healing skills; Abe doubted he'd make another trip to his great uncle's trailer.

He'd rushed through his morning routine: surgical soap in the shower and antibiotic ointment afterward to fight infection, then prescription medical tape and gauze to cover up (he'd started with store-bought, labeled "For Sensitive Skin!" but it caused puffy lines that cracked and bled). At breakfast his stomach had been too twisted to eat, partially from the throbbing pain in his groin, but mostly from worrying what he was going to learn from Dr. Weisberg. Abe's father had insisted on driving Abe to the Canadian side of Ahkwesáhsne to use the Wi-Fi at Iohahi:io, The Good Road, an adult education center less than fifteen minutes from the house. Abe suspected it was so they could share quality time.

If Abe'd known how bad Dad's driving had gotten, he wouldn't have been so anxious to leave. His father has been blind in one eye most of his life; the story is that he came down a playground slide face-first and sand scratched his cornea. Before today, Abe had never noticed any difference between Dad's one-eyed navigation and the way fully sighted people tackle the road, but it's been a while since his father has driven him anywhere. Dad half-assed his way up the road to Fort Covington, details like trash cans, curbs, and lanes be damned. Worse, he didn't seem to notice when he weaved over the lines or struck anything. Abe was glad to see so many cars at the check-point; it forced Dad to inch forward instead of swerving around.

Abe assumed he'd be freaking out—inside, anyway—right up until he saw Rheumatologist Weisberg's face appear on his laptop.

But combine his lack of sleep with the car's heater, the gentle vibration of the engine as they wait for their turn through the checkpoint, and the sound of Beck lamenting his lost love, and it's putting Abe out. He nods off, then sits up. He grabs his earlobe and twists it, trying to stay awake.

"Why do you and Mom have such shitty internet?" he mutters.

"Hey." Dad sounds wounded. "We have cable now."

With his umber eyes and tawny skin, Dad has always been ambiguously ethnic. He's growing his hair long again, and it falls to his shoulders in gray and silver waves. Now that he's getting older, you could get away with parking him at a campfire between Chris Hemsworth and Tom Hardy to dispense some First Nations wisdom.

"Did you read the new Ross Gay yet?" Dad asks. "Or Ada Limón?" *Catalog of Unabashed Gratitude* and *Bright Dead Things* have just come out.

"I'm a little behind on my reading lately, Dad."

"Aw, you gotta catch your rabbit," Dad says. Not *you don't know what you're missing*, not *I loved them, you should give them a day in court*, but *you gotta catch your rabbit*. Dad means, "You need to catch your rabbit to cook it," which was all advice he'd offered when Abe had mentioned becoming a writer himself, just before moving to Miami. It's Dad's way of saying if Abe wants to write, then he needs to do a lot of reading. Which isn't wrong, but Abe had been hoping for encouragement, not advice.

"Terrance Hayes has a new one out," Abe says. "*American Sonnets for My Past and Future Assassin.* I read that."

"You gotta read something besides your favorites. Get out there, see what's doing."

"Yeah, I know." Abe braces his arm in the doorframe, foot stomping an imaginary brake as Dad stops just short of rear-ending the car ahead of them. Abe pulls his wallet from his back pocket and fishes out his tribal ID.

"How was it, though?"

Abe had wanted to tattoo some of the lines on his chest and run screaming through the streets with his shirt off. "I liked it," he says.

Looking at his ID, Abe remembers applying for it in hopes of helping to pay for college with tribal grants. He hears the voice his Uncle Asher—an artist who'd occupied Alcatraz Island with Richard Oakes in 1969—who'd said to Abe, "I heard you got your Star of David." Abe wasn't the only one who had—in order for him to join the Saint Regis rolls, his parents were required to enroll first. All three of their cards had arrived in the mail on the same day, numbered one after the other. They'd jumped around the kitchen, waving the letters from the tribal clerk over their heads, yelling, "We're Indians, we're Indians!" and laughing at the absurdity of it all.

Once he got to college, Abe learned the real reason he'd gotten his tribal ID. It turned out to have nothing to do with financial add.

SYRACUSE, 1992

When Abe was growing up, he had an Irish uncle who owned a bar half an hour off the Rez. He was the richest guy Abe had ever known personally. He owned a boat, and he'd motor Abe and his siblings (a term that includes his cousins, so if you see it, just know we could be talking two people, or twelve) up and down the Saint Lawrence River. The wind would whip their hair behind them like ribbons, and they'd feel like royalty. One summer, Abe's uncle had even taken them all the way to Boldt Castle, the view from the water like something from a fairy tale. But apart from those trips, Abe had never been off the Rez. He'd gone to school at Salmon Run Central, which serviced pre-K through twelfth grade for Ahkwesáhsne and the surrounding area—just over one thousand students in total.

While Abe never considered his elders or his ancestors to be uneducated, only Aunt Abby and Uncle Asher had gone to college (for an MBA and a BFA respectively). After showing Abe how to do some basic sketching, Asher had moved to a shack in the New Mexico desert. He lived hand-to-mouth selling paintings at an open-air market in Sante Fe, dating poets and smoking pipe tobacco. It sounded impossibly romantic to Abe. The domestic life his siblings were settling into held no interest for him, and he knew if he stayed he'd be sucked in—get his girlfriend pregnant, have to get a job to support them, get drunk on the weekends with his siblings, and have Sunday dinners with his parents in perpetuity. Abe wanted to follow in his uncle's footsteps, leaving the Rez and doing something artistic somewhere cool—sculpt in a lakeside cabin, maybe, or paint in a mountain lodge. To do so, he would need an education like Asher's; at college, Abe was certain he would swell to fill the big life he deserved.

When it came time for him to go to college, he was surprised to find out his parents had nothing to give him. I don't know if he was too self-centered to notice how frugally his parents lived, or if he was just optimistic. Thankfully, Syracuse University offered him a partial scholarship, and since he didn't have money for anywhere else, SU became his only choice. The university was barely three hours from Ahkwesáhsne, but it felt like another country. SU alone had nearly twice as many people as the entirety of Ahkwesáhsne's population, never mind Syracuse itself. To Abe the college town was a booming metropolis.

And what was this grand destiny he was confident he'd fulfill? He didn't know. Maybe if the rage that turned his knuckles bruised and bloody couldn't find him, that would be enough. Wandering the quad, Abe wore a goofy grin. He said a big "hi!" to everyone he passed. After he saw a poster for an upcoming lecture by Kathy Acker, Abe stopped by Bird Library and checked out *Blood and Guts in High School* (the only book of hers they had on hand). Sitting on the landing at Crouse College, propped against the red brick wall with downtown Syracuse at the bottom of The SU Hill before him,

Abe cracked open a book he'd never heard of from an author he'd only learned of an hour before, and felt very, very collegiate. That was how he first met Alexandria East.

Her laugh drew his attention and her features held it. Her skin was clear as cream, and her eyes were the same brilliant blue as the autumn sky overhead. She was exiting Crouse's double doors with five other students, smiling like a toothpaste model. Studies show that marginalized folks often subconsciously seek acceptance from the dominant culture through relationships with partners from that culture (in other words, America might not love you but at least an "All-American" type could). If you believe those studies, then you'd say Alex was exactly the kind of girl Abe would fall for once he left the Rez.

Alex wasn't a dainty blonde, though. She towered over the three girls and two boys she'd left the building with. Her hair wasn't White Girl Perfect, either. In 1992, people still sported eighties hair. Whether gelled and crunched into large helmets or pulled tight to the scalp like a swimming cap, eighties hair was meant to never move. Alex had a thick mass of dishwater-blonde hair tumbling down her back like the tangled pelt of some mountainous beast. She sported a pair of brown corduroy overall shorts, a red pinstriped men's button-down shirt, and pink high-heeled jelly sandals.

Alex felt Abe staring over the top of his book and met his gaze. Abe didn't look away. He meant to but couldn't make himself drop his eyes. He was just shy of gawking when he regained control of himself, giving her an upward nod and turning his overlong look into a greeting.

"Hey, do you know how to get to Montgomery Street?" Alex asked. "It's downtown."

"What for?" Abe didn't know how to get to Montgomery Street, of course, but he wanted to buy time.

"There's a dance studio there. We're musical theater majors." She walked toward him, waving a hand toward the other students. "We

need to try out so they know what level to put us in. The voice program is at Crouse, so we came here. But they said—"

"Yeah, I'm supposed to try out, too." Abe stood and tucked the
slim volume into his back pocket. In heels, Alex was right at his eye
level. "I was just killing time."

"Where's your stuff?" She indicated the yellow duffel slung over
her shoulder, a promotional bag from Chiquita banana.

"Oh, I don't have dance clothes." Abe smiled. "I'm a singer. They
just need to, you know, see me dance. Because of my major. Musical
theater."

"You can get us to Montgomery Street?" she asked.

"Sure, I'm from Syracuse." He couldn't remember the last time
he'd lied, and here he was lying twice in practically the same breath.
But a simple *Mind if I walk with you?* would have left room for her
to turn him down, and he couldn't let her walk away without him.

"Awesome." She put her hand out. "I'm Alexandria, like the city
in Egypt. Call me Alex."

He wanted to make a joke about the library, or the lighthouse,
but nothing sounded witty in his head, and he was worried she'd
heard it all, so he said, "I'm Abraham. Abe."

"You ever heard 'Story of Isaac'?" Her handshake was firm.

Abe admitted he hadn't.

"Leonard Cohen. You don't know what you're missing." She
closed her eyes and made circles with her thumbs and forefingers,
drawing them apart like she was stretching an invisible piece of
string. Then she called over her shoulder, telling her classmates Abe
could get them all to the dance studio. She adjusted her bag and
nodded toward the staircase leading down The Hill. "After you."

"Ladies first."

"I don't know where I'm going."

Then we're even, Abe thought, yet he started down the stairs.
Maybe if he wandered, his feet would naturally take him where he
needed to be. It worked hunting for plant Medicine in the woods;

maybe it would work for the dance studio in downtown Syracuse. Their little group managed to hook up with the rest of the incoming freshman streaming out of Archbold Theatre at the bottom of The Hill, and they followed the other students carrying dance bags to tryouts, so it kind of did.

Abe might have never had a dance lesson, but he liked his chances. You know his Tóta had danced around the fire in her ninth decade, but you don't know she'd also been famous for rocking the dance floor in the decades before that. Rez-famous, anyway.

To honor her joy, here's a story of Tóta dancing.

About twenty years before her funeral, you could find Tóta and the Jacobs sisters at a sock hop fundraiser—Aunt Abby, the youngest, she of the MBA; Aunt Maisy, the oldest, who you know is the boisterous new matriarch; and Abe's mother, Haricot, or Hari. Hari is the quietest of the three Jacobs sisters but her spine is pure steel, a fact that isn't relevant to the dance story, just one I offer for your edification going forward.

The sock hop had a four-dollar admission to raise money for the Ahkwesáhsne Freedom School, which, six years after opening, had decided to develop a language-immersion program. Most people gave a five-dollar bill and called it square so they could feel extra-generous, which had been the organizers' plan all along. Half the Rez turned up to listen to fifties pop and do the Mashed Potato.

For ambiance, the organizers had a couple of ringers, like Johnny and Penny in *Dirty Dancing*, so even if you couldn't Peppermint Twist, you at least got a good show. Their "Johnny" was a twenty-five-year-old whose Smoke Dances and Grass Dances made pow-wow crowds whoop. He had studied and practiced those old dances for the sock hop (as best he could before videos of those steps were an internet click away), put on a leather jacket, and greased his long hair into a giant pompadour. All his preparations had made him overly confident, so Johnny Rez got it in his head to dance battle with Tóta. He must've thought it would be cute, the young dude versus the old lady; he didn't know Tóta had taught her daughters how to move back when those dances were new, or how fit she still was under her oversized paisley dress. They traded dances back and forth, Johnny looking like a marionette, Tóta tearing it up like the world's oldest bobby-soxer. As a final flourish, Tóta, aged seventy-two (or three or four), dropped to the floor in a split and popped back to her feet as neat as you'd please. By then, people had their cameras out. In pictures taken immediately after the split, Tóta is leaping with both arms raised in triumph, her fingers spread into jazz hands. A smile splits her face, light reflects off the lenses of her glasses, and her hair is a silver corona. It looks like she was so filled with happiness that it lit her up and lifted her into the air. On the floor in front of her, the pompadoured "Johnny" is genuflecting.

Everyone in the family has managed to get a copy of that photo, Tóta dancing in wallets, across walls, over shelves, and inside photo albums, as inspirational and aspirational as any Punch.

Unfortunately, Abe learned at musical theater tryouts that he had not inherited his Tóta's rhythm or fluidity. At the audition he floundered around the floorboards of the dance studio in downtown Syracuse, struggling to mimic his fellow freshman. Finally one of the dance instructors—a fast-talking New Yorker—pulled him aside.

"Look around," the instructor said. "You're the biggest guy here. All eyes are going to be drawn to you the second you step on a stage. If you don't have every step absolutely perfect, then there won't be anywhere for you to hide up there. You have a lot of work to do, you understand?"

Abe nodded. *All eyes are going to be drawn to you the second you step on a stage*, he thought. Until he heard that the adulation of a crowd might be in his future, Abe had no idea it was something he wanted. But the New Yorker's words made Abe's spine tingle, pulled at a void he didn't know he had inside. At that moment, Abe decided to major in musical theater.

■ ■ ■

And you're wondering what that has to do with Abe's tribal ID. The proof of Abe's enrollment status came up shortly after he met Alex because she was shocked to learn Abe was Native.

After she made fun of Abe's dance audition ("You looked like a zombie from the 'Thriller' video, but bad"), they wandered the campus chatting until they ended up at Schine Dining Hall. It was too late for lunch and too early for dinner, but Abe got an apple pie with whipped cream and a coffee and Alex got a bowl of chili and a Coke. As they ate, they argued over Anita Hill's testimony against Supreme Court nominee Clarence Thomas. Coverage of the hearing dominated television at the time, bringing "sexual harassment" out of academic texts and obscure court cases and into the popular lexicon for the first time. Anita Hill reminded Abe of his Aunt Abby, who was often the only woman or person of color at her corporate job; he believed every word Hill said. Alex, who'd navigated some asshole managers and coworkers in the course of her working life, rolled her eyes at the whole thing.

"I bet her boss kept pushing for a date, to the point where he made a nuisance of himself. I'm also sure he talked about sex and pornography when she didn't want to hear it." Alex swirled her spoon in her bowl, making designs in the remaining bit of chili. "But I don't know if that's harassment."

"So these douchebags grilling her are right?" Abe had asked, referring to the congressional panel scrutinizing Thomas's nomination.

"I never said that. That's a room full of condescending shitheads. Fuck all of them." With her bowl empty, Alex swiped a finger through the whipped cream on Abe's pie.

"Hey, I don't know where your hand has been." He pulled his face into an exaggerated moue.

"I'll make it up to you." Alex made a show of bringing the cream to her mouth and licking it off. Abe laughed. Her come-hither expression was as over-the-top as his disgust had been, but he still felt a tingle in his belly.

"I never got into the whole *9 ½ Weeks* thing," Abe said, "mixing sex and food."

"That just means you haven't done it right."

They talked about past lovers—the positions they'd tried, the longest sessions they'd enjoyed, the most orgasms they'd had in a single day, the craziest places they'd had sex. Alex was talking about many lovers. Abe kept pace with the stories, hinting at a vast array of girlfriends, but he was only talking about one girl. He'd dated Cheryl Curly Head for two years, his first and only. She was a year ahead of Abe and dumped him when she left for college. Since then, Abe had forgotten how it felt to want. Talking with Alex about sex made him feel like he was sunning himself on railroad tracks, the vibrations of an oncoming train thrumming throughout his body. He had no idea if her joking display meant anything, but Abe figured Alex must like him at least a little to swap sex stories.

"I have to tell you something," he said.

"Tell me everything." Alex gave him the sideways grin he was already falling for. She'd just told him about her two girlfriends, saying she hadn't gone down on a woman but couldn't wait to start in college. Since Abe had been matching her story for story, he imagined she expected to hear about his same-sex encounters. From what I've read, a lot of boys fool around with other boys when they hit puberty, but Abe never had. Not at that point, anyway.

"I'm not from Syracuse," he said.

"Really?"

Her tone was inscrutable. He'd been trying to make her laugh most of the afternoon, so Alex may have thought Abe was messing with her. Either that, or his failure to direct them anywhere (beyond agreeing with every stranger they stopped to ask for directions) had given him away, and she'd been humoring him the whole time.

"I'm from Saint Regis."

The sound of her laughter put his heart into his throat. He wanted to make her laugh forever.

"So you're a missionary."

"Yes, my child." He made prayer hands. "Kneel before me and accept the Holy Communion."

"Like I'm failing for that." She squinted across the table at him. "What're you, really?"

"What do you mean?"

"My dad's Jewish. My mom—the hippy? She's half Hungarian Romani and half WASP. What are you?"

"Hungarian Romani?"

"The racial epithet would be 'gypsy.'"

"Huh. Guess I won't be using that one anymore."

"So . . ." She gestured like *come on*. "What are you?"

The question made Abe feel alien, but she'd offered her own pedigree first.

"Ahkwesáhsne Kanien'kehá:ka."

She frowned. He tried again.

"Mohawk Indian."

"Get the fuck out."

"Yeah."

"No way. I would have guessed Costa Rican, or maybe Peruvian. A Mohawk, for real? You're really Mohawk?"

"I can show you my ID." He offered as a joke, trying to sidestep his annoyance, but her eyes lit up.

"Cool, whip it out."

Abe grabbed his wallet, feeling stupid . . . but also feeling his neck prickle at the specific flirty emphasis Alex used when she said, *Whip it out*. He found the card and passed it over. She looked at it for a long time, and when she handed it back her fingers gripped his.

"I've never been with an Indian," she said, peering into his eyes.

Abe needed a moment to process the look she was giving him, so he took his time putting the card and wallet away. With the scent of greasy dining hall food and the steamy fart smell of the industrial dishwashing equipment wafting from the kitchen, at that moment the grants seemed like a perk. The gleam in Alex's eyes was the actual reason Abe had gotten a bullshit ID from the government declaring him a "real" Indian, he just hadn't known it until then.

"Usually when a woman says that to me," Abe cleared his throat, "she's Michelle Pfeiffer and I'm alone in my bedroom."

Alex threw back her head and laughed.

"Well, shit, let's get out of here," she said, pushing away from the table.

Alex lived on North Campus, a few miles walk past The Hill. Much more private than the dorms, North Campus complexes were made up of split-level two-bedroom apartments.

"How'd you get a place up there?" Abe asked. For the first time, Alex seemed distant.

"Are you a transfer student?" Abe pressed. He hadn't asked her age. "I tried to get a place there but they said only upperclassman can live on North Campus."

She looked up at The Hill, her brow furrowed. Before Abe could ask what was wrong, Alex pulled him close and kissed him, right there on the sidewalk. It began slowly, then they pressed their bodies together, getting serious. She wrapped her arms around his shoulders. His hands found the wild tumble of her hair. When Alex pushed away, smiling, her face had flushed in twin spots of red on her cheeks.

"I lost my virginity at thirteen," she said quietly, walking backward, away from him. "My mom lost hers at fourteen. His name was Rob Sharpe. Mine, not my mom's. He was Haitian. He spoke English, Spanish, French, and Creole. His parents had a yacht and a home recording studio. I thought he was kind of stuck on himself, honestly. But I wanted to beat Mom, and Rob Sharpe is who I was dating at the time."

She shrugged, still looking at Abe as she walked backward, trusting her feet would find the sidewalk. Every so often, she'd glance back to find her way. Mostly, she kept her eyes trained on Abe's.

"We were on South Beach. It was after midnight. He looked really big in the moonlight. His penis, I mean. I changed my mind. He said it would be fine, so I said okay. And he was right, it was fine. Since then, I've been with fifty-three boys and two girls. Seventy boys, if you include blow jobs. I always say yes. Do you want to know why, Abe?"

He tried to answer but his mouth had gone dry. He nodded instead.

"Because. Life's too short for no."

He couldn't see a flaw in her sex logic.

"I've fucked white guys, but never really dated any. I've dated Cubans, Black guys, Jews. If it's a country south of America, then I've dated them, too. But you know the sad part?"

Abe shook his head.

"I've never been with a Native American."

Being the object of someone's First Nations fetish generally makes your skin crawl, but Alex didn't creep Abe out. It felt like being seduced by a gorgeous, experienced woman. He felt sexy and special; chosen. Alex didn't just talk a good game, either. Once they got to her bedroom, she pulled out every trick she'd ever learned. By the time the sun came up the following day, he was in love.

Of course, he didn't know her well enough to be truly in love. But by the time his initial infatuation wore off he was in deep.

AHKWESÁHSNE, 2016

"ID, please." The border agent's voice startles Abe back to the present. His dad is already putting his own ID away. Abe holds the little plastic square out and the officer waves him on without asking any questions. Customs delays for Mohawk citizens are a source of perpetual tension between the governments of Canada, the United States, and Ahkwesáhsne; every few years politicians talk about adding an express lane for Ahkwesáhsne residents, but it never happens.

"Now's the time to read, Abe. Especially poetry." Dad pulls away from the border station. In Miami a luxury condo would block the view, but up here the road hugs the Saint Lawrence River. It's a gorgeous view, rippled water under the morning sun, the greenery warm with fall colors. "You're husked out. Humble. Present in a way people rarely are. It's a gift. If you let it be."

Abe nods. He doesn't argue because he already knows how it would end. Whenever they argue, it circles back to Abe "doing something with his work," like he'd tried when he'd first moved to Miami.

Abe would say, *I sent out dozens of poems and got back nothing but rejection.*

His father would reply, *That was one time twenty years ago,*

and Abe would say, *No one's been asking,*

and Dad would say, *You're hiding,*

and Abe would say, *The graduation poem that made you cry was decades ago, get over it already.*

and Dad would ask, *Are you still writing?*

A little here and there

Maybe it's time to try again

I don't know if I could recover from another drubbing

You've got to toughen up

Hello, I'm your son; have we met?

I think it's sweet, the way his dad supports him, but Abe only sees how he and his father butt heads. It's not like his dad ever told Abe to get a real job, some high-paying gig requiring a suit and a degree. As a child, Abe's pudgy little fingers had traced the spines of Dad's book collection, thick volumes that took his father places he found so compelling he chose them over spending time with his kids. Now that he's grown, Abe works in a bookstore and dreams of being a poet, but being a part of the literary world hasn't helped Abe know his father any better.

The car loops back, and they're already on The Good Road's campus. Abe puts his ID and wallet away, rubbing his face. He wonders how many years passed before he and Alex had stopped trying to blow each other's minds and started having transactional sex. They still had it most afternoons before Abe started dinner, mainly at Alex's insistence. The way it went down put Abe in mind of changing the oil in the car; maintenance, really.

The four jobs Abe complained to his mother about back in college were working at a deli counter, clerking at a drug store, a work-study job at Bird Library, and delivering pizzas in the wee hours. Still, Abe would stay awake talking with Alex in her North Campus apartment until the sun came up. He got three hours of sleep on a good night.

Now, even after being apart for weeks, they're barely texting. Abe tells himself the shitty Wi-Fi makes trying to communicate too annoying. Whatever reasons Alex has for texting so infrequently, Abe refuses to contemplate.

So far his parents haven't pried into what's keeping Alex in Miami, but his sister is a different matter. Don't know if it makes a difference at this point, but I swear I'm not being lazy calling Abe's sister "Sis." As a girl she used to curb boys by saying, "You don't want me, you want my sister" and pointing toward whatever random girl happened to be walking by. It became a habit, and the name stuck. At certain angles, Sis is a dead ringer for a nineties-era Tantoo Cardinal—though it's less about looks and more about fierce charisma. Tantoo Cardinal is one of those actresses who is a damn legend in Native circles but who does a lot of blink-and-you'll-miss-it roles in mainstream cinema

Over a hearty soup of tortellini, carrot, cabbage, artichoke, red and white onion, and deer sausage floating in a savory, fragrant broth of backyard mushrooms and anti-inflammatory herbs she'd made for dinner, Sis and her husband, Robert, didn't hold back.

Sis: "You guys having problems?"

Robert: "What, she finally get sick a you?"

Sis: "She can't handle the idea that she might have to take care of you for once, instead of the other way around?"

Robert: "She take off with some groupie?"

It had an air of *teasing-but-tell-us-all-about-it-if-you-want*, which Abe appreciated; it told him they cared while letting him avoid answering anything directly. It had also made him urgently need to hear Alex's voice. Sis had some sort of mini dish pointed at a commercial tower that gave her house good wireless service, so after dinner Abe had stepped out on Sis's back porch and tried Alex's cell.

"Hey, babe," she'd answered, drawing words out, infusing them with longing and affection, as though they hadn't screamed at each other before he left Miami. Like I said, the rheumatologist delaying his diagnosis by three weeks was the first time Abe had felt steroid-induced rage; the second time happened the same day, when Alex had returned from work. Scrolling his phone during dinner, Abe had started reading aloud—descriptions of various illnesses that matched his symptoms. In response, Alex had scarfed her meal, dropped her dishes in the sink, and tried to get past Abe to their bedroom.

Abe had stood from the table and blocked her from getting through the doorway, still reading from his phone. Alex turned and walked from room to room, trying to get away. He'd been so desperate to get her to face him that he'd raised his voice louder and louder as he followed her. So loud that she finally put her hands over her ears and yelled, "Stop it!" And then, "Wait for the fucking doctors, Abe!" And then, "Shut up, shut up, shut up!"

Abe had grabbed Alex, spun her around, and screamed in her face. He has no idea what he screamed, can't even remember if he used words. In response, Alex had slapped him across the face, which finally shut Abe up.

In nearly a quarter of a century together, Abe and Alex had never touched with anything but love. In the aftermath, they stood panting, faces warped by shock, anger, fear. They froze for a time, as though any movement would shatter their world. Then Alex grabbed twin handfuls of Abe's shirt and dropped to the floor, dragging him down on top of her for angry, violent sex. As roughly as they treated each other's bodies, it didn't relieve the tension inside Abe. It was a mechanical simulation of lust. Afterward, he felt more distant from her than ever.

He'd asked for a leave of absence from the bookstore the next day without any clear idea of his next step; he was just afraid staying with Alex might lead to more violence, the sort that couldn't be channeled into sex. He'd bought the plane tickets—Miami to Boston, then Boston to Massena, twenty-five minutes outside of Ahkwesáhsne—and packed the big travel bag. Alex hadn't even asked him to stay, or offered to join him.

"It's good to hear your voice," Abe said softly. He felt like he might cry.

"You, too, babe." Something was off. She sounded too chipper. Years ago, when the bookstore had sent Abe to an expo in Los Angeles, Abe had called Alex to tell her about the cool publishers' dinners he'd been enjoying. To cover her jealousy, she'd responded using the same upbeat tone. "How's the Rez?"

Abe thought, *Are we really doing this?* The pause he took was probably a bit too long, but he said, "Everyone's asking about you."

"Aw, give them my love." Like he was on vacation, like she was taking a few extra work days in Miami and would join him soon.

"I've got that call next week."

"Yeah?" It sounded like Alex had the TV muted but was scrolling for something to watch, concentrating on her streaming choices more than the call.

"My diagnosis." Abe clenched his jaw. The last thing he wanted was to start yelling again. It had been a relief to take a break from the day-to-day—work, grocery shopping, menu planning, cooking, dishes, and cleaning house. What Abe hadn't realized was that it had also been nice to take a break from Alex's breezy attitude toward his illness. A dark thought bloomed in his mind: *At least if I lose my temper, I won't be able to hurt her over the phone.* He barked a shameful laugh.

"What's funny?" Alex said, her voice sounding normal for the first time.

"Not much these days," Abe said. They'd been apart for a long stretch once before and Abe had missed her like crazy; Alex had called him every night, and sometimes they'd talked for hours. *Doesn't it bother you that we're not in contact for days at a time?* he wanted to ask. But he wasn't sure it actually bothered him, so he didn't. Instead, they made small talk. Promised to text more. Abe said he'd call her once he had his diagnosis. They'd exchanged I love you's and hung up.

Dad pulls the car up outside The Good Road's computer lab. His hubcaps scrape against the curb, and he doesn't so much brake as bump into the concrete.

"You sure you don't want me to wait around?" Dad asks, letting the car idle. "Maybe come in with you?"

"I'm good." Abe gets out of the car, grabs his laptop bag from the back, and raises a hand to his father.

"Call me when you're done then." Dad looks worried. "I love you."

"Love you, too." Abe turns away and heads into the lab.

AKHTSÍ:'A (MY BIG SISTER)

by Dominick Deer Woods

When I find her to say goodbye for the twelfth time
my sister's eyes are bleary with craft brew growlers
remember when she wants to know
remember when
and I think of the time we talked about our dreams
and I think I know what it is to be a small, scared thing
    trying to be invisible in the world because I have shrunk
    myself into corners while a giant raged outside
my sister described an enormous hand stretching the
    doorway to cracking and my body prickled like the skin
    of a raw chicken

we shared the same dream because we share the same father

remember when she wants to know
and I think of the time she drank so much Southern
    Comfort her boyfriend refused to let her ride in the cab
    of his truck
so we rode in the bed and I held her hair from her face
while she covered it and us with SoCo vomit and we gagged
    and we giggled
and she cried and told me about the trio of pale men who
    preyed on her when she was walking home from work
    like she always did

how they ran her down in an orange Chevy and dragged her
    back to the bed and made an ash woman of her
and I pretended not to have made sense of her words as they
    spewed
out and she pretended she'd never said anything
but after that night we shared an understanding

do you remember she asks
and I think of the time she drank Fireball Cinnamon Whisky
    and we laughed
hard enough to fly a false tooth from her mouth
and we laughed even harder
and I chased her around the rest of the night trying
to get a picture of her gap-toothed smile
and I knew the only reason she'd have a fake tooth I didn't
    know about was
because of a man
who made her briefly a women of makeup and bows
to contour the lumps and cover the bruises
a bow to pull her hair tight on one side and make the eyes
    look even
but if I stopped laughing and trying to capture an image
    then she'll know I know so I keep trying and we keep
    laughing

remember when
and I think of how she taught me about picklebacks
a shot of Jameson with a pickle juice chaser
and we laughed until she peed herself
and I thought of her birthing her good, strong boys
so much like her handsome husband
how they broke her body on the way out
and made her something she never knew she wanted to be

so the twelfth time I say goodbye
and we're toasting with strong craft beer poured from
growlers and she pulls me in and on a wave
of beer breath tells me how a basswood tree
explodes with seeds before it dies
and when you see a cluster of basswood trunks
what you don't see is the one that died
years before to create that abundance
and she tells me she is the tree
and her house and her husband and her boys
are the abundance and I think she's finally
too sloppy to remember and I think of later how
this memory will glitter in my mind like a treasure

Four

be and Sis sit in Adirondack chairs on their parents' back porch, the evening air sweet with blackberry from a patch of bushes near the shed and the faint traces of the ham Mom baked for dinner.

"What is it, again?" Sis asks.

"Systemic Necrotizing Periarteritis." Abe tries not to sound annoyed; she's asked him to name his autoimmune diagnosis half a dozen times since he got home from The Good Road. Abe started out picking his way over each syllable like a novice hiker working a mountain, but now he's almost got it down. Systemic Necrotizing Periarteritis, acronym: SNiP.

"SNiP" puts him in mind of Greek myths—the three Fates who spun mortal's lives, allotted their length, and cut them accordingly. Clotho weaved this disorder into Abe's life, Lachesis is spooling out his final months, and Atropos is getting ready to cut. Only it won't be shears for Abe, nothing so clean and quick. No, SNiP will saw at the thread of him like a rusty nail file.

He has browser tabs open to Johns Hopkins' and the National Organization for Rare Disorders' pages for SNiP, along with a tab from the Alzheimer's Association. Vascular dementia is going to hit him in a matter of months. Soon his brain will start to rot, giving him strange moods and stranger habits, stealing days at first, and then years, erasing his friends, his family, Alex, everyone he's ever known.

Since the rheumatologist gave him the diagnosis Abe has been praying. Not to avoid his fate—they don't know what causes SNiP, and there is no cure—but to be happy, not mean or violent. He imagines himself opening his arms to everyone for a hug, calling out, "Hey, stranger"—either a warm greeting for a new friend (or nurse, more likely) or a clever "joke" if the person turns out to be family. *It's me, Abe—your sister,* Cass will say. *I know,* he'll laugh, knowing nothing of the sort. Picturing his future is like mourning himself, like he's already gone.

Their parents are doing the dishes with Louis Prima playing faintly in the background. Listening to Prima sing about the loveliest way to pass an evening, Abe curses himself for every song, every album he's ever listened to. He laments every book, movie, or TV show he's ever given his time. What was it Roberto Bolaño said, "We never stop living, although death is certain"? Abe wonders if he would have done anything differently, knowing what he does now. He likes to think he would have, but Alex had always been the one pushing for them to live every day like tomorrow wouldn't come.

Abe keeps shifting in his seat but there's no escaping the pain. His lids are sandpaper against his eyes. He feels like a sack of soil. On their call, the doctor told him they're stepping him down from steroids and putting him on something targeted. The list of side effects from quitting steroids—exhaustion, muscle weakness and aches, body and joint pain, loss of appetite and nausea, etc. etc.—overlap what Abe's immune system is doing to him. If you love irony, you've got to love that. Then there's a whole host of fun mental side effects from weaning off steroids, things like irritability, depression, and mood swings. And since Abe has learned he's got about eighteen months before his brain turns to oatmeal, he's guessing he's going to be irritable, depressed, and moody for much of them.

Abe looks at his sister, lounging in her chair, mug in one hand and cigarette in the other. Sis is an herbalist. Her day job is as an intake receptionist at a hospital, but since Abe left home his parents and sister have taken classes, trying to bring back some of the old, precolonial ways. Dad's been flintknapping stone arrowheads, Mom's been braiding sweetgrass baskets, and Sis decided to grow and harvest herbs, walking the land to find plant Medicine. She's smoked since she was thirteen. Adding osha root and coltsfoot to her tobacco, drinking thyme and eucalyptus with her tea—those are nods to approaching fifty and still being a smoker. The idea of Sis becoming a stranger to him terrifies Abe.

"And there's no cure?" Sis is looking at the setting sun, not at Abe.

"What the hell happened to the Barnharts' lawn?" Abe asks, pointing his chin to the left. There isn't a shred of green out front, just rutted dirt. It looks like construction vehicles have been doing donuts in it.

"Mrs. Barnhart moved to the trailer out back." Sis points her lips at a double-wide parked in the Barnhart's backyard, which is marginally greener. "The main house is actually a casino now."

"What the fuck, seriously?"

"Seriously." Sis's mouth opens and closes, like she's going to press Abe about his disorder, then she plunges on. "Mrs. Barnhart had the grand opening last year. She sold off the furniture and moved in a bunch of gaming tables, but she didn't do anything with the plumbing. All the extra traffic busted out the pipes. You shoulda seen it, these guys in tuxedoes with their dicks in the wind, these ladies in high heels sinking in the mud, hiking up their skirts to squat in the bushes. She had Yonder working security, if you can believe it."

"Yonder Curly Head?" Abe can't keep the disdain—or the fear—from his voice. As a kid, Cheryl's older brother had thought dipping a stray cat's tail in gasoline and lighting it on fire was the height of wit, and he'd never liked Abe. "She couldn't do any better than him?"

"Well, she used to be his stepmom, and you know how it is with family. But Yonder's in Jamesville now. They got him on Grand Larceny for stealing Herc Leaf's Buick."

"Hardly seems worth it." Abe feels sad to lose another Mohawk to the system, but he can't deny being relieved to hear Yonder is out of circulation. Strange, given how on edge Abe already is, that just hearing his old bully's name can agitate him further.

Sis squints at their neighbors over her dangling cigarette. When she speaks again, her voice is low. "What're you going to do?"

Breath in and out for as long as I can, Abe thinks. *Get blind drunk from sunup to sundown*, Abe thinks. *I have no idea*, Abe thinks.

"How's the plumbing over there now?" Abe's voice is full of false cheer, his smile hollow, a ghoul's grin.

"Works good, from what I hear." Sis sighs. "What does Alex think?"

"I'm supposed to FaceTime her on Friday."

"Supposed to?" Sis frowns. "Is she—"

Abe cuts her off. "When did the Gravel Pit go?"

The Gravel Pit is the Jacobs' name for the acres of woods and streams behind the house, filled with the trails where they spent most of their childhood. At the edge of the Jacobs' property there's still the same tree line and bushes you'd pass through to reach their old stomping ground. But immediately beyond, some damn fool had leveled the land and thrown up a strip mall.

"A few years after Tóta died." Sis shakes her head. "Seems like it happened overnight."

"How come I never noticed?"

"You been staying with me'n Robert too much when you visit." She smiles at him. "It's good you're here with Mom n' Dad."

Abe nods in agreement. He'd always felt a little guilty choosing his sister's house, knowing his parents weren't getting any younger.

But life being the carnival of surprises that it is, they would now both outlive him.

"What the hell was so great about those woods, anyway?" Sis waves her hand dismissively. "Bunch of snakes and rusted old crap. Trees covered in so much bird shit you had to shower after you climbed them. Killer ants, kamikaze squirrels."

"I know, right?" Abe grunts. "All that fresh air hurt my lungs."

"Those berries stained my hands."

"I got pinched digging for crayfish."

"This one time, the Gravel Pit killed my dog."

"Fuck the Gravel Pit."

"Fuck the Gravel Pit, man."

Abe bites his lip, trying not to laugh. When Sis gets going ("What am I going to do with a new car? A new car would choke to death on Rez gas. I need an engine twenty, twenty-five years old, one that's part Mohawk.") it always kills him.

"You hear from A-Hole?" Abe asks. A-Hole is Adam's Rez nickname, so I guess Toots ain't so bad all things considered. Abe texts their brother and his wife in the same group chat; he can't remember the last time he got an answer directly from Adam. A five-year, seven-year age gap is nothing when you're grown, but the difference between Abe at eight years old, and Sis starting to party, and Adam getting his learner's permit? They might as well have been different species, and so far only he and Sis have found each other as grown-ups.

Sis takes a slow drag of her smoke and levels her gaze at Abe.

"Why don't we talk about Uncle Budge?"

"Oh, right. The healer." Abe blows air through his nose, a mocking sound. But he wonders what Sis will say about their great uncle while their parents are out of earshot.

"That's what they say."

"'They,' who's 'they'?" Abe asks. "People he's healed?"

"What do you want? Do you want to hear how he visited a hospital and pulled some kid out of a wheelchair? How he wiped scar tissue from a burn victim's face?"

"Is there a story like that?"

Sis cocks an eyebrow at Abe; *don't be a dipshit*, the look says.

"Okay," Abe says, "so he doesn't make the lame walk. Does he at least make the blind see?"

"If he could, don't you think he would've fixed Dad's eye for him?"

Right, Dad's blind eye. The story is sand in his eye on the playground; what really happened was, Grandpa hit him hard enough to detach his optic nerve. Sorry if you feel like telling the story before the truth makes me a liar, but you've gotta admit that the made-for-TV version is nicer.

"All right, then tell me what makes Budge a healer?"

Sis thinks for a moment.

"Remember Mrs. Lewis up the road?" she asks. "She used to make that blackberry jam Mom liked so much?"

"Yeah, sure."

Sis gives Abe a look. "No you don't."

"Then why'd you ask? No, I don't. I don't remember Mrs. Lewis. But I hear she lives up the road and makes a mean blackberry jam."

"Whoever told you that must be one cool genius."

"Are you going to tell me about this woman or not?"

Sis rolls her eyes, then leans back in her chair and makes a sweeping gesture over the back lawn, as though the story is written there for Abe to read.

"Not much to it, really. She was dying of cancer. She had so much pain that morphine couldn't touch it. If they shot her up enough to kill the pain, it made her incoherent. Or else it put her to sleep. If they tried to keep her awake, well, she was mean as hell. Basically, she was dying young, which pissed her off, and she took it out on anyone who came into the room. So Budge went to see her."

"And her cancer went into remission?"

"No, ijit, she died two weeks later. But those last two weeks she wasn't in any pain. She was weak, could barely even stomach broth, and she couldn't leave her bed. But she wasn't in pain. And she stopped raging. Her family got her back. For two weeks before she died, her family got her back."

Great, Abe thinks. *Perfect.* Sweat beads in his temples, despite the cool air. His heart speeds up and his ribs feel too tight for his lungs.

"I don't need a spiritual healing, Sis." He wills his breathing to slow before he starts hyperventilating and presses the palms of his hands into his eyes. He's no longer wearing the mittens. Between the diagnosis and the inflammation in his knuckles, it's easy for him to pass off the scabs as a symptom. Current situation aside, he's always been a quick healer.

Abe tries to remember the last time he'd punished his hands like that. A fight with Alex over something stupid? The time his boss yelled at him? He can't remember. He'd learned to handle it better at Syracuse, in no small part because Alex had seen him as easygoing, and Abe desperately wanted to preserve that image. Plus there wasn't enough privacy on campus; all he could get away with was a single blow to an alley wall or public notice board in passing. Sometimes hard enough to draw blood, but never hard enough to pacify his turmoil. In the days after, the livid red marks on his knuckles would fade to bruises, the sight filling Abe with shame. Fear that Alex would notice the damage kept him from melting down too often, until eventually he couldn't remember the last time he'd lost control.

"How do you know what you need?" Sis is looking into the evening, her voice low. It's dark despite the early hour. There are fewer buildings and houses putting off light than Abe's used to as well. Her face is in shadow. "I love you, but you're so far up your own ass, you can see daylight coming through your nostrils. Maybe Uncle Budge'll get you out of your own way."

"Sounds like you've made up your mind that I should ask him to heal me."

She shrugs, settles back in her chair. "Why else're you here?"

Abe opens his mouth, closes it. *Because if I stayed in Miami, I might have done something terrible.* Instead, he asks what Mrs. Blackberry Jam's doctors said about how she died.

"The doctors called it 'Twilight Euphoria.' They say it happens sometimes; lucid, pain-free moments right before death. It's usually just hours, though. Or a day, maybe. Never—not two weeks."

"So . . . we don't know."

"What do we ever know? Richard Pike used to see Budge once a week before he died, and Richard Pike—"

"Has Budge ever healed anyone who lived?"

"Richard Pike had bad kidneys," Sis says over Abe, not quite yelling. She's generally low-key but her tone tells Abe she's close to getting pissed. "Richard Pike saw Budge every week, and he lived without dialysis for eight years."

Which begs the question of how long he might have lived on dialysis, but Abe is not going to bring that up to Sis when she's in a mood.

The porch light comes on. The kitchen door opens, then the screen door creaks and slaps against the wall as Mom and Dad emerge. Dad closes the door behind him to keep the chill air from taking over the kitchen. Sis stands and leans against the porch railing. Abe follows suit, trying to make it look as easy as she did. At least the watery feeling in his thighs has passed. He leans against the railing opposite his sister, hands in his pockets to keep from fidgeting. Before she sits, Mom pulls Abe into a hug. They usually only hug at the end of the day when Abe visits.

Their parents take the seats Abe and Sis vacated.

"Tell me again, Abe." Mom groans as she settles in. She has olive skin in sharp contrast to a crown of striking silver hair. She started seriously going gray at thirty, and Abe has never feared his own gray because of her beautiful shade. Of course, the first time she saw a gray eyebrow hair, she ran around the house in her bathrobe, pulling at her brow and yelling "I'm old, I'm old," so she's not all wisdom and light. She has her own cup of Sis's tea, and she rests it on the arm of her chair, exactly where Sis had hers.

"They call it SNiP," Abe says. "Basically, my immune system is attacking my blood vessels. They don't know what causes it. There's no cure. They don't know how to treat it. If they can get me to go into remission . . ." Abe shakes his head. What Weisberg called his five-year differential was aligned with the deadliest cancers, like brain and pancreatic, but it all hinges on remission. And what are the odds of remission, when Johns Hopkins and NORD can't even decide on a name for the thing you have? For a time, the four of them sit under a pall of silence.

"I was telling Toots about Richard Pike," Sis says.

"Richard Pike, Richard Pike," Dad mumbles. His hands are wrapped around his mug, coffee instead of tea. The man can drink coffee at any hour and it never seems to do anything to him.

"Richard Pike," Mom says sharply, her tone telling Dad he knows who he is.

"Levi Pike's cousin?"

Mom nods.

"Okay, what about him?" Dad asks. "We talking about how he wasted eight years seeing Budge?"

Looking at Sis, Abe gestures at their Dad like, *There you go.*

"You shouldn't talk like that," Mom says, exasperated.

"Why not?"

"Well . . ." Mom looks at Abe, then back at Dad. She's been taking song and dance classes, learning about healing, like Sis with her plants.

"How much healing you get from any Medicine comes from your faith in it," Sis says. She opens her cigarette case, peeks into it, and puts it back in her pocket without removing a smoke. Another reason she rolls her own: whenever she wants to smoke Sis has to weigh the desire for nicotine against knowing if she fires up, she'll be one cigarette closer to the project of rolling more. "You should know that, Dad. How can you say Richard Pike wasted his time?"

"How could I doubt my own uncle-in-law?" Dads says, mock aghast.

"You can't possibly know, Dad."

Dad leans forward in his chair. With the porch light casting shadows on his face, he looks like a prophet. Gazing up at Sis, he points to his blind eye.

"This eye isn't dead, you know. It sees into men's souls."

Mom rolls her eyes.

"Hilarious," Sis deadpans. Her lips press into a thin line. Her mood has not improved since Abe got under her skin.

"I have looked into Budge's soul," Dad says, "and what I've seen there is a whole heap of bullshit."

Sis decides on the cigarette after all, casting her eyes heavenward. "That must be why the two of you get along so well." She inhales, then lets out a plume of smoke that smells sweet and green.

"Must be." Dad grins. "Budge had one good healing in him, you have to give him that. But this business"—he waggles his hands in the air—"this idea of him laying hands on people. I just don't know." Dad shakes his head. He can call bullshit as a joke, but it seems he can't quite bring himself to call Budge a fraud.

"You've lived here all your life," Sis says. "It's like you've never heard a single story anyone's ever told."

"Oh, I've heard 'em all. Most of them twice. Then heard some more for good measure. Even told a few myself, come to think of it. But the truth is, I ain't seen shit. With either eye."

"What's Budge's one good healing?" Abe assumes he's going to hear about Budge's sister Maggie and their horrid stepfather. In other words, a spiritual healing, like Mrs. Blackberry Jam.

Mom and Dad exchange a look. Dad crosses his arms, resting his chin in one hand, coffee mug in the other. This is the pose he assumes when he puts on some old vinyl record with the intention of doing nothing but sitting and listening to it. Mom takes a deep breath, her oval face creasing into a frown. As she gathers herself for this story, Abe can see past the fact that she raised him to what others must see when they look at her: she's becoming an Elder.

They might not "look Indian" (in the way Abraham Jacobs is not an "Indian" name), but Abe has always thought you could build a fine Hollywood Indian from his family's bits and pieces; Sis's fall of raven hair and killer jawline, Mom's black eyes and heavy lips, Dad's blade of nose (the dead eye is a nice touch, too, especially for a villain), Adam's broad forehead and high cheekbones. Abe has lived in Miami long enough to contribute the right skin tone. It doesn't matter what you are, as long as you have the Look. Just ask Johnny Depp, who played Tonto in *The Lone Ranger* movie. That Missing and Murdered Indigenous Woman movie has a Taiwanese girl playing Arapaho, too. If you can count on Hollywood for anything, it's that they'll fuck up Native representation nine ways to Sunday. And even if everyone on screen is Native as hell, I know for damn sure it'd still be white folks telling our stories for us. What's genocide, after all, but a vehicle for Jeremy Renner to Learn Something Profound.

"It was 1978," Mom says. "He was a year younger than your brother, so he would have been twelve years old."

"Who's this now?" Abe asks.

"Tsítso Papineau. Tsítso means fox. His dad was James Papineau, a man who loved to drink. Mean as poison, too. People used to call him O'serón:ni, 'the Frenchman,' because of his last name. But I think we also called him that because we didn't want to claim him. Like saying he was more French than Mohawk, even though most of us have a little French blood somewhere in our family tree. We were kidding ourselves, really. But I suppose when someone does something like that . . .

"The Frenchman, his wife died of diabetes and she wasn't even thirty. After that he bounced from woman to woman. The

Frenchman could catch a woman, but they never stuck around when they saw how he got when he was drunk. So mostly it was just the Frenchman and little Tsítso, all alone.

"Tsítso started turning up to school with bruises. Your Uncle Dan—Dan was on the Tribal Police back then—Dan got wind of it and went to their house. I guess he figured, since they grew up together, O'serón:ni would listen to him. Tsítso was okay for a month or two after that, then he turned up to school with handprints on his arms. Those marks, you could see the Frenchman grabbing poor Tsítso and shaking him. Dan went out there again and told the Frenchman that was it. If Tsítso got so much as a scratch, Tsítso was going into foster care and the Frenchman was going to jail.

"Dan wasn't even Tribal Police for a year yet. I don't know what he would have done if he'd been there longer. No one wants to lose another baby because some fool judge thinks a white family can raise them better. But Tsítso, he was in a terrible situation.

"Not two days later, Dan gets a call from the Papineau's next-door neighbor. She heard Tsítso screaming. So Dan went over there. The Frenchman answered the door. Dan said he stunk like cheap rye. 'You're just in time,' he says, and he invites Dan in. Tsítso was sitting in the living room, hunched over, dangling his arms between his legs so they wouldn't touch anything. He was crying and pale as a corpse. What happened was, the Frenchman caught a notion. He wanted to see whether he could break Tsítso's bones with his bare hands. So he broke Tsítso's forearms, and his upper arms, and he was trying to break his legs. He says to Dan, 'I just about gave up tryin' before you showed up.' He asked for Dan's help. Not in calling an ambulance for his son. Not with fixing whatever was wrong in his head. No, the Frenchman asked for Dan's help breaking Tsítso's legs. He asked it easy, like he wanted help moving a piece of furniture."

"Jesus," Abe says softly, really forgetting his diagnosis for the first time that day.

"Dan called me," Mom says.

Abe had been staring off, picturing the awful scene, but he looks at his mother sharply when she says this last bit. He guesses it makes sense, given how much younger the uncles are than Mom and the aunts.

"He should have called another deputy, or the sheriff, but he called me," Mom repeats, nodding at Abe. "He hadn't been doing it long, like I said. Dan was always sensitive. And it was such a terrible thing. He asked me to drive Tsítso to the hospital while he took O'serón:ni to the station, so of course I went.

"Tóta watched y'all while I drove Tsítso to the hospital. Except I didn't know whether to go to Massena or Malone. Either one was a half hour drive, and Tsítso looked so miserable. He wasn't even crying, just leaking tears. Every time we went over a bump, he . . . I knew no matter what hospital I picked, he'd feel every bump the whole way. I pulled into the Health Center to get my bearings, but I knew if I walked in there, we might never see Tsítso again outside of a courtroom. Then I thought, maybe my friend Millie'd be working. She could give the poor kid a shot for his pain. I'd be in and out right quick, before anyone knew anything. Well who's out front but Uncle Budge. Budge was getting his forehead stitched up because he got drunk and walked into a shelf. He might even have opened a door and hit himself in the face, now that I'm thinking about it.

"I got Tsítso out of the car as gently as I could. Uncle Budge saw me with Tsítso, walked over, and blocked our way going in. He went, 'Hari, it's good to see you.' All excited, like he was throwing a barbecue and I'd just walked in with the cornbread.

"I said, 'Can't really talk now, Uncle Budge.' I tried to get by, keeping myself between Tsítso and Budge. I didn't want Budge patting Tsítso on the back or ruffling his hair or something, making the poor kid's pain worse.

"Budge looked around me and spotted Tsítso. He frowned and sort of leaned back, and he had this look on his face. He said, 'Nope, nope, nope, that won't do, I don't like that one bit.' He stepped right around me like he had places to be. He scooped up Tsítso's hand and pulled him into a handshake. At least, that's what it looked like to me. Like Budge thought I was embarrassed of him so he side-stepped me to introduce himself. Tsítso made this one little noise, like *huh!* Then his mouth dropped open, and his eyes got all big.

"'Better innit?' Budge said. 'Whattaya say we do t'other one?' Tsítso's mouth was still hanging open, but he nodded real slow. Budge held Tsítso's other hand and pulled that arm tight. Tsítso bit his lip but he didn't yelp that second time. This all happened, right in front of me.

"Tsítso flexed his arms, looking up at Budge like he's—I don't know. Bruce Springsteen or someone. Then the boy smiled. It was like the sun came out. He threw his arms around Budge, and Budge, he started laughing. He called Tsítso a big faker, and Tsítso laughed right back. He still had tears on his cheeks, but he was laughing. He arms weren't red anymore, and the swelling was already going down. You could tell there wasn't a thing wrong with him anymore.

"Budge looks at me, bandage on his forehead, sweating beer, and says, 'You got time to catch up now?'"

Sis and Dad laugh, and Mom chuckles. Abe wears the sort of grin you use when everyone else gets the joke except you. "One good healing," his father had said. It flashes through Abe's mind unbidden, the little boy screaming for help, playing a form of possum to get his dad to lay off, believing the lie so totally he convinced himself, snapped out of it by Budge's good cheer.

"So Tsítso Papineau never had an X-ray?"

"Oh, Abe." Mom shakes her head, frowning and smiling all at once. Sis makes a *tsk* noise. Even Dad looks annoyed.

"I think you might need a mud bath, son," he says. "Get the earth back in you. You wouldn't mind, would you?"

"Then tell me Budge is a healer, Dad." Abe's voice is flint, a tone he learned from the man he's looking at. "Come on, let's hear the words."

The one eye that sees him is hard. The expression is the ghost of the father Abe remembers, the one who wore sobriety like a shirt of razor blades, the one pained by talking, or by silence, or by the wind. The one who it was best to avoid, lest his simmering rage boil over into his fists.

"Maybe he is and maybe he's not," Dad says slowly. "But I know a healing when it happens."

"Abe." Mom's voice is pitched so low, Abe has to strain to hear her. "I drove that poor baby back to the station to meet with his father. The whole drive, he kept flexing his arms. 'I heard them snap,' he said. 'I felt it.' Outside the Health Center it felt . . . well, I don't know exactly. Not any way I can put in words. But it felt good. It felt right. On the drive, the farther away we got from . . . whatever it was, I started to get scared."

"You took him back to his father?"

"Well, I drove him back to the station. Dan called Tsítso's istá. She took him in."

In Kanien'kéha, istá means both mother and aunt. Since Tsítso's mother was dead, Abe understands Mom is referring to Tsítso's aunt. Abe rubs his face, trying to center himself. The agony in his hips, knees, and stomach has been unrelenting. It's like being trapped in a building that's on fire. Not the pain of burning flesh, but the skin-crawling panic of having no way out. He's scared of dying young. He's angry Budge's healing didn't do anything. Further, he feels stupid and embarrassed for being angry. It's his body betraying him, not his family. Taking a deep breath, Abe manages to keep his voice even. "Why didn't she take the kid in the first place? Why let him get abused for so long?"

"Abe, I don't know." Mom shrugs. "Probably she doesn't, either."

"It had to happen like it did," Dad says, swigging the last of his coffee.

Abe wants to rail at him: *You were mocking Budge five minutes ago, make up your mind.*

"When Tóta heard the story," Mom says, "it was like something clicked. She confronted Budge and he got sober. Maybe that's why it had to happen like it did; he's a lot better for the world sober. We wouldn't have Sharon in our lives, or her husband, or their daughter. You wouldn't be here."

"Come on, Mom. I would—"

"Would you?" She's not a crying woman, but Abe can tell she's getting emotional. Her voice is soft and slow in a way it only gets when she's telling hard truth, when her words are fighting to come. "I think if you hadn't remembered meeting Budge at Tóta's funeral, you would've stayed in Miami. We wouldn't have heard about your sickness until it had been cured or it had killed you. We don't talk about things that matter until they're behind us. By then either everything's okay and it stopped mattering, or someone's dead and it can't matter."

Abe takes a moment to reflect and realizes his mom is right— except about Budge. She reminded Abe about his great uncle the healer *after* he'd arrived from Miami and told everyone about his health problems. What he hadn't told them was why he'd left Miami.

"I don't know about y'all," Abe says, absently rubbing his stomach, as though he could relieve the ache, "but I'm calling it a night."

Abe isn't a clean freak but he needs another shower for his second daily disinfection. The shower curtain has a spray of sunflowers to really lean in to the yellow tile everywhere. Growing up, Abe hated that the only bathroom was just off the kitchen, where everyone gathered all the time. Like most of the house, the room is an add-on. The door is thin as a Nutty Buddy wafer, the gap underneath three fingers wide. Once, as a teenager, Abe complained he was tired of ripping ass with an audience.

"You're welcome to use the outhouse, like we did," his mother invited sweetly. Thankfully, this wasn't a real threat; by the time Abe came along, the only people using the outhouse were wasps. He did stop complaining, though.

Soaping up, Abe thinks about the first time he brought Alex home from college, how self-conscious he'd felt in front of his big-city girl-friend. The green Formica table and matching vinyl chairs in the Jacobs' kitchen would've made a hipster drool forty years earlier, when it was all new. By the time Alex came into Abe's life, the table's surface had dulled and the vinyl seats had split and been "repaired" with clear packing tape. At breakfast, Abe sped to the chair closest to the window, the one with more tape than vinyl. Stupid, considering everything he couldn't cover up—the mismatched rugs, the cracked windowpanes, the outdated decor, his dad's crass humor (when Abe asked why he and Alex had to sleep in separate beds, for instance, Dad answered, "You're just in a touch-hole relationship," with Alex standing right there).

At that point he'd never been to Alex's house in South Miami, but he'd leafed through a photo album. Her mother had made a complete turn away from her former hippy ways, furnishing Alex with a life out of a design magazine. Seeing Alex eat eggs and rez hash (basically mashed potatoes with ground beef or pork, mixed together and browned) with mismatched utensils at the faded table had put Abe on edge. She'd been gracious, though. The guest room was near the living room, where Tóta played the TV at window-rattling volume while she fell asleep in her favorite chair. Still, Alex claimed she'd slept like a baby.

As their time together went on, Abe would learn that Alex's artsy parents had kept them just above the poverty line. Once, without a morsel of food or a parental figure in sight, Alex had eaten an entire box of chocolate squares she found in the bathroom—which, of course, turned out to be Ex-Lax. Alex's first job had been hustling backyard mangoes by the side of the road as a preteen, and it was the first time she'd been able to buy new clothes. Did she jump fences and steal those mangoes from people's lawns? You bet she did. She liked getting not-thrifted clothes so much, she started climbing trees at her parents' house to harvest the coconuts, giving her something to hawk roadside year-round.

For twenty years Abe and Alex had managed to live in Coral Gables, the fanciest zip code in Miami (if you didn't count Fisher Island, where all the celebrities live). Coral Gables was built in the 1920s as a playground for the rich, centered around gorgeous Mediterranean-style rock coral structures—a quarry pool with grottos and waterfalls, a country club and golf course, and a grand hotel. Ornate archways surrounded the neighborhood, and fountains were peppered throughout. Abe had no business living there, is what I'm saying, and neither did Alex. Here's how it happened: when they'd first moved to Miami they'd lived out west in a suburb called Kendall, and Alex had worked as a host at a chain restaurant. One of the regulars was a woman named Judy, who sat at the bar most afternoons drinking Schnebly's Beach Rose, an atrocious guava-avocado concoction from a local winery the bartender kept on hand just for her. Eventually it came out that Judy owned a duplex in Coral Gables. She lived on the top floor and she'd had "bad luck" with renters, so for five years, the bottom floor had been sitting empty.

The place was huge, built in 1918, with all the original details still intact—fourteen-foot ceilings, glass doorknobs, narrow-plank hardwood floors, a giant sunroom in the front with Spanish tile, a stone Spanish-revival fireplace, jalousie windows, and tiny black and white hexagon tiles in the bathroom, which of course had a claw-foot tub. The living room even boasted a telephone nook. It was all a bit rundown, but Judy let them move in without putting up the last month's rent or a security deposit, and she charged a third of what she could've gotten, so they really couldn't complain. The condition was, as Judy put it, "If you ever hear a thud on your ceiling one night, you have to come up and collect the body."

In Coral Gables, Southern live oaks, banyans, shady black olive trees, and slash pine provided a thick canopy over the sidewalks and streets. Orchids and air plants exploded from the trunks. People landscaped their lawns with all manner of palm and flowering trees. Trellises crawling with pink trumpet vines adorned moss-covered limestone piazzas. There were pocket parks decorated with bright red royal poinciana and thickets of pink shower trees like something out of a Japanese garden. If Abe was having a bad day, often all it took was a walk around the block, enjoying the greenery, to set his mind right. He'd hoped to work some magic on his mental state in this way the night before his flight to Ahkwesáhsne, in fact.

Abe had lain awake, replaying the fight with Alex, adrenaline coursing through his body. At some point he'd drifted off, because he'd woke in pitch blackness, an image of his fingers sunk into Alex's arm as he grabbed her and forced her to face him seared into his mind. The sound of Alex's contented breathing beside him chewed away any notion of sleep. Abe decided a predawn run, watching the sunrise in a garden paradise, would be just the thing. Not only would it clear his head, the endorphins would alleviate his pain. For the first time in months, Abe wore shorts. The bandages covering his lesions flashed beneath him in the dark as he moved. Ignoring the pain in his knees and hips, brushing the crab spiders' and orb weavers' webs from his face and hair, Abe tried to increase his speed, looking for relief.

Snails trailed back and forth across the sidewalk, crunching beneath his sneakers. Abe switched to the street, where he slipped on strings of fallen pine seeds. As the morning went on, the pungent orange seeds—each about the size of a grape tomato, but firm as an apple—would be smashed by passing cars, attracting clouds of bees and hornets. In the darkness, the little seeds just wanted to trip him up.

Was it the steroids that made him move back to the sidewalk? Possibly. Watching for pine seeds, he couldn't build up enough speed to clear his head. Every step vibrated painfully through his knees. The third time he slipped, Abe nearly lost his feet. *Fuck it,* he thought, hopping back up to the walkway. There were times in his life accidentally stepping on a snail had brought tears to his eyes. Now, though? Deliberately? Blood thrumming with steroids and frustration? The crunching sounds gave Abe a mean pleasure. *Whatever is happening might kill me,* Abe thought, *but I'll outlive these fucking snails.*

On the heels of this cruel idea, as if proving how much more important to the Gables ecosystem they were than him, Abe crushed a snail and slipped. His kneecap slammed down on the sidewalk, erasing a crescent-shaped smile of skin. "Goddammit." Anger overrode the pain. His legs looked bad enough, and there he was skinning part of his flesh that was clean. Rage turned his blood into a bassline, vibrating his temples. He clawed at the bandages on his lower legs, prepared to rip them off, to tear them to pieces and throw them in the bushes like confetti. Then he saw the shadows moving at the edge of his vision. His rage dissolved into fear. The harbingers of death had found him at last, as they had found Tóta during her last meal. Kneeling in the dark, he wasn't surprised to be surrounded by crawling shadows; his flesh was rotting off his bones, after all. Only when Abe looked directly at the shadows to disperse them with his living gaze, they still circled him, creeping over the sidewalk—not shadow-harbingers at all but snails with their shells as black as dollops of tar. The improbable soldiers crawled all around him, glistening in the predawn. For a moment, Abe felt relieved. Soon, looking at them filled him with atavistic revulsion. He loved all of God's creatures, was on a catch-and-release program with any pest in his house that wasn't a roach or a mosquito, but these creatures did not seem to be of God.

Abe's breath trembled as he slowly stood, careful not to step on any of them. He backed away, toeing snails aside to find his footing. His sneakers squeaking through snail slime sounded both muffled and too clear, like an echo of sound instead of the sound itself. It felt like he'd stepped out of time. The air left a coating in his mouth. Never in life had there been snails with shells so black, like holes in reality. Like the lesions on his lower legs. Abe moved back, heart pounding with fear, looking all around, desperate not to kill another. Once he was clear of the nightmare snails, Abe turned and walked back to the house, arriving just as the sun came up. He knew he'd made the right decision to return to Ahkwesáhsne. The black snails were like an arrow, pointing toward his childhood home.

Freshly showered, sanitized, and bandaged up, Abe heads for his old bedroom. Since Uncle Ghost is on the night shift at the casino, Abe's got the room to himself. Masturbating would alleviate his pain for a short while, the way drinking or exercise would, long enough for him to fall asleep. He knows one of the many boxes up here holds old *Playboys* and *Penthouses*, but his thoughts are too chaotic. He sits on his bed, marveling that his old room still smells the same after all these years. Even with the crazy neighbors, and the Gravel Pit gone, spending time with his parents under this old roof has given him glimpses of calm. If only he could string some of those moments together.

Abe sees the notebook Budge gave him sitting on the nightstand. It's wraparound buckskin leather with Coptic stitching and heavy pages, like something someone cosplaying a wizard might carry. It's beautiful and ridiculous and Abe loves the heft of it in his hand, the trace smell of leather it leaves on his fingertips. Abe hopes Budge made it himself; otherwise, Abe might have to rethink his hatred of the tourist-kitsch shops. He flips through the blank pages, surprised at how they call to him. Abe hasn't written anything in months apart from complaints about his marriage, self-pitying tripe over the state of his body, and dire speculation about his future, all logged on his laptop. Maybe he should give his computer a rest, shake up his routine. The notebook might not be the key to rediscovering his voice, but holding it makes him feel like maybe he could trust the run of his thoughts again. And what a blessing that would be.

SOME DEEDS ARE STRONGER THAN MUSIC

by Dominick Deer Woods

When the Creator blew strength into my cousin She coughed
    and he almost exploded.
He didn't look like much but his hug could crack a rib.
If you didn't know him, you might say he was too quiet.

My cousin left the Rez and took his guitar to the Big City,
a dying factory town steeped in resentment and racism
with a university on top like a single
staple on a festering slash of wound.

My cousin found a biker bar.
A biker bar with live blues and a tonk piano can't be
a genuine boogie-woogie without at least one "Indian,"
so they let him drink for free.
My cousin let his one free draft sweat into the bar
while he listened.

Compare my cousin to the rough men around him,
you might say he wasn't enjoying himself.
You wouldn't notice him drinking the music into his bones.
On the reservation, music like that is an event. In the
    Big City,
college town boogie-woogie, it was an average weeknight.

My cousin's hands itched with unshed songs.
His thick fingers bled when he played,
a dishwasher's hands, squelching over the notes.
If you saw them, revulsion might wrinkle your nose.

One night in the boogie-woogie my cousin met a dead man.
The man didn't know he was dead. Not when he introduced
    himself
with the barked insults such men use. Not when he escalated
    to threats
and violence. Not even when he pulled a switch knife from
    his pocket.
The dead man only grasped his fate when my cousin,
who, as the saying goes, doesn't know his own strength,
fought back.

A biker bar with live blues
and a tonk piano can't be a genuine boogie-woogie without
blood seeped into the floorboards.

My cousin returned to the Rez,
dragging the dead man behind him.

His guitar never made it back.

Five

Allow me to introduce myself. Hello, I'm Dominick. Dominick Deer Woods. I wonder what you've made of my occasional intrusions, or if you've even noticed them. Mostly, I wonder what you think the relationship between me, your proud narrator, and Abe, our humble protagonist, might be.

Wait, you didn't notice the note at the beginning wasn't from Abraham Jacobs? What about the poems? TV started the Great American Brain Rot and the internet is finishing the job. Stop amusing yourself to death and pay attention, hey.

You might not remember your birth, being a baby at the time and all. That puts me one up on you, because I was seventeen when I was born. The graduation poem that made Abe's dad cry, his high school English teacher must've recommended Abe to the principal at Salmon Run. The principal guaranteed Abe an A if he wrote something for the occasion and read it aloud (with an ominous hint that his grades would suffer if he didn't). Abe wanted to say no—his teacher and principal expected him not just to write to a specific event, but to then read it in front of all these kids he wasn't friendly with and their parents, while his bullies sniggered behind their hands. Then again, it was a guaranteed A; what's a studious boy to do?

Dollars to donuts he was getting an A anyway, but that never occurred to him. His family kept him naive, like I said.

Abraham Jacobs is not an Indian name. We've covered how it's a Native name but that doesn't make it an Indian name. Dominick Deer Woods, though? You could light a peace pipe with it. Dominick came from Abe's cousin, who was fighting an involuntary manslaughter charge Abe's senior year. Deer Woods was for the White Gaze. Thanks to missionary . . . let's call it "zeal," you'd be hard-pressed to find a Mohawk surname you can't find in Oxford (and I mean the one in England). Abe came up with Deer Woods because it's close to the Kanien'kéha name Tóta gave him. The anglicized version of it, anyway. Once he had the name, thinking of a graduation poem became a simple WWDDWD—What Would Dominick Deer Woods Do?

I didn't spring to life fully formed at high school graduation; I was more of a zygote. Later, when Abe had to perform in front of his theater "classmates" at Syracuse University, that's when I became me. Abe never changed his major from English. Instead, he followed Alex to her classes and told everyone (except for her) that he was a musical theater major. Abe risked his scholarships and tribal grants (and, of course, the idea that a college degree would open up a larger world to him) in order to spend as much time as possible with a girl he'd just met.

Why, you ask? Because he was a broken boy. I don't know whether you expected the Mohawk version of *Angela's Ashes*, but if you did, then I'm sorry, because I don't want to tell it. At the same time, you need enough for some understanding of why Abe is how he is, so here's something from his childhood I don't like to talk about. If it helps, tell yourself it's just a story.

One night as they lay in bed at Alex's North Campus apartment, waiting to see whether they'd drift off to sleep or rally for another round of sex, Alex shared the first nonsalacious intimate detail she'd ever divulged to him.

"I used to be bulimic."

"Imagine, you could've been taller than me," Abe said.

She tweaked his nipple, making him yelp.

"What I meant to say was, 'How sad, tell me more.'"

"That's not even true." Alex frowned. "I made myself throw up once. But I told everyone I was bulimic. My mother made me see a psychiatrist. I don't think I told him a single thing that was true."

"What's the point of lying to your psychiatrist?" Abe asked. When his parents had taken him to a psychologist in middle school, Abe had been as honest as possible.

"Oh, I lie to everybody."

"Why?" Streetlight from the window played over Alex's body. Abe caressed her idly, wondering how he'd gotten so lucky that such a gorgeous creature could want him.

"This from the guy telling everyone he's a musical theater major." She grabbed Abe's hand, holding it still. "According to the new shrink I'm seeing, it's a control thing."

"So you're not lying to him?" Abe asked. "Or you're at least being truthful about lying to everyone else?"

"I'm trying to be honest with this one, so I don't kill myself."

"Kill yourself?" Abe was unable to keep the surprise from his voice. On the Rez, suicide happens so often it's practically a natural cause. The statistics would be even worse if you counted drinking yourself to death, or overdosing on meth. When people talk about substance abuse and suicide on the Rez, they love to use the word "epidemic." That doesn't sit well with me. First, diseases don't have intent. Second, it implies there's some defect of Native character that gives these problems room to grow. Both issues have the same root cause, and there's nothing natural about it. Pick at most any problem in Ahkwesáhsne, or anywhere in Indian Country, and sooner or later you'll end up talking about white supremacy.

Broader issues aside, there's Cheryl Curly Head. Abe's First Everything sometimes broke down and begged him not to leave until the sun came up, so she knew she'd live to see another day. Then there's Abe himself . . . but we're almost there. For the moment, let's just say Alex suggesting she'd considered suicide took him aback. She was upbeat in contrast to Abe's negativity, restless where he was mellow, outgoing to his introversion. Where Abe had self-esteem issues, Alex came across as confident to the point of arrogant (when the theater faculty asked where she saw her career in ten years, for instance, Alex said she'd be an icon). She really seemed to understand the absurdity of life and how to live it lightly.

"I don't think I could do it," Alex said. "I'm just sad lately."

Abe waited for her to say why, but she didn't.

"Being away from home?" he ventured.

"I'll tell you some day," she said. "Not tonight."

Alex's candor brought out emotions and secrets which he normally struggled to express, or deliberately kept hidden. "I tried to kill myself," Abe said. He'd never spoken the words aloud, not to his psychologist, and not to Cheryl, but he told Alex that night. "I jumped out of my bedroom window when I was seven."

"Oh my God."

"It's okay. There was snow on the ground. It broke my fall."

"No, I mean—why? I mean . . . seven."

Abe took a deep breath, staring at the ceiling. As easy as she was to talk to, did Alex need to know he'd snuck a steak knife into his room and kept it hidden there for weeks? Did she need the visual of him holding it in his little hands after school, trying to summon the courage to stab himself through the heart? Did she need to know he tried to hang himself, his child's mind thinking a thumbtack pushed through the belt of his bathrobe into the ceiling would hold him?

When Tóta died, shoeboxes of old photographs sat on the kitchen table for people to sift through. Abe found a picture of himself from this time. Second grade, shoulder-length hair combed to the side, suit jacket buttoned over a turtleneck, mouth stretched into an over-wide grin. The photo was black-and-white but Abe immediately recognized the dark red jacket he'd worn every day for two months, which he'd gotten from a church donation bin. He'd started wearing the jacket to school because it was the dressiest piece of clothing he owned. He'd given away his *Star Wars* figures and Micronauts to his friends, had kept the room he shared with his brother, Adam, spotless, did whatever his parents told him without complaint. Abe wanted the people he was leaving behind to have good memories of him.

With no children in his life on a regular basis, Abe had only a vague sense of himself as a second grader. On the rare occasions he pictured this time, he was an abstraction, a smaller version of the Abe looking back. Seeing a picture of the child who jumped out the window shifted something inside of Abe, like he'd somehow captured his inner child on film. How much of this picture did Alex need to see?

"My dad was an alcoholic," Abe said. "Well, *is* an alcoholic. It's like being a Marine, you know? No matter how long you were one, you're one for the rest of your life. In alcoholic families, children take on certain roles. The first born is the Hero. Adam kicked ass at pretty much everything. I couldn't go anywhere on the Rez without someone calling me 'Adam's little brother.' The second born is the Scapegoat. Sis got in a lot of fights. She got kicked out of school and ended up in rehab. I was the third born, the Lost Child. They kill themselves. I'll tell you, you haven't lived until you've seen the worst truth of your life typed out in a little pamphlet."

"Your heart's beating so fast," Alex whispered.

Abe breathed a shaky, nervous laugh. "I remember lying there in the snow, looking up at the sky until it got dark. By the time Mom came to get me for dinner, my body was numb. I'd locked my bedroom door. She had to open it with a screwdriver. I bet the room was freezing, with the window wide-open like that. I saw her lean out. She was just a silhouette, blocking the light. She yelled down, asking me what had happened. I told her I'd jumped. She asked me why . . .

"I was that weirdo kid who tied a blanket around his neck and said it was a cape, you know? I'd wear it for weeks, say I was Batman, say I was Dracula. Mom probably expected me to say I was trying to fly." Abe snorted, bitterly. Alex found his hand in the dark and squeezed. "Instead, I yelled up that I wanted to kill myself. She said, '*What?*' in this shocked voice. So I said it again. Then she asked me why. Again."

Years of one-on-one counseling to get in touch with his emotions, family counseling to help them communicate, Children of Alcoholics meetings to open him up, AlaTeen to keep him sober, and Abe still only has the vaguest idea of what he may have been thinking. There was something fundamentally wrong with his family, something broken from the time he was born. Acting like it was normal, like he wasn't in emotional turmoil, was excruciating. His only thought was he could end it. The relief this idea brought was profound. It was when he started dressing up every day.

"Why did you?" Alex asked.

"Why are you?" Abe countered.

"That's not fair," she said.

"Well, I didn't." Not for lack of trying, of course. If he'd been older, he would have been better at it. He would have found a place higher than twenty-something feet to jump from. He would have tied himself to something sturdier. He would have drawn a hot bath and found a razor blade. So I guess it's good he tried as a child. All the counseling, keeping a diary, it saved him as a teen. Not from darkness, never that, but from snuffing the light.

Hey, you want to hear something funny? Now Abe is killing himself for real, only it's via an involuntary illness. Well . . . it's funny ironic, not laugh-out-loud funny.

Alex rested her hand on Abe's stomach, and he took another shaking breath. "Whatever the reason, when I jumped, that was Dad's rock bottom."

Now he was lying. If that was Dad's bottoming out, then it took a good five years for it to really hit home. Abe is sure they didn't start counseling until he turned twelve. He despised talking about his feelings, so on the way home after one of those first sessions, Abe had demanded to know how long he was expected to go. "It took twelve years for you to get this messed up," Mom had answered. "It might take another twelve to fix you." The answer had made him want to scream.

Once he fell silent, Alex rolled over in bed and held him. Abe didn't cry, only took deep breaths until he didn't feel like crying anymore. After a time, he wrapped his arms around Alex and began to drift off. Her voice brought him back. "Did Hurricane Andrew make the news up here?"

"Oh, yeah." The month before, Andrew had been the first Category 5 to hit the country in sixty years. It had killed scores of people and leveled Miami neighborhoods, leaving thousands homeless. Abe had seen helicopter shots of the military's tent cities, watched interviews with grim-eyed homeowners who promised death to looters. "I've wanted to ask you about it."

"Two big trees smashed into our house," Alex said. "We still have a bedroom and part of the living room tarped off. Mom has to wait for the insurance people to see it before she can fix it, and they're backed up with all the claims. Believe it or not, you get used to the heat. It's the sameness that drives you crazy. Like, if I eat one more can of tuna I'm gonna lose it, you know?"

Abe didn't, but he agreed with Alex to keep her talking.

"Most of the time, hurricanes miss. Or they become tropical storms. Andrew was the first storm of the year, and we hadn't been hit in forever. Besides buying chips and beer, no one was ready.

Instead of a couple of days without power, it was weeks. You couldn't drink the water without boiling it, and you couldn't boil it without gas. We were lucky, because my father was a little paranoid. They both had real jobs by this point, so he'd stocked us up. So much we even had enough to share with our neighbors. We had even more to go around, after . . .

"You're not supposed to drive. That's the thing. There are no traffic lights, and the roads are full of debris. It's supposed to be emergency travel only, just the power guys and the tree guys. I guess running out of beer qualifies as an emergency for some people. My father was out clearing our lawn. He was pushing a wheelbarrow with a tree stump in it. A drunk driver blew through the stop sign in front of our house and ran him over."

"Oh, babe." Abe tightened his arms around her.

She continued her story, speaking into his chest. "He died right away, so that's something." She choked back a sob. "The driver stopped, too. I guess we should be glad he didn't take off. That was almost worse, though. Our world ended, and we have this stranger kneeling on our front lawn, wailing at the sky. I might even have comforted him at one point?"

Alex stopped holding back; she broke down. Abe thought of his mother during one of their family counseling sessions. "How fucked-up are we?" she'd asked, a painful smile quivering on her lips. "I want to cry right now and I can't. That's how fucked-up I am. I want to cry in front of my own family and I can't." In that moment, holding Alex, stroking her back until she quieted, Abe realized Alex would be good for him. He held everything inside; she let everything out.

"I went to my father's funeral two weeks after Hurricane Andrew," Alex said, once she could speak again. "That was a Monday. We got power back at the house on Thursday. I flew here Friday. The Monday after the funeral, I met you."

Abe held her. He didn't know what else to do. She'd gotten special dispensation to live alone because of her recent loss, which is why she'd gotten cagey about having a place on North Campus.

You know, now that I'm thinking about it, I can't say for sure they shared these pains the same night, confession to confession like that. But they had so many late nights and when they weren't having sex, Alex and Abe talked, so it's tough to say when all of this came out. What you need to know is, they didn't hold back.

Did they bond mentally and emotionally because the sex was good? Or was the sex good because of their bond? The word for that first stage of getting together—when your brain is all oxytocin, dopamine, and intrusive thoughts of your lover—is "limerence." Basically, when you think you've found your soulmate, it's the drugs talking. Not to shit on their early days, I'm just saying sooner or later limerence fades and you have to decide whether or not to get to know the actual person behind your idealized projections. I guess since they eventually got married, you know that Abe and Alex decided to try.

Hey, you want to hear something else funny? Abe's family never talked about his suicide attempt, not in counseling, and certainly not with each other. Everyone gathered around the dinner table the night he jumped must've heard Abe and his mother yelling through the house's clapboard walls. After their exchange, his mother came outside, pulled Abe from the snow, and brought him to the kitchen table. Then Abe's family ate dinner. It's not ha-ha funny, more like horrify-people-over-cocktails funny, but it's still a hell of a punchline. It's also how I know some forms of silence make the air almost too thick to breath.

SYRACUSE, 1992

My childhood was much nicer than Abe's. Surrounded by New York City theater kids who'd been taking dance and vocal lessons since grade school, Abe stuck out with his wooden line readings, lumbering dance moves, and off-key warblings. I stepped in to loosen Abe up, take the edge off his performance anxiety.

The professors kept bragging about how much they'd expanded the theater program that year, admitting a freshman class as large as the prior four classes combined. Abe convinced the professors he'd appear on their rolls once the bursar's office fixed a screwup with his grant money. This bought him a month in the program. Abe still remembers the preppy redheaded song study professor, Miss Karp, who finally called him out. The look on her face as she peered over her reading glasses and said, "Please, please leave and quit wasting everyone's time," haunts Abe, especially when he's already feeling down on himself.

Abe left the theater classes, but he brought me with him. He wanted to give performing a shot, so he started to write in my voice to give himself something to say. I became Henry Chinaski to Abe's Charles Bukowski. Or, Indigenously, the Miss Chief Eagle Testickle to Abe's Kent Monkman.

Before Starbucks came along in the aughts and killed it, Zopie's Caffeine Fix was SU's coffee shop. On Wednesday nights they hosted open mic nights, and Abe and Alex started frequenting them. Inhabiting the basement of a corner lot beneath a chain drugstore, Zopie's had low ceilings but a lot of floor space. It was shaped like a capital *L*, with steps leading up to the sidewalk at either end and a coffee counter in the bend. Everything was painted white, with graffiti-covered wooden tables and a rotating gallery of student artwork hanging on the walls. Only one end of the *L* allowed smoking. Since the stage was in the nonsmoking end, you could at least see through the haze of secondhand smoke.

In general, Abe dressed preppy some days and punk on others (where "preppy" means khakis, flannel button-downs, and black Chuck Taylors, and "punk" means ripped jeans, classic rock tees, and Doc Martens). On performing nights, to get into character, Abe spent the day dressed in what he imagined I would wear—thrift store Red Wing boots, jeans, and a denim jacket. No matter what time of year, he went shirtless underneath the jacket. He didn't have William "Sonny" Landham's abs, but he was skinny enough at the time. Plus, folks liked the novelty of seeing bare skin in cold weather. He didn't have Sonny Landham's cheekbones, either, but when Abe braided his hair and wrapped a rolled-up paisley bandanna around his head, people got the point.

Who's Sonny Landham? Native actor whose heyday was the eighties. His biggest roles were in the original *Predator* with Arnold Schwarzenegger and *48 Hrs.* with Eddie Murphy. Sonny did the same thing in both; he played the Indian.

When Abe stepped to the mic as me, we didn't slam, we recited. Still, I was a force. I could wed Judith beheading Holofernes to settlers scalping Indians, blackface Shakespearean actors to redface in Hollywood, and diplomatic immunity in *Lethal Weapon 2* to US laws allowing non-Indians to commit crimes on reservations, all in one poem.

On the best nights, the entire coffee house went silent, register and espresso machine on pause, customers keeping their cups and spoons still so they wouldn't miss a word. I felt like my poetry could make flowers bloom, defeat colonialism, and melt the panties off every woman in hearing distance. On the worst nights—people sitting stone-faced and borderline hostile—it was so humiliating that had a sinkhole opened at my feet, I would have stepped into it with a grateful sigh.

However the poems went over, Abe still got his coffee for free. And Alex loved to watch. "Your writing gets me wet," I believe were her exact words after one of those early readings. She was talking shit but she did it with a gleam in her eye.

"Are you even paying attention?" Abe asked her. "This is not sexy stuff I'm reading." They were sitting at a table away from the stage, against the wall, watching the other performers—students, for the most part, with the occasional local thrown in (mostly gay men with devastating stories of losing lovers to AIDS, since this was the early nineties).

"Whatever you say, shirtless." Alex closed her eyes and tilted her head back. "You should see yourself up there." She made an *uhn* noise deep in her throat.

"So what you're saying is you've got a thing for Dominick."

"Oh my God." Alex sat up straight, giving Abe a wide-eyed, eager look. "Do you think he'd like me?"

"I'm sure he'd be happy to ravage your body with five hundred years of colonized rage."

Alex barked a laugh. She ran a hand up Abe's thigh. Too far up for public consumption, but no one noticed.

"Maybe he'll join us tonight?" she asked.

"I should warn you . . ." Abe eyed her over the rim of his coffee cup, taking a slow sip. "Dom's libido is too large to be contained to one woman."

"A man after my own heart." Alex was always seeing at least one person outside of their relationship, usually a woman. One memorable month, she'd had four extra lovers—two boys and two girls. Not because she didn't love Abe and didn't see them lasting, but for the opposite reason. She said they'd be together until they died, and nineteen was too young to never sleep with anyone else. Again, Abe didn't see a flaw in her sex logic.

As for Abe? By that point, Abe had heard that he was gay so often he worried their theater friends knew something about him that he didn't know about himself. Drama and musical theater majors were coming out of the closet left and right, to the cheers of their class-mates. Maybe Abe was one of them . . . except it didn't feel right. Abe had a lesbian cousin, a gay uncle, and plenty of butch women in his family who didn't give much of a shit how they presented to the world. Mohawk men, I'll admit many of them have fallen prey to white patriarchal norms. Our precolonial conception of same-sex love (which is that they embody the Creator as equally as opposite-sex lovers) has been tainted by American prejudice. There's a Mohawk contingent whose understanding of what it means to be a "warrior" is steeped in toxic, macho bullshit. Still, most rez folks don't give a flying fuck how you identify or who you sleep with. When the popular notion of what is right and good doesn't include you, that makes it very easy to embrace people living outside those arbitrary definitions of "right" and "good." All this to say, if Abe had wanted to be with other guys, I think he would have just dated other guys. Alex would have welcomed it. Logically, he thought her sex philosophy made sense, but—beyond a few drunken make-outs—he hadn't been able to make his body follow her lead.

Every weekend, Abe, Alex, various theater students, and a gang of local outcasts hung out at Syracuse's one gay club, Traxx. Dancing among people who'd lost so many loved ones to AIDS was to take part in a collective expulsion of grief, a deliberate break from reality, a celebration of life that I'm struggling to capture with mere words. Douse your clothes in vodka, light yourself on fire, then twirl around in the rain, and maybe you'll have some inkling of what those nights felt like. They'd dance until the lights came on and Celine Dion's "It's All Coming Back to Me Now" blared from the speakers. Afterward, they'd get breakfast at a twenty-four-hour diner called the All Night Egg Plant, laughing as the sun came up.

One night, a big group of them sat at a table in the alley behind Traxx. When the bouncer ran a hand up Abe's thigh, Abe thought, *What the hell? I'll see where this leads.* After Celine Dion's voice shook the rafters, instead of getting breakfast, Abe went back to the bouncer's apartment.

The place smelled like reworn laundry. They sat on the bouncer's futon couch, a muted TV providing the mood lighting. If I can interject here, I'd like to say Abe could have done a lot better for his first time with a guy than that bouncer. He was a big, brown-haired, pear-shaped doofus, barely even cute, who everyone thought was a straight guy there for the paycheck. They kissed and Abe didn't particularly care for it, but he went through the motions. No matter how much passion he faked, his erection wouldn't last longer than a few seconds at a time. But the bouncer was good and hard, so Abe worked with that.

Abe unzipped the bouncer's jeans and released his penis, stroking as they made out. He was shocked at how quickly the man came. He'd planned on using his mouth—any experiment worth trying is worth doing right—but the bouncer's speed didn't give Abe a chance. Abe would have been mortified over such a quick orgasm, but the bouncer didn't seem remotely self-conscious. After coming, the man also lost interest in the whole encounter with equal speed.

"You wanna fuck me?" the bouncer said. Abe imagined he would use the same resigned, flat tone suggesting fast food for dinner. Abe declined, washed his hands in a sink littered with stubble shavings, and left. He parked his old K-car at the base of The Hill in the morning sun, then slept through classes while his alarm bleated for unknowable time, entering dreams where he drove around the city fighting fires.

His limp penis—and the inability to inhabit his body rather than judge the scene from a distance (disassociation, I believe the kids call it, and by "kids" I mean "mental health professionals")—should have told Abe what he needed to know about whether he harbored desires for gay sex. But our boy Abe kept trying. After months of hearing how gay he was, he felt obligated to fool around with most any guy who showed interest. He gave a lot of head and a few hand jobs, and even spread his legs once. For all the orgasms Abe gave while he "experimented" with guys, the only orgasms he was gifted came from Alex.

Hearing about his encounters with guys drove her wild. "Tell me," she'd say, "tell me," slowly riding him while he whispered in her ear. Sometimes she'd take him into her mouth as he narrated. She'd start to voice those deep groans he loved to hear, so Abe embellished, erasing the doubt, self-consciousness, and discomfort he'd felt while he was in the moment. Retroactively, he made it sound sexy.

Try not to judge Abe too harshly. Didn't you read somewhere that he's the child of an alcoholic? He had childhood trauma, self-esteem issues. As shameful as it sounds, he went with guys he wasn't attracted to because it felt good to be wanted.

You, on the other hand, might call yourself straight, but I say heterosexuality untested is no heterosexuality at all.

Sleep on that, my friend.

Looking back, I'd imagine Abe got taken for gay because no one knew what to make of Indigenous masculinity. In pictures from college, he looks androgynous as hell: long hair, soft features, oval face, thick eyelashes, full lips. So I get it. My two cents? His performance problem didn't stem from being with other boys, it happened because—even under the umbrella of an open relationship—being with someone besides Alex always felt like cheating.

Depending on the crowd and general mood, Abe's performances at Zopie's Caffeine Fix were hit-or-miss. Unless he had a heckler. Butting up against someone guaranteed Abe a good night.

I don't have to tell some of you that being surrounded by white folks for the first time—going from human to something people wanted to catalog—was an experience for Abe. Alex may have been the first person to ask him, "What are you?" but it became a litany. Not believing the answer also turned out to be standard practice; Abe heard "you don't look Indian" a lot.

When fellow students learned Abe was Native, they'd tell him about a TV show with a Native character, or a documentary they'd seen on some tribe, regardless of whether it involved Mohawks or not. Students asked if Abe had ever scalped anyone, did he live in a tipi, shit like that. One wit asked Abe if he had ever fucked a buffalo—what are you supposed to do with that? And oh my, how they loved to shuffle their feet and pop a hand against their lips while yodeling at him. Some even added the "Tomahawk Chop," the latest fad in synchronized racism at the time. The real bitch of it? These students meant well. Even the jokesters believed they were being friendly. Do I need to point out that most of them were white students? Probably not.

Not to say white folks have a monopoly on the droplets of prejudice we've come to call "microaggressions"; we all have a lot to learn about each other. But any time Abe met a fellow student who did *not* mean well, that student was always white. They often started as jokers, but after a few drinks the "jokes" morphed into anger.

"Mohawk my ass. All the real Indians are dead."

"Oh, so you're Indian? Nice Converse you got on."

"My taxes paid for your tuition . . . not that you'd know anything about paying taxes. Go clean my fucking dorm room. Reparations, bitch."

The angry students liked to call Abe a "post-contact Indian." Meanwhile, everyone here is post-contact with us. Take a look at the neoclassical statue of George Washington at the National Museum of American History, wearing a Roman toga and holding a sword. If it wasn't for Mohawks, the United States of America would have appointed "his excellency" George Washington its first king. Abe's classmates should have thanked Abe for representational democracy, maple syrup, and popcorn, and then shut the hell up.

Exhaustion, the sort that comes from deciding how much of yourself to be, and how to handle the times when being yourself seems problematic for others, meant Abe mostly laughed these encounters off. Not to mention fearing for his safety—a crowd of young white men drinking raised his hackles in a way few other things could. But remove Abe's shirt, braid his hair, and put him on a stage . . . Ask yourself, WWDDWD if someone yelled some bullshit? What Dominick Deer Woods did was smite colonizers with righteous anger.

Losing what he imagined to be great improv pained him, so Abe started to bring a pocket tape recorder to his readings. Then if he got heckled, Abe could bring my extemporaneous brilliance home and spin it into gold on the page. The first night Abe recorded, there were five of them, guys who'd played high school sports but were too small or slow to play at a Division I college. At SU, they'd morphed into hardcore Orangeman fans, decked out in school jerseys and sweatshirts. Four of the five wore baseball caps with the same Greek letters across the front. The second time one of them shouted, "Bring on the dancing girls!" while Abe read a poem about his cousin's legal troubles, he reached into the pocket of his jean jacket and pressed record.

"Great contribution, thanks," I said on the tape—I think it was me, anyway. I enunciate better, project louder. Abe wants to blend in; I want to be heard. "Would you even know what to do with a girl?"

On the tape a voice responded, faint but clear, "I think I'm looking at one."

"Ha, Ha, Ha. A long-haired boy must be a woman. There's one I've never heard."

The tape recorded a couple half-hearted laughs at this.

"You wish I was a woman," I continued, even louder. "Then you wouldn't have to freak out over the semi I'm giving you. I know it's scary and confusing for you. But don't worry, you're not my type. For one, you wear Docksiders. Two, I'm picturing *Full Metal Jacket* under those hats. I like a head of hair I can grab onto while I'm fucking. So how about you quiet down and enjoy the show?"

"How about I kick your ass?" came the reply.

"How about you kick my ass?" Possessed by my bravado, Abe sounded amused. "Look out, folks, we've found ourselves an open mic tough guy." A chorus of titters greeted this. "Well, riddle me this,

Open Mic Tough Guy; how's that going to work? Are we talking just you, or you and your forty-four buddies?"

Like I said, there were five of them, but 44's was the name of the sports bar around the corner, named for the number Jim Brown, Ernie Davis, and Floyd Little all wore when they played football for SU. If those names mean nothing to you, then imagine SU Hill is Mount Rushmore. Jim Brown, Ernie Davis, and Floyd Little would be three of the faces carved on it, with Larry Csonka being the fourth. And not to detour further during a digression, but it would be a disservice to the Lakota—and to Natives in general—to mention Mount Rushmore without unpacking its significance.

First off, "Mount Rushmore" is a desecration of the Six Grandfathers, a mountain sacred to the Lakota as a site for prayer and provisions. After decades of activism, the Supreme Court awarded the Lakota Nation four hundred million dollars; the Lakota—as nicely as possible—told them to shove the money and give them their land back. To add insult to profanity, the presidents represented there all committed atrocities in Indian Country.

Abraham Lincoln ordered the largest mass execution in US history: the simultaneous hanging of thirty-eight Dakota on made-up charges.

In the Declaration of Independence, Thomas Jefferson wrote "merciless Indian savages" practiced "warfare which is an undistinguished destruction of all ages, sexes, and conditions." This was, of course, how settlers treated Natives, not the other way around. According to his private letters, Jefferson baked this into the founding of the US in the hope that everyday citizens would "take up the hatchet and never lay it down until all Indians are exterminated."

Theodore Roosevelt's first speech as governor of New York included these gems: "This continent needed to be won. We could not leave this domain the hunting ground of squalid savages. It had to be taken by the white race." Roosevelt also joked about the axiom "The only good Indian is a dead Indian," saying "I don't go so far as to think that the only good Indian is the dead Indian, but I believe nine out of every ten are, and I shouldn't like to inquire too closely into the case of the tenth."

Three of the Greatest Presidents in American History, folks.

And how did the original president, good old George Washington, lay the foundation for future presidential dealings with Natives? Kanien'kehá:ka knew Washington personally. In 1779, as commander in chief of the Continental Army, Washington told his men, "Do not listen to any overture of peace before the total ruin of every Indian settlement." By that point we'd been calling him Town Destroyer for twenty-five years, a name he started using in letters, he was so proud of it.

Our history, friends and neighbors, and it's about time we face it.

Anyway, back to the battle of Dominick Deer Woods vs. 44 Frat Bros at Zopie's Caffeine Fix. I've demanded to know whether I'm expected to fight just the speaker or all five of them, "because," I continued on the tape, which recorded a muffled electronic crinkle from the microphone as I pulled it from the stand, "I have to say, without hyperbole, you don't stand a chance in a fight against me." Clearing my throat, I let my passion build. "Every step you take gets supported in everything you do. But me? America is trying to reject me like a virus. Your people have been trying to end mine for five hundred years, and I'm still fucking standing here."

I thundered this last bit into the mic, my voice echoing off the walls. The crowd whooped and cheered in response. Everybody loves a guy reckless enough to antagonize a table full of drunks, especially people who were probably ridiculed as weirdos by kids who looked a lot like those frat bros. I waited until the crowd quieted to continue.

"There's a reason why a hunting party of twenty could take on five hundred soldiers, so if it's all five of you, well . . . let's take that outside and see where we end up."

"Damn," some onlooker in the crowd said, to more laughter.

"So, gentleman—what's it going to be?"

Overlapping voices answered. If you close your eyes, focus, and replay the tape a few times, you'd catch "Fuck you, Tonto," "Big talk," and a certain homophobic epithet. The crowd at Zopie's began to boo.

"I don't think that's going to go over well, gents," I said. "Not with this crowd, anyway. But let's get one thing straight. Tonto ain't real; I am from Ahkwesáhsne. You don't know where Ahkwesáhsne is but don't even worry about it. Keep this up and I will bring Ahkwesáhsne to you."

Abe didn't get an apology. Or a beating, come to that. But he did get five drunken fools booed out of a coffee house. Once they were gone, I reread "The Bikers, Bartenders, and Blues Players all Vouched for the Indian" from beginning to end. The coffee house was silent as a confessional. When I followed it up with "This One's for the Colonizers," it brought the house down.

Abe listened to the tape exactly once before erasing it and leaving the recorder at home for good. It wasn't cleverness, it was hostility and ridicule. The biggest hearts in the room probably beat beneath the muscled chests of those five drunken frat bros; that's why they fought so hard against their feelings. I should have brought them to my side, introduced them to their better selves, but that's an old person's game. Elders charm you with wit and wisdom, and the next thing you know, you're evolving against your will just by knowing them. I wish young me could've been more like that. Hell, I still wish I could be more like that. But it's an Elder's trick because it takes a lifetime to learn.

THE WRITERS' ROOM IN
THE GOLDEN AGE OF TELEVISION

by Dominick Deer Woods

White men are the only group of people
whose self-esteem rises when they watch TV.
   Women
and men of other ethnicities
feed their self-hatred
to varying degrees.

I tried telling a white writer being clever
his ironic reappropriation
is a bulwark not a bombshell.

I told him if the joke is
"look at the brown person
who thinks it's people"
then you're telling on yourself.

And you'll never get it
even as we explain ad nauseam
while your narrative
scribbles over ours.

Six

few days after Abe's diagnosis, over dinner, a cousin tells him the truck stop where she works has a café with free public Wi-Fi. She offers to drop him off for his Friday FaceTime with Alex, but exercise is supposed to help him feel better, so Abe says he'll hoof it. He doesn't mind using the landline with his doctors, but he wants to keep his conversations with Alex to himself. The steroids are still in his system, and he's started his new treatment—Dalimuterin, a cancer pill that's sometimes used as a last resort for autoimmune disorders. Not quite the "targeted approach" Abe's doctors promised. His aching and exhaustion remain unchanged, but he hasn't grown any new lesions after stepping off the steroids, so his doctors are very pleased with themselves.

After dinner, the Jacobs watch a new sitcom starring Joey from *Friends*. Mom sits in Tóta's old recliner, Abe and Dad get the ugly couch with all the support of a flat tire, and his cousin and Aunt Abby use the pretty one that feels like velvet laid over concrete. Abe's parents bought the concrete to replace the deflated tire but wound up keeping both because the new couch was so uncomfortable. Abe wishes they'd trash them both and finally buy something decent, but doing that would require them to change personalities first. No, they'd made a mistake spending money on a new couch and so now everyone has to live with the consequences.

Dad makes popcorn on the stove, which he does a few times a week. The popcorn sits in paper shopping bags in the corners of the living room, butter darkening the paper, and he combines the old batches and reuses the empty bag for the fresh-popped. Warm and fresh is good, but Abe likes it even better after it's been sitting for a few days.

"You've finally got cable and we're watching this," Abe says.

"What's wrong with this?" Aunt Abby asks, her tone overly innocent. She knows TV generally isn't his thing. The year Abe introduced the family to *Pulp Fiction*, Aunt Abby railed about it for half an hour afterward. Then she stole Abe's tape and took it home. "I didn't say I didn't like it," Abby explained, "I said it didn't make sense." Aunt Abby still likes to ask Abe what "thing that doesn't make sense" he's watched lately.

Abe doesn't have a problem with a cozy sitcom. There are times when all Abe wants is the comfort of the completely expected, but watching pabulum with a laugh track isn't enough to keep his failing health from his mind. Pabulum in the form of a formulaic procedural, on the other hand? That Abe can do.

"C'mon," he says, "there's got to be a *Law & Order* marathon somewhere."

"If Abby wants to watch it, let her watch it." Mom sounds annoyed. She immediately becomes invested in anything you put on TV. Abe thinks it's because television was invented during her lifetime, so she didn't have time to build up an immunity to it. Even if she doesn't particularly care for a show, she hates missing the dialogue.

On screen, the sitcom wife—worried about her daughter's future—takes a moment to think of the worst fate she might have. "She could wind up . . . a cocktail waitress at an Indian casino."

"Oh." Abe says with a grin. "Anti-Indigenous."

"What?" Aunt Abby sounds genuinely confused.

"Kaolin is a cocktail waitress at an Indian casino," Abe points out.

The cousin in question smirks at Abe but holds her tongue, content to let the older folks duke it out.

"Abe." Mom flaps her hand like, Stop talking. "Get a sense of humor."

"Damn," he says, "you've changed your tune. What happened to the woman who used to throw her shoes at the television any time those Mazola ads came on? You taught me everything I know about hating TV. Hell, you had me cursing out 'feminine hygiene' commercials."

"Can't you shut it until the commercials?" Mom leans forward in her chair, looking genuinely pained. She angles her head toward the set, covering the ear facing Abe with one hand.

"What else should I expect from a Redskins fan?" Abe knows Mom's love for the team stems from a lack of representation during her childhood, but he finds annoying her a lot more entertaining than watching the show. Which Mom knows.

"Stop trying to get my goat, Abe," she says.

"Better the Redskins than the Cowboys." Dad shoots Abe a look.

"Is it, though?" Abe looks to his young cousin for backup. "Surely, cheering for a racial slur is worse than cheering for the Cowboys. I mean, there are Native cowboys. The Cheyenne—"

Mom cuts him off, her voice conversational as she throws a piece of popcorn at Abe with every syllable. "Please. Be. Qui. Et. Shush. Shush. Shush."

"Hey, you're wasting popcorn," Abe says, but he's smiling. "You're not missing anything, Mom. Here's how it's gonna go. Matt LeBlanc is going to win his daughter's teacher back. He'll end up class dad again. His wife is going to be so grateful, they'll bang it out. But they'll use innuendo, because it's network TV. Plus, they're over fifty and no one wants to see that. Oh, and he'll trick Kevin Nealon into eating that hot pepper."

His cousin giggles.

"Why are you like this?" Mom groans.

"You let me watch too much TV."

Abe hasn't thought of his illness for several minutes; then he scratches his head. He's been keeping his hair short for a couple of years. He had called Mom before he'd cut it, in fact. "It's really hot down here," he'd said. "Do you think it's okay if I cut my hair?"

"Why're you asking me? It's your hair."

He'd had to remind himself his mom had lived on the Rez her whole life. Still, she watched TV. She watched movies. She had to know the stereotypes.

"Because," he'd said. "Will it make me . . . I don't know . . . less Mohawk or something?"

"Oh, Abe."

"*What?*" Abe heard Aunt Abby ask in the background, having caught Mom's tone.

"Abe wants to know if it's okay for him to cut his hair," Mom called to Aunt Abby.

"*Short?*" his Aunt called back faintly.

"Short?" Mom asked Abe.

"Short," he agreed.

"Short," Mom called to Abby.

Then Aunt Abby had wanted to know how short, so Abe kept trying to name actors she might know for comparison, and I'll spare you that exchange. They had finally settled on Tom Selleck.

"Weh, if you're so worried about being Mohawk, then why don't you wear braids all the time?" By then his aunt had picked up the phone, caring enough to make her point in person. Aunt Abby had worn her hair in a short, take-me-seriously-as-a-businesswoman-coif for as long as Abe could remember. She had a series of navy and black suits and usually wore white button-downs on her days off. "You could wear a feathered headband and a beaded vest. You could wear arrowhead jewelry and moccasins. Typical Indian."

"I've got it, Aunt Abby."

Now, sitting on his parent's couch in front of the so-so sitcom, scratching his head feels weird to Abe. There's something tickling his hand and scalp. *Is it a spider?* he wonders. *A spiderweb?* Dropping his hand, a flash of black catches the corner of his eye. Abe looks down to see a small pile of hair.

"What's that?" Dad asks.

"Nothing." Abe closes his hand and forces his fist into his pocket to hide the hair.

"Is that your hair?" Dad looks shocked and scared, which is how Abe feels, too. It must show on his face, because Dad stands, pulling Abe to his feet and into a hug. Mom joins in on the other side. Aunt Abby leans over the three of them, and Abe feels his cousin's hand on his arm. None of them tell Abe he'll be okay, for which he's thankful.

The next day Abe walks to Truck Stop #9. The air is cold over his temple, where the clump of hair fell out. Since none of his relatives joked about shaving a stray dog's ass to make a toupee, Abe's knows his traitorous immune system has him properly fucked. Hopefully the walk will give him some idea of how to share the good news with Alex.

The angle of the morning sunlight, his breath pluming in front of him, the distinctly northern foliage, the sparse houses; it all feels real in a way his new home doesn't. On some level, Miami has always felt to Abe like a set, too sun-bright and washed-out to be real.

Ahkwesáhsne doesn't need a fancy destination casino like some Nations build to bring in revenue. Since Route 37 is the only east–west option this far north, visitors will pass through no matter what. Still, we want their money when they do, which is why all the gas stations have a slot machine and there are tobacco stores every ten feet. Abe doesn't remember there being any smoke shops when he was a kid besides the Bear's Den, and that was a general store which happened to carry a lot of cigarettes.

If his knees, hips, and stomach didn't hurt so much, Abe could be walking with his childhood buddies to Lou Bonds. Once there, they'd buy five different flavors of Adirondack soda for a dollar and pass them around out front, belching and giggling and vibrating from the sugar rush. When he visits his family, generally Abe keeps to the house. Walking the Rez now, he sees the houses are a lot nicer than they used to be, heritage brick instead of aluminum siding, Cape Cods rather than ranch homes. He assumes it's all the cigarette and casino money coming to fruition. There's so many more businesses, too, freshly painted and inviting. The trading community Abe remembers has been consumed by consumerism. Abe hopes they recognize it's time to ease up.

Here he is, walking Route 37 like the decades in between never happened, creeping toward death in the home where he was born. The thought—*Did I come back home to die?*—makes him briefly lose his footing. When he left for college, Abe hadn't meant for it to be permanent. He'd fallen in love, is all. Over his first Christmas break at SU, Abe had told his parents that when the second semester started, he was moving in with Alex off campus.

"After five months?" His mother had sounded skeptical. "That's awfully fast."

"We were married after five months," Dad had said, "remember?"

"Well, don't tell him that," Mom snapped.

Turns out a lot of his classmates had gone to SU because they found it "quaint," which meant Abe and Alex had a place to crash in half a dozen major US cities. During summer breaks, Abe and Alex drove around the country in the K-car, praying it wouldn't break down. Chicago, Boston, New York City, Philadelphia, Santa Monica, and Los Angeles, visiting friends for weeks at a time. Between you and me, once he'd seen so much of the country, Abe never considered moving back to Ahkwesáhsne.

After graduation (or rather, after Alex graduated; Abe made it two years before he ran out of money and had to drop out), they'd followed Alex to her job at a theme park in Virginia.

Abe's been thinking about their stint in Virginia a lot lately. The time he'd spent away from Alex there, when he was all restless and panicky. It's worth hearing about, and we have time while Abe makes his way to the truck stop. But to tell you that story, I need you to know Kanien'kehá:ka are psychic.

B ack in the day, Kanien'kehá:ka had conversations without ever opening our mouths. We could heal ourselves and each other, shape-shift, control the weather, all sorts of fun stuff. Ask around. Visit the Rez; Elders would be happy to tell you all about it, if the sun is shining and you ask them right.

There isn't much of that left in the average Mohawk save for stuff you've probably experienced yourself—you think of someone and they text you, you know what song the algorithm is about to throw at you, you start humming a jingle stuck in someone else's head, that sort of thing. Collectively, though? Rez life can get a little like a guy turning up on your doorstep with a deer carcass after your hungry family was up all night praying for a miracle, like hitting a three-hundred-and-fifty-dollar bingo pot when you're three-hundred-and-forty-dollars short on rent money, like finding an eyebright plant on your daily walk when you're out of allergy medication. And that's Medicine diluted by centuries of colonization, so just imagine us when we had this side of the earth to ourselves.

Maybe you think I'm crazy. That's fine. Not to boil your noodle but I've been called crazy before. Or maybe you don't think I'm crazy. Maybe you're just wondering if Abe has any of that in him.

If you ask Abe then he'd say no, so it's ace he made me up, innit. Abe seems to know more about his loved ones than they tell him, whether they're friends or family. He's heard, "How did you know that?" more times than I can count. The question always surprises Abe; "You told me, remember?" he answers. He chalks it up to imagination, a writer's affinity for story filling in the gaps to people's narratives. I say ancestors walk where they want, see what they see, and whisper to people who have ears to hear them.

For example, a few years back, a woman Abe was having lunch with said, "I just read the most amazing book." *A Gift Upon the Shore*, Abe thought. The book was eight years old, from a publishing house that no longer existed, written under a nom de plume. The author was a moderately successful thriller writer, but *A Gift Upon the Shore* was a postapocalyptic one-off. Maybe the fact Abe works in a bookstore hedges the bet, but thousands of books are published each year. No reason for Abe to know which book she meant; the name popped in his head the way your subconscious might kick up the name of an actor you've been struggling to remember.

Abe didn't say the title aloud. He watched her pull the hardcover with the ratty dust jacket from her bag and show it off, talking about how she'd gotten it for two dollars at the Goodwill Superstore. Abe nodded, feeling very strange, like the blood in his skull had fermented. As weird as Abe felt, imagine how she would have felt if Abe had told her the title before she took it from her bag.

When you fight these things—the moments when it seems there's more to the world than what's on the surface—they happen to you less and less. If it goes unused, even the strongest Medicine will fade.

I told you all of that so I could tell you about the shadows Abe saw in Virginia. I don't want to fall into the trap of "real" NDNs always do blank, or "real" NDNs never do blah. There are hundreds of Nations and millions of Natives and—much like human beings— we have a variety of outlooks, opinions, and demeanors. But I will say this: if you meet a Native who tells you a straight story, with no digressions or sidebars, then that Native is suspect.

AHKWESÁHSNE, 1996

Abe and Alex's one-on-one basketball game took place on a gorgeous day in June, shortly after they'd graduated from college. It was Alex's first visit to the Rez not centered around Thanksgiving. All too aware of the "no sleeping together unless you're married" rule at Abe's parents', they stayed with Sis and Robert. All week long, family came to visit because Abe was in town, and Abe and Alex talked up the big match.

"All state, two years in a row." Alex would slowly shrug, a *come on, now* look on her face. "I'll make quick work of him, then we'll have barbecue."

"Okay, at a gym?" Abe would nod. "Sure. But at the hoop nailed to my parent's garage? You got no chance."

They had a lot of family coming through not just to celebrate their visit, but because Abe and Alex had come to say goodbye. I know I told you lack of funds forced Abe to drop out of college, but he frittered away any time he might have spent doing schoolwork on Alex anyway. If he hadn't met her, then I'm betting Abe still would've flunked out. Make a case for an Abe who isn't juggling four jobs graduating and I'll hear it, but at the same time, going to college just to go—with no clear goal of what you want to get out of it, or where you're headed—is a recipe for failure.

Alex, on the other hand, had a newly minted Bachelor of Arts and a job offer in Virginia. Her scholarships hadn't covered all of her fees, but she'd graduated debt-free because a lawyer had convinced Mrs. East to sue the driver who'd killed her husband. The settlement had also afforded Alex a brand-new Toyota Camry, and the plan was to drive down after this visit.

Alex had issued the one-on-one challenge. Winter games weren't kind to her; she always seemed to pick a bad-luck board for Pokeno (an old-timey game that combines bingo and poker, which the

Jacobs played for penny ante), and her athleticism never helped her master Kick the Can.

If you're unfamiliar with the greatest thing you can do with an old Folgers can, Kick the Can is like hide-and-go-seek meets tag, only the person who's It can't tag you. Instead, whoever's It has to run back to the can, put a foot on it, and yell, "One-two-three on Abe behind the garage." If you name the wrong person (easy to do in the dark), or if they beat you back to the can and kick it before you complete the one-two-three call out, then anyone who's been caught gets freed.

As fast as Alex was, she hadn't grown up with the Jacobs. She didn't realize they were swapping hats, scarves, and coats to screw with her when she tried to name people. She didn't know the best hiding spots, or tricks like Hide in Plain Sight (an Adam special, blending in around the bonfire with the family members who weren't playing, casually drinking his beer, then moseying over to nudge the can when he was the last one left). Her other problem is she'd lived in city night her whole life, and that's a whole 'nother animal compared to country night. Barely able to see, she moved hesitantly, a different Alex than daytime Alex. In four years of visits, she'd only kicked people free once, and had eventually given up both times she'd been It.

When Abe and Alex took to the driveway at the Jacobs' house, more than two dozen onlookers—friends and family both—sat in folding chairs or stood watching. They'd brought beer and snacks for the occasion. Abe gave Alex first ups, as he claimed he had home-court advantage. The dusty gray asphalt had twin ruts made by the passage of cars over the years; cracks ran through the surface, and whole chunks were missing. Abe doubted she'd even be able to dribble.

"We call this driveway Candyland, babe." Abe rocked his weight from foot to foot. "You know why? Because it's loopy like ribbon candy."

"Just check the ball."

"Careful," he said. "Watch that crack."

They bounced the ball between them to start the game, and it managed to stay on course.

"You sure you want to take that stance?" Alex asked. In a bid to keep her from getting around him, Abe had planted his feet extra wide.

"Quit stalling," he said, waving and rocking.

"I tried." Alex bounced the ball between Abe's legs, darted around him like liquid from a water gun, and picked up her own pass. Moving easily wherever the treacherous driveway kicked the ball back to her, Alex dribbled in for an effortless layup. Abe's family roared approval, especially Sis and his varsity basketball–playing cousin, who stood and pumped their fists.

"You should've seen the court at Pine Lake Elementary," Alex said. "Whew. I don't know what they were thinking, laying acrylic outside in that heat. Check."

In short order, Alex was up ten to two. As she scored, she ran down a litany of shitty courts she'd been forced to play on in Miami growing up. Abe's only highlight (his baskets were both ugly, lucky affairs) was reading one of Alex's pump fakes at the end. He swatted her jump shot down, sending the ball bouncing across the road (where Mrs. Cook had come out to her porch to watch).

"That's right, this is my house!" Abe had walked around the driveway with his chest puffed out, waving his arms like he was hyping up an imaginary crowd. His family laughed and cheered him on. One-on-one is played to eleven for some reason and each basket is a single point (don't ask me why), so his behavior was extra-ridiculous. "Look out, comeback of the century starts right now."

He'd touched the ball last, so it was still Alex's play. They checked the ball, and Abe told her to get ready for the heat, stifling a laugh that blew snot from his nose. Alex had a hard time standing up straight, she was giggling so hard. For her winning point, Alex repeated her self-pass between Abe's legs, cruising in for a layup while Abe knelt with his arms raised to the heavens.

"I'm sorry, I'm sorry," Alex said between snorts of laughter, "I couldn't help myself." Sis laughed so hard, she fell over sideways in her lawn chair.

After the game, the chairs and refreshments moved to the picnic table behind the Jacobs' house. The family brought cornbread, fruit salad, potato salad, spinach salad, and tossed salad. Dad prepped the grill for hamburgers, hot dogs, barbecue chicken, ears of corn, and slices of squash. Sis's husband, Robert, had also pulled a bit of deer sausage from his freezer for the occasion.

"The ancestors are pissed you let a white girl beat you, Tootashay," Adam said, passing Abe a beer (going full toddler nickname to let Abe know how low he'd fallen).

"They let me down, what can I say."

"Too bad they couldn't play for you."

"I've never had venison," Alex said, grabbing her own beer. "I'm getting some of those sausages."

"Last chance, Miami." Brad Brown, Abe's oldest half-Irish cousin, grinned across the table at Alex. Soon he'd join the middle Brown brother in the Florida panhandle, and Adam would move to Syracuse, but until then the two of them made Rez life hard on Abe. Like his brothers, Brad's Irish genes dominated his looks; he had a lanky frame, blue eyes, and a head of curly brown hair pushed halfway back on his head. "You gonna dump this loser and get yourself a real man?"

"Why," Alex said without missing a beat, "you know any?"

The table exploded with laughter, Brad included.

"Shit." Brad shook his head. "This one's too quick for you, Toots."

"You got no idea." A bitterness Abe hadn't intended must've seeped into his tone, because Sis shot him a warning look. At that point, Sis was the only one who knew that Abe and Alex had an open relationship. He took enough ribbing being the youngest. If the older boys knew the gorgeous creature he was moving to Virginia with also bedded other people, Abe'd never be able to speak without them bringing it up, and the subject was already sensitive enough.

After the basketball game, they indulged in a rare summer bonfire, cooking hot dogs over the flames. Once the sun set, they played Kick the Can. It was moonless, the sort of night where all it took to hide was wearing dark clothes and lying flat far enough from the bonfire to blend in with the shadows. Abe and Alex ended up lying side by side in the big field behind the house, letting the game go on around them while they stared up at the sky. Only years later would Abe understand why Alex found the layered blankets of stars glittering from horizon to horizon over Ahkwesáhsne so moving. She'd grown up in Miami. No one would look at that sky, scuddy with light pollution, and posit a Skyworld beyond it. But it wasn't just that. Alex loved that they could have so much fun with nothing but an old coffee can, and she said as much to Abe.

"Thanks for this," she'd whispered, her voice thick with emotion.

RICHMOND, 1996

Hoping for Disney money, Paramount had bought several regional theme parks and used "the magic of the movies" to spice things up for their patrons (things like the NASCAR simulator being rebranded Days of Thunder after the Tom Cruise movie). The job they'd followed to Virginia was Alex donning false eyelashes, a blonde wig, and an iconic white cocktail dress to mingle with guests at Paramount's Kings Dominion. In addition to the Marilyn Monroe–esque "Diva," Alex swapped the sultry eye makeup and padded bra for a puffy pink gown and Strawberry Shortcake "Damsel" curls twice a week. But her favorite gig was covering days off for the girl who played "Ghost Host" during the ice show. Sure, it meant Alex worked six days a week, but as Ghost Host, Alex stayed in air-conditioning the entire day. Plus, she got to fly.

At the beginning of each show, Alex would intone spooky vocals through the speakers. Then she'd fly over the skaters while wearing white-out makeup and a platinum marcelled wig, her flying harness concealed beneath a gauzy silver dress. She'd land center stage and introduce herself as an ingénue who died on the set of 1923's *The Ten Commandments* (a joke referencing Cecil B. DeMille's pre-safety-code shoots that even in 1996 went over most people's heads). Ice skaters performed versions of scenes from beloved movies, while Alex—unhooked—vamped as the sets and costumes changed. During the song-and-skate medley at the end of the show, they'd hook Alex back to the wires and hoist her overhead as the skaters struck their final pose.

By contrast, Alex's walk-around days were hot and dull. So Virginia's punishing heat wouldn't overwhelm them, characters were strictly limited to ten-minute walks at the top of each hour, four before lunch and three afterward. But even sweating in ten-minute increments can wear on an outfit, which is where Abe came in. His job title was "costumer" because he occasionally had to tighten up a button or repair a seam, but the work mostly entailed sitting around in the communal green room with Alex, waiting to do laundry at the end of the day.

Evenings in Virginia usually started with dinner and drinks, then more drinks at a bar, then either a house party or driving to a DC dance club. Abe had to wait for the costumes to come out of the dryer, so he'd join up at whatever bar the crowd had picked that night. If Alex pulled someone in for a threesome, they usually figured it out at the bar, and Abe's night out would be cut short. And thanks to Alex, she of the lamp-like blue eyes, dazzling smile, and bottomless charisma, Abe had plenty of abbreviated nights out.

In the morning after their threesomes, Abe would make everyone breakfast. The guy or girl Alex had seduced would lean over their coffee mug, talking low, for Alex's ears only. The sight always filled Abe with pity. No matter how many times Alex tried to make it clear that Abe and Alex would always be Abe and Alex, the thirds she brought home often fell hard. "Doesn't it feel like we're using people to make our sex lives sexier?" Abe asked her once. Alex looked annoyed. "I'm always honest," she protested. "I can't help it if some people refuse to believe me."

One memorable July evening they pushed it too far for Abe's taste. They had tickets to Tori Amos's *Under the Pink* tour, and Alex brought an ice skater named Wendy. Normally the skaters kept their own company, as they considered themselves to be athletes more than performers. Leave it to Alex to lure one of the life-size goddesses away. Wendy had a black pixie cut, an aquiline nose, and the powerful build common to all the skaters. Abe took a costumer who worked in a different building with the plush costumes, Hanna-Barbera characters like Hong Kong Phooey and the Flintstones. On the way to the concert—Abe driving and his partner Michael in the passenger seat, with Alex and Wendy in the back— Alex told them about piano prodigy Tori Amos.

"She got kicked out of the Peabody Institute when she was eleven because she wanted to play rock and roll," Alex said.

"What's the Peabody Institute?" Michael asked. Slight of build, with soft features and hair in a tight fade, Michael sometimes wore a curly wig, dressed in what he called "street drag," and went by Marissa. In precolonial terms, people who live on the spectrum beyond gender constructs embody the Creator more than those locked into a binary. Early in their dating, Abe had tried expressing as much to Michael/Marissa.

"If angels exist," he'd said, "then they're neither male nor female. You're exactly how I picture an angel."

Michael/Marissa had grinned. "Aw, that's sweet, babe, but honestly, I see myself more bigender."

"Then I guess that makes you my 'bothfriend.'" After that, they became inseparable.

"The Peabody is the conservatory at Johns Hopkins," Alex said. "I saw her play the summer before college, at this tiny club in New York City. She has long red hair and these luscious lips. She looks like a Delacroix painting. She played sideways, straddling the bench, pumping her hips like she was fucking it." Glancing in the rearview mirror, Abe saw she had her eyes closed, taken by the memory. "She spent the whole concert eyeballing the front row, doing little tongue tricks between lines. I fell in love."

At the Firehouse Theatre, a nineteenth-century fire station modified into a venue for a few hundred people, Abe paid the attendant five bucks and parked the Camry.

"Here we go." From the back seat, Wendy held her hand out. In the harsh sodium-globe lighting coming from the parking lot, Abe saw four little white pills in Wendy's palm. Abe's Uncle Dan, the former cop, had once warned him never to do "white drugs," that pills and powders would fuck you up. "Stick with mushrooms and pot," Uncle Dan had said, "things that come from the earth." Yet when presented with a mystery pill, Abe didn't hesitate. They all took one, dry swallowing them down.

Inside the theater, the audience was mostly women around their age. The four of them took their seats, Abe and Alex next to each other, Michael/Marissa and Wendy making bookends. They chatted while the place filled up (Alex: "She sings like a valkyrie!" "She doesn't read sheet music; instead of notes, she sees colors!"). I'm probably wrong, but I remember the pill kicking in just as the lights went down and the crowd started to cheer. Whenever it happened, the pill wrapped the world in a warm, fuzzy blanket. The opener walked out, a tall guy wearing denim head-to-toe, with long black hair held back from his face by a cowboy hat. He had an acoustic guitar slung over his shoulder.

Alex elbowed Abe, who nodded in response, grinning. They'd had no idea who the opening act was, and seeing a Native dude was a pleasant surprise. His playing ranged from gentle to violent, expressing emotion and technical prowess by turns with the virtuosity of a lifetime of playing. He sung in a powerful baritone, telling stories of rural and reservation life which would have been at home on any country music station. Collectively, everyone was too eager for Tori Amos to pay much attention to the lone Indian with a guitar, so Abe clapped thunderously to make up for it.

Then the guitar player performed a medium-tempo blues number and Abe's neck prickled. The song was called, "Listen to Me," the lyrics an account of the genocide committed against Natives. Abe had seen Indigenous bodies fall on film (or bodies meant to be taken as Indigenous, anyway) but never from a First Nations perspective. And the specific atrocities the song described, Abe had never witnessed in art—not from a movie, TV show, or a song. As Abe took the lyrics in, the world shrank down to him, the man singing, and the song. The lone Indian wailed the chorus into the microphone, crying out feelings inside Abe he'd never been able to express, rage and melancholy braided together. Tears ran down his face. He crossed his arms over his chest, hugging himself, covering his mouth to stifle the sobs.

When the last note fell away he managed to choke out, "I've got to go buy this," before pushing past the row of legs and hustling to the merch table in the lobby. He didn't want to lose the song, a real possibility at the time. Bill Miller turned out to be Algonquin—Mohican, specifically—but Abe couldn't hold that against him. Miller wooed the crowd the longer he played, and the house went wild when he ended with a smoking version of "Folsom Prison Blues." Abe barely heard it. He stood by the stage with a dozen or so others, waiting for

Miller to finish his set and sign their CDs. Abe stayed back so he'd be the last person, trying to think of what he could possibly say to encapsulate the enormity of his emotions, to express to the musician what hearing his song had meant.

You wrote that song for me, he wanted to tell Miller. Instead, he handed the CD over for an autograph, words choking in his throat. As a final strange touch, the theme from *Rawhide* blared through the speakers as the headliner strode out. After signing Abe's CD, Miller disappeared backstage. Abe walked away, opened a side exit door, and stepped into the alley. The night was muggy, the breaths he took sticky with humidity. He slumped against the theater's brick wall, head in his hands, letting the tearful fit have its way with him.

He squatted there for some while, the wall swelling and receding at his back with the piano's pounding rhythm as the headliner performed. A hand fell softly on his neck, startling him. The touch traveled down his spine like a trickle of light. He looked up and saw Alex, gazing down at him kindly.

"You okay?" She rubbed the back of his neck, the sensation making him lean in to her touch like a cat. "Bad trip?" She didn't mean it literally; they'd left their LSD days behind them in Syracuse. But he knew what she meant. Abe shook his head.

"What're you doing out here?" he asked. In the alley's safety lights, flattering to no one, Alex still managed to look impossibly beautiful.

"Looking for you."

He couldn't speak, so he held the CD out to her. She took it, nodding like she understood. "You're missing Tori," Abe said.

"She's not all that." For a wonder, her tone really sounded like she was all right being in the alley with him instead of in the audience, listening to a performer she idolized.

"Okay." He stood, wiping his nose and eyes, then wiping his hands on his jeans. He hugged her, and the heat melted their bodies into one.

"I thought you were sick," she said over his shoulder. "I checked the bathrooms, and you weren't there."

"We should go see your girl."

When they walked back inside, Abe couldn't tell how long he'd been in the alley. Amos sat alone on a darkened stage, a figure in white at the piano, glowing in the spotlight like a fairy. Her voice washed into Abe, the surreal lyrics heightening his altered state. As enthusiastically as the crowd clapped and cheered, no one left their seats. It almost felt more like a recital than a pop-rock concert.

Abe took his seat in a daze, listening to the half dozen songs left in the show, songs that wailed through him for what felt like hour upon hour. Michael/Marissa caressed his arm on one side, Alex caressed his arm on the other, and the two of them kept Abe from floating into the rafters.

Afterward, they waited in the alley with a few dozen fans to meet Amos. It's a blur—her face, whatever any of them may have said to each other. Abe remembers a corona of red curls and a billowing white dress. Amos spoke with everyone in the alley and signed whatever was put in front of her. Their foursome watched her Town Car pull away, then they took a collective breath, like coming out of a spell. Wendy, who was on the whatever pill for the second night in a row, and so wasn't being hit so hard by the effects, drove them all back to Abe and Alex's apartment. In the car, they couldn't keep their hands still, idly caressing each other's skin.

"Did you see her—"

"—when she played 'The Waitress,' I—"

"—couldn't believe how good she—"

"—what I told you, she's so—"

"—like a siren or something—"

Once behind closed doors, the four of them let their caresses become more fervent. Abe and Alex kissed their dates, at first, then they kissed each other, and the move from one set of lips to another confused the whole idea of who was supposed to be kissing who, and all four of them eased toward the bedroom together. They stripped off their clothes. If it wasn't the pills or the amazing concert, then I blame the ice skater's abs. Three soft-bellied individuals found the sight sigh-worthy. They pressed their fingers over Wendy's firm torso, marveling at the power beneath her skin. They kissed Wendy's lips and neck, then Abe and Alex worked down to her nipples, over her stomach, then farther down to where she'd grown slick with excitement.

"You've taught each other things, haven't you," Wendy said, making them laugh. After licking inside her thigh, Abe left Wendy's most sensitive places to Alex. Abe moved to Michael/Marissa instead, taking his lover into his mouth. Michael/Marissa moaned, pressing their hips forward. Wendy caressed them, and the two of them ran their hands over her body as Alex worked between her legs. Hands stroked Abe's shoulders, ran through his hair, dug into his back. Watching Wendy's joy, hearing Michael/Marissa moan, Abe felt powerful and mindless, sexy and alive. Seeing Alex revel in her task, while he used his mouth on Michael/Marissa and felt Wendy's muscles clenching and unclenching, it all made him feel unhinged, like his skull might crack open from desire.

After Wendy begged them to stop, Alex turned to Abe and took him into her mouth. He cried out in surprise and pleasure, falling back as Michael/Marissa pulled away from him. Then Michael/ Marissa's mouth found Abe's chest and neck as Wendy grabbed his jaw, kissing him, muffling his cries. Alex smelled and tasted like home, everywhere he put his mouth on her. Over the weeks he'd grown used to Michael/Marissa as well. Wendy's chemistry was disconcerting in its foreignness, yet exciting for the same reason. Wendy's eyes were open and Abe saw her and Michael/Marissa watching Alex work on him, the way he'd watched Alex pleasure Wendy. He moaned into Wendy's mouth, kissing her as Michael/ Marissa explored his chest, while Alex used her mouth on his penis. He'd wondered if desire could give him some sort of stroke moments before, but then he moved beyond wonder. No thoughts, only sensation. He was sure he would crack, spilling everything inside, destroying himself. But Alex knew his body, knew how to catch him on the brink, and so she did. She pulled her mouth away, listening for his breath to level off. She'd put him in a space where she could straddle his hips and take her pleasure, as long and as often as she wanted. Wendy kept kissing Abe, one hand stroking between her own legs, as Alex pulled condoms and lubrication from the bedside table. They spent the night forming and reforming, connecting and pulling away, various pairs side by side, egging each other on to new heights, or three of them leaving the fourth gasping for air.

Abe didn't make breakfast that morning. He feigned sleep until he had the bed to himself, then he waited until he heard the voices outside the bedroom door stop. None of their previous threesomes had affected him like this foursome. During the trios, Abe had mostly stepped outside his body, letting Alex take the lead. He'd found them fun but unfulfilling, nothing like the way he and Alex could whittle the world outside their bedroom away until only the two of them existed, moving toward a state of consciousness where every sense was present and alive, a pleasure so intense that the aftermath, when they returned to themselves, felt like they'd been renewed in body and mind. The night after the concert was the first time Abe reached that ecstatic state in a group. Lying there, waiting for their guests to leave, images from the foursome kept flashing in his mind. He couldn't believe the things that had happened to him, and the things he'd done.

For the next several days, Abe couldn't focus. He'd stay stopped at a green light until the car behind him honked, he'd put a movie on and end up staring off into space until the credits rolled. That week, Abe and Alex went to the Old Stone House—the oldest building in the city—on their day off, to visit the Edgar Allan Poe Museum. Turned out, while Poe had lived in Richmond, he'd never lived in the house. Once Abe heard that, he pretty much tuned out the rest.

For days he hadn't really left that tangle of bedsheets, those four shades of skin, the mingled scent of their bodies, the harmony of their voices. Abe and Alex saw Poe's childhood bed, a vest he wore, and a swirl of loose hairs supposedly trimmed from his head after he'd died that looked to Abe like something you'd pull out of a brush. When they got to the garden outside, Abe couldn't keep it in any longer.

"I'm out, Alex." Not a "honey" or a "babe," but using her name to let her know how serious he was.

Alex squatted to scratch one of the garden's many black cats before she addressed his non sequitur. "Out of what?"

"Threesomes. Foursomes. I can't do it anymore."

"Why?" Alex had looked up at him like he'd said he would never have ice cream again.

"I'm not saying you can't, you know. Sleep with whoever. I'm just saying that for me, I don't want to do it again."

"You didn't seem to have a problem with it the last time." Alex stood, and they followed the brick path along the stone wall of the house. "In fact, you seemed to enjoy yourself quite a bit. I know I did. I know they did."

"It was one of the greatest nights of my life. That's the problem." Their sex life was a free-for-all, an amusement park that got hastily slapped together and might hurt people.

"Maybe you don't know how to have fun," Alex countered.

"Common trait of adult children of alcoholics." Abe sighed. He cut away from the wall, taking the path toward one of the slowly trickling fountains. "Or so I'm told."

"Is this a Catholic thing?"

"My parents were raised Catholic," Abe said. "I wasn't."

"Guilt by osmosis?"

Abe snorted a laugh. "Maybe. Or maybe you're projecting."

"I don't feel guilty." Alex took one of the benches facing the fountain. "We talk about these things for a reason. And who are you, giving me permission to 'sleep with whoever'? Who died and left you boss of my vagina?"

"I'd be a good boss of your vagina," Abe mused, sitting beside her.

Alex pointed her toes, trying to reach the stone lip around the fountain; she was a good foot short. "Do you love Mich?" She pronounced it "Meesh," referring to Michael/Marissa.

"What?" Abe hadn't thought about it, so he took a moment to answer. "They're the closest I've come to it, next to you. Why?"

"Just curious." She shrugged. "I think being in love with two people at the same time would be awful."

No danger there. Abe could see himself with Michael/Marissa if Alex wasn't in the picture, but there was no way for anyone else to access his heart as long as it was full of her.

After the foursome, Abe never knew if Alex's nights out involved one lover or two (or more). The closest he came to asking was seeing her smile wistfully over her coffee one morning. "Penny for your thoughts," he'd said.

"I've decided the only way to have a threesome," Alex replied, "is when you're the guest star."

Listen, I know plenty of folks who would love it if their relationships could be a little looser. Isn't that what everyone wants, to be in a fun, loving home, but still take advantage of outside opportunities when they present themselves? Openly and without lies? It's very French. Or Indigenous, depending on your Nation. Well, there's nothing wrong when two people of that mindset share a life. Alas, unlike Alex, Abe is the one-woman sort.

Sorry, all this sex talk made me forget we're in Virginia for a near-death experience, but we've worked our way back around to it. One night, chopping onions for the rare dinner at home, Abe saw black moths fluttering in the corner of his vision. He swiped at the moths, but there was nothing there. It happened a few more times, shadows dancing around him, shadows that disappeared when he looked directly their way. Abe felt uneasy, almost scared. You've heard tell of these shadows twice now, but this was Abe's first experience with them. The fourth time a shadowy, sly thing appeared and vanished in his peripheral vision, Abe put his butcher knife down, picked up the kitchen phone, and called home.

"Yello?" Abe's father only put the *y* in "hello" when he felt especially fine.

"Is everyone okay?" Abe asked.

"Did you have a dream?"

They hadn't spoken in a month but phone calls with his parents felt like resuming a meal that was always on the table.

"No, it—just now I saw . . ." But what had Abe seen, exactly? Black flowers blooming outside his vision? Shadow butterflies flapping in the corners of his eyes? "Something," he finished lamely.

"Sounds serious," Dad mused. "Like what?"

"Like . . . black shadows, I guess." Abe felt stupid. "Just out of range of where I could see them."

"Uh-oh."

"What, is that bad?"

"Nope," Dad said. "Just means you're your mother's son."

Abe heard the muffled clunk of the phone dropping on piled papers. He could picture the dining room, the tiny phone desk stuffed with bills and letters crammed between the doorway to the living room and the doorway to the kitchen, boxes of fabric and spools of thread on the table, the tabletop covered with whatever quilt Tóta was working on at the moment. Abe heard his father call his mother to the phone, and when Mom picked up, Abe explained what he'd seen. Aunt Abby had come for dinner, and Mom asked if she'd smelled oranges lately; Abby (who, remember, smelled oranges when someone was about to die) had not.

"Is that what the shadows mean, that someone's going to die?"

"Oh, could be danger," Mom said. "Could be death. The more shadows there are, the bigger the danger. And if you see a really big shadow, shaped like a person? Look out, you're really in trouble."

"Oh."

"Did you see a big shadow? Or a lot of little ones?"

"Little ones, I think. But everyone's okay?"

"Well, Tóta's hearing is getting worse, and your Uncle Asher is supposed to be on a visit, but he's practically out the door before he's done chewing . . ."

Her easy tone soothed Abe. When he'd dialed the phone, he'd been sure bad news would be waiting on the other end. But Mom knew all about the shadows and she didn't sound worried, so he decided to let it go. If Abe had thought about it more, he would have realized his mother's equanimity wasn't because there was nothing to worry about, but because there was nothing they could do about it. How is it Abe could accept this—along with Aunt Maisy dreaming of flowers when someone catches pregnant, and his own mother talking to any dog like it was human and having said dog follow her instructions more often than not—but still doubt Budge when the man comes into his life? Maybe it's self-sabotage. Maybe it came from living in the city too long. I wish I knew, so I could undo it.

Over the next two weeks after his first sighting, the shadows got worse. Any time Abe stared off into space, one or the other side of his vision would flutter with movement. Then one night, as he walked to the bathroom, a man-sized shadow stood at the corner of Abe's eyeline. The figure faded below the knees like an unfinished sketch. Abe froze, hand still inside the bathroom doorway, finger on the light switch. The figure drew closer. Abe whipped around, heart in his throat. The hallway was empty.

Abe took a steadying breath. As he was telling himself to calm down, the phone rang. Abe's stomach felt heavy. He was sure it would be bad news on the other end. It turned out to be Mom.

"Is everything okay?" she asked quietly.

"I don't know," Abe said. "I saw the big shadow you told me about, a man-shaped one."

"I saw him, too." She sighed. "He was bald, and had a beard, and was holding a baby. I tried to get a closer look at the baby, but the man held it away from me and used his body to block the view. Then they were gone."

"Your guy had a face?"

"Well, sure."

"Maybe I'm doing this wrong," Abe said.

"No, you're fine," Mom told him. "Be safe."

The next day, the shadows were so thick they gave Abe tunnel vision. Rattling around the apartment, he felt like he'd eaten too little food and drunk too much coffee. When the phone rang, it was Wendy, the ice skater, her voice full of tears. It was one of the days Alex covered for the Ghost Host. A carabiner on her harness hadn't been screwed down all the way. As she'd flown over the stage to start the show, Alex had fallen thirty feet to the ice, breaking her neck. They'd helicoptered her to Inova Trauma Center.

Somewhere in the course of Abe's two-hour drive to the hospital, he realized the shadows that had been dancing around his vision all morning had gone.

TEN LITTLE INDIANS

by Dominick Deer Woods

Elizabeth II is ninety years old.
She was twenty-five when she visited
The Mohawk Institute Residential School

Ten Little Indians kissed her feet
(were made to)
twenty flower petals breezing over royal skin
an arrangement selected by
Elizabeth Windsor Herself

Better they be made to kiss the feet of a gravedigger
a butcher
a maid

Ten Little Indians
picnicked in the woods
with Elizabeth Windsor Herself
made to skip off and never return

Years afterward
The Mohawk Institute Residential School
closed
    Government trucks
blanketed the surrounding grounds

beneath twenty feet of earth
for no reason at all

America stopped advertising cigarettes on TV
baby boomers demanded Nixon lower the voting age to
    eighteen
Jimi Hendrix died
Walt Disney World opened
Tina Fey and Karen Kilgariff were born

In those days they believed
twenty feet of earth
would forever hide their sins

They call it forensic anthropology
when instruments render soil invisible
and you can see all the way to the decade that birthed me

Born to be kidnapped
and raised where they
Kill the Indian
to
Save the Man
but are known to be overzealous

Untied from the rack in the basement
released from chains on the walls
given leave from electroshock and rape
for a third of an hour a day
to run beneath gray skies
air cold on my shorn scalp
the stench of my cousins' corpses puffing from the soil
beneath my government-issue shoes

One day I'd meet the Queen
that I might kiss her feet
on threat of being thrown
into the Mush Hole and forgotten

The Government-sponsored
Church-run
boarding school buried my diploma
underground
with six thousand Mohawk children
planted like corn seeds

Inside
the hallways shadowed
windows shattered
chairs and desks piled and covered in dust
pillory and tramp chair burned to ashes
restraints pulled from basement walls leave holes like empty
    eye sockets

Outside
the Mush Hole filled
grounds run to bramble
while I'm cozy
beneath my blanket of earth
twenty feet thick
gifted me
by Elizabeth Windsor Herself

Seven

With its blue walls, gray tile floors, and beige granite countertops, the Three Feathers Internet Café looks more like a bank than a place to eat. There are no booths, just metal tables and chairs. Normally the lack of cushioning would not be a concern, but with his recent weight loss it feels like Abe's hip bones are resting directly on the metal. The cases by the counter are filled with enticing cakes, pies, pastry logs, and to-go salads. One bite of his toast told Abe they make their bread on site. His western omelet tastes delicious, but his stomach feels off, so he's pushing it around his plate more than eating it.

Behind his food, his laptop sits open on the table. He's wearing headphones, and Alex's number is keyed into the FaceTime app and ready to go. He watches the clock. He's not looking forward to the conversation, but Abe feels as anxious to see her face as he did twenty years ago, after she'd broken her neck and spent nearly three months in Miami recovering. In all the years since, they've barely been apart. It feels like an age since he's seen her face or heard her voice.

The walk to the café had given him a headache. He hadn't had coffee before he left the house, so he thought it might be caffeine withdrawal, but the Three Feathers brew is making it worse instead of helping. He's on his second water, wondering if it's dehydration. Even though the sun isn't as strong, the air is a lot dryer up here than he's used to. *At least your legs stopped hurting while you were walking*, I point out, *that's something*. It's a bit of a lie. His muscles stopped aching, and his joints hurt less; an abatement, not an abolishment.

If the pain stayed the same day-to-day, even morning to afternoon, then Abe feels like he would be able handle it better, tune it out. Instead, it manifests in new and interesting ways from moment to moment. As he sits, the pain in his torso is getting worse, twisting inside his guts, throbbing down his testicles like he's been kicked. His shoulder feels like he fell off his bike and hit the pavement with his full weight on it, and his knee and ankle on that side feel clunky, like ill-fitting gears.

At ten o'clock Abe clicks the FaceTime icon and hears the shrill *brinnnggg* as his computer connects to Alex's phone. Abe is suddenly sure she won't answer. He can see himself on the laptop screen; his expression is anxious. He looks wan. Thinner than when he left Miami, but that's probably his imagination. He shakes his head quickly, as though he could shake the worry from his face. *Heart failure*, he thinks. *Emphysema . . . Kidney failure . . . Or will it be one of the ones you can't pronounce, where they cut away parts of your intestinal tract until you're using an IV to eat and a bag to shit?*

Then the screen shrinks to a rectangle down the center, filled with Alex's face. For a moment, Abe doesn't recognize her. With Virginia so much on his mind, he'd expected more Farrah Fawcett than Ruby Rose. But apart from the short, undercut bob, some extra laugh lines around her eyes, and a deepening of the smile lines framing her lips, Alex at forty-three looks almost exactly like Alex at twenty-three. Abe feels the knot behind his chest loosen.

"It's really good to see you, babe," he says.

"Good to see you, too." She frowns. "Where are you?"

"Three Feathers, remember?" He leans down, moving the computer so she can see the mostly empty café.

"Oh, yeah. Food any good?"

"Well, it's no Jimmy's but it's decent." It's actually better than Jimmy's Eastside, but the diner on Biscayne Boulevard is their favorite place for a greasy all-American breakfast. Abe is trying to tell Alex he misses her without sounding desperate. Then he blurts it out anyway. "I miss you."

"How's everyone?" she asks. He can't tell if that was a snub, or if she's half listening, the way she forgot his whole explanation of the shitty Wi-Fi at the house, and how he had to call from the café up the road. Abe responds with a rundown of doings on the Rez, tells her the family misses her.

"Aw, give them all my love."

"Whatcha been doing?" Abe smiles. "Sitting on the couch with the TV off, staring out the window, wondering when I'll be home?"

"Working. Rehearsals. Judy comes down for dinner on Fridays. You know." Alex shrugs. Judy is the landlord.

"Judy still coming down? What are you feeding her?" He's gently teasing Alex about her lack of kitchen prowess. It doesn't feel like too long ago when Alex would've joked back, *Yes, that's what I do, sit in the dark waiting for my man. I don't have a widow's walk so I loop around the block . . . I feed her compliments and herbal tea . . .*

"We order Sushi Siam."

Abe rubs his temples, wishing he'd asked the counter guy for an aspirin. "Listen, I finally got a diagnosis."

She knows he got a diagnosis—it's the point of the FaceTime—and he knows she knows, but he has to start somewhere. Alex shifts her gaze. Abe realizes it's the first time she's looked at him instead of her own face on the screen. She opens her mouth, then closes it and nods for him to continue.

He breaks down Systemic Necrotizing Periarteritis for Alex, his immune system attacking his blood vessels, no known cause and no known cure. He manages to keep his voice steady. Her face in his laptop screen crumples by increments.

"You said they don't . . . they don't know how to treat you?" Alex's lips press flat together, making her mouth into a horizontal slash. Her eyes are wounded. He sees this is not the news she expected.

"I mean, they have treatments. I'm on some new pills. It's just so rare, they don't know if it'll work. They're basically guessing."

Dr. Weisberg told him one percent of the world's population has rheumatoid arthritis—one and a half million souls in the US. Meanwhile, only four other Americans have what Abe has, maybe a dozen total worldwide. The eight percent who survive SNiP for five years—mathematically, nearly one whole person—are ones who have gone into remission. They haven't found anything common to the remission patients, either.

Inside the frame, Alex's face grows smaller as the hand gripping her phone goes soft. Behind her, Abe sees the curved entry to the hallway running down the middle of their house. He realizes she's at their dining room table, their least comfortable seating by a wide margin. Does she want to make short work of this call? Then he's looking at Alex's hair and the place where the wall meets the ceiling.

"Babe, you there?"

"I'm here." Again, her face fills the rectangle in the middle of Abe's screen, blinking rapidly. Her lips remain a grim line.

Abe takes a deep breath, grateful there's no table service, glad to be across the room from the nearest person. "Even if they can get me to go into remission, it's still going to kill an organ." He makes a chuffing sound, a laugh without humor. "Well, technically it'll kill the blood vessels feeding an organ, but you know. Same difference."

"What about a transplant?"

"I guess if we had an unlimited supply of donors, sure. I could burn through hearts and they could keep giving me new ones. But as it stands, organs tend to go to people whose blood vessels won't kill them, you know?" Abe is going for flippant, brave-in-the-face-of-the-inevitable, but the FaceTime call feeds an echo of his voice back to him. He hears bitterness and fear . . . maybe even anger. Is he mad at Alex because she asked a perfectly innocent question, or because she's been downplaying his symptoms ever since they started? Maybe he's angry to be dying before he's ready. "You know the numb spots on my hands?"

Alex nods, but she looks lost. Abe can't tell if it's from the shock of his diagnosis, or if she's forgotten in the weeks they've been apart.

"SNiP affects systems," Abe says. "Like, your liver dies, but it's because the circulatory system feeding it dies. Or it attacks your renal system and kills your kidneys, right? Those numb spots mean it's attacking my nervous system."

"Your nervous system?" Alex looks like she's been slapped.

When the disorder goes after the nervous system, then brain degeneration starts about two years after the first lesions appear. This gives him a year and a half. Of course, if you believe in Medicine (not Western medicine but the way Hotinonshón:ni use Medicine, a word that—like "Indian"—is shorthand for an idea too complicated to get into), then you know by imagining his immune system would attack his brain, Abe willed it to happen. But you know the old joke—try not thinking of a brown bear with blue eyes. And if you don't know it, well . . . now you're thinking of a brown bear with blue eyes, get it? Thoughts are slippery little eels, tough to herd. You can only do it by changing the entire topography of your mind. That takes years, time Abe no longer has.

"We're talking balance problems, weakness, vision loss . . ." *Headaches*, Abe realizes. Except the one he has now isn't as severe as the ones he's read about. Then again, some people found the skin lesions agonizing, so how could he possibly know? "Confusion, forgetfulness, seizures, ministrokes . . ."

"Jesus, Abe." Like his own tone earlier, Alex sounds all wrong. Closer to annoyance than concern.

"Yeah." Abe smiles weakly. "Based on when the lesions started, I should be experiencing vascular dementia right around my forty-fifth birthday."

Alex's jaw works. Abe hears the phone clatter to the kitchen table, and suddenly he's looking at the ceiling above their dining room.

RICHMOND, 1996

Lying in a hospital bed at Fairfax Medical Center, Alex opened her eyes. She took in the sight of Abe, Abe's parents and brother, her mother, and her new stepfather, the whole lot gathered around her. She smiled weakly. "I feel like a TV."

"Well, you do love being the center of attention," Abe said.

Alex had been moved from the intensive care unit at Inova Trauma Center that morning, fitted with a halo, and given a standard room. Abe recognized the contraption they'd put on her head, holding her skull and spine in alignment so her neck could heal. He'd seen it before in *Fight Club*, *Mean Girls*, *ER*, *Fringe*, *Grey's Anatomy*, and *Breaking Bad*. He can't blame all those movies and shows for featuring the device; it's very cinematic looking. Alex wore a fleece-lined plastic vest with four steel bars sticking up from the shoulders, two in the front, two in the back. Bolted to the four bars was the steel halo around her head. Keeping Alex's neck in traction were four pins drilled through the halo and directly into her skull. They called the fitting a nonsurgical procedure, but a surgeon had still done it.

You wouldn't know it from the screen, where seeing actor's faces is important, but doctors normally place the two front pins toward the center of the forehead for the greatest stability. Alex's front pins, however, were drilled into her temples, like she was already a movie star. "We didn't want to scar your pretty face," the surgeon had told her.

After arriving at the trauma center the night before, Abe had paced the ICU waiting room until the early morning, waiting for their parents to arrive and visiting Alex whenever the nurses came to get him. Mrs. East and her new husband had arrived first on the red eye from Miami. Abe's parents had driven down from Ahkwesáhsne, swinging through Syracuse to pick up Adam. They had walked in at dawn, just in time for the doctor to show them Alex's X-ray in the waiting room.

"Let me start by saying that Alex is the luckiest patient I have ever personally encountered," Dr. Diome had said with the sonorous voice of an Old Testament prophet. Short and stout, with a full, neat beard and a head of black hair threaded with gray at the temples, Diome was the sort of Indian that Christopher Columbus had expected to find when he'd set sail. He held a large, mustard-colored envelope.

"What? What does that mean?" Mrs. East—packed into a tailored navy suit, her hippy days long behind her—had been dialed up to eleven the whole night. Abe wanted to tell her to let the doctor talk. He found her emotional displays unseemly, though he didn't understand why. I'd say it was because they made it harder for Abe to bury his own emotional turmoil, but hey—that's just my guess. Maybe Abe wanted all the pity points for Alex's condition to himself.

"Alex has a C2 fracture. What we call a hangman's fracture." Dr. Diome reached into the envelope and pulled out an X-ray, raising it so the fluorescent light shone through. He stood to the side so everyone could see.

"Oh my God, oh my God," Mrs. East said, putting her hands to her mouth, rocking back and forth. Her husband, a dapper man who looked like a college professor, put his arm over her shoulders, shaking his head at the X-ray. Abe's family stared as if bearing witness would help. Abe couldn't pull his eyes away, either. He flashed back to the time, as a child, when he'd wanted to see what Barbie looked like naked. Her hair had gotten tangled up in her clothes and he'd accidentally popped her head off. When he'd heard his sister coming up the stairs, he'd dropped the doll. Barbie had landed on the floor with her head and neck side-by-side, much the way the pieces of Alex's neck appeared on the X-ray now.

"Yes," the doctor said, his tone as resonant as Moses's speaking the Ten Commandments. "Only a small percentage of the population has enough space between their vertebra and spine for a break like this to not sever the spinal cord outright." He held the top of the X-ray in one hand and pointed to some ghostly lines and smudges with the other. "Of that small percentage of people, only an equally small percentage have enough elasticity in their spinal cord that it would move with the break. Here, you can see the spinal sheath isn't even damaged." Watching Dr. Diome's finger trace Alex's spinal cord as it ran from her skull, made a sideways *S* shape, and entered down into her spine, made Abe's stomach flop. "Ninety-nine point oh six percent of the population would not have walked away from a break this severe."

"You say she walked away?" Adam asked softly.

"Well, no." The doctor chuckled. "Though from what I'm told, she tried. The dancers forced her to lie still."

"Dancers?" Mrs. East's panic level made even that one-word inquiry into an explosion of feeling.

"I think he means the ice skaters," Abe said.

"That's right." Dr. Diome smiled. "It's a one-in-a-million break. Well, technically, it's a four-hundred-in-a-million break. Four hundredths of one percent of the population. We will set her neck correctly. She will wear a halo vest for three months. Then, in all likelihood, she will be fine."

"In all likelihood?" Abe couldn't reconcile the X-ray with the doctor's words. "What does that mean?"

"Well, her body has undergone a terrible shock." Jesus, Dr. Diome's voice. Somewhere between truck commercial and tent revival. He takes it down a register to put Abe at ease, and it totally works. He would make an excellent cult leader. "Sometimes in cases like this, we see bruising. We see swelling. She may have problems with her coordination for several days. Nothing a couple of months of rest won't cure. She's young, strong, healthy. In three months, you will never know she suffered such a terrible injury." He looked around at their shocked faces. "As I said, she is the luckiest patient I have ever seen."

Later, they'd all waited in Alex's room until the orderlies wheeled her bed in. Alex had smiled and raised a hand, responded to their greetings, then promptly passed out. When she woke again for real, she told them what happened.

"It felt like time slowed down almost, except it didn't, really," Alex said. She laughed nervously, like she couldn't actually believe she'd survived. "Even though it felt like slow motion, I didn't even have time to think, 'Oh shit.' I was like, 'Ohsh—' then, *fwhoo*, I was falling."

"Oh." Mrs. East sounded like she'd been goosed.

"It's weird." Alex voiced another nervous chuckle. "I felt something cradling me. Someone, I mean. I think Dad was with me. Is that crazy?" Alex looked at her mother, who smiled and frowned all at once. "It felt like he cushioned my fall. Maybe not. But I should have died. At the very least, I should be paralyzed. But I'm not."

"What did your father look like?" Abe's mom asked.

Alex described him as a large, heavyset bald man with a shaggy beard: "Like a Hells Angel, only nice."

"Abe, do you remember?" Mom looked at him, lips quirked. "That's exactly how he looked as a shadow."

Abe kept silent as his mother described the shadow man she'd seen, hiding a baby behind the bulk of his body. Over the phone, late at night, having just been scared by his own shadow man, Abe had accepted the story. It felt the same as if his mother had told him she'd seen the reddest cardinal ever perched on the laundry line. Now, under the artificial lights, with Alex's mother and stepfather present, smelling the miasma of industrial disinfectant and bodily fluids, Abe had the urge to clamp his hands over his mother's mouth. No one scoffed, or called her a lunatic, or told her to keep that spirit mumbo jumbo on the Rez. This bothered Abe even more, as though he could sense condescension in Mrs. East's silence.

"Let's get donuts to go with this coffee," Abe said. "Adam, help me carry them?"

Once they were outside in the hallway, Abe pitched his voice low. "You believe that stuff Mom was running?"

Adam glanced at him, his impossibly handsome face rumpled with confusion.

"You know..." Abe gestured back toward the room, "the stuff about the shadow man. Do you think she does it for attention?"

Adam stopped short. He put his hands on his hips and laughed briefly to himself. "You know I love you," Adam said, looking up with a wounded smile. "So I'm going to pretend you never said that."

Abe's brother turned around and walked back to Alex's room, leaving Abe slack-jawed. For thousands of years, Mohawks have known trauma lives in the body and is passed on to future generations. Whitescience never listened to us. Thankfully, Whitescience "discovered" epigenetic trauma by torturing mice, so we can add that to the Natives-told-you-so pile. I remember reading an account of a Tuscarora Medicine Man talking about his witchy shit with colonizers around. The Tuscarora—who would eventually join the Five Nations and make them Six—had come up from the Carolinas in 1713, twenty years after the Salem witch trials. The Five Nations had to explain to the Medicine Man that colonizers didn't like witchy shit. I'd guess that once upon a time, discussing Medicine in mixed company got Abe's ancestors killed, and the surviving witnesses passed that experience on, and eventually the trauma ended up lodged in Abe's stress response system. That's about as kind as I can be to Abe for his behavior in that hospital.

Abe took the elevator down to the cafeteria, bought donuts, and pushed anything about the fall he couldn't read in an X-ray from his mind.

AHKWESÁHSNE, 2016

Sitting in the Three Feathers Café, computer screen showing the ceiling over his dining room table, Abe waits for Alex to reappear. When she does, wiping her face, finger-brushing her hair back, her eyes are red but her face is stony. For a time, they simply look at each other.

"What do you think?" Abe finally asks.

"What do . . ." She looks toward the heavens and barks a laugh. "I don't . . . This is a lot, Abe. I don't know what to think."

"Yeah, me neither. It's just . . ." But what is it, just? Trying to form a thought about it is like trying to funnel a demolition derby onto a highway. "That last poetry reading I went to, one of the panelists didn't publish her first poem until she was sixty-three. She raised her kids, and helped raise her grandkids. Then she decided to start writing again. There are a lot of stories like that in the book business, you know? I just . . . I thought I had all this time."

"You're not going to die, Abe."

They're silent for a time.

"Are you coming up for Thanksgiving?" Abe knows she doesn't like taking time off, but she always comes up for the holiday, at least.

Part of him feels sorry for being a middle-aged bookseller who's paid a pittance. Once Alex started making a decent living as a teacher, Abe's meager salary became supplemental, making sure they could save for trips and go out to eat whenever he didn't feel like cooking. But even with Judy giving them a break on rent (she only raises it every few years, and never more than sixty dollars at a time), the cost of gas, groceries, and evenings out kept going up.

From looking at their bank account online, Abe knows Alex hasn't chipped away at the settlement to make rent yet, but he worries over how much longer she'll be able to manage alone.

"You're staying there that long?"

"Well. I mean . . . I'm not going to miss Thanksgiving." Over the years, sharing dreams for the future and opening up about past hurts had been replaced by discussing the minutia of keeping house. Abe can't remember the last time he's done something as simple as waking Alex for comfort after he had a nightmare. How to put into words, the way seeing his family had cooled his state of mind? "I feel more even-keeled up here. And I should spend as much time with my family as possible. Right?"

"So you're what? . . . Done with Miami?"

Had she been about to say, *Done with me?* Abe thought maybe so. What he couldn't account for was the relief in her tone.

"No. I don't think so. Well . . . shit. I don't know right now. I haven't really thought about that. Thought that far ahead, I mean. I guess I just pictured you up here with me."

"I can't just quit my job, Abe."

Except she can. They signed a one-year lease with Judy in 1998 and have never renewed it on paper. Between vacation, sick days, and accrued personal time, Alex could leave with a month's worth of pay. Sis and Robert's boys are grown and out of the house, so they have room to spare. Alex could teach up here if she wants a job. If she doesn't want to work, then she could use some of the settlement to cover the scant months before Abe no longer recognizes her and her presence won't make a difference. Of course, Abe had the chance to live with Tóta during her last months, between her time in hospice and when she came home to die, and he'd stayed in Miami instead. Maybe this is his karma.

He doesn't want to fight. Not in public, not over a computer.

"I'll be up here until at least Thanksgiving." *My second-to-last one*, Abe thinks. Since Alex's family is limited to her mother (and now, stepfather), she's always loved hanging out with Abe's huge family. If the Jacobs' biggest holiday celebration of the year can't get her up north, then nothing will. "You should come. Everyone would love to see you."

A subtle smile passes Alex's lips, there and gone in a flash. "Is Aunt Ella making her peanut butter blossoms?" she asks.

Abe gives her a half grin. "Always."

RICHMOND, 1996

Mrs. East insisted Alex fly back to Miami with her to recover from the broken neck. Abe, physically exhausted and emotionally strung out from his time being "strong" in the hospital, didn't have it in him to fight her. His own family stayed with him briefly, then he was alone in a strange city, with a job and friend circle that were only fun with Alex around, tied to a lease that wouldn't be up until after Alex's halo was already off.

To distract himself from his loneliness, over nearly three months where time stretched like salt-water taffy, Abe cleaned. He made weekly chores into dailies, and monthly projects into weeklies. With the place looking ready for a visit from the Queen, Abe rearranged their entertainment—CDs, DVDs, and books—chromatically, then chronologically, then autobiographically. Once satisfied he'd never be able to find shit he was looking for, Abe rearranged the rooms.

Before he could start painting walls or refinishing furniture, I reminded him how much fun he'd once had tending our garden of words. Before Alex's fall, Abe hadn't listened to me all that often. Now that he wasn't performing in front of a crowd, I'd stopped being anything special, just one of a number of voices calling for his attention. One voice told him a shot or two of whiskey would make being alone a lot more bearable; Abe ignored that one, because he got the sense it would have no bottom. Other voices said he should learn to play guitar, or model clay figures, or start painting. Easy enough to ignore those voices, whose invitations entailed buying materials and making a space to work. Guess who won the day thanks to needing nothing but a pen and pad?

Our conversations felt wooden, choppy. Still, I have a fondness for the words Abe and I knocked around while Alex convalesced in Miami. We'd almost found our groove again when, after eleven weeks recovering in her childhood home, Alex decided she didn't have a twelfth week to give. "You sure you can't stick it out?" Abe asked. "It's only one more week."

"I don't have one more day," Alex whispered, so he told her he'd be at the airport when she needed him. She'd sounded strained over the phone, obviously missing Abe as much as he missed her, but she hadn't elaborated. Turned out proximity to her hovering mother hadn't allowed Alex to have her full say. The whole drive from the airport, walking to their apartment, and inside on the couch, Alex vented—a forty-minute spiel on everything that had driven her crazy in Miami over the previous weeks. It culminated in the pronouncement that she never wanted to see her mother again.

Abe listened from across the room, afraid to approach when Alex was raging. It felt incredible to hear her voice again, to see her face. Abe knew her words were bunk. Family is family, and her rant consisted primarily of childhood angst triggered by living together again now that Alex had tasted independence. Still, Abe agreed. "Screw her, you're an orphan now. Once the doctors take that getup off, we'll go on a road trip cross country, just the two of us."

Alex took a moment to look into Abe's eyes. Tears spilled down her face. "It's so good to see you," she whispered.

"It's good to see you, too." He walked over and knelt down. He held her hands, clammy from Miami sweat and the plane ride. Her hair was inexplicably wild, twined around the halo and the rods bolted to her vest.

"Do you want a sponge bath?" Abe asked, stroking Alex's face.

"Yes," she breathed.

The challenge of washing her hair around the contraption explained why it had become such a mess. Her mother had clearly gotten tired of dealing with it. As Alex leaned over the tub, Abe worked slowly, methodically, pouring pitchers of warm water over her head that made her sigh, massaging her scalp with a gentle rhythm that made her groan. With her hair cleaned and rinsed, Abe used a cream conditioner and brushed it out as best he could. He put her hair in a simple braid, then he sponged her body, starting with her torso beneath the vest. The down cushioning inside had gone from puffy and white to a matted dinge. The plastic had dulled, and he saw scratches in a few places. Abe wondered at everything he'd missed while they'd been apart.

As awkward as working around and inside the vest was, Abe loved touching her body again. Alex hadn't used a razor the whole time, and Abe found he didn't mind. She didn't seem to care, either; no self-deprecating *stubble is so sexy* or *ugh, I feel gross*, just a blissful smile. The more he touched Alex, the more he felt the tension leaving her body. With Alex's body clean, Abe shook her hair loose, rinsed the conditioner off, and rebraided it, a little tighter the second time.

Abe helped her up, patted her dry, wrapped her in his bathrobe, and guided her to the couch. He popped a VHS tape of *The Little Mermaid* into the VCR. Alex made a contented noise deep in her throat, smiling up at him. Leaving her in the living room hurt (he'd barely gotten her back) but Abe did, mopping the mess of suds and water from the bathroom floor in a rush so he could get back to her as quickly as possible.

"Hey, babe?" she called.

"Yeah?" he called back, easy as anything. Like she'd been there all along, like he hadn't felt rudderless without her. He put the mop away and returned to the living room, wiping his hands on his t-shirt like it was a dish towel. On the TV screen the tape was paused with King Triton frozen in place talking to the crab, all but invisible behind a line of static. Alex dropped the VCR remote and beckoned Abe forward, reaching out for him. She grabbed his hands, held him in front of her. Her blue eyes, shining with emotion, pinned him in place.

"It's you, Abe," she said. "It's always been you. I want to take you to Miami. You'll love it so much down there, I promise. We'll be together, just the two of us. No one else. Forever."

"Yes," Abe said, tears in his eyes. It was all he'd ever wanted to hear from her. "Yes."

Poor Abe. Smart enough to know Alex was just blowing off steam when she talked about never seeing her family again, but too naive to question what else might have been said in the heat of the moment.

SOLATIUM

by Dominick Deer Woods

Refraction

One of the most beautiful things I've ever seen was a
    full double rainbow arcing over the water at South Beach.

Like every year
we were there to sell cookbooks
penned by celebrity chefs.
Tickets cost a month of our rent.
Festivalgoers dropped it like it was nothing
to chase artisanal nibbles for an afternoon.
To gape their mouths like tarpon
begging for blasts from vodka shotguns
wielded by women
in corporate bathing suits.
To take pics, lips peeled away from sweaty teeth,
leaning against the autograph table
as a TV face in sunglasses leans back.
Lagasse. Guy. Tsai. Irvine.
Gotta post them all.

Dispersion

A line of security guards marched,
elbows locked across the sand,
herding the final swigs, the last snatched morsels.

A storm front thought better of itself and
the twin arcs appeared.
We stopped packing to gape.
Beachgoers rattled each other from dozing and
stopped throwing frisbees and flirting to
point stiff, feverish fingers into the sky.

Reflection

Before the Food Network devoured us
the festival felt radical.
No one else put on food and wine festivals
before Miami put on food and wine festivals.
We slept overnight in the cookbook tents
to guard our inventory from weather and wanderers.
Before the icy tubs of water *sponsored by*—
attendees got dangerously drunk.
Pulling off clothes and stomping them into the sand drunk.
Passed out and carted away by paramedics drunk.
Rush the demo stage and
make off waving a stolen kabob like a victory flag drunk.
But my God, the lines to buy books stretched across
    the sand.
We sold over five hundred copies of Giada's first.
It never occurred to me to do the math
to see if I was getting paid enough
because it was free food and free booze people were paying
    hundreds for.
It was holding Wolfgang's newborn so he could sign stock.
It was standing with Nigella looking like she was something
    out of a storybook
under a sun umbrella that matched her dress.
It was seeing a teenager built like a tetherball pole
in a Ramones t-shirt walking away from me,

and when I snorted, "What the hell do you know about the
   Ramones?"
him turning around to reveal not a teenager but
Anthony Bourdain with his crooked grin
demanding to know what I knew about the Ramones,
and we laughed and I told him *Kitchen Confidential*
was one of my favorite books
and he blushed,
the man blushed.

Internal Refraction

When we stopped working to look at a double rainbow
we swore to ourselves and each other
this year will be different from all the others when
we worked too much and left too little for ourselves,
but of course we worked too much anyway.
Later I think of Anthony Bourdain
and of how he left this world,
despite showing us the best of it,
and it makes me mad,
and I don't mean angry, I mean crazed,
I mean will I never be through with this shit,
with these dark thoughts of
twin rainbows
and how seeing them changed nothing.

Eight

Outside the Three Feathers Café, Truck Stop #9 looks like a collection of corrugated buildings that barely hint at the businesses inside—casino, kitsch shop, the café, a tobacco store. Abe feels wrung out, emotionally and physically. It took more convincing to get Alex to come for Thanksgiving than he thought it would, and she's not even taking extra days off. Abe hopes the walk home will get his blood pumping. The headache is gone at least; he tries to feel grateful for that.

He crosses the road for a bit of a different view on the walk home, trading the tobacco store at Truck Stop #9 for the tobacco store across the street. Tax-free cigarettes coming or going, like the ancestors always dreamed. The sun is higher than on the walk over, warming the day slightly, but to Abe it feels hotter than it should. In the time it takes to get from the Mohawk Bingo Palace to the Ahkwesáhsne Mohawk Casino Resort (you can gamble coming or going, too), Abe removes Dad's hunting jacket and threads it through the straps of his laptop bag. He wipes sweat from his face, wondering how he can be hot and shivering at the same time.

He passes two nondescript rectangular buildings. Squinting at the sign out front, Abe sees it's the admin office for the Saint Regis

Mohawk Tribe, which issued Abe his fabled tribal ID. In 1973, after nearly a century of insisting the people of Ahkwesáhsne start using an elected government, New York State and the national Bureau of Indian Affairs had forced the SRMT on the Mohawk people. Founded in the 1920s, the BIA took fifty years to staff their Native offices with Natives, so at least the SRMT started with an all-Mohawk staff. No shade to our neighbors for collecting a paycheck, but we recognized it for the long con that it was—the latest tool of assimilation.

Sure, we can bring treaty violations to the office, cases where land has been ceded to us on paper, but the government has used it anyway. But the SRMT only goes to the negotiation table after the Mohawk Nation Council of Chiefs—the traditional government, which we call the Longhouse—has done years, or even decades, of activism. We also reported pollution problems to the office for twenty-four years, but the federal government didn't do anything about Alcoa or GM or Reynolds Metals dumping toxicants on our land and in our waters until locals got together and created the Ahkwesáhsne Task Force on the Environment.

And of course, if you want the government to acknowledge you're Mohawk, then you need an ID card from the SRMT. But what if the older generations of your family—who were born on the Rez, lived on the Rez, and died on the Rez—hadn't given a damn about getting an ID themselves? Well, then you're shit out of luck because for you to get a card, your parents had to have a card, and for your parents to get a card, their parents had to have a card. So I guess you're not really Mohawk. Never mind the college aid, health care, and housing that will be denied to you, you'll spend your whole life fighting for your identity in the white world because you don't have some bit of plastic.

Like a portion of the Rez, the Billings part of Abe's family claim the Longhouse is the sole governmental body on Ahkwesáhsne (both the US and Canadian sides, of course, because Ahkwesáhsne predates both). Abe respects the Longhouse, and he still feels guilty sometimes about caving in to the tribal ID scam when he needed money for college. But it had stopped feeling like his fight in the early aughts, somewhere around the time he did his third beach cleanup and started embracing his new home.

A car speeds by, briefly toot-tooting its horn. Abe doesn't recognize it, but he lifts a hand anyway. He passes another tobacco shop—Smokey's, with a good old-fashioned cigar store Indian out front, Native kitsch at its finest. Abe is heating up again. He takes his hoodie off and drapes it over the shoulder bag, on top of his dad's jacket. He feels dampness around his hairline, cool in the breeze. His dress shirt sticks at the pits and down his back.

After more gas stations and tobacco stores, he passes the marker where his walk becomes less commercial and more residential—a by God Dunkin' Donuts. Abe's glad they've avoided the pitfalls some Nations have had with casinos creating microcosms of American capitalism, where one big resort benefits a select few council members while most of the tribe members struggle to pay their bills. On the other end, the Miccosukee Tribe in Miami distributes tens of thousands in tax-free gaming revenue to every one of their members, money the US is after. The federal government also has a stranglehold on enrollment, trying to make sure the six hundred fifty remaining Miccosukee are the last of their tribe, no matter who they marry. Imagine being told your children are not your own. Shenanigans like that are what keep the Longhouse strong; when fighting for sovereignty, they can cite treaties going back centuries before the SRMT.

As he continues walking, Abe's legs start to feel weird, like his feet aren't there anymore. Looking down at them, they seem to be stepping normally; still it's strange, watching his feet land and feeling the impact start at his ankles. *Numbness*, he thinks. Abe slows his gait, worried he might trip. He lets his boots scrape with each step, the sound telling him his feet are connecting with the ground, even as sensation has stopped.

By the time he's halfway home, Abe is outright sweating. He takes off his dress shirt, down to a t-shirt underneath. The sun makes wearing nothing but a t-shirt in fifty-two-degree weather okay. Or at least he thinks it does. Despite the sweat pouring down his face, his skin feels cold. *Hypothermia*, I tell him. *You're gonna keep stripping off layers until eventually you'll be running around naked in the freezing cold.* The idea makes him chuckle. If exposure to sunny, low-fifties temperatures really is cold enough to kill him, then he's got hours and hours before it does.

MIAMI, 2002

Looking across the pool at Benny—a muscular, v-shaped, action figure type with a shaved head—Abe wondered why he let Alex talk him into coming to this pig roast in west Miami. Alex and Abe's typical nights were spent downtown, where the back porches of four rambling houses—built one hundred years before by Bahamian shipbuilders—overlooked the same patch of grass. They were friends with couples in three of the four houses, which basically made the courtyard theirs. They'd drink beer, pass a bong, and chatter away. Sometimes, the group would head to a party at one of the other conch houses in the neighborhood. Sure, they knew folks who'd gotten robbed at gunpoint right around the corner, but the eight of them believed singing a passable "No Scrubs" en route to a house party would keep them safe. And you know what? It always did. At the next house a party would be in full swing, and Abe would meet a Peruvian vegan who worked as a sound engineer and have the most fascinating conversation of his life. Until the next weekend, when he met a Cuban DJ who did biochemistry during the day and had invented a dye that made it easier to track cancer cells. Or the next weekend, when he met a middle-aged French expat who'd done porn in the seventies but was now a pilot. And on and on—a boundless collection of oddballs and art freaks who had found community in the dilapidated rental properties downtown.

This Benny fellow's party, on the other hand, was not Abe's scene. First, there was the house. A newly built cinder block bunker trying to disguise itself as a Coconut Grove bungalow, without any of the foliage or architectural flourishes. Sure, it was nice to have trimmed grass without rotting fast food or broken glass in it, but it looked more like a putting green than a lawn. An overhang ran the length of the back of the house, covering a cement slab of patio that abutted a cheerless, kidney-shaped cement hole of a swimming pool. Second, there was the crowd. It was a pool party pig roast, and the chiseled, buff figures compared how many hours they spent in the gym each week. The women wore their diamonds and gold in the pool. The men wore bulky watches with names Abe had never heard of, introducing them like they were friends, *This is my Bulova.* Worst of all, Benny—who was maybe five years younger than Abe and Alex—owned the place outright. Alex's mother kept hectoring her to buy one of those houses in the Design District downtown, the same ones where they party-hopped. Mrs. East knew Alex still had enough left over from her father's settlement for a down payment, and wouldn't let it go.

"You're there practically every night, anyway," Mrs. East would say, usually weekly, over dinner at her house. "Miami built interstates through there in the sixties and it drove the property values right down, Wynwood and Little Haiti, too. But before long, you're going to see the same thing happening in those neighborhoods that's been happening in Brooklyn for the last ten years. Renting, you might as well be flushing your money down the toilet."

The first time she'd heard this speech, Alex had grimaced. "We're one U-Haul away from a new city, Mom. Any time we want, we can drop everything and have a fresh life somewhere else." Her mother's counterargument was that if she moved away, Alex could rent the place until the neighborhood hit, then sell it and be a millionaire.

After that, whenever the subject came up, Alex would smile and promise to think about it, even as she told Abe in private, "No way I'm being tied down to Miami the rest of my life."

Abe knew the drop that had broken her neck had fucked with Alex's head. Not physically, but in the sense that Alex thought she'd been saved to do something significant with her life. She'd joked about becoming an icon because she was so talented, but feeling she'd been spared death by a higher power made her want to be more altruistic.

For his part, Abe stayed out of the real-estate discussion. He hadn't exactly fallen for Miami, but he had a good job (in five years he'd moved from kitchen work at a mid-level chain to a corporate coffee house to the aforementioned independent bookstore), friends (mostly a mix of Alex's high school crew and like-minded work colleagues he'd collected over the years). And as an added bonus, no one ever asked Abe what he was. True, they assumed he was some sort of Latino, which might as well have been white in Miami. But after feeling like a perpetual outsider in Syracuse and Richmond, Abe was ready to be invisible.

"How do you know this guy, again?" Abe sat at a dark table in the corner of Benny's pool area with Valentina and her best friends, a pair of Italian sisters. Valentina, a heavily tattooed Brazilian American woman with limbs chiseled by Muay Thai and lust for life in her gap-toothed smile, worked with Abe at the bookstore. When it came to handselling, the rest of them competed for second place behind Val.

"He's Annie's little brother," said Valentina.

"Annie, right." Valentina and the DeSocio sisters were regulars at the downtown get togethers ("getties" in Miami-speak, bro), but Abe was still wrapping his mind around Annie. He'd met her tonight for the first time—along with Amber, Carrie, Christine, and Christa, Valentina's sorority sisters. "I still can't believe you were in a sorority."

"It's a good thing."

"The Greek system is a bitchy sorting hat, only everyone's house is Slytherin."

"You watch too much TV."

Abe grunted in response.

Alex had spent most of her time moving between the pool and the hot tub beside it. At first she'd catch Abe's eye in the crowd, throwing him a smile or a wink or a raised brow, and he'd bring her a beer. He'd watched as she'd listened to a beefy dude they called the Shermanator, her unbroken eye contact with the guy hypnotizing even at a distance. Mrs. Sherman (one of the C-named sorority sisters, though Abe wasn't sure which one) had offered Abe an OxyContin earlier in the evening.

"I'm good," Abe had replied, trying not to judge her for popping opioids while carrying her newborn on one hip.

Valentina elbowed Abe, gesturing toward the hot tub. "Does that bother you?"

Abe smiled, almost laughed. When they'd first moved to Miami, Abe and Alex had had several conversations to establish what their monogamy would look like. Flirting was encouraged, anything up until the point of silent eye contact where all you can imagine is kissing. That was the line. If potential temptation arose, they had to be honest. *I think I have a crush on that new barista,* one of them might confess, *the one with the nose ring. Come here,* the other would answer, *and let me fuck that right out of your system.* In the meantime, they practiced hot monogamy before that became a buzz phrase or a self-help book. If being Daddy meant keeping Alex to himself, then fine, Abe could play Daddy. He could be pirate to her wench, cowboy to her saloon gal, Solo to her Leia. Or vice versa if the mood struck. They had toys, props, outfits, and all.

"Not really," Abe told Valentina. He was feeling loose and boozy, so he let her in on their open relationship prior to Miami. Valentina was a good listener, so he got fairly explicit.

"You ever miss sucking dick?" she asked when Abe was done, making him laugh for real.

"What's between our legs is just spare parts," he said shrugging. "Plumbing, really."

"I dunno ... Once I went six months without sex. I took Marco home"—she gestured with her beer hand toward the pool, where a hirsute guy swam with a dead ringer for Missy Elliott—"and he had this surface-to-air-missile dick. I was like, lovin' on it. For hours. He got scared I was going to eat it."

"How long you been together?"

Valentina gave him a look; *get serious.* "Let's just say Marco has a gift he doesn't know how to use."

"Aw," one of the DeSocio sisters—Sara or Lara—said, "I hate when you say that part of the story."

"Totally ruins the fantasy," the other DeSocio sister agreed.

"On that note." Abe upended his beer. "I'm going to find out when this pig will be ready."

He really didn't want to stand shirtless next to Benny, but he didn't have much of a choice. He faked confidence, shoulders back, beer belly sucked in, chest out as he walked.

One of their downtown friends had done two semesters at Johnson & Wales Culinary Academy and always concocted kick-ass snacks for their get-togethers. Abe himself would never invite anyone over without a spread. Benny hadn't coordinated anything with the guests, so other than a bag of corn chips with some salsa devoured in a flash around three o'clock, forty people were watching the sun go down, surrounded by coolers full of beer, waiting for the caja asadora to finish roasting a whole pig. Besides the beer, Benny had a counter crowded with liquor bottles in the open window between the patio and the kitchen; Abe had counted five types of flavored vodka alone. A girl named Haley stood at this makeshift bar, serving mixed drinks. Every time she used the shaker, one of her breasts popped out of her bikini top. When she poured the cocktail or the shots, she'd shrug the loose flesh back in; sometimes she said "peek-a-boo" and laughed. Alex had offered to retie her strings at the neck, but Haley said, "Nah, the girls need their air from time to time."

In addition to the OxyContin from C. Sherman, Abe had been proffered both cocaine and ketamine, as well as hits of nitrous oxide ("I don't have it on me, bro, but if you go to the red Sebring out front, my man'll hook you up"). Each time, Abe said he was good. It's not that the downtown freaks were teetotalers, but they stuck to weed and a beer or wine buzz, maybe the occasional shroom if it was Halloween or a birthday. The crowd at Benny's, they went hard. And on empty stomachs. If Abe had known the deal going in, he would have brought side dishes.

"Yo, Benny," Abe said, doing his impression of an outgoing person.

"Yeah, man." Benny clinked Abe's beer with his own. "Thanks for coming. Abe, right?"

"Yeah, that's right."

Benny grinned wide, a twenty-five-year-old with his own home and two clubs on Washington Ave. his father had bought for him to run. His limbs looked like they'd been carved out of oak; the muscles in his lower torso formed an arrow pointing toward his low-slung shorts.

"How much longer on this pig?" Abe asked.

"Just did the last dusting of charcoal."

Abe nodded; it meant nothing to him. "Okay, so . . . ?"

"Stella's been marinating in my hot tub all weekend."

Abe looked at the hot tub, frowning.

"Nah, the one in the master, bro." Benny dug into his pocket. "Check this out."

Benny pulled out an oblong cell phone that fit in the palm of his hand. He pressed the top corner and it flipped open. Against his will, Abe was impressed. Benny pulled up a grainy photo on the little screen; the pig, soaking in an icy mojo sauce, head above the slurry, sunglasses perched on its snout, a cigar hanging out of its mouth. Abe chuckled, shaking his head.

"That's some funny shit, right?" Benny said, laughing hard enough to double over.

Abe glanced back toward the outdoor hot tub. It was full of people, but Alex and the Shermanator were not among them. Alex hadn't given him any reason to think she was unhappy with their monogamy, and Shermanator's wife and child were kicking around somewhere, but Abe still felt a pang of worry in his stomach. There was a whole house for them to explore, plenty of cars parked out front.

Abe tried to focus on Benny, who wanted to talk about the VIP room at ReBar. Apparently, an actress who used to be on *General Hospital* in the eighties snorted heroin off of Benny's dick there once. Abe hadn't heard of the actress and had never tried heroin, so he wasn't sure how to respond.

"That's excellent," he finally said, which made Benny crack up.

Abe stared over the pool, letting Benny's monologue wash over him.

Benny's shaved skull bleeds sweat
like an urgent cock throbbing with fluid

I've mentioned how Abe sent out a bunch of work and received a slew of rejection letters for his pain. That happened when Abe first got to Miami. He'd also tried an open mic at Churchill's in Little Haiti, but the crowd had caught his nervousness like a virus and he'd bombed. Since then, Abe and I had drifted apart. But I sensed his discomfort at the pig roast, so I searched for poetry in the dark, trying to put him at ease.

nightcrawler veins pulse
along Benny's bowling pin forearms

Abe finally saw Alex, coming by the patio for a beer. He didn't ask where she'd been, but her lips looked normal (meaning friction free, meaning unkissed), her hair damp and flat (meaning it hadn't been grabbed or tousled in a sexual frenzy).

"Hey, babe." She gave Abe a quick peck, then hugged him and whispered in his ear, "You can call me Valentina tonight, if you want." She pulled away, smiling. "What? I saw you talking to her."

That was Alex in a nutshell. She'd once told Abe she loved hanging out with gay men. "There are no limits," she'd gushed. "No feeling that hanging out might go too far." Abe had asked if she worried about that with everyone else she encountered. "Well . . . yeah," she'd said. "Don't you?" When Abe had said he only felt sexual attraction toward her, she'd laughed. "Christ, that makes you practically asexual." He'd had no idea what she'd meant by that, but her words had still stung. Because Alex smelled sex everywhere, maybe she imagined Abe was attracted to Valentina. Or maybe she'd misread Abe's concern over her disappearance at Benny's party as guilt. "C'mon, admit it," she said. "I saw the way you were looking at her. It's no big deal."

"I was admiring her tattoos," Abe said, "not lusting after her."

"You know you wish I had those tig ol' biddies."

"See, this just makes me think you wish I was built like the Shermanator."

"The who?"

"The guy you were talking to in the hot tub. You don't know his name?"

"Babe, you know I only have eyes for you."

Benny had Abe help him dump the ashes. The smell of roasted pig wafted out when they lifted the tray off the top of the caja asadora, filling Abe's mouth with smoke and saliva. He helped his host flip the rack holding the pig. Benny used his butcher knife to score the skin, and they replaced the charcoal tray.

"Thirty minutes that shit'll be crispy as fuck," Benny called out, fist raised. Most of the partygoers cheered, but some of them booed, having thought the pig was done. Benny pointed his knife at Abe. "You get first pick, bro."

Half an hour later, Benny rolled a large kitchen rack topped with a butcher block out to the patio. The smell of the pig hitting it was incredible. A crowd gathered around. Benny nodded to Abe. "What'll it be, bro?"

Abe pointed to a plump, crisp cheek.

"See, I knew it," Benny said. "You're quiet but you're on point, bro. Okay, one cheek for you and one cheek for me." He addressed the crowd at large. "Yo. Forty minutes and we can cut this sucker."

A collective groan went up.

"Hey, I cut it now, all those juices'll just drain right out. Stella needs a rest."

Mostly the protest was good-natured, but Abe felt a moody undercurrent. For a moment, our poem went dark.

starving revelers heave the butcher block
into the pool it goes
molten grease floats to the surface
shining like a wishing well
the spit roast box crashes
coals comet through the night
the water alights
swimmers sink below
forced to choose between drowning and burning alive

Abe, having downed beers on an empty stomach for hours by then, realized his head was spinning. He pushed the images away, worried he might somehow call forth the maiming and drowning of these partygoers.

When Abe finally got his pork cheek, it melted in his mouth—tender, smoky-sweet, and delicious. The skin had a satisfying, chewy crunch, tempered by the savory fat beneath. All the awkwardness of the preceding hours fell away. Once they'd eaten their fill, Abe and Alex jumped into the pool. They spent the rest of the night playing pool games, laughing under the Miami moon.

Alex continued to cling to a romantic notion of being unfettered, but the mood to pack up and move to a new city never struck. She loved being able to picnic on the beach whenever she felt like it, the mix of people, the food, and the weather (and, as much as she would never admit it, enjoyed butting heads with her mother every week). She went back to school and got a job as an elementary school teacher in a rough neighborhood. She liked to joke, "I've got to teach these kids we're not all devils," the "we" in question being white folks. Even though her father had been a teacher, Abe got the sense that an Alex who hadn't broken her neck would never have considered following his lead.

At night, Alex sang and played in various local bands without the expectation of any of them making it big. Abe joked about Alex's need for anonymous adulation—"What, my love ain't enough for you?"—but still, he never begrudged her for feeding on the adoration of strangers. It would have been nice if Abe had taken as much time to push the cursor with me as Alex had taken with her music, but you saw how it went. I'd whisper lines to him, but he rarely listened and he never wrote anything down.

AHKWESÁHSNE, 2016

Abe continues the endless walk home from Truck Stop #9, wiping the sweat off his face with the bag load of clothing he's carrying. His legs are starting to feel weak, unsteady. As the last businesses fall behind him, Abe wishes he'd called home from the truck stop. But more than halfway back to the house, it seems silly to bother anyone.

At some point, the houses stop on his side of the road, and the ones across the street become few and far between. The speed limit increases to fifty-five, the occasional car zooming by. To be safe, Abe moves farther from the road, from the soft shoulder to the grass. Abe recognizes this short stretch of woods. Once he passes them, the clatch of houses that includes his won't be long, but the distance seems to be dragging on. Every patch of woods he's come across seems smaller than when he was a child, except for this one. This one has grown.

"I'm afraid to lose my mind," he mutters. "I'm lonely, which doesn't make any sense since I'm surrounded by the people who love me most."

Abe is doing a trick one of his many uncles taught him when he was a kid—"Any time you have a problem, walk the woods and tell it to the trees." The woods soak up words like raindrops.

"I think dying sets me apart from them, and that's why I feel alone. I'm scared of how little time I have left. I'm afraid of not knowing anyone at the end." Abe becomes aware he's speaking aloud and closes his mouth, moving slower than ever. It doesn't feel like he's walking so much as piling his legs in front of himself, bit-by-bit from the feet up, then pushing forward to balance on them. "At least if I fall," Abe says, "the grass will be soft."

He borrowed his dad's coat for this walk, thinking he'd be cold. He digs through the pockets, finding receipts, hair ties, an empty pack of gum, two peppermint hard candies, and, hidden in the zipper of the inside flap, a single Isotoner glove. Everything except his phone.

"That's weird," he says. "I must've missed a pocket, or else I would've found it." He checks again, moving the detritus in his dad's coat to one pocket for easier sifting. When he still comes up empty, he checks the hoodie, then his pants and bag. Maybe he left the phone at the café? But he remembers checking the temperature, both on the way to the truck stop and on the way back, so he had it when he started this walk home.

The odds of someone he knows driving by—or someone he once knew, at least—are good but not great, given it's a weekday. Why is he shivering? Abe puts his hoodie back on, zips it all the way up, and pulls the hood over his head. As he does, a drop of sweat falls off the end of his nose. He wonders if he has food poisoning. He wonders if he's about to pass out in the grass on the side of the road.

"I'm afraid if I pass out here, then . . ." Speaking takes a lot of effort, so he looks at the tree he's passing and finishes the thought in his mind, *no one will notice me in the grass.*

Abe plods on. He digs into his computer bag again, not expecting to find his phone, only knowing he checked the coat twice and the bag once. Or maybe he hasn't checked the bag yet, because the phone is there, right in the main compartment beside his laptop.

He pulls his phone out. Predictably, there aren't any bars. He holds the home button, staring at the screen for a time, wondering why it won't open. Remembering the reason takes some time. Side-of-the-road time, which moves differently than time in other places. Then he lands on the answer: the temperature difference between Miami and the Rez has made his thumbprint stop working, and he's been too lazy to figure out how to update it. His attempts to key in his passcode don't go so well either. Abe doesn't know if his brain is going early or what, all he knows is that staying on his feet is becoming more and more of an effort. All he wants is to curl up into a ball and sleep for a week.

Abe wills himself to stop weaving, the phone to stop going blurry, his fingers to stop trembling. His will falls short; he's helpless in the face of whatever's happening. Whiteness permeates his vision. Hot fear rises inside him, cutting through the haze. Adrenaline brings him back from whatever curtain was trying to fall over his consciousness. Slowly, slowly, color bleeds into the day. Patterns resolve themselves into recognizable shapes. Abe nearly sobs with relief. Still cradling the phone, he moves his fingers over the correct passcode.

He texts Sis first; "Feeling sick. Walking route 37. Come pick me up." It's desperation erasing common sense; his sister averages three weeks to return a text. Besides, she's working. *Dad*, Abe thinks, *he'll be at home.* Abe texts him, "I don't feel good. Walking back. Come pick me up." He can't tell if the texts get through. In his muzzy state, the colored bubbles mean nothing to him. He texts Mom, Sharon Oaks, Aunt Maisy. He texts Adam, "No service up here. I'm walking route 37 and I'm about to pass out. Call someone to come get me."

Abe looks up the road, as though trying to see the house will make it appear. He's close, less than a mile to go, but he's never been so exhausted in his life. He has to keep on his feet and he'll make it, that's all. But his watery legs betray him, and he stumbles. Abe catches his elbows on his knees, a back-saving squat Tóta taught him, useful for gardening all day. And, apparently, for keeping your feet when you're woozy.

The reprieve is temporary. One more step and the day washes over white again. This time Abe slumps into the grass. *If only*—is the last thing he thinks before oblivion takes him.

THE ONLY INDIAN IN THE ROOM

by Dominick Deer Woods

At a screening for *Paterson* I see another Native in the lobby so I tell her Mohawks invented popcorn and she smiles. I can't tell whether the smile means she already knows this or she wants me to flirt or both. We shake hands and the earth trembles. The Turtle shivers one might say. I ask and she answers Otoe Tribe, Owl Clan. "Really? I'm Turtle Clan. That makes us the wisest motherfuckers in the room." Alone in this crowd we'd have no shelter, no Medicine, no Song. Two Natives in one room can make a drum and a rattle into a rhythm into a bacchanal into a snarl of limbs into generations of terpsichorean hordes. Two Natives will fulfill the duty passed on from prior generations and make future generations, the only Indigenous thing we know for sure how to do.

She is every woman in my family and I am every man in hers.

We could build a home with the bones of our ancestors but the director is doing a Q&A afterward so we take our separate places in the dark and the earth settles back to sleep.

Nine

Three days after passing out by the side of the road, Abe sits in the passenger seat of Sharon Oaks's nineties Subaru, on the way to her father's trailer. From what he heard afterwards, Abe's texts had caused a flurry of activity, calls and messages from Syracuse to Montreal. Mom had taken Tóta's old Buick before anyone else could react. Dad drove a little behind, bringing along an uncle and a cousin. The two cars drove slowly up the road and spotted Abe pretty easily. He was groggy when Dad and Uncle Ghost picked him up and put him in Mom's car. He only remembers flashes: head lying in Mom's lap in the back seat of the Buick; a home renovation show in the hospital waiting room in Malone; a student trying repeatedly to draw blood from his wrist (according to Dad, Abe had said, "Alice Hyde is a teaching hospital" every time the student tried and failed to find a vein, but he has no recollection of this). When Abe came to, it happened all at once, like waking from a long sleep.

His lesions are in stasis, his blood markers say his organs are fine, and a contrast scan of his brain turned up nothing. The doctors in Malone don't know what caused him to lose consciousness, and his Miami doctors concur. They cite the change in weather, his lack of exercise compared to all the biking he did in Miami, the stress of his diagnosis. The Malone doctors wrote him a prescription for a cane and called it good. The Miami doctors switched his pills from Dalimuterin to Amethopterone, to be on the safe side.

Once he saw the aluminum cane on offer at the health center, Abe raided Tóta's old collection, picking a maple cane with a smooth brass knob on top and brass cap for a toe. Tóta lost a lot of height over the years, but she'd liked a tall cane she could hold in front of herself and lean in to. Abe, by contrast, keeps it low, tucked against his leg. He tells his youngest niece that Tóta imbued the wood with Medicine to make it work for whoever uses it, no matter their size. Because if you're not messing with your relations, are you even Mohawk?

Abe isn't sure how to feel about going to Budge's place for the second part of his healing. His pain has gotten worse, grinding into his knees and hips, twisting in his gut to the point of nausea, making him walk like a rickety old man. It doesn't occur to Abe to think Budge might have pissed off something inside his body, some lurking Thing that likes his suffering just as it is.

Sharon Oaks has the driver's side window cracked open and she's puffing a Seneca from the red pack. Besides being one of the Six Nations, Seneca is a local brand made on the Seneca Reservation that goes for a fourth of what you'd pay for a Marlboro or a Newport. Brands like Seneca—or on Ahkwesáhsne, Signal and Niagara's— you can taste the savings in every puff. But if you're desperate (read, "poor") enough, you can get used to choking them down, as Sharon apparently has.

Her back seat is adrift with fast-food bags, and crumpled cellophane and old gum fill her ashtray. A fine coat of cigarette ash and dust covers every surface, the dashboard streaked clean where she moves cassette tapes in and out of the deck. Growing up, the few cars Abe rode in had the same gamey closet smell, the same lived-in layers. I don't know if it's salt on the roads rusting bodies or winter sludge coating everything with grime, but no one gives a shit what their vehicle looks like up north. Living in Miami, a place where a clean car is considered more virtuous than a kind demeanor, Abe has missed this carelessness toward a possession that simply means you don't have to take the bus.

Today, Sharon has swapped her tie-dye for a faded Bart Simpson t-shirt. Bart advises Abe not to have a cow, man. If Sharon wasn't on a reservation on the Saint Lawrence River it'd be full of cool irony, but there's nothing ironic about a woman wearing men's Wranglers. Well, not hipster ironic. It's probably ironic to whoever invented Wranglers. Sharon drives them down the same route that defeated Abe earlier in the week, past the truck stop. Traveling through the main drag between the Raquette River and Saint Regis River, Abe shakes his head and gestures out the window. "You know what this reminds me of?"

Sharon pulls a long drag from her shitty Seneca cigarette, squinting against the smoke. She takes in the view she sees every day, trying to see what Abe sees in the gas stations, smoke shops, and casinos, both mini and grand. "Home?" she offers, her tone deadpan.

"Not even. This is that scene in every movie where they land in a foreign country, and when they walk down the street, they're mobbed by street urchins."

"'They' who?"

"You know." Abe moves a hand dismissively. "Our Heroes. Brad Pitt and Sandra Bullock or whoever. It's like, 'Look at these weird foods hanging from hooks. Look at these crazy outfits. These people are so desperate that they're foaming at the mouth for our spare change.' This is like that."

"'This' what?" Sharon asks.

"All of this shit. When I left, there were old farms, trees."

"There's still old farms and trees."

"Yeah, but back then you could pull over anywhere along here and pick berries until you got sick of them. Now, whether it's gas or cigarettes or gambling, what they're really selling is Indian kitsch.

Some of these places have totem poles out front. Fucking totem poles. Do you know where totem poles come from?"

"The Haida."

Abe is surprised she knows it, and it must show in how he stops talking and looks at her.

"Yeah, I said Haida, hater," Sharon says, changing the pronunciation so they rhyme. Abe laughs, and Sharon laughs, and it's the kind of shared laughter that gives birth to friendships. He's lucky she's so forgiving, like she was during the ceremony for Tóta's passing ten years before. When she'd called the fry bread she served with her Corn Soup "scones," Abe had chuckled over the word choice. "You making fun a me, cuz?" she'd said, her face hard. Abe had frozen. First he'd kissed her cheek, then he'd laughed at her; he was fucking up coming and going. His face must've looked priceless because Sharon had laughed until tears popped in the corners of her eyes. "Didn't know they took life so serious down in Miami."

I seem to remember promising to tell you about a Mohawk funeral. Thing is, I'm not supposed to. Not because you're an outsider or anything . . . although there is a certain glee in withholding information. Or telling flat-out lies. My favorite example of that is the Inuit, who told white anthropologists they used seal shit to brush their teeth (a test of humor the scientists, alas, failed). No, it's more the idea that writing down a ceremony defeats the purpose. Once you have some rule book to follow, the danger is it will become rote. There's no room for evolution or growth. Besides, I have to confess, it gives me a lot of pleasure to jump around in time and resurrect Tóta over and over, but let's finally put her to rest.

Tóta's burial ceremony was the first time Adam, Sis, Abe, and their half-Irish cousins, Aunt Maisy's boys, had been together in decades. When the Jacobs Kids and the Brown Boys got together at last, even though they were there to see Tóta interred, they couldn't deny the energy felt like a party. Brennan bought a case of Labatt's Blue to get the evening started. It wouldn't be enough to get them

all drunk but it would lubricate the cogs. If history was any indica-
tor, it would lead to more trips into town and escalating beer buys.
Eventually, they'd stop messing around and buy enough beer for a
whole regiment to feel no pain, with enough left over to start the
cycle again the next evening.

The six of them brought that first case of Blue behind the house
and lit kindling in the trash barrel. They stood around this makeshift fire and toasted to Tóta's memory, to family, and to all of them
being together. They'd barely taken their first sips when Uncle Dan
joined in. The timbre of Dan's voice lived in the subbasement next
to Johnny Cash, and he had the complex handsomeness of a Javier
Bardem. Uncle Dan always joined the Thanksgiving bonfire, and
would even play a round or two of Kick the Can, so his presence
wasn't unusual. However, the request he made was.

"Can I get one of those?" he asked. Dan rarely cracked a smile,
his wit as dry as January powder. No one had ever known him to ask
for a beer; Abe assumed Uncle Dan was sad over his mother's death
and wanted a beer cushion to land on for the night.

"Sure," Adam said, after a beat. Abe's brother? His handsomeness
wasn't complicated at all. It was right out there for the world to love,
and he smiled almost constantly. In fact, he was smiling big when he
handed their uncle a can. Instead of drinking the beer, Uncle Dan
cracked it open and poured in into the burning trash barrel, where
it hissed and steamed.

"Wow, that hit the spot," he rumbled, passing the empty back.
"How about another?"

He'd committed alcohol abuse of the highest order, but Uncle
Dan was Adam's uncle. No longer smiling, Adam passed Dan a fresh
one. Their uncle did the same thing with the second can, cracking it
open and pouring the beer into the burning barrel.

"Whoo, that'll wake you up." Uncle Dan walked over and brushed
past Adam to grab the rest of the case. He rested it on the edge of the
barrel. "Let's get this party started."

He opened one can at a time and tipped them into the barrel. He invited his nephews, niece, and grandnephews to do the same with the beers they held. As the firelight died, an acrid smell filled the air.

"We don't light fires during the ceremony," Uncle Dan said. The hard edge had left his tone. He sounded sad and tired. "We don't drink during the ceremony. That means no booze of no kind, not beer, not wine, not liquor, not rum butter taffy."

Pouring their unfinished beers into the trash barrel felt like a ritual. The flames hissed out, and Abe's family became darker shadows under the cover of night. They stood in the dark, smelling the smoky damp acrid reek, unsure of what to do with themselves. Abe felt like he was six years old again, the time he'd used Mom's lipstick to graffiti the word "ASS" on the side of the toilet tank, and she'd confronted him in front of the whole family.

"We didn't know, Uncle Dan," Adam said.

Uncle Dan rested a hand on his shoulder. "Now you do." His subbasement timbre made those simple words a pronouncement, a closing of whatever strange ceremony the dousing of the fire had been. Then Uncle Dan walked up the porch steps and back inside the house.

"Well, shit," Brad said softly. Then they followed their uncle up the steps, and inside, where they spent time with family and mourned the loss of their matriarch. They weren't the only ones who unwittingly broke ceremony protocol. Abe's nephews got bored and hit up a casino, an offense that earned them a chewing out from Aunt Maisy. The boys took their guilt to a tattoo parlor, getting ink to commemorate Tóta—her date of birth to her date of death. Since Tóta had three different birth dates and there were three of them, it worked out well. Until they came back to the house and showed off their tattoos, an offense against the ceremony that earned them a tongue lashing from Aunt Abby. Why didn't the older folks just enumerate the rules at the beginning of the ceremony and save everyone some guilt? I don't know, but I'm sure there's Indigenous wisdom in it somewhere. I will say, the shame really made Abe focus on losing Tóta.

As far as the ceremony itself, let's go broad, and only with the understanding that none of this is set in stone (despite what you read on the internet, where it sounds like there's a checklist burned into a sacred deer hide somewhere). For the most part, the Jacobs followed the rituals outlined in the Kaianere'kó:wa you'd find online, what non-Mohawks usually call The Great Law of Peace, which is really The Great Good Way, a system of philosophy, religion, and governance that's intertwined and inseparable—and why the Mohawk Nation Council of Chiefs' refusal to give up and let the government ID crew completely take over is so important. For nine days, Tóta was never alone. Someone in the family watched over her body, day and night. For nine days, friends and family gathered and told stories about her. They sang songs and hymns. They listened to Methodist preaching, Catholic benedictions, and prayers to Kateri Tekakwitha (Lily of the Mohawks, the first Native American to achieve sainthood). The Billings side of the family—Priscilla, Maggie, Budge, and their cousins, children, and grandchildren—fed the Jacobs family and their guests, and kept the house clean.

They buried Tóta on a beautiful afternoon, one of those blue sky, cotton cloud days that feel so rare in the Saint Lawrence Valley. Outside the church, Abe watched the sun glinting off the water and thought of how Tóta and Skahiónhati had planned to meet at the river. He realized the sun was shining for them, not for the family they'd left behind.

I mentioned this in passing but let's spell it out. When they learned Tóta wasn't long for the world, Abe could've come back to Ahkwesáhsne and lived with her during those last few months. He could have heard all of Tóta's stories (the ones she was willing to tell, at any rate), maybe even written them all down. But he'd chosen not to. He got as far as telling Alex he was thinking about it, then stayed in Miami to sell books and drink beer and talk shit on old porches and eat Cuban toast and watch movies.

If not at hospice, then in the few months she spent at home afterward, everyone in the family got a chance to say goodbye to Tóta before she walked on. Of her six surviving children, nine surviving grandchildren, and six great-grandchildren, Tóta only said "I love you" back to Abe's cousin Brennan Brown, Aunt Maisy's youngest. Brennan is also the only one Tóta visited after she died. I hope Brennan, with his Irish father and Mohawk mother, the only grandchild who Tóta professed love for, the one who stayed on the Rez, will hear all the stories Abe missed, passed on by her children. (Yes, Sis still lives on Ahkwesáhsne, too, but she's more warrior than poet.) Then Brennan can write *The Collected Stories of Three Sisters: Being the Jacobs Sisters, Maisy, Haricot, and Abobora.* Barely anyone will read it, but it will last until the Turtle collapses, a record for anyone who wants the truth of our people at this point in time.

I bring Brennan up because if he passed by, you'd see a brown-haired, blue-eyed fella and likely have no idea he's Kanien'kehá:ka. I bring Brennan up because you should know he's the best of us. I bring Brennan up because Tóta chose him, not Abe, and that's important enough for you to know it, too.

How did Abe feel when he told Tóta he loved her in hospice and got a curt nod in return? There's no word in Kanien'kéha for "love." But sometimes, for those of us born to the English language, "I love you" is all we want to hear.

AHKWESÁHSNE, 2016

Riding to Budge Billings's house, Abe tells Sharon, "I'm sorry. Most people don't know the provenance of totem poles."

"I'm not most people."

No, she's a Mohawk woman, and proud of it. Which means Abe—even though he's got the better part of a decade on her—would do well to remember Sharon's been up here fighting for her identity while he's been chilling in Miami, passing for white. Miami-white, anyway.

"Okay, so tell me how a totem pole makes it off the island, then all the way across Canada, then over the Saint Lawrence and into the parking lot of the Trading Post," Abe says, pointing toward a gas station they're passing.

"Prolly inchworm-style across the land, innit? Then like a snake in the water, then back to inchworm." She shrugs. "Easy."

"Get serious," Abe says, but he's smiling. "I'm trying to make a point over here."

They hit a pothole, and the giant Dutch oven Abe's brought jangles open and closed in the back seat. There are grocery bags back there as well, filled with cans of beans, cans of hominy, onions, carrots, cabbage, rutabaga, chicken bouillon, and a gallon Ziploc bag of bones trimmed from a cut of deer Abe's brother-in-law shot; the makings of Corn Soup.

When he asked Aunt Maisy how much of a "tribute" she thought would be appropriate to bring for his healing, she voiced her signature full-throated cackle (the Jacobs sisters are full of humor, but Aunt Maisy's laugh takes over her whole body, like Tóta's used to do). After ribbing Abe for losing brain cells in the Miami heat, Aunt Maisy set him straight on what sort of things make a proper tribute, tokens from the heart rather than the wallet. So today Abe will cook for Budge, and Budge will . . . I don't know. Continue the healing, I guess.

"Well, I'd be happy to tell you exactly how that totem pole got there," Sharon says, crushing her cigarette butt into the overflowing ashtray. They cross the bridge over the Saint Regis River, which opens out onto the Saint Lawrence. The tribe recently won a two-hundred-year land battle, which allowed them to dismantle a dam that had been blocking half a dozen species of fish from migrating. The dam has been gone for less than two months. Passing over an honest river, instead of the lake of rocks he remembers, Abe realizes not all the changes since his childhood have been bad.

Thinking of the rocks under the bridge, covered now by water, makes a memory of his first girlfriend float to the surface of his mind. Walking home in eight-degree weather, he and Cheryl Curly Head once stopped to kiss under that bridge. Lips frozen and mouths warm, a mad urge struck them. Shadows concealed them as she tugged at Abe's belt, her fingers like cuts of meat. His numb fingers unzipped her jeans and slipped into her panties. The cold air stabbed his thighs as she yanked his clothes down. His fingers worked furiously, stealing her warmth for himself, and Cheryl hissed through clenched teeth as she came. Then, she wrapped an icy hand around him, stroking fast to bring him over the edge, and Abe groaned with a mix of pleasure and pain. The shiver-inducing cold had gotten tangled up in their post-orgasmic trembling, and they'd started giggling until they realized how dangerous it was to be out in the freezing cold.

Abe wishes his last time with Alex hadn't felt so strange, then maybe a pleasant, horny teenage memory wouldn't be making him feel so guilty. When was the last time they'd been a pair of wanting, sweating engines, destroying the world together one moment and bringing it back with laughter the next, rather than two people engaged in a mutually orgasmic paint by numbers? In retrospect, they never should have gotten married.

But that's a story for another time. Right now, Sharon is talking to Abe. Before she explains how a totem pole actually made it to Ahkwesáhsne, Sharon wants something from him. His cousin points with her lips beyond the mouth of the Saint Regis, toward the intimidating gray band of the Saint Lawrence, with its rocky shores and majestic breadth. "First, you've to tell me the name of the river."

And just like that, their budding friendship is troubled. Mohawks might know words or phrases here and there, but not the actual language. Asking relatives to repeat words to get the pronunciation right is embarrassing, because in doing so we're admitting we don't know and are therefore not Indian enough. We're reluctant to repeat what little we know for the next generation because we might be quizzed and found lacking. Maybe we can tell you "teacher" is iakorihonnién:ni and how to pronounce it, but what iakorihonnién:ni means? "Shows you how to be"? "Speaks true until we understand"? "Holds us captive until they clang that noisy ringer"? Most of us don't know. "Teacher," we'll say impatiently, feeling how inadequate we are as teachers ourselves.

The few lucky enough to be immersed in the language like to weaponize it. Abe recalls walking this road when he was twelve or thirteen, how the Ahkwesáhsne Freedom School kids surrounded him on their bikes.

What road're we on, cuz?

Route 37.

Wrong, Nohawk—it's Saterati. Where's your blood?

But Sharon Oaks is Abe's blood. For her, he'll get over himself and try. "I don't know it, but I imagine it's something like Big Water."

"Hey, Miami," Sharon says, sounding impressed. "The sun ain't completely fried your brain. I'll give you that one. It's Big Water*way*, Kaniatrowanenneh."

He feels absurdly proud of himself.

"Here's the thing," Sharon says, "the problem isn't a Haida totem pole on Mohawk land. The problem is you, thinking it's a totem pole."

"It's not? 'Cause it sure looks like one."

"Nope." Sharon glances away from the road, shooting him a look. "It's a test. If you think that's a Mohawk totem pole, that there's even such a thing as a Mohawk totem pole, then we know we're dealing with an ijit. Or maybe you don't care. Either way, we can do business, we can be civil, but we're not going out for beers any time soon."

"Okay," Abe says, like *hold on*. "But aren't you feeding the stereotypes? Well, no, not the stereotypes. The . . . homogenization. You know, lumping us all together, like we're one culture." Abe waves his hand, the word right on the tip of his tongue.

"Pan-Indianism."

"Right."

Sharon takes a turn, pulling the car away from the water. "Well first off, I don't own one of these tourist traps. I take soil and water samples for environmental surveys. So watch those 'yous,' you. Second, I'll say it again: the people who are dumb enough to lump us all together are never going to know the difference between a dreamcatcher and a spirit shield. So we make their idiocy work for us. Like a filter, innit."

Abe sees Budge's house coming up. He wishes Ahkwesáhsne was longer, larger, covering the entire earth so Sharon Oaks could keep driving and they could talk forever.

"So we're in on the joke," he tells her. "Good for us. But being outside of the joke . . . or you know, putting people outside of a joke they don't even know is a joke. We're feeding the system."

"Whether we feed it, or it's feeding on us, the system gets fed." Sharon swings into her father's driveway and rolls the windows down, letting the crisp air in. She kills the engine, drops the keys in her purse, and turns toward Abe. "Did you see the billboard when you first came in? The spray-painted one?"

He nods, and Sharon speaks Kanien'kéha. Nothing Abe catches or will retain, but hearing it aloud feels like a sacrament. Beneath her words, the car ticks as the engine cools. "The sign says we're an independent nation, that the land is Kanien'kehá:ka land and always has been. It asks visitors to show the same respect any native population deserves from visiting foreigners. Someone climbed up there and spray-painted that. Every time it fades out, someone else gets up there and paints the same message all over again. That's who we really are, innit."

"Sure. But can anyone see it past the neon?"

Sharon smirks at Abe. "We can."

MOHAWK FUNERAL

by Dominick Deer Woods

no one told us the rules
before
we broke them

Drinking
Gambling
Lighting fires

tarnishing Tóta's memory
honoring her imperfectly

but we came
and we wept
and it's never enough

Ten

"Keep it up and this soup is going to taste like fear," Abe tells Budge. He's standing in Budge's kitchen, prepping the ingredients for his Corn Soup tribute. Every once in a while, he leans on the counter with both hands, taking some of the weight from his legs. His great uncle keeps quizzing him about his health. Abe usually downplays how bad he feels any time someone asks, so it's something of a relief to be able to talk about it frankly.

"Fear don' hurt flavor," Budge says. He's perched on a stool at the counter shared by the living room and kitchen, elbows resting on the linoleum, watching Abe chop vegetables. He's sporting another tee from a band Abe hasn't heard of, Minor Threat. There's a corked bottle on the front wearing a leather jacket. "Sadness, anger. Even a little bitterness. These seasonings are all okay."

"Yeah?"

"Yeah."

"You're the boss," Abe says.

From the first lesion, Abe had known something he'd never experienced before was happening to him. It started as three tiny markings on his shin, like the points of a triangle. They looked like scabs that had been scratched off, only there had never been any scabs.

Or bleeding for that matter. The color was like nothing he'd ever seen on a body; the punctures in his skin seemed to reveal another world, some purple-black starless void. The three marks grew until they merged to form a rough hole the size of a dime, surrounded by angry skin. Then the process began again; a new patch of skin, more trios of marks. When it looked like he'd developed a flesh-eating bacteria from the knees down, Abe finally saw a doctor. Abe is explaining all this to Budge, basically bringing him up to speed with things you already know. But what Abe doesn't need to explain to Budge is why he waited for his legs to get so grisly before he saw a doctor. You probably do, though.

First, doctors sterilized several women in his family without their knowledge. In Indian Country, back in the day, doctors sterilized any Native woman who came into their office. Didn't matter if their office was part of Indian Health Services or if they were private practitioners. Sometimes they'd make up an excuse to get her on the operating table, sometimes they'd destroy the woman's fallopian tubes by leaving Mepacrine capsules in her uterus after pelvic exams. Because crimes against Natives tend to take place on reservations, and the criminals—doctors mutilating Indigenous women, in this case—are tried off the reservation by non-Indians (if they're tried at all), they never faced consequences. Not a day in jail, nary an arrest, not even a lost job.

This went on until word got out in the seventies and the practice became frowned upon. So in the 1970s—not the 1870s but the time of disco, *The Godfather*, and the first five novels of an up-and-coming author named Stephen King—hospitals included a sterilization form with the rest of the admission paperwork. They'd have the woman sign everything after the drugs kicked in. Or they'd deny her pain medication until she signed. Then while the doctor had her open and unconscious, he would snip her tubes. Or, if he was feeling especially frisky that day, he'd give her a hysterectomy. The woman would have no idea she'd been rendered infertile until she realized her cycle had stopped following Grandmother Moon. The permission form shifted the blame. It also made the experience more traumatic; imagine learning you'd been robbed of your ability to bear children supposedly by your own hand. The women whom the doctors targeted? Most were younger than twenty.

Do I need to tell you this practice spread beyond Indian Country, to Black women, to Puerto Ricans, to immigrants? Probably not. Eventually awareness of involuntary sterilization spread, which is a way of saying White Folks Who Gave a Shit found out. Which is proof we need more white folks to have our backs, if any was needed (and I mean have our backs, as opposed to telling us which way to go).

Abe's parents are in the "here-sign-this-don't-worry-about-it" generation, his Tóta was in the "your-appendix-looks-inflamed-let's-get-you-prepped-for-surgery" generation. Is that progress from the "point-your-rifle-at-anything-savage-and-shoot-PS-we'll-pay-you-for-scalps" generation, which is how the one before Tóta's handled what they called the "Indian Problem"? It sure is more civilized. About as civilized as the court-ordered Depo-Provera injections for "troubled" Native youth happening right now.

IHS offered these doctors no financial incentive, nor did the Public Health Service, the American Medical Association, or later, the American Board of Physician Specialties. If there's paperwork with damning letterhead recommending involuntary sterilization for Native women, or grainy film footage promoting it, none has survived. No aging whistleblower has stepped forward, no doctor has confessed on his deathbed. This is grassroots racism at its finest, thousands of different doctors from across the country attending hundreds of different medical schools, and somehow they all managed to learn which parts of America belonged and which should be cut out.

Fun fact: the Kanien'kéha word for white supremacy is "civilized."

The second reason Abe doesn't care for doctors is because Indians don't get pain medication in the same doses as white patients. We're either refused meds because we're junkies faking pain to get drugs, or we're given watered-down doses because—according to legend— our pain tolerance is higher than white folks'. Diluting pain medication is also a cost-saving measure, and who better to use weak pain meds on than a powerless population? I'm afraid this is an experience shared by non-Native Black, Latin, and South Asian folks, too.

I apologize for not leading with this one because it's less horror-inducing than involuntary sterilization and I realize you need to weigh each atrocity to keep the progression logical, hey. But I'm ending with the pain meds problem because Abe has experienced it himself. He had four wisdom teeth pulled in middle school and felt the whole procedure; dulled, but not absent. He was given Tylenol afterward. "Take this when the Novocaine wears off," the dentist said. Abe had immediately ripped the packets open and swallowed the pills, for all the good they did. The dentist rolled his eyes at his assistant. "You see what I mean?" The woman nodded; she hadn't looked at Abe once during the whole visit.

Trying not to gloat too much, Abe described how he'd put the fear of outbreak into the medical establishment during his first meeting with Dermatologist Unger. At her chichi Bal Harbour office, she'd probably forgotten the last time she'd done something besides remove a mole or inject toxic bacteria into someone's face. As Dr. Unger removed Abe's bandages to examine the wounds on his leg, her glove had gotten caught in the medical tape. When she saw the lesions, she'd quickly rolled her chair back, pulling off a line of squares all at once; the leg beneath looked rotten.

"Oh, yes, okay," Unger said, trying to appear calm while her eyes vibrated in their sockets. "Obviously, there's an issue there."

The nurse was shaking so much she couldn't even take pictures once they had all the bandages off, but Dr. Unger's panic was short-lived. With fresh gloves and a surgical mask, she held the iPad close and took her own shots. "Hello," she breathed.

She zoomed in on the pictures, showing Abe which dots of his rash were likely to form new lesions. Unger's iPad showed dribbling yellows and fine threads of purple-red which he'd missed when looking at the pictures he'd taken with his phone. Probably because he'd documented the wounds less to see them and more to have a bit of distance, some semblance of control over the situation. Just as his primary had been stumped and brought in the dermatologist, Unger was stumped and brought in the rheumatologist. The one who lived in her same Key Biscayne high-rise, if you recall.

"When they were still trying to diagnose me, Dr. Weisberg called me 'fascinating.'"

"Like Spock?" Budge asks.

"A little, I guess. More like how you looked at me after that first . . . time, though."

Given how he lost consciousness the other day, Abe can't bring himself to say, *After that first healing.* He looks at the cutting board, heaped with neatly separated piles of minced garlic, finely diced onions, peeled and sliced carrots, and rutabaga scrubbed and cut into chunks. The chicken bouillon has been dissolved in a pot, since Budge doesn't have a big measuring cup. It's time to start cooking, so Abe splots some of Budge's grease into the Dutch oven. If you don't have family who keeps a tub of grease in the fridge, here's the deal: I'm sure you know you don't want to dump grease down the drain and clog your pipes, or into the trash where it'll melt your trash bag, so you pour it into a jar. Once it cools off, of course, it's okay to toss it out, but cooks know that stuff is where all the flavor ends up, so instead of throwing the jar away, they keep it to season future dishes. Budge's grease smells like it's mostly bacon, which'll work just fine. Once it's sizzling over medium heat, Abe dumps the onion into the pot, stirring to keep it from browning.

"She'n Indian?" Budge asks.

"No, I'm pretty sure she's Jewish."

Budge isn't being funny. Abe was in college before he registered what being Jewish even meant, and that certain surnames likely meant you were a Member of the Tribe.

"I mean, she looks at me the way you look at me. I noticed it the first time you had me over." Abe adjusts the flame down, stirring a bit faster because Budge's gas stove runs hot. He flexes his fingers between movements. Sometimes the pain makes Abe feel like any motion will crack his joints in two; working them a little assures him they still function despite the sensation. About to stand? Why not give the knees a couple of practice bends first? It's a new habit that's quickly become something of a tic. "This was my second visit. She checked off practically the whole testing sheet and they still had nothing. She stared at me for a long time. Then she said, 'You're fascinating.'"

"Man, that's just what you want a doctor to say, innit?" Budge chuckles. "'I ain' never seen somethin' like this, you're all kinds of messed up.'"

Abe snorts in agreement. Once the onions are clear, Abe adds the garlic, sautéing it until it's slightly browned. Then he adds sliced carrots and rutabaga to the pot. The grease is being soaked up so Abe adds a bit more, raising the heat accordingly.

"They put me on steroids, still with no idea what they were treating," he continues. "They lived a few floors apart in the same condominium, so they'd have dinner and come up with theories. They called every night to quiz me."

"So you were the Dinner Party Case."

"Maybe." Abe keeps the veggies moving at a brisk pace, putting an edge on them before adding the liquid so they don't get too soft while the soup simmers. No disrespect to some folks' conception of Corn Soup, but a soggy veggie is an affront to a Jacobs' kitchen.

"Don't you watch *Grey's*?"

Abe gives his uncle a blank look.

"*Grey's Anatomy*?"

"Can't say I do, Uncle Budge."

"Oh, man. You dunno what y'missin."

Abe can't argue with that.

"First season, they're all living together in one house," Budge says. "When they eat, they talk about their mystery patients. They argue over who has the right diagnosis. Sometimes they make bets, even though they know it's wrong."

"Then yeah, that's exactly what I picture. A little pasta, a bottle of wine, and let's play 'what's wrong with the Mohawk dude.'" Abe leans his face over the pot, inhaling deeply.

"But now you know."

"Yeah. It's an autoimmune disorder called Systemic Necrotizing Periarteritis." Bam, rat-a-tat-tat, like he's been saying it his whole life.

"Sounds fancy."

"Yup. Only top-shelf diseases for me." Abe adds the concentrated bouillon to the veggies, along with the deer bones, then uses the smaller pot to fill the Dutch oven three-quarters of the way. In half an hour the veggies will give up their secrets, but the bones will continue to add flavor the longer they simmer. Abe cranks the heat up, waiting for it all to boil.

"You know how people always say, 'I've never been sick a day in my life'?" Abe looks at Budge, who nods. "Well, I've been sick, but not much. I've had the flu and all of that, maybe three or four times. Huh . . . about once a decade, now that I think about it. And now that I'm really sick, it's with some shit no one's ever heard of."

Abe opens and closes cabinet doors. Budge asks what he's looking for, then directs him on where to find a can opener and a colander. Abe puts the colander in the sink, opens the beans and hominy, and dumps them in. Abe would've preferred to use a variety of dried beans, but he forgot to start them soaking last night.

"What the hell is Systemic Necco Wafer Perrier?"

"Systemic Necrotizing Periarteritis." He can't keep the smile from his voice, but a cynical part of Abe says his uncle already knows. Abe has told everyone at the house, along with Sis and her husband, and word gets around. Teierihwenhawíhtha, you know? Budge has probably heard and has already consulted Dr. Google so he knows what sort of "healing" to provide. Still, Abe answers his great uncle in good faith.

"My immune system is attacking my blood vessels." Turning the faucet on, Abe goes to shake the colander under the water, but he misjudges where his fingertips curl underneath the colander's edge. The colander drops in the sink with a clang.

"Easy there, Killer," Budge says.

Abe's suspected he's been losing more feeling in his hands, but this is the first time he's dropped something. He grips the edge of the colander firmly, holding the hominy and beans beneath the stream of water, mentally chanting "it's fine, it's fine, it's fine" with every shake.

Budge points with his lips toward the pot. "Smells good."

"Onion and garlic sautéing in bacon grease, sure it does. We've got a ways to go on it, though." Abe learned the secret of good cooking from his mother and aunts: make whoever's eating smell your food for several hours before they ever get a taste. By the time it's in their mouths, they'll swear it's the best meal they've ever had. Abe turns the faucet off and shakes the excess water from the hominy and beans, careful to keep his grip tight this time.

"So, necrotizing whassitz," Budge says. "Your immune system trying to kill your blood vessels. Fascinating." Budge arches his brow like a certain Vulcan science officer; Abe gives him a sour look. "What causes it?"

"It's idiopathic."

This time, Budge raises both eyebrows.

"They don't know what causes it," Abe says. The pot starts to boil, so Abe lowers the gas until the flame is little more than a blue ring.

"That's not the main thing, though. You ask five doctors about it and you'll get five different treatments. Meanwhile, it's going after your heart, your lungs, your liver, your intestines. The doctors just chase it around, trying to buy you time."

He grinds pepper into a pile across the liquid, then stirs it in, along with some salt, watching the steam rise. Abe wants to cool the pot enough to crack the lid and leave it simmering without it boiling over. There's something soothing about the spoon's movement, the familiar smell. It's hypnotic.

"Last time you said something about your brain," Budge says.

"Yeah. Nerves, the brain, it's all one system. I've got these numb spots on my fingers . . ." Abe glances up. Sympathy has deepened the lifelines etched around the old man's eyes and mouth. Abe stares back into the pot. Anything not to look into Budge's concerned round face.

"You can cry, kid," Budge says. "Ain' no shame in it."

"Of the few people who've had it, when it picked the brain . . ." Abe's words are as soft as that blue ring of flame beneath the pot, like if he says it low enough God won't hear him, and it won't be real. "I've got maybe a year and a half before my brain starts to rot like my legs are. Every time I'm stuck on a word, or I leave the oven on, I think, 'Is this it? Is it starting now?'" He can barely get the words out, but some deep part of Abe feels that if he hides anything from Budge, he'll block the healing from working. "You know I work in a bookstore? Well, I've always wanted to be a writer. Sure, there's those lists. Best writers under thirty or whatever. But there are so many writers who didn't start until they were my age."

"You ain' old, kid," his great uncle says kindly.

Abe tells Budge about the seventy-two-year-old poet who visited his store. "I thought the writing would always be there, you know? When I was ready."

"Usin' the journal I gave you?"

"No, not really." Abe swipes at his eyes and nose. "My life has been garbage, and I don't have enough time left to make up for wasting it. It's already too late."

"Have you loved?" Budge asks softly.

Abe nods.

"Have you been loved?"

Abe nods again.

"Then your life ain' garbage."

The smell of simmering Corn Soup fills Budge's trailer. Abe sits on the stool beside Budge's while they're waiting for the flavors to come together. When he needs to stir the soup, Abe braces himself on the counter to stand and leans heavily on it as he works his way around to the kitchen side of the counter and to the stove. Abe doesn't ask for help and Budge doesn't offer; it's Abe's tribute, after all.

The chat includes Budge telling Abe to add walnuts to his salad and cereals for brain health (part of a larger discussion explaining how foods resemble the parts of the body they're good for). Abe tells Budge flax seeds are good, too, even though they just look like seeds. Budge tells Abe that movie stars are generally tiny but Rock Hudson and John Wayne were both six feet, four inches tall, which is what made them seem larger than life. He tells Abe in order to be steadily employed, you need to be two of three things: reliable, well-liked, or effective. Abe asks which ones Budge picked. "People love me so much the other two don' matter," he replied, a statement that doesn't exactly fill Abe with hope.

Budge tells Abe a story about colonists asking for help with constipation. The Mohawks gave them goldenrod tea. It was so effective, the colonists asked for help with diarrhea as well. So the Mohawks gave them goldenrod tea. The colonists complained that constipation and diarrhea were two different problems. Mohawks explained that goldenrod aided your guts, no matter what the issue was, and asked the colonists to trust both them and the plants. The colonist walked away from that exchange thinking they'd been cured by pure dumb luck, rather than generations of knowledge.

Budge tells Abe his father (Budge's, not Abe's) had some knowledge of Medicine, which often requires the sacrifice of your first-born child if you plan on practicing for real, only Budge's father died before he made the choice. He tells Abe plants and animals know what they're doing and why they're here, but humans don't, that we did once but we've since forgotten, and that frustration gives rise to a feeling of loss we keep trying to fill with the wrong things.

After two hours of talking shit and stirring the pot from time to time, Abe sees the shreds of meat have lifted from the bones. It's time to finish off the soup. He dumps the rinsed beans and hominy into the pot, adding more salt and pepper. He normally would add a heap of thyme, some rosemary, and a dash of oregano, but the fact that Robert (Sis's husband) had the deer bones on hand made Abe want to keep things old school. Meaning precolonial. Although to be really authentic it would've had to be turkey broth rather than chicken bouillon, but Abe doubts the ancestors begrudge him this one small cheat. As if in answer, a song emerges from Abe's mouth, and into the soup.

Abe owns a few CDs of traditional Native music: drums, flutes, rattles, and the sort of singing white folks like to call "chanting." There are no words, only vocalizations that express things inside the singer that are beyond words. The CDs aren't something he consumes daily, but when he feels like connecting with his roots, he puts them on. As many times as he's played one of those CDs over the years, I promise you, he's never once tried to sing along.

As Abe stirs the Corn Soup, something like one of the songs he's heard comes out, a sort of *ya-ay, aya-oh*, repeated, ending with *ya-hey-hi-yo, hey-a-hi-yo* ... remember when I told you I felt like a fraud performing Indigenousness by talking about the Indian name Tóta gave Abe? Trying to describe this moment feels like that. Maybe if you were traveling through Italy and someone asked you for directions and you apologized for not speaking the language, only you said it in fluent Italian, then you'd understand Abe's surprise. But like I said, Abe isn't speaking Kanien'kéha, he's voicing everything he can't articulate with words into a song. His first song without words.

Abe sings the same refrain several times, his confidence and volume increasing with each repetition. He keeps stirring the pot, and it's like he's stirring his words—and the feeling behind them—into the soup. When the song ends, Abe waits for embarrassment to fill the silence. It doesn't come. The song feels as natural as a sneeze. In fact, when he looks at Budge, his great uncle is nodding, looking through the blinds of his kitchen window. He lives in a pocket of woods. Outside, the trees have dropped their leaves, exposing the trunks of black ash, tall and thin with spindly branches; box elders, splayed out from a focal point like a troll doll's hair; and gray birch, spotted like the legs of a bird dog. There's white pine out there, too, the only year-round greenery, with their five needles for Six Nations minus Tuscarora. It seems like Abe's song has given Budge food for thought, but he doesn't appear surprised.

Abe takes a breath, then ladles up two bowls and moves them to the counter. He butters two slices of Wonder Bread, cuts them in half, puts them on a plate, and sets it between the bowls. The Wonder Bread elicits the dubious look from Budge that his song did not.

"Trust me," he says, using the counter for support as he makes his way around to join his uncle. The song has stirred something in Abe. He wonders whether his shortened lifeline means he can't afford to waste days idling around, singing and talking to trees, or if he should spend all of his time idling around, singing and talking to trees. It feels good to have a legitimate conundrum to mull over, instead of listening to a chaotic wind roar inside his skull. He's sure it's his uncle's presence.

Budge tastes the soup, groaning with satisfaction. Corn Soup is not a fancy dish that rearranges taste buds or broadens perceptions; it's entirely expected. Comfort food, its own sort of culinary glory. Abe takes the stool beside his uncle, wishing someone else had made the soup so he could enjoy it instead of critiquing himself. His mother and aunts claim you put too much of yourself into a dish to be able to fully enjoy it, so food always tastes better when someone else makes it. Predictably, Abe finds the soup almost flavorless.

"You know..." Budge downs a large spoonful with a satisfied grunt. He dunks the Wonder Bread and bites off a chunk, chuffing through his nose in surprise. "I'm no fool."

"I never said you were, Uncle Budge."

"What I mean is..." Budge takes another spoonful, making a show of savoring it before wiping his lips and leaning towards Abe conspiratorially. "I know why you got sick."

"Lay it on me, Uncle Budge." Abe doesn't care what caused his immune system to go haywire. He assumes Budge is going to talk about generational trauma in the genes. Or General Motors, Reynolds Metals, and Alcoa polluting their water and soil, even though Abe hasn't lived here since he was eighteen so his exposure is much lower than most of his family's. But thanks to these companies, if it's not your immune system coming up with ways to make your life interesting (Dad with his Sjögren's; Aunt Abby, Aunt Maisy, and Uncle Dan with their various rheumatoid problems, to name a few) then it's cancer.

But Uncle Budge has something else in mind, and Abe knows it from his first words. "It was the time when dogs could talk. The Hotinonshón:ni were all pretty darned pleased with ourselves. Other than a few squabbles with our neighbors, we had peace for thousands of years. We controlled the weather. We commanded the elements. We communed with animals and plants. We were learning to fly. Everything was going so great we got the idea it should maybe last forever, so we started thinking we should use the one Medicine we don't ever use.

"We weren't the only ones. From ocean to ocean, everyone had an inkling to use the Forever Medicine. Horse people, salmon people, people who build, seal people, plains people, desert people, people who move, whale people, buffalo people, plateau people, people of the swamp—everyone sent Medicine folk to meet in the middle.

"Medicine folk, Two-Spirits, Teachers, Herbalists, Elders, Witches—over a thousand of 'em gathered on the plains. They shared food 'n drink. Besides the tribes who came from the same regions, there was no common tongue. So they sang, they danced, they conjured spirits. The plan was to make the Medicine we never use, the one that makes you live forever."

Budge's bowl is empty, so Abe returns to the stove and refills it. He butters more Wonder Bread while he's at it, putting the slices on the plate before moving back to his seat. Budge continues his story in the meantime.

"As the day goes on, they start showin' off. Callin' birds to perch on their shoulders and sing mournin' songs, turnin' the clouds into sky pictures, makin' coyotes Smoke Dance, that kind of thing. Arrogant, you know, but not dangerous. Only they got so caught up, they forgot all about the Forever Medicine an' kept practicin' after the sun went down."

Abe has been off the Rez for decades, but since childhood he's known this is a big no-no.

"Some say we hadn't learned the lesson yet, that it started w'this gatherin'. Others say they were so arrogant, they didn't even care it was nighttime. Th' Medicine went bad, a course. Called out somethin' it shouldn't've.

"A man climbed up on top of a big rock in the middle a the plains. No one had seen him before. Every tribe had their own idea of who stood on that rock. We say it was Flint, Tawiskaron, his own self, breakin' out of his prison underground to make a special appearance. Whoever it was, when he spoke, everyone understood.

"He described a world. A brash, upstart world something like ours. The people who lived there had insatiable appetites, and gaping mouths where their souls should have been. They were so hungry they couldn't stand to see anyone else fed. Their bodies were squat and broad, their skin pale but furry like a bear. They had blue eyes, cold as ice water. The ocean would vomit them onto our land, and they would wash over us like a flood. We'd be swallowed whole.

"None a that sounded so great, you know? Th' Medicine folks, they said no thanks. They apologized for playin' around. They begged the stranger, Tawiskaron or whoever he was, to take it all back. But it was too late.

"'They're already here,' the stranger said. He climbed down from the rock an' disappeared into the dark. The silence he left behind was so deep, the Medicine folk could hear conquistadors making landfall, the first of the hungry souls who were almost human. We'd gathered there with the intention a livin' forever. Instead, we created our own doom."

Abe feels the skin on the back of his neck prickle.

"We broke the world that night, kid." Budge scoops the last three spoonfuls from his bowl into his mouth in rapid succession, and speaks around a mouth full of food. "Good thing we healed it last year."

"What do you mean?"

Budge finishes his second bowl, swiping bread inside to soak up anything he missed. He crams the bread into his mouth with the last bites of soup, cheeks puffed out, making rapturous sounds as he chews. Abe pushes his own bowl over to Uncle Budge and takes the empty one for himself. Once Budge has chewed and swallowed, he winks at Abe.

"Standing Rock."

"Get the hell out," Abe says, topping off their bowls.

"They got every Nation out there," Budge says, stretching his arm out as though he's pointing all the way to North Dakota. "They're prayin', dancin'. Takin' care of each other. Tryin' to get people to listen to the earth. Look at a map, Abe. That camp is dead center to the whole thing."

Abe waits to see if Budge is having him on, then he pulls out his phone. First, he looks up the location of Sacred Stone Camp, which leads him to look up Cannonball, North Dakota, then he touches the map and zooms out. It takes a lot longer than it would off the Rez, but soon enough they're looking at a red pin at the top of the United States.

"Budge, that shit is way north." He can't keep the relief from his voice. The story of the Forever Medicine has put him on edge. He shows his screen to Budge. "See?"

Budge gives Abe a kind, yet withering look. "Abe, would you please stop lookin' at that map like you weren't born here? That's just a line someone drew on a piece a paper, innit."

Abe realizes his great uncle is right: the camp protesting construction of the oil pipeline in North Dakota isn't in the middle of the United States, it's in the middle of the continent. The realization overwhelms him into silence.

"That's where the tribes met the first time," Budge says, "that's where we broke the Turtle's shell, and that's where we healed it, too. People see shit gettin' worse. I see all of us fightin' together, harder'n ever. But it ain' about one pipeline. Maybe it gets built, maybe it doesn't. But seven generations from now, the idea of a pipeline is gonna be unthinkable."

"Wow." Swirling a spoon through his soup, Abe remembers why Budge supposedly told him the story. "Thanks for the story, Budge. Seriously, thank you. But I don't understand what it has to do with me being sick."

"You never got sick before."

"Not really, no."

"Your immune system killed everythin' that came after you."

"Sure."

"Now your immune system is killin' you."

"Yeah."

Budge spreads his arms like, *There you go.* "Your immune system got cocky, like we all did back in the day," he says. "Now you're like those Medicine folk messin' around th' plains all them years ago, doin' everythin' but what they meant to do. You called this up, Abe. Your body went old school Indian and conjured its own death."

A t Budge's request, Abe has stripped to his underwear. He's lying on a mustard-colored sheet spread over his great uncle's living room rug. Budge is kneeling on the floor beside him, his hands resting on top of Abe's feet. They're warm on Abe's toes, which have been frozen since he came back up North. Budge nods to indicate Abe's shins.

"I need to take these off." He wants to remove the bandages on Abe's lower legs. "That okay?"

"Do you have to?" Abe can't keep the slight whine from his voice. Alex had only seen the beginning stages; otherwise so far, only Unger and Weisberg have seen the damage his immune system has wrought, pics sent to them each day.

"Need to see what I'm dealin' with here."

"Let me." If Abe had known he'd be removing them, he would've brought more supplies. He carefully loosens the edges of the bandages. The squares of gauze start below his knees and stop at his ankles, covering his shins and calves, so many that it looks like he's wearing weird argyle socks. He gently peels the bandages off, trying not to let them ball up, ignoring the stains that have seeped into the material. He saves the bandages for reuse by laying them messy-side-up on Budge's couch.

"I've got gauze, you know," Budge says. "Medical tape, too."

The prescription tape thing feels like too much to explain, so Abe says it's better if he reuses the gauze with the antibiotic ointment on it. Removing them so carefully is a pain in the ass. He probably should've just used whatever Budge had and swapped when he got home.

"Hell, you think I can't get ointment?" Budge asks. "I got a tin 'a herbal balm that'll work better'n the crap they got you smearin' on yourself. Might even help the joint pain, too."

"Really?" Abe is okay with sounding eager—relief from the pain sounds amazing—but he's afraid he also sounds desperate.

"Sure. Fifty bucks."

And here it is at last, the big bilk. Abe knows the kind of tins Budge is talking about, like those little travel chewing tobaccos that wear rings in the pockets of truckers' jeans. Gas stations up here sell them at the checkout counter, Magic Mohawk Unguent, Three Feather Thrills, Grizzly Grease, all of them offering the cure for what ails your body, none of them any more effective than a tube of Bengay.

"What would fifty bucks get me, Uncle Budge, a lifetime supply?" Abe puts it in his voice; *I've been away a while, but don't treat me like I'm some idiot stopping for gas and a dreamcatcher to hang from my rearview mirror.*

"I'm kiddin' kid, relax. You're gonna give yourself an aneurysm." Budge huffs in his throat. "Cass makes it. For you I'm thinkin' we can do a special offer of on th' house."

"What Cass? My Cass? Sis?"

"That's her."

"Does she sell it in the kitsch shops, too?"

"She's been known to, when she can be bothered to make a batch."

Sis isn't one to make a fast buck with minty grease, even at a tourist's expense; she must think it's the real deal. On the heels of this thought comes another—*That's why she didn't tell you about it; you stayed invisible in Miami so long you disappeared.* Has living in Miami fully colonized Abe's mind? Surely not. It's not a bad place for magic. Caribbean folks have their Santería and Voodoo, Africans have their Hoodoo. There's even a ration of Wiccans. Then of course, Catholics, Protestants, Baptists, and Jews are popular, and there's a smattering of Hindus, Buddhists, and Muslims. Because so many people of different faiths mingle every day, there's a saying in Miami; "I don't believe, but I respect." Whatever gets your neighbor through the night, you respect it, even if it's not what gets you through yours. But respect for Mohawk traditions isn't going to help Abe here.

He doesn't know exactly what brought him home, but his family has put him in Budge's hands and he needs to believe, to have faith in his great uncle, for this healing to have a shot. Each year he's spent away from Ahkwesáhsne has made it easier for Abe to ignore when reality reveals how thin it is; his mind has hardened against it like clay left out too long. The universe has mostly given up trying to reach him. He's become a skeptic, the type of Indian who would dismiss a Rez story as coincidence, who'd say the Peacemaker's given name right out loud, forgetting it pushes us closer toward the fall of civilization. If it wasn't forty degrees out, Abe would take his father up on the offer of a mud bath. Might help get his mind right.

When his attention returns to the trailer, Abe realizes his great uncle has been staring at the ravaged skin on his lower legs. Looking at them, sweat prickles on Abe's scalp. Much like when he saw the dermatologist's iPad pictures, he feels like he's looking at the lesions for the first time. Abe can handle the maroon splotches and rash on his skin, the waxy edges around his wounds, even the pus and blood. All of it looks awful, but at least it's human. It's the color of the lesions themselves, like the black snail shells surrounding him on his run, like the darkness inside a sealed tomb still finding a way to grin. Revulsion and despair fill Abe.

"This don' hurt you," Budge says, his tone somewhere between question and statement. Abe has explained several times that the lesions developed painlessly, but clearly Budge is struggling to reconcile this with the horror show of skin before him. Abe can barely bring himself to look, either—it's too easy to picture these same rotting holes forming in his brain. Still, while the muscles in Abe's thighs ache so badly he's almost trembling, his lesions merely itch. The painlessness makes it surreal.

"Feels irritating, like when a scab is loose but not ready to fall off." Abe keeps his voice light.

Budge grunts. "So your joints and muscles hurt but they look normal, and your legs don't hurt but they look like bad pasta."

Abe surprises himself by laughing. "You've got a way with words, Uncle Budge."

"So they tell me. The Necco Wafer . . ." Budge waves a hand up and down, indicating the whole of Abe's body. Abe admires his uncle's dedication to never calling his disorder by its rightful name. *Trying to get me to be less afraid of it*, Abe thinks. "Is that why you lost all this weight?" his uncle asks.

"I've been wondering that myself."

Through shitty diet and a sedentary lifestyle (he'd always been more of a sit-at-the-computer-ordering-books-type bookseller than a carry-stacks-of-books-around-the-store-and-up-and-down-ladders-type bookseller), Abe had gradually put on enough weight over his time in Miami that his descriptor to strangers switched from "the tall guy" to "the big guy." He'd become aware of his belly as a separate entity, a slab that pressed between him and Alex when they had sex, that robbed him of air when he was tying his shoes. He'd had abrasions on his waist from his belt digging in. At two hundred and fifty pounds, Abe had felt sluggish, with chronic back pain and probably a host of internal problems he'd need a doctor to tell him about. Abe hadn't understood that his problem was not excess weight, rather that his excess weight was a symptom of the lethargic way he was drifting through life. He'd only realized this because of the Jetty Giant.

DESTIN, 2008

The Jetty Giant story is a two-parter. The second part is what made me think of it, but fair warning—the first part doesn't end so nice. I hope you won't judge Alex too harshly. When a polyamorous person and a monogamous person couple up, trouble is inevitable.

Abe first brought up marriage when they'd spent a week without power after a hurricane, playing board games in their underwear, living on Red Stripe beer and potato chips, and having sex on the cool tile floor of their sunroom. More than the break from normal, Tóta's recent passing had likely put the idea in his mind, if only because it had reminded him of the importance of family. Alex had not been interested in marriage; at all. She'd said they didn't need a piece of paper to prove anything to anyone else, and certainly not to each other. Abe had never hounded her about it, merely brought it up from time to time.

Two years later, as they drove to a movie at the Shops at Sunset, Abe accidentally found Alex's tipping point. Driving past a bridal shop, he said, "You think you'll wear white to our wedding?" the same way he might've asked if she wanted a milkshake when they passed Swensen's Ice Cream.

"Fine," she snapped, pulling into a parking space. She turned off the car, unbuckled her seatbelt, and rounded on Abe. "But only if we do it at the courthouse, we don't get rings, and you never, ever bring it up again. Now can we please go watch Angelina Jolie shoot some people?"

All the beautiful sentiments any man would look for in his newly betrothed.

Alex didn't want to make the wedding a "thing," but Mrs. East insisted they use her as a witness instead of some stranger. Because of that, there are pictures of the wedding. Thirty-four years old, Abe looked to be just out of college (he'd been getting gray hair since high school, but not enough to show up in pictures). His face was fleshy (though not as full as it would become) and the off-the-rack suit he'd bought for the occasion fit poorly. Yet Abe smiled like a kid in an amusement park. Alex wore a parent-teacher-night outfit— dress pants, a vest, and a long-sleeve button-down shirt—her Ruby Rose hair slicked back.

At first glance, Alex's smile matched his. Looking at the pictures after things between them went stale, Abe would feel retroactive embarrassment. Sure, Alex was smiling, but it was her I'm-trapped-in-a-conversation-with-someone-I-can't-stand smile. Thankfully, they never posted the pictures on Facebook; anyone would have seen it. Except Abe. No, Abe looked at Alex's bare teeth and chose to see joy.

They'd already scheduled a trip to Destin the following week to visit Abe's cousins, Brad and Blaine, two-thirds of the Brown Boys (the other third being Brennan, the Boy Who Stayed). The coincidence led them to call it the Not-Honeymoon. Abe and Alex's first night in town, the lot of them went out to Fisherman's Wharf, a rambling restaurant on stilts that resembled a wooden ship turned upside down. A little cheesy, maybe, but it had great seafood and a gorgeous view of the Gulf of Mexico.

As the hostess led them to their table, they passed a wall of framed photographs with a sign overhead reading, "I Beat the Jetty Giant!" One man in a white hat and shades was given pride of place—centered on the wall, no other pictures within two feet. "The Machine: 19 minutes, 30 seconds" the frame read.

"You should do it." Alex pointed to the sign as they passed.

Abe smiled quizzically.

"What, it's fun." Alex bumped his shoulder, smiling. His cousins and their families thought Alex had a fine idea. As the group took their seats, Abe said he'd think about it.

He was very much looking forward to his 863 Amber Lager from the Florida Brewery, but when the waitress brought their beers over, Alex playfully swatted Abe's forearm.

"Don't drink that," she said. She turned her lamplight attention on the waitress, smiling like they shared a sexy secret. "Tell me about this Jetty Giant."

The gist: if Abe finished the Jetty Giant in an hour—five pounds of shrimp po' boy, fries, and coleslaw—he'd get it free and they'd hang his picture on the wall. Abe wasn't all that into it, but he was meeting Brad and Blaine's wives and children for the first time and wanted to impress them. Plus, Alex was right—it could be fun.

"The guy on the wall who did it in nineteen minutes had the right idea," Abe told the table. "It takes twenty minutes for your stomach to tell your brain you're full. If I don't finish this thing in less than twenty minutes, it's never going to happen."

A group of servers delivered the shrimp po' boy on a platter, announcing to the restaurant that a patron had accepted the Jetty Giant challenge. Abe played it up, cracking his neck, swinging his shoulders back and forth, stretching his arms. The crowd started clapping and wishing him luck.

Alex had ordered surf and turf, so she used her steak knife to cut the sub into fourths. Abe divided the fries into four equal piles, too. He cleared half the platter in five minutes. The restaurant rapidly lost interest. The third wedge, with fries between bites, took Abe nearly ten minutes. His brain might not've gotten the message he was full, but he felt pressure building in his gut all the same. Abe groaned, wiping his brow.

"Why did I want to do this, again?"

Alex rubbed his back.

"Oh God, don't touch me," Abe said, laughing despite his discomfort. He really wanted a swig of beer to wash down what he'd eaten, but he didn't want to give up the real estate in his stomach. He picked up the last wedge of po' boy, as his family urged him on. The restaurant turned its attention toward him again, the other patrons joining Abe's family, shouting encouragement. The waitress came to the table, timer in hand.

"We might be looking at a new record, people!"

His family yelled and pounded the table, rattling dishware. Abe's stomach still hadn't sounded the alarm, so Abe popped the remainder of the po' boy in his mouth. It felt like food had backed up to his esophagus, like the back of someone's hand was propping up his jaw. But the crowd could not be denied. Resting both hands on the table, Abe chewed like mad, swallowed, and washed it down with a slug of beer to show off. He opened his empty mouth and the waitress stopped the timer.

"Eighteen minutes, forty-five seconds," she cried. "We have a new record."

Cheers filled the restaurant. Abe stood and lofted the empty platter over his head, screaming. When the waitress took his picture for the wall, Alex made Abe pose with his fingers spelling "305," the area code for Miami-Dade.

After dinner, Abe and Alex walked alone on the pier overlooking the gulf. They watched the ships come back in, the fishermen gutting their catch at the dock with the sun setting behind them. Beyond the pier, there were only a few other couples on the length of the boardwalk.

"I'm never gonna eat again," Abe groaned.

"This is such a gorgeous view," Alex said. "Better than the Keys."

As gorgeous as the sunset views in the Keys were, Alex was right: the view from Destin's boardwalk was better. The still water gave the reflection of the setting sun a peacefulness he'd never seen outside of a painting. They walked in silence, looking at the horizon. Abe understood how the Tequesta could see their souls reflected in the water, why they made the shoreline their sacred ground.

"Kyle's brother gave me a ride home from rehearsal the other night," Alex said. When she wasn't performing, rehearsals kept Alex on an even keel. In order for her to work in a Florida suburb where half the population lived below the poverty line during the day, she needed to be on stage at night. Whether singing backup and playing tambourine for modern bossa nova band Puta Madre, or playing lead guitar, songwriting, and singing backup for a rock group called the B-Sides, or billing herself as Miss Entertainment and doing whatever the hell she felt like doing, Alex called her endeavors in Miami's music scene "sanity gigs."

Around the time of their trip to Destin, the B-Sides had wanted Alex to sing lead on some songs so she'd started to rehearse with them even more. It wasn't unusual for Abe to already be asleep by the time Alex got back home. Abe understood her passions. By this time, he'd found a writers' group. Though they drank martinis at Fox's Lounge as much as they shared work, Abe always found himself in a better mood when they met regularly.

"Which one's Kyle?" Abe asked.

"He's the bass player, the one with the smiley face tattoos on his hands?"

"Right."

"His brother is ten years younger. Comes to rehearsals to watch. Mostly, to watch me."

"Oh, really?" It had been a while since Alex had confessed a crush to spice things up. Abe thought perhaps the not-Honeymoon was inspiring her to lure him into a public tryst, something she hadn't done in many years. The timing couldn't be worse—he felt like the kid from that Christmas movie so bundled up he couldn't put his arms down, only Abe's pressure was pushing out from the Jetty Giant bloating his stomach.

"You know that little alcove outside the back gate of our complex?" Alex continued. "I had him park there when we got back. I sucked his cock until he came in my mouth. Then I took my panties off and pulled my dress up. He ate my ass while I played with my clit. I came really, really hard."

Abe knew she meant it, that it had happened exactly as she'd described it. If she'd wanted him to pull her under the boardwalk, push her against one of the supports, and fuck her hard and fast as they watched the sun go down, then she would have worded it differently. *I thought about having him pull over on the drive back . . . What would you do if I told you I sucked him off? Can you see my mouth falling open because I'm hungry to taste him?* Instead, Abe recognized her tone, the one he'd heard throughout their years in Syracuse and Richmond, when it had been a different sort of game. "Tell me what you did," Abe would whisper, moving on top of her. Alex would be as graphic as possible, encouraging him to fuck her better, to be the only one who mattered again. She could have said it differently now and Abe would never have known the difference. But she'd wanted Abe to know; she wanted to see what he'd do.

Abe stopped walking and grabbed the railing in both hands, watching Alex's face in the setting sun. "Was it the first time?" he asked.

"Not at all," Alex said. "That was the . . . ninth time. Although we usually go to his place. Rehearsal ran late, so we were in a hurry."

"How long have you been seeing him?" *Seeing him*, Abe thought. *Christ*. They never used euphemisms for sex unless they were joking; *will we be making love tonight, dahling?* He felt sick, and not only from his full stomach.

"Two months," Alex said. Ever since she'd agreed to marry him. In the sunlight, her blue eyes were contrite and defiant at the same time.

"Are you going to do it again?" Quiet, almost a whisper.

"What if I do, Abe?" She turned away from the sunset, looking at him from beneath a lowered brow, a challenge, an invitation, in her eyes.

"I—" Abe's voice cracked. He choked back a sob as tears prickled the edges of his eyes. Alex's jaw fell open. He'd never cried in front of her before. He'd teared up talking about his childhood, sure, but crying? I don't think so. But in that moment, Abe put his face in his hands and sobbed. I don't know what Alex had expected, but it wasn't that. She started crying as well.

"I'm sorry," she said, wrapping her arms around him. "I'm so sorry. I won't do it again, I swear. I promise, it's done, it's over."

Once Abe's crying jag ended, they continued walking well into the evening. Abe told Alex he understood. He'd pressured her into a marriage she didn't want and she'd reacted, that's all.

In the years to come, they settled back into their routine, rushing through the motions of sex, sort of like dinner prep. In Alex's words, "Why take forty minutes to do something you can do in four?" It almost made Abe wish he could forget the tricks to getting her off.

From time to time, though, Alex would get especially frisky— waking Abe with blowjobs, sexting him during the day. But it felt fretful rather than lusty, a passing storm. The second time it happened, Abe caught a whiff of cologne that wasn't his. He didn't push her to tell him anything, though. I'm guessing Abe figured Alex's need to step outside their marriage would fade as they grew older. In the meantime, there were worse manifestations of an affair than morning head on a Thursday.

Abe never revealed his suspicions. Oren Lyons, Faithkeeper of the Turtle Clan, once said, "Never accept a man's love when he doesn't love himself." Or maybe I saw it on Insta, I'm not sure. Either way, it's a truism. If Abe had loved himself more, he would've demanded better, or at least set some boundaries. He would've been fully present in his relationship, instead of drifting along, telling himself he was happy. He'd had a lot of practice at that growing up. And it was just as effective as when he was a child jumping out the window. Just ask his immune system.

Part two of the Jetty Giant is less dramatic. Five years after visiting Destin, Abe received a package. Fisherman's Wharf had shut down, so Abe's oldest cousin had collected the framed photograph of Abe from the wall of the restaurant, cocooned it in bubble wrap, and sent it to Miami. As big as Abe had been when the picture was taken, he'd gained more weight and was approaching three hundred pounds. Looking at the photo, Abe remembered the devastating confession Alex had made not long after it was taken. Worse, he remembered how quickly he'd hustled them past it, desperate to get to a place of normalcy. Shame filled his heart. Making him cry had changed Alex's combative mood to contrition. But when Abe forgave her a scant two hours later, Alex hadn't seemed relieved. She'd worn the expression of a scientist whose experiment had gone horribly wrong.

AHKWESÁHSNE, 2016

"Let's get going here." Budge makes a twirling gesture with his finger.

Abe rolls onto his stomach. While Abe talks, Budge massages his back. His uncle's touch makes Abe feel like he's melting. He tells Budge how looking at the Jetty Giant picture his cousin sent made him question his life choices. He didn't do anything special to lose weight, just started eating better, stopped drinking beer every night, and started working out. He piled boxes under his computer at work, turning it into a standing desk, and he started walking and biking to his shifts. He felt more energized after only a few months and even started writing again. It took losing fifty pounds before anyone else noticed. He fed on compliments from friends and coworkers, eventually losing eighty pounds in total, before he got on the newest drug and his weight loss got away from him.

"Maybe I never got healthy," he tells Budge. "Maybe this disease has been chipping away at me the last few years, and I didn't realize it."

Budge grunts agreement, running his knuckles along Abe's spine. "You got a doctor up here?"

"I call my doctors in Miami," Abe says. "Uncle Dan, Aunt Maisy, and Aunt Abby, they all see the same guy down in Malone. They took me to him when I passed out."

"They got the same thing as you?"

"Nah, but it's all in the rheumatoid family. They all get different treatments."

Budge nods, then scoots across the floor. Abe marvels at the old man's spryness. His rough hands massage the long muscles of Abe's thighs. He asks Abe to flip onto his back. He knee-walks until he's squatting over Abe's torso, massaging his upper chest, shoulders, and arms. He massages Abe's stomach; the bit of Corn Soup Abe ingested gurgles under his fingers. Abe smiles, doubting this is an approved massage technique.

Budge massages Abe's forearm and hand, spending a while kneading his fingers and thumb. He squat-shuffles around and repeats the hand massage on Abe's other side. Mapping the numb areas on his own knuckles and fingers is largely guesswork for Abe. Being touched by Budge, it's easy to picture his hands as carved from Swiss cheese.

"Are you afraid of death?" Uncle Budge asks. He massages the front of Abe's thighs and his knees. Skipping Abe's lower legs, and the lesions there, Budge moves on to his feet. With Budge's big thumbs digging into the arches of his foot, and his strong fingers wrapped around his instep, Abe feels like he's stepped into heaven.

Abe has no idea how long Budge has been massaging him, but he feels perfectly content. He looks around inside his head, searching for a fear of the end. He's relieved to find it's not there. Of course, there's more to fear than death. There are enough blood vessels in your body to circle the earth four times. One hundred thousand miles of blood vessels run through the meat of you like roots in the ground, like ants tunneling the earth, like rivulets trickling among pebbles. One hundred thousand miles for your traitorous immune system to explore before setting up camp. Heart or lungs. Kidneys or liver. Intestines. Nerves. It's the dying part he's scared of. "Not of actual death, no."

Budge's massage reaches Abe's toes. The floors at his parents' house have been so cold, his feet haven't heated all the way up even in the hottest shower. Or so he'd thought. Budge's touch makes Abe realize the truth, that some of his toes have lost sensation at the tips, and others have lost feeling completely, just like in his fingers. Abe starts to tremble. The calm he felt moments before evaporates. He's hyperventilating. He's either going to lose consciousness or vomit, he's not sure which.

"You're okay, kid, you're okay." Budge moves quickly, kneeling above Abe's head. His strong fingers dig into Abe's scalp. His voice is low and soothing. Abe doesn't puke, and he doesn't pass out. As fast as Abe's mind can create a worry, Budge's fingers smooth it away. "Shh, shhh shh. I'm right here, kid. Talk to me."

"I'm going to die," Abe whispers. Tears roll down his cheeks, puddling in his ears. "And that's okay, but I want it to matter that I was here."

Budge grunts his understanding. "It's good to want, kid. Want means you're thinkin' a th'future. You can't get there without thinkin' on it first."

"I don't want to be alone," Abe says, speaking so quietly it's little more than thought. "I don't want to lose my mind. If I look at my own family and don't recognize them, who am I?"

"Good, kid."

Abe takes a deep breath. It's shaky, and there are tears in it, but it's still cleansing. He's breathing poison out, breathing out everything until he's hollow. He takes in a breath tinged with Corn Soup and the ghost of the wood-burning stove and an old Indian. Budge has massaged Abe from scalp to knees and worked magic on his feet. Abe is over any awkwardness that kept him from enjoying himself during their first session, weeks ago that seem more like half a lifetime. He feels no more substantial than dandelion seeds; only the pain threaded into his body keeps him from floating away.

"I want to work your legs," Budge says.

"Okay." Abe knows Budge means his lower legs, where the lesions are. Abe chooses to trust him.

"I'm going to go get your sister's balm. We'll rub that in and see what happens."

"Sure."

Budge rises, taking more time to straighten his limbs than he did to squat or move around the floor. As Abe listens to Budge rummaging around in another room, his dandelion seed body begins to feel heavy again. He realizes the absurdity of what he's doing. He's nearly naked, separated from a questionable rug by a mustard-yellow bed sheet, waiting for his great uncle to apply a home remedy his sister made. His disorder is capable of killing him in a dozen different ways, and his defense is a pair of aged hands and some backyard weeds.

When Budge returns, Abe is caught between laughter and tears. Budge kneels and rests a rough, warm hand on Abe's forehead. Between the massage and how long he's been holding back, Abe has no defenses left.

"It's not enough time, Uncle Budge." Abe's voice breaks. "I don't have enough time."

"There's never enough time, kid." His voice is as gentle as the touch of his hand. "If you're not doin' the work, then it's never enough time."

What work? Abe wants to ask, but he sobs instead. Budge waits until the tears pass.

"Shit, you leave the room for two minutes and I'm a blubbering mess." Abe wipes his eyes.

"Can't keep calm all the time," Budge says. "Sometimes you gotta let it out."

Abe takes a shuddering breath, somewhat under control again. Sis's balm looks exactly like Abe pictured it, right down to the hippy-dippy font reading "Magic Mend." Budge turns the little tab on the side of the tin, popping it open.

"Let's keep going an' see where we get," Budge says.

Abe nods.

"That works for my livin' room an' for life, by the way." Budge cups the tin in one hand, digging his fingers in with the other. The smell of a breeze blowing through a field of wild herbs and sweet grass fills the room. Budge sets the tin down and rubs his palms together, warming the paste into a greasy goo. He wraps his hands around Abe's left ankle. The closer you get to your feet, the more vascular your skin is—more medical knowledge Abe has acquired against his will. Budge's palms are on the worst of the damage.

"Is this okay?"

"Yep."

Abe always steels himself when he disinfects the lesions. It's superstitious, and even though he knows it's not how the disorder works, part of him is afraid touching the lesions will spread them to his hands. Budge, though, doesn't hesitate. He also doesn't use the targeted approach Abe uses, carefully applying a dollop to each individual lesion. Instead, Budge works quickly, rubbing the balm from ankle to knee on both of Abe's legs, dipping into Sis's Magic Mend as he goes. The itching at the edges of his lesions turns tingly instead. Budge massages the extra herb balm into Abe's feet. After ten minutes, Abe's feet feel like they've been filled with warm molasses. Even if he's not a healer, Uncle Budge gives one hell of a massage.

"Okay." The old man sits back and wipes his hands on the sheet. He stretches his arms over his head and his shoulders pop like twin reports from a .22. Then he leans down and clasps both hands around Abe's knees, first one and then the other, saying "here" both times. He lays his hands on Abe's thighs and says it again, "Here."

He cups Abe's right calf. "Here."

His hands drop to Abe's left ankle. "Here."

Abe had been on the verge of dozing, but now his eyes go wide. A chill infuses his body, like he's chugged icy soda on a summer day. Still on his knees, Budge scoots up and wraps his hands around Abe's left elbow, then his left wrist. "Here. Here."

Mohawks were given the drum to mimic our heartbeat. With the drum, we'll always have a way to communicate without words. Inside the cage of his chest, Abe's drum beats wildly. Budge is mapping his pain.

Budge's hand engulfs Abe's left thumb. "Here."

One by one, Budge touches the arch of Abe's left hand, his middle knuckle, and all the knuckles of his index finger. "Here, and here. Here, here, and here."

The middle knuckles of the ring finger and pinky on Abe's right hand, "Here. Here."

Budge scoops up Abe's left hip, thick fingers pressing the joint. It's the first time he's touched anything covered by Abe's underwear, and his voice is hesitant. "Here?"

Abe nods, and Budge moves back. He kneels with his hands resting palm up on his thighs, head bowed, eyes closed. Leaning forward, he scoops Abe's right hip, then finishes by leaning down and brushing the top of his right foot. "Here and here."

Budge stands, knees popping. If his shoulders were .22s, then his knees are .38s. He balls his hands into fists, pressing them in the base of his spine and leaning backwards, eliciting a soft *crink*. Finally, Budge crosses his arms, heavy lips twisted in a satisfied grin. "So . . . we on the right track?"

Budge has mapped Abe's pain, not as it was yesterday or when Abe woke this morning, but exactly as it is at this moment. Abe sees a pregnant Skywoman falling from a hole in the universe, sees ocean birds carrying her to the Turtle's back, sees a muskrat bringing earth from the ocean floor for her to use to plant the seeds she snatched while dangling from the Tree of Life. In an instant, he believes the Earth grew from Skywoman's love and care, that her daughter, Breath of the Wind, died birthing twins and became Mother Earth, that Skywoman became Grandmother Moon, that when the Turtle collapses the world will end. It's always been a story, but in that moment it feels like a story the way the invention of the airplane is a story. In that moment, Abe believes Budge can stop his body from killing him.

"Well . . ." Abe says, when he's finally able to speak, "I'm glad my balls didn't hurt today."

Budge throws his head back and laughs.

IMPOSTER SYNDROME

by Dominick Deer Woods

Every Mohawk exists in twain.
Or rather, Skywoman's twin grandsons
   Sky-Holder (called Standing Sap, called Good Mind)
and Flint (called Swampy Elm, called Bad Mind)
exist in every Mohawk.

Whichever one you foster is the one
who survives and all'a dat.
Two wolves inside you and all'a dat.
Eight tracks beside yours
become four tracks
because one wolf carries you home.

Good Mind wore a scalp lock
and a face tattoo.
Bad Mind got a fade
lookin' *GQ* smoov.

Good Mind browned
under Miami's sun,
a melanin declaration.
Bad Mind left home and

left his capital P People (of the Flint)
behind.

Good Mind wore dresses
because fuck your gender roles.
Home composed his heart's sap.
Knotwood fingers whittled
the chip on his shoulder
into a clan symbol.

Bad Mind mucked that chip
at South Beach.
Sobriety is anti-colonial;
like Bad Mind gave a shit.
Pumping through his body
booze felt like benediction.

Decades ago in Syracuse
I strutted the sidewalk
arm in arm
with my boyfriend,
staring factory workers down.
The white community cast me out,
so I castigated them
whenever and wherever,
prepared to take a beating
rather than pretend.

Now I have brunch with conservative Latinos,
tongue clamped in my jaws to still it
from asking the man joking

about the woke mob
   if he's ever lived
outside the 305 to test his "whiteness."
Mouth full of blood, I
push from the table
and wander Ocean Drive
wondering what I'm
arm in arm with
now.

Eleven

Abe is sitting at the picnic table in front of KT's Market, a glacier smothered in onion and green peppers in one hand and a copy of Danez Smith's *[insert] boy* in the other, when he sees Cheryl Curly Head approaching. A glacier is a Glazier's hot dog, an all-beef red dog made in the area which isn't any great shakes given all the artisan dogs on offer nowadays. Glazier's was special to an older generation of folks who presented it to their children as amazing, who in turn served them to their children as amazing, thus perpetuating the ongoing cycle of mediocre hot dogs. Abe is feeling nostalgic about being home, so the glacier scratches that particular itch.

Danez Smith is a poet who presented their collection at the Miami Book Fair two years prior, and *[insert] boy* proves a genius at spoken word can also bring fire to the page, which gives Abe hope. The poems are Black and queer, mighty and vulnerable, and reading them keeps Abe's mind malleable, exactly how he needs it to be.

His cane leans against a support beneath the table. Even after the second part of the healing the week before, Abe still feels unsteady on his feet. If you scroll through the pictures he sends to his doctors in rapid succession, it appears his lesions are opening and closing like morning glories. They're not multiplying, and even though they largely keep growing, the doctors are excited by the occasional shrinking. The pain is still there, but Abe thinks it may have stayed put since Budge mapped it. Even if it has moved, it's still easier to tune out now. The joy this gives Abe has inspired him to pick up the journal Budge gave him and start writing.

Now that we know where we're at, we can address Cheryl Curly Head—Abe's sometimes suicidal, prone to giving hand jobs under frozen bridges, First Everything—in more depth. As a girl, Cheryl had been hurt the way a lot of rez women are hurt, first by a family member, and later by white men from off Rez who prowl the streets, prey violently on whoever they can find, and drive home with impunity. Cheryl had approached Abe when she was a junior and he was a sophomore, and used him to help heal her sexuality. She'd sensed—correctly—that he was behind his peers in that regard. At fifteen, he'd been content to masturbate on the rare occasions he'd found time alone, but had been too shy to so much as flirt with another person. Cheryl had taught him everything she knew, and in taking the lead in their sex lives reclaimed her own body. Abe had been devastated when she'd dumped him before leaving for college her senior year. He's only seen her once since then, at a bar on a Thanksgiving visit. It was packed enough that Abe dodged her in the crowd.

Now Cheryl is approaching KT's Market and she's not alone: she has two kids and a man in tow. Abe isn't the best judge of kids' ages, but the boy is roughly Cheryl's height while the girl barely reaches her thigh. Cheryl holds the girl's hand, the two of them looking down at the pavement, navigating the potholes.

Cheryl's face and body are thicker than Abe remembers, her hair streaked with gray. She's no less compelling than she was in high school. He's never seen her as a mother, hasn't seen her in maybe a dozen years, yet Abe instantly knows her—swatting at her son's shoulder to get him off his phone and out of the car, the way she runs her hand up and down the strap of her purse three times to get it just so after putting it over her shoulder. Her voice—"Do you wan' mac n cheese again, Shelly?" "Babe, grab the keys for me." And of course, the hair. In this case it's a legit surname, not a nickname, and most in her family share the trait.

Just as Abe is trying to decide whether to hail her or hide behind his book, Cheryl sees him. A bemused expression crosses her face, followed by joy. "Now there goes Abe Jacobs," Cheryl says.

The man, who we'll assume is her husband, turns backs. When he sees where Cheryl is looking, he frowns. He doesn't know Abe, but Abe has his father's jacket open and the clothes underneath are a little too . . . let's say "Miami" for the locals.

Abe puts his hot dog and book down, and wipes his hand clean. He leaves his cane out of sight, pressing his fingers on the table's edge as he moves around it. They hug hard, shoulder to shoulder, and back away quickly. Cheryl makes introductions, confirming her companions are in fact her husband, son, and daughter. The husband smiles when he shakes Abe's hand, but it's not exactly warm. Cheryl's face is arranged in careful lines of bubbly excitement, but her eyes are doing something different. Abe feels a pang, like his body is a guitar string that's been plucked.

Cheryl—Bero nowadays rather than Curly Head—sends her family inside the market. The husband doesn't look thrilled to be leaving his wife at the picnic table without him.

"How are you?" Cheryl sits opposite Abe. "Who are you?"

He could grab her hands across the table and be right back in old times, if not for the rings on their fingers. Abe provides a highlight reel of the more than two decades since she broke his heart—where he's lived, big vacations, major injuries endured, marriage, jobs. Normally Abe would relay the information between bites of his lunch, but he doesn't want Cheryl to see his mouth full of mashed red dog and potato salad.

"Where's your better half?" Cheryl looks around, as if Alex might appear from behind the market, or walking down the street.

"Back in Miami," Abe says. "She'll be up for Thanksgiving."

"What's she like?"

Abe smiles. He and Cheryl had been young when they were together, but their relationship had lasted two years; decades, in high school time. Cheryl was the only person besides Alex who'd gotten close to his heart.

"Tall." Abe says. When Cheryl gives him a *do better* look, he thinks on it. "If you were bored, you'd want her there. She can make going to the DMV a good time."

"Who's this?" the husband asks. He's back with the kids, putting food on the picnic table. Mac n' cheese for the girl, a sub for the boy, and lasagna for him and Cheryl.

"My wife," Abe says.

"Where's she at?"

"Back in Miami." Abe reiterates that Alex'll be up for Thanksgiving. Abe picks up his hot dog, which is no longer hot, and asks Cheryl what she's been up to. She waves her hand around the table toward her family like, *What more do you need to know?*

Still, while helping her daughter with her food, Cheryl gives Abe the run down. She graduated SUNY Plattsburgh, did her sophomore year in Denmark. She quit the gas station and got a job in hospital administration. The husband works for UPS and they knew each other from the deliveries he made. Plus he coaches kids' lacrosse, so they met for real because Cheryl's niece is on the team he coaches. They rented a camper and drove out to Yellowstone a few years back, when the son was the daughter's age and the daughter was a dream. Cheryl's father died and she's glad the piece of shit won't be around anymore to pop up with a check, hassling her for forgiveness. Her mother is alive and she's glad for that, too. Her brother got released from Jamesville Penitentiary in the spring and she's still deciding how to feel about that.

Abe can't imagine Yonder Curly Head has spared him a single thought in decades, but he still feels a twinge of childhood panic. He tells himself he's being ridiculous, but in his gut Abe knows Yonder has a way of turning up like a bad penny.

AHKWESÁHSNE, 1982

When they were nine and ten years old, respectively, Abe Jacobs and Cheryl Curly Head had started walking to school together every morning, splitting up where Route 37 meets the bridge to the Ahkwesáhsne Freedom School. From there Abe would continue on to Salmon Run with the white teachers, while Cheryl learned from Kanien'kehá:ka who actively practiced anti-colonialism and Native spirituality at the Ahkwesáhsne Freedom School. You might remember the AFS from when Tóta danced at a fundraiser for a new language-immersion program. Or maybe you remember the dance and forgot the fundraiser. Don't worry; you're on the same page as most people who were there.

Some Mohawks called AFS the "Free to Be Dumb School." Rumor had it AFS students didn't need to learn math, science, and history like in the public school, they only needed to learn to be "fully Mohawk," whatever that meant (what it meant is that AFS wanted students to attain ultimate enlightenment, but naysayers are gonna nay). The rumor wasn't true. AFS taught everything the public school did, only with the nationalism removed. They also taught classes on Kanien'kehá:ka language and culture. Of course, being false made the rumor that much harder to shake, and the "Free to Be Dumb" moniker stuck for several years after it opened—including during Cheryl Curly Head's tenure. Meanwhile, public school dressed Abe as a Pilgrim for a reenactment of the First Thanksgiving, taught him Christopher Columbus was a great explorer, and made sure Abe venerated good ol' cherry tree chopping George Washington. We've covered Genocidal George, all you need to know about Columbus is that he fed Taíno children to dogs in front of their parents as a negotiation tactic, and we'll get into Thanksgiving later. This might explain why even though Abe and Cheryl were children, the Curly Heads didn't like her hanging out with a Jacobs, even for the span between the Jacobs' house and the bridge to AFS.

One fine early winter's morning, maybe a month into this companionable walking arrangement, Cheryl stopped in the snow at the base of the bridge, where they parted ways every morning and met back up most afternoons. As Abe opened his mouth to say goodbye, Cheryl said, "Kiss me."

"What?" Abe stumbled over his own feet but managed to keep his face neutral. The idea had never crossed his mind.

"Kiss me," Cheryl repeated.

Abe snuck a glance at her face, round beneath a Toronto Maple Leafs toque and a fur-lined hood. Her chubby cheeks were red with cold, and stray hair whipped in the wind. Expectation filled her black eyes and a slight grin quirked her lips. "Do it."

Low-grade panic made Abe sweat. Now that Cheryl brought it up, Abe realized he did want to kiss her. He wanted it very much, in fact. On the heels of that want came fear; what if he did it wrong? He looked up and down the road, but no one was coming to help him.

"Do it," she said again. Abe leaned forward and pressed his mouth against Cheryl's. Her lips started off cool from the winter air, so he stayed in place until they warmed up. When they pulled apart, she smiled. Abe answered with a goofy grin so large it threatened to reach his ears and knock them askew, looking around again to see if anyone had witnessed him become a man of the world.

All day he wondered what the kiss meant. He didn't see Cheryl on the way home, but he kissed her goodbye again when their routes diverged the following morning. That day on his walk home, a high schooler stood at the intersection of Route 37 and the bridge to

AFS, smoking a cigarette and glaring at him. The teen's open denim jacket, lined with fleece, flapped in the wind. He wore his hair in a single heavy braid. The air was so cold the teen's whole head seemed to disappear when he blew smoke out.

"You Abe Jacobs?" The teenager stepped forward, glaring down at Abe.

"Ye-es," Abe said. He swallowed hard.

The teen grabbed Abe's collar in one hand, pulling him to the tip of his toes. With the other hand, he pointed the cigarette into Abe's face. Abe felt the heat from the glowing tip. "Stay the fuck away from my sister, you got that?"

"Who?"

"You a fuckin' owl?" The teen tossed his cigarette and used both hands to shake Abe. "She told us what you did at dinner last night."

"What I did at dinner?" Abe was mystified, terrified.

The teen muttered something that sounded to Abe like "zaluxa." He heard the same from Aunt Abby whenever she was frustrated, or couldn't believe her ears.

"Are you some kind of moron?" The teenager brought his face inches from Abe's. His breath smelled like an ashtray filled with salami. With his eyes wide as Moon Pies, he spoke slowly and loudly. "My sister is Cheryl Curly Head. She told us you kissed her. If you kiss her again, I'm going to beat the shit out of you. Am I getting through your thick skull?"

Abe's mouth worked but no sound came out. Cheryl's big brother shook him like a rag doll.

"Say yes, dipshit."

"Yes!"

"Yes, what?"

"Yes, no more kissing!"

"All right. All right, good." Cheryl's big brother dropped Abe and stepped back. "You okay?"

Abe nodded, wiping his nose on the sleeve of his jacket.

The older boy slapped at Abe's shoulders and the back of his coat, not unkindly, working his clothes back into place. "You're all right, kid. Didn't even cry or nothing. Tough kid. All you gotta do, stay away from my sister and we're cool. Okay?"

Abe nodded again, feeling like he might still cry, only with relief that it hadn't been worse. White light filled his vision as the teenager's balled fist rammed into his stomach. Abe hadn't seen it coming, and all the tension he'd built up in his body had been draining away. Pain rushed into the white space, like nothing he'd ever felt. His siblings took it easy on him because he was quick to cry. His father struck with an open hand, and Abe generally knew it was coming, because Dad had gone after larger targets first. He slumped to the snowy ground and curled into a ball, wondering if he'd ever draw another breath, sure his stomach had split in two. When he managed to suck in air, the cold burned his throat. Abe saw Cheryl's brother looking down at him, his face blank.

"Remember it, kid."

In the two years he'd dated Cheryl in high school, Abe had only seen Yonder once. Yonder had been "interred" for car theft at the time, what they called Interim Probation Supervision. When Abe had come by to see Cheryl, Yonder was sitting on their parents' front porch, drunk and high. He'd cut his braid at some point and replaced it with a feathered seventies shag that exploded from under a Marlboro Miles snapback. Yonder asked Abe if he'd ever seen a match burn twice.

That weed's not going to do much for your piss test, Abe thought. What Abe said was, "Yes, I have."

If you don't have older brothers or cousins—or worse, parents—who've showed you the trick, it goes like this: Light a match and blow it out, that's once. For twice, you hold the hot match head to the skin of the kid dumb enough to answer no.

Yonder didn't like Abe's answer. He frowned, giving Abe a dead-eyed stare.

"Not like this you aint." After lighting the cigarette dangling from his lips, Yonder shook the flame out, then pressed the glowing match head to the tender skin inside his own wrist. Eyes locked with Abe the whole time, Yonder used his thumb to grind the match out.

"You think I don't remember you?" He grinned slowly. "Fuck off my porch."

No, Abe didn't forget.

AHKWESÁHSNE, 2016

Abe finishes his lunch as he listens to Cheryl's highlight reel, watching the husband and son on their phones. The husband clearly isn't actually paying attention to his phone, though, rather listening to what his wife is choosing to say and how she's choosing to say it. When Cheryl finally tucks into her lasagna, the husband speaks up. "Heard'ja come back for a healin' with Budge Billings."

Abe looks at him, then back at Cheryl. Even the teenager stops looking at his phone. The only one not looking at Abe is the little girl, who is frowning into her Styrofoam bowl, stabbing one cheesy noodle at a time. So the word is out about his healing. Teierihwenhawíhtha, you've got to love it. With a nod, Abe confirms that what people are saying is so.

Thinking of his second session, Abe recalls his mother's words when she related the story of Tsítso Papineau's healing. *It felt good. It felt right. The further we got away from it, I started to get scared.* When Budge had mapped Abe's pain, Abe had felt the presence of God. Or a power so close to God it meant the same thing. Afterward, getting dressed in a daze, Abe had felt his own insignificance crashing down on him. Why in all the universe would God bother to look his way? Because an old man from Abe's own family had the power to bend His will? The idea was ludicrous. And terrifying. It felt safer to push Budge's mapping to a corner of his mind and forget about it.

"What's the occasion?" the husband presses. No flies on this man. He knows there's something beneath his wife's casual interaction with her old high school boyfriend and he wants Cheryl to know exactly how sick Abe is. The man smiles, his face the picture of innocence. "If you don' mind me askin."

"He's my great uncle," Abe says.

The man holds one palm up and tilts his head back and forth. *Go on*, the gesture says.

They're all still looking at him, so Abe pushes on. "I have an autoimmune disorder."

Cheryl and the husband nod. The teenager goes back to his phone. They must know a friend or have a family member. *Leslie's knees froze up on her . . . Richie's hair started falling out . . . Wendy got the rheumatiz, like her mom.* Intergenerational trauma and industrial pollution are a poisonous cocktail. Like I said, dig at any problem on the Rez and you'll end up talking about white supremacy.

"It's kicking my ass pretty bad," Abe admits. "Doctors aren't much help, so . . ."

"Uncle Budge?" Cheryl asks, her brow crumpled with concern.

"Uncle Budge," Abe agrees.

"I'm sorry." The husband does manage to sound sorry, at least, despite pushing for Abe to spill his secrets over lunch. "Good luck to you." The husband raises his Coke, toasting to Abe.

What kind of a grown man drinks soda? Abe thinks. The husband gulps the can down. He smacks his lips on his daughter's head, making kissing noises. "Hair napkin," he says, when he pulls away.

The girl squeals, swatting at her dad as he laughs, the gesture so like Cheryl that surreality washes over Abe. The daughter grabs her dad's arm, using his sleeve to wipe cheese and bits of noodle off her face. "Arm napkin, arm napkin, arm napkin," she cries gleefully, and Abe feels normal again.

Laughing softly, Cheryl's husband rubs the sleeve of his flannel shirt across the edge of the picnic table to clean up the mess. He reminds Cheryl of someplace they need to be and goads the son into helping him clear the trash from the table. Cheryl finishes her lasagna in several rapid bites. She comes around the table for another quick hug.

"He seems like a nice guy." Abe pitches his voice low.

"I did okay," she says, just as softly. Then louder, "I'll prolly see you."

Abe is sure she means around the Rez. But a worried piece of him sees the hungry look she gave him when her family wasn't around.

MY COUSINS ARE A QUILT

by Dominick Deer Woods

My cousins' laughter
is the raucous crackle
of yard detritus burning,
their calloused hands rubbing
over the bonfire
the hiss
of a pulled beer tab.

When I say cousins please know I mean cuzzins.

As Rez rascals my blue-eyed, half-Irish (cuzzins)
grew taming the basketball hoop
nailed over our garage door.

Trouble was they played too good.
Trouble was full bloods sneering
Where's your blood?

When I say full bloods please know
I understand the irony.
When I say full bloods please think of
apples that are red on the outside
and white on the inside.

My blue-eyed half-Irish cousins carried trouble
like they carried bonfires
like they carried drink
like Irishmen at a wake
which is to say like Indians
which is to say they had fists of cord wood
ready to swell shut the eyes of anyone who asked for blood.

When I say my cousins drink like Indians
please know Indians drink nothing to prove we don't need it.
Indians drink in moderation to show we're in control.
Indians drink all the drinks because we ain't got shit to
    prove.

My cuzzins blood plods like a double bass
bops like a clarinet
playing toward oblivion
hefty arms slung over howling shoulders.

Their blood sings a song as old as the land
a song without language.
Their blood sings Whiskey in the Jar.

My cousins drink around the bonfire
like the Irish Indians they are.
Watching them I think they must
be the happiest people on Earth.

Twelve

Nearly a month ago, when Alex asked Abe if he was done with Miami, the question had thrown him for a loop. Tonight, sitting at the bar in Pyke's Place, a shot of Herradura Reposado between his palms, listening to a group of drunk dudes tunelessly warble a karaoke version of "Surfin' U.S.A.," Abe can picture living in Ahkwesáhsne again. Usually when he and Alex visit, his cousins take them out to Cricket's or Rhonda's—dimly lit dives with vinyl flooring and low ceilings, faux wooden wall panels from the seventies, and a beery smell no amount of mopping can touch. Pyke's Place opened so recently Joseph Pyke hasn't even had a chance to stain the wood. Inside, it looks like some rich dude from the city built himself a grand, country-modern cabin retreat then turned it into a bar at the last minute.

Tuesday karaoke draws a crowd, but what would be an uncomfortable press of bodies at the dive bars is loose and relaxed here. People talk in clumps around the bar, or cluster at the tables, leaving plenty of room to breathe. Abe would like to think it's just a preference for clean-smelling bathrooms and personal space that endears Pyke's to him, but the truth is, Mohawks and folks off the Rez mix the most at the dives, and drunken comradery has a way of turning sour when closing time approaches. Massena, Brasher, Bombay, and Fort Covington haven't found Pyke's yet, so Abe feels safe.

Earlier that day, his cousins—Brennan Brown (Maisy's youngest, the Boy Who Stayed) and Louis and Moses (mirror twins on his dad's side, who you haven't met)—brought a six-pack over to the house. All afternoon, they nursed their beers and played pitch with Abe. His cousins are down the hall in the pool room. Abe begged off joining them for a bit, wanting a moment alone to recharge. In the mirror behind the bar, Abe appears gaunt, his face a stranger's, full of shadows. The new meds are eating him alive even as they fight the disease. He looks away.

Abe is nervous about seeing Alex when she comes for Thanksgiving in two weeks. Alex had stopped dabbling in multiple bands and formed her own Pat Benatar tribute act called the Right Kind of Sinners. She's developed a following, and even contributed to a movie soundtrack—two Benatar soundalikes to save the producers money over using the originals, and one blue-eyed soul version of "Blue Moon." She used the money from the gig to self-release an album, *Tall Potatoes*, which the *Miami New Times* called, "a gleeful, sarcastic, maverick romp through indie-pop and cowpunk... Think Ani DiFranco, if she had her roots in vaudeville." Alex liked to brag that *Tall Potatoes* had "gone wood."

On the other hand, our boy Abe had some false starts in Miami. He injured his knee the first time he tried to go running and he immediately gave up working out. He took a couple of poetry workshops that inspired him, but the momentum fizzled quickly. The Jetty Giant picture, though. When he received it, Abe didn't know that picture would be the talisman that would change his life, give him sustained momentum. Over a couple of years, Abe gradually got healthy. He wrote in the morning and took classes for no particular reason other than curiosity—book making, bartending, pottery; he even attended a "circus school" run by a former Cirque du Soleil performer, where he got to trapeze jump.

His renewed enthusiasm for life brought Alex back to him in little ways. They rolled *Inside Amy Schumer* sketches into new private jokes and talked about what *Jessica Jones* exploring trauma and misogyny meant for the world. Instead of telling him to make whatever he felt like, she helped him plan the menus for the week. Like most people, Alex didn't notice Abe's weight loss until it was significant. Once she did, she started teasing him about his "sidepiece." Alex called this figment of her imagination, Talulah, as in, "Talulah likes her men fit."

Abe decided his new body deserved a new wardrobe. He was getting older, and wearing the same baggy clothes he'd had since the nineties wasn't doing anything good for his self-image. The first morning he dressed for work in an outfit that displayed the lines of his slimmed-down body, Abe felt profoundly stupid. He was wearing thrifted Hugo Boss pants that could only be called "trousers" and a vintage Ely Cattleman button-down from the Salvation Army. Looking at himself in the full-length mirror, picking at the fabric, shifting his weight from foot to foot, he heard ghost voices from the Rez.

Hey, how was court?

Where's the funeral, cuz?

You get lost on the red carpet?

Not crabs in a bucket, just general ragging to make sure you knew dressy clothes didn't make you better than anyone else (the summer before ninth grade, Abe had a classmate who made the mistake of bragging that his parents bought him four pairs of pants for school; to this day, people still call the guy Spider). Who was Abe trying to be? Some dress-for-success, salt-and-pepper stud? Why bother? He was just going to get all sweaty on the bike ride in to work anyway.

Muy guapo, I whispered to him.

Abe grinned at the little voice in his head pumping him up.

Rico Suave, I said.

Abe decided to fake it. He took a deep breath and walked out of the bedroom. He and Alex had already had breakfast; she was in the kitchen, twirling cream and sugar into a travel coffee tumbler.

"Is that new?" Alex asked, dropping her spoon in the sink.

"Salvatore Armani, your favorite."

After a childhood of nothing but, Alex refused to set foot in thrift stores. Still, she laughed. "Have a good day, my sharp-dressed man."

She'd kissed him on the cheek, grabbed her purse, and taken off. It was a welcome shift from barely glancing up from her phone in the mornings. She'd not only registered his presence, she'd appreciated what she'd seen. Not long after, when Alex suggested they host a dinner party for her birthday, Abe felt like they'd finally stepped out of their rut. Somewhere along the line they'd stopped having people over; the party meant Alex felt they had a home worth celebrating with friends again.

"I don't want to sit out in the living room while you do everything, though," she said, sounding a little shy.

"I'll let you clean the house, how about that?"

"Oh, can I?" Alex said, her sarcasm laid thick enough to make him laugh. "I know it's my dinner, but let me help."

"Sounds lovely," Abe said. In Syracuse, and sometimes in Virginia, they would split a bottle of wine, crank their CD player, and sing along while they cooked together. Gradually over the years in Miami, Abe had taken over all of the cooking duties. To hear Alex tell it, he'd turned into a "Kitchen Nazi." Abe, a former line cook, believed in "clean as you go" culture. Alex's tendency to drop a bomb on the kitchen and clean it up later drove him crazy. Plus, she never knew where anything was. The story became, if it wasn't for Abe, then Alex would starve to death. Of course, flying solo in the kitchen turned something that was once done out of love into a burden, and Abe started to resent cooking. Losing the obligation and rediscovering the love sounded like a great way to celebrate Alex's birthday.

To prepare for their guests, Abe and Alex cleaned the house together. Alex surprised him by hooking up her old MP3 player to their sound system in the living room. It was loaded with late nineties and early aughts hits they'd burned from CDs years before. Normally, once the place was clean, Alex would get ready, then veg on the couch watching TV while Abe cooked. Abe would get ready at the last minute when people started to arrive. That night, they met in the dining room, still in their cleaning grubs. One of the classes he'd taken was on wine tasting, with a focus on finding bottles under fifteen dollars that drank like they'd cost fifty. Abe had opened a cheap bottle of red wine to let it breathe: Donna Laura's Ali.

"I've got to fire up the grill," Abe said, handing her a glass. "So you can get ready now if you want."

"No, we're not doing that." Alex sipped her wine, *hmm*-ing in her throat in a way that let Abe know the class was paying off. "Show me everything."

"I feel like I'm dying or something, and I've got to show you the ropes before I go."

Alex laughed. "I just want to be with you. On my birthday," she added pointedly.

So Abe helped Alex dust off her kitchen skills. They took the marinating chicken halves out of the fridge so they could come to room temperature, then soaked pimento sticks, bay leaves, and allspice cloves in water.

"You'd think anywhere in Miami would have pimento sticks," Abe made a point of telling Alex, "but you'd be wrong; you have to order them online."

Their landlord had a detached garage out back, overgrown with palms, that held the washer and dryer (and a bunch of old crap she couldn't admit the humidity had destroyed). Abe pulled out the grill, but when he went to open it so he could clean the ashes out, Alex put an arm across his chest. "Allow me."

Abe gestured; *be my guest.* When she was reaching for the handle Abe said, "Gotta warn you, though. Sometimes there's a roach hiding under the lid."

She let Abe take over cleaning the grill, but she insisted on dumping the briquets in and lighting them up. While the briquets became coals, they went back inside and preheated the oven. They put butter, cream cheese, and heavy cream on the counter to come to room temperature for their potatoes, scrubbed and stabbed the potatoes themselves, then put them to bake on a cookie sheet. They scrubbed and sliced squash, salting them and putting them to the side. Alex asked why and Abe replied, "It sweats the water out so they don't get mushy when you grill them." For jeweled rice, they sliced Vidalia onions, orange peels, carrots, and scallions; peeled and smashed garlic cloves; and measured out pomegranate seeds, slivered almonds, golden raisins, saffron, cumin, and allspice. For the black beans, they chopped white and purple onion, celery, and red pepper.

Alex asked if she was "getting the size right" on her chopping so often that Abe accused her of playing the helpless maiden.

"You know you don't need to do that with me," he joked. "I accept you as the strong, independent woman you are."

"But sir," she said, batting her big blue eyes at him, "I don't know what I'm doing, and this knife is sooo heavy."

Abe puffed his chest out as he crossed the kitchen, approaching her at the cutting board. "No, no, no—you're doing it all wrong," he purred. He spooned his body against hers, hands covering Alex's as she held the knife in one hand and an onion in the other. "Let me show you how a *man* does it."

He "helped" her chop for a minute, moving his body in waves, making little oo's and ah's as the blade sliced through the onion and hit the cutting board.

"Thanks," she said, smiling, back to her normal tone. "I think I've got it now."

With smoke from the pimento sticks flavoring the chicken halves, there wasn't anything left to do but assemble everything. Prep had gone on longer than they'd planned, so they had to shower together to get ready for company. They quickly swapped the hot spot under the spray, lathering like mad to get clean. They were in a hurry, but Alex gave Abe a look when he started soaping his body up.

"Oh no," she said, mimicking Abe's sultry tone from earlier. "You're doing that all wrong." She lathered up her hands with body wash, rubbing between Abe's legs and down his penis. Once he got hard, Alex rinsed herself off and hopped out of the shower. "See how that's better?" she asked.

Abe half laughed, half groaned, rinsing himself off. "This is just one big tease," he said. They spent the rest of their time getting ready kissing and telling each other to stop messing around because company was coming.

They had invited three couples and Alex's newly divorced friend Susa (you really don't need the others' names but I mention Susa because she comes to bear). Abe crisped the chicken skin and presented it on a platter, to much exclaiming from the arriving guests. Everyone gathered at the dining room table and drooled over the chicken and rice. Abe mixed the dairy ingredients and brown sugar into the sweet potatoes and set the dish out. Alex poured the drinks. The air crackled with conversation. Whenever Abe caught Alex's eye, she'd grin.

After everyone had eaten to their heart's content, Abe called their attention by clinking his fork against his wine stem. He raised his glass, offering a toast. "To the birthday girl, whose voice can rock the house or rock the cradle, whose lyrics have been known to make grown men cry or propose, who does more for future generations in one day at Florida City than most of us do in a lifetime, and who seems to grow more beautiful as the years go on." Some people are embarrassed by public praise; Alex is not one of them. Her face glowed.

Their guests whooped and clapped, but Abe held up a hand. "I wrote a little something for the occasion."

"No, you didn't." Alex smiled, her eyes shining.

"Sure, I did. Thanks to your help, I had plenty of time between meal prep," he said, smirking—in truth, he'd been revising it for a couple of weeks.

Alex responded by offering a toast to Abe's food. She bragged about how Abe had been working on the meal all week, which wasn't exactly true. He'd planned the menu the week before, but he'd been working on the meal—shopping, paying expedited shipping for the pimento sticks, making the marinade, and soaking the chicken—for four days at the most. But if she felt like bragging about him, Abe wasn't about to stop her.

He pulled the poem he'd written from his pocket and made a show of unfolding it, clearing his throat, squinting at the paper, adjusting the distance from his face, bugging his eyes. The relaxed, boozy atmosphere garnered this bit of vaudeville a much bigger reaction than it deserved, but Abe hadn't done it solely for laughs. He was nervous and stalling. Alex had a drawer full of love poems from their early days together, but he hadn't written to her—for her—in years. And he'd never read one aloud to her, let alone in front of people.

Abe read:

Alex,
there's no Mohawk word for love
so I'm calling it cerulean,
the most prized color
because it's the only pigment that can render
true shades of sky and sea.

Cerulean is not the color of the sky
we met beneath,
or the color of your eyes,

but if your eyes had a name it would be
the color everyone wants
and if love had a word in Mohawk it would be Alex.

We kissed and I closed my eyes and opened them
twenty-four years later.
There's no Mohawk word for love so let's say
I stepped beyond time to be with you.

And then my journey's end,
my beginning,
my release,
my renewal,
my home,
my light,
my sun,
my earth,
my moon,
my Alex.

There's no Mohawk word for love so let's say
I'm so very lucky to be alive while you are.

This is ours, I think,
this meal,
this moment,
these hours,
these years,
ours.

There's no Mohawk word for love so let's say
the world is green because
I sleep circled in your arms.

Abe got through it without choking up. No one spoke. He saw tears standing in Alex's eyes. Her smile, the one he'd decided so long ago to try and ignite as often as he could, radiated.

"I love you, Alex." He raised his wine glass. "Here's to the next twenty-four years."

Alex, Susa, and the three couples cheered, and drank. Susa leaned over and said something in Alex's ear that made her laugh. Afterward, Abe and Alex moved to the kitchen to French press coffee and get the dessert ready. While Alex sliced strawberries, Abe made a blackberry compote to go with the shortbread he'd made the day before. He asked what it was Susa had said. Alex set her knife down and turned toward Abe, making sure she had his eye.

"She said, 'This is you having problems?' She said she should've been so lucky." Both of them smiled, but neither laughed. It was the closest they'd ever come to admitting their marriage, their relationship, had lost its spark. But instead of talking once their guests left, they tore each other's clothes off the minute they had the place to themselves. Alex's fingers dug into the back of Abe's neck, her lips pressed to his nearly hard enough to bruise. It felt like she was drowning, like she needed his mouth for air. He pinned her to the wall and she wrapped her legs around his, feet braced against his calves. They moaned together as Abe slid inside her.

If they planned to talk about the nadir their marriage had hit, those intentions got derailed by the "weird mark" on the outside of his calf that one of their friends pointed out when he was leaving. The next morning, Alex examined it and said Abe should see a doctor, something she'd been trying to get him to do ever since he turned forty. Abe had never spelled out why he hated doctors; it was too depressing.

"So they can charge me five hundred dollars to tell me it's a scab?" he snapped. "Why don't you worry about your own bullshit."

"Fine," she said, and they didn't say much else that morning.

Abe sips his Herradura, the barstool at Pyke's Place pressing into his pelvic bones. He misses the padding he used to have. He's also amazed the good feelings between him and Alex, so hard-fought, could be so short-lived. He waits for the tequila to mellow the gnawing in his joints, the pain in his muscles.

Just as Abe and Alex never talked about her affair with the bass player's brother, they never discussed how their relationship had stagnated, how they'd come to feel more like roommates than lovers. As things improved, Abe felt relieved—perhaps they could bridge the distance between them without ever having to talk about it. He assumed Alex felt the same. Of course, like his suspicions about her affairs, he'd never asked.

Lost in his thoughts, Abe doesn't register the person sitting next to him, has no idea how long the dark silhouette has even been in the corner of his vision. For a moment he thinks the shadows have found him, then the figure takes a sip of beer. Abe steals a glance. He doesn't recognize the man, slim with silver and iron hair slicked back to the collar of his red flannel shirt. Over the flannel, the man wears a bulky Carhartt jacket.

"Howzit?" Carhartt doesn't look at Abe when he offers this opening sally, but Abe recognizes the voice immediately. Yonder Curly Head. The only bully who had ever really frightened him. Yonder's eyes are black and dead, like abandoned caves, and he wears a little grin. He's prison-trim, not out long enough to put the comfort weight of decent food back on.

"Yonder." Abe keeps his voice even. He's not nine years old anymore. Not seventeen, either, come to that. He has a mad urge to add, *How'd you like prison?* Instead, he says, "Been a minute."

Yonder grunts. "Took off, dintcha there?" He quaffs half his beer in one go. "You always were too good for the rest of us."

"I wouldn't say that." Abe doesn't like where this is going, and the speed with which it's getting there. Holding his shot glass, Abe sneaks his other hand beneath the bar, grabbing the cane, and pulling it between his legs to hide it. He takes another sedate sip of his tequila.

"Who knows what coulda happened if you stuck around. Shit, me'n Adam used to pal around all the time."

"Yeah?" If it's true, this is news to Abe.

"Shit, yeah. I had the best weed back then. Schwag compared to what's out there now, but what the hell did we know?" Yonder laughs, takes a large gulp of beer. "Your brother was a bitch but his money was green."

Beneath the bar, Abe's grip tightens around his cane. He should make his move first, catch Yonder off guard. As if in answer to his thought, Yonder moves like a snake. One moment he's casually holding his beer, the next his hand clamps around Abe's wrist.

"You want to stay with me, now." Yonder's tone is mild, his grip iron.

Then Abe feels his shirttail pulled free of his pants, and something hard and thin presses against the side of his back, just over his kidney. The object is cold against his skin. Another man sits on Abe's other side, pulling his stool chummily close. Abe feels his pulse in his temples, thrumming in his throat. A third figure joins Yonder on his other side, then more at Abe's back, blocking the arm holding what is certainly a knife from prying eyes. In the mirror, Abe counts six of them including Yonder. Their faces are vaguely familiar. Guys Abe sees around when he visits, hanging out at the bars, filling up at the gas pumps, smoking in front of Lou Bond's. The oldest probably has a score of years on Yonder, while two of them look like they aren't even old enough to be in the bar. Young relatives, if I had to guess. When you're out drinking you gotta show these kids how to take an imagined slight to some illogical extreme, otherwise they might just get a buzz on, have a few laughs, and go home. Then where would we be as a people?

Abe sizes them up for all the good it will do. Despite the bravado I put forth to the frat bros at Zopie's all those years ago, Abe is not a fighter. He fears he's about to find out what would've happened if that verbal sparring at the coffee shop had gone badly.

"Let's you and I talk," Yonder says.

A be knows people who, when dragged outside a bar by six men, would not be afraid. Would, in fact, be excited. The Browns, for instance. Aunt Maisy's boys, Abe's half-Irish cousins, have been taking on grown-ass men in bar fights since they were teenagers. Then there's Sis's husband, Robert, a Marine who Abe once witnessed taking down five drunken off-duty sheriffs in less than a minute. When someone gets in their faces, there's a contentment beneath the anger of these men in Abe's life, a sense they can finally stop holding back and let their inner demons out. Abe's demons—self-sabotage, poor self-esteem, depression—aren't going to help him in this situation, which is the men from the bar pinning him against the wall out back, between the dumpsters. Their boots scrape the gravel. Abe smells stale beer from the recycling bin and gentle rot from the trash bin, tempered by the cold.

There's a door above a short flight of concrete steps. Abe wills the door to open, for Joseph Pyke to come out and yell, *What's all this now?* It wouldn't scare Yonder off but Joseph would get Abe's cousins, even up the odds a little. Hell of a time for Abe to find out he's neither a Fight nor a Flight but a Freeze, innit? He doesn't struggle, not consciously, but a great negation of what's happening heaves though his body from toes to scalp, a cramp that first pulls the men toward him and then pushes them back.

"Easy, big fella." Yonder's voice is cheery; he's having the time of his life. Yonder didn't leave a lookout at either corner of the bar; does that mean he wants this over with quickly? Or does he want as many hands on Abe as possible? "Hold him."

The men grip Abe's arms and shoulders. He tightens his stomach muscles, but when Yonder drives a fist into his gut, Abe feels every weight the man lifted over the years. The sound is a dull, meaty *thwack*. White flowers fill Abe's vision. A grunt escapes him, a noise that makes the men giggle. Yonder punches him in the stomach several more times, really winding up for each blow. Abe sees the flowers of light each time, releases involuntary grunts each time, hears their excited titters each time.

Abe thought he'd felt adrenaline in the bar, but these blows make his skeleton thrum inside his skin, his brain vibrate inside his skull. At the same time, his legs curl up toward his body. If the men let go, he'll tumble to the ground.

"Keep him up." Yonder sounds out of breath.

Not much cardio down in Jamesville, huh? Abe thinks.

"Hold his head," Yonder says.

Abe decides he's had enough. He's going to throw himself backward into the building as hard as he can. If he's lucky, he'll crack their forearms against the wall, break their grip. If not, he'll start biting hands, throw himself to the ground on purpose and start elbowing nutsacks. He's past caring.

But as he finds his legs, rough hands grab his neck and hair, yanking him upright. Yonder's knuckles crash into his cheek, his chin, they mash his lips back against his teeth, crack into his nose, pound his eye. He's on the ground, looking up at Yonder. Wetness trickles down his face, runs over his lips. Tears or blood, Abe doesn't know. Yonder shakes his hands out, grinning.

"Damn, you got a head like a fuckin' rock, boy." Yonder drives the toe of his boot into Abe's chest, and Abe cries out. It's like a signal. Boots and sneakers fly at Abe from all sides. He curls into a ball, covering his face with his forearms. They stomp at his ribs, his thighs, his shoulders, they kick at his shins and arms. Abe is utterly helpless, filled with terror. Their feet are shadows flying at him in the dark, and it all makes sense. The shadows weren't harbingers of danger, they were premonitions of this moment. *This is how I die*, Abe thinks.

"Look at that, boys, he's turtling," Yonder cries, joyous. "He's Turtle Clan and he's turtling, look at 'im!"

As they kick and stomp, the men get the giggles. They lean on each other to keep upright, snorting with laughter. Good cheer weakens their blows a little, but Abe feels like if he's forced to endure their laughter while they continue to beat him, he might choke on his own vomit.

At that moment, there's a commotion—bodies hitting bodies, yelps of pain, crashes as something slams into the wooden siding of Pyke's. As if by unspoken agreement, the men stop kicking him. Abe draws a breath thick with snot and tears and blood, and chances a look from between his forearms. Brennan Brown, Abe's half-Irish cousin, the One Who Stayed, and his mirror twin cousins, Louis and Moses, have arrived at last. The men were having such a grand time beating Abe, they hadn't seen the attack coming.

The white-haired man is hopping around, accusing Brennan of breaking his ass, while Brennan throws punches into Yonder's torso and face. Abe's old nemesis backs away, yelping in pain and surprise. Lois and Moses have their hands braced against the wall, kicking the pair of men they've tackled to keep them from getting up.

The last two men . . . well, one man and one barely more than a boy (who is getting one hell of a lesson, I must say) are just looking around. I'm giving you this piece by piece, but really, it's all happening in a blur. Abe isn't forming thoughts, only impressions; he wants to help his cousins, keep the momentum on their side before Yonder and his boys can recover, before whoever brought the knife remembers he's got it. He drives the heel of his Doc Marten into the kid's leg.

The kid voices a hellish, guttural cry and falls to the ground, gripping his knee in both hands. All the men behind Pyke's stop, watch as the kid rocks back and forth, moaning through clenched teeth.

"Get off'n him, get off'n him." This from one of the men around Abe's age, clearly an uncle, much older brother, or the sort of father who thinks six against one behind a bar is a fine life lesson. No one is actually attacking the boy, but the man doesn't notice. For him, the kid's choked whimpering is all there is in the world. He's trying to get past the twin who tackled him, but Louis or Moses keeps kicking him back down.

Abe pushes himself into a sitting position. The adrenaline has snuffed his joint and muscle pain. Shock is making it impossible to tell where he's hurt, or how badly. He presses a hand to his face and it comes away bloody. He looks up at the only unscathed member of Yonder's group, some guy in his thirties with a long ponytail. If Ponytail tries something, Abe is ready to elbow him in the crotch. But it looks like the fight has drained from him. In fact, the tone of the scene behind Pyke's has shifted. All the men are just watching the kid Abe kicked trying to comfort himself. Even the old man has ceased his hopping around; he stands there, rubbing his tailbone, eyeing the boy.

The men steal glances at Abe. You'd think they'd look guilty, or even sorry, right? But that's not the case. There's resentment in those looks. Abe has violated the unspoken rule of bar fights—you're supposed to take your lumps and get some new scars, but Abe's taken all the fun out of it by causing what might be a permanent injury. Maybe Abe should feel bad, but he can't escape the sensation of being surrounded by men laughing and kicking him into the gravel.

Yonder uses his sleeve to wipe a trickle of blood from beneath his nose. He clears his throat and spits, then looks at Abe. For a moment it could go either way, but Yonder must think Abe's face is bloodied enough. "Charlie, Matt. Help Paul get his kid to the hospital."

Abe's mirror twin cousins offer a hand to the guys they took down. The younger one doesn't know any better, so he accepts the help.

Paul wants nothing to do with Louis's (or Moses's?) hand, slapping it away and standing on his own. Paul and the thirty-something who went untouched help the kid to his feet, being as gentle as they can. The kid slings his arms over their shoulders, leg kicked out in front of him like a bird's broken wing.

Now it's just Yonder and the old party, who mutters to himself (Abe is pretty sure it's "broke my ass") and shoots a wounded glance at Brennan. Brennan helps Abe stand, while the twins flank them, ready for anything.

"We done here?" Brennan asks, glaring at Yonder.

"That's okay," Abe says. Brennan is still in bounds, sticking up for a cousin. Anything more and Yonder might become Brennan's problem as well, and Abe doesn't want that. Fella like Yonder, though? I guess you don't need me to tell you, he has a way of being everyone's problem.

"Yeah, Brownie," Yonder says. "I was just leaving."

He and the old guy walk off, but Yonder stops at the edge of the building. "Wasn't gonna really hurt you, ya know."

Abe nods, not knowing any such thing. Once they're out of sight, Abe asks one of the twins to go inside the bar and collect Tóta's cane.

Thirteen

People are sometimes surprised to learn of Abe's love for Thanksgiving. I admit, many Natives—plenty of them living in Ahkwesáhsne, in fact—believe Thanksgiving is bullshit, a whitewashing both of Native history in general and the Wampanoag genocide in particular. Obviously, the story of generic, unnamed "Indians" showing up, welcoming the Pilgrims, feeding them, then fading into obscurity, while the Pilgrims peacefully inhabit the "New World," without displacing or slaughtering anyone, is a lie that represents how American History largely overlooks the genocide of Natives. Today the Wampanoag live on Martha's Vineyard, unrecognized by the federal government. For them, Thanksgiving is a day of mourning.

I don't have research to back me up, and my guts may have shit for brains, but my gut tells me Thanksgiving became more accepted among the Hotinonshón:ni because of our Thanksgiving Address. The Ohèn:ton Karihwatéhkwen, the Words We Say Before All Else (or What We Say Before We Do Anything Important, or Words Spoken Before All Others). We start every gathering by giving thanks to all aspects of creation—people, plants, animals, the wind and waters, the sun, moon, and stars. The Ohèn:ton Karihwatéhkwen is different each time, based on whatever's in the speaker's heart at that moment. You might stand and spend an hour naming every bird you've ever encountered on your land, then everyone will say, "Now our minds are one," and you'll sit back down. You probably won't be asked to give the Thanksgiving Address again, but your backyard bird tour would still count. Because our religious practices were banned until 1978, my theory is Hotinonshón:ni started hiding our traditions within the confines of this new holiday, and we never stopped embracing it.

In the Jacobs family, in addition to the Thanksgiving feast, Aunt Maisy makes chicken and rice on Tuesday, spaghetti with meatballs and sausage on Wednesday, and pork loin on Friday. Anyone visiting for the holiday who doesn't feel like squeezing in at Maisy's place—a converted mobile home with additions, where a couch or bit of floor and a layer of quilts counts as accommodations—stays with Brennan, Sis, Aunt Abby, or Abe's parents. After breakfast, the family spends the days together at Aunt Maisy's house. Able-bodied youngsters might have a chore or two to "earn" food—mostly involving firewood. If you're a teenager you'll be chopping, storing, moving, or tarping wood before lunch. Adults help with meal prep, desserts, and dishes. The real youngsters gather stray wood from all over the property and pile it out back to start the nightly bonfires. Other than that, each day is board games and card games until dinner.

After dinner it's a movie, and finally Pokeno inside and a bonfire and Kick the Can for those up to braving the cold. Depending on how much drinking occurred around the bonfire and the general mood, after hours happen at one of the local bars or—more and more likely as the years have gone on—Brennan or Sis's house. For over forty years, nothing has stopped Aunt Maisy from hosting and preparing four delicious evening meals—not snowstorms, not divorce, not rheumatoid arthritis, not breast cancer.

Everyone is dressed nicely for Thanksgiving 2016, impatiently waiting for three o'clock. Abe's nephews and young cousins have taken two folding tables and several folding chairs out of the garage and lined them up, extending the dining room table from the kitchen to the living room couch. Even though they're slightly different heights (and the dining room table is ovoid), two huge tablecloths have been tossed over them in an attempt to make it look like one long table. Chairs and stools have been gathered from all corners of the house.

A bit before three, Abe's nieces and nephews bring cold food to the table—olives, pickles, cranberry sauce, banana bread, pistachio whip, and celery filled with cream cheese. Mom and the aunts bring sides to the table: single bowls of acorn, banana, buttercup, butternut, and spaghetti squash that have been sliced in half and roasted with butter and pepper; thirty pounds of mashed potatoes in three bowls; fifteen pounds of roasted sweet potatoes in two bowls; ten pounds of green beans piled in two baking dishes; twenty-five ears of corn, broken in half and served in one giant deep-dish platter; sage bread stuffing, divided into two dishes; four gravy tureens; and a large basket of dinner rolls. This year Aunt Maisy has roasted two turkeys, a twenty-two-pounder that comes to the table on two large platters, with an eighteen-pounder resting in the kitchen, which will be used for turkey sandwiches and take-home leftovers as the week moves on. The drinks are pitchers of iced tea and lemonade and gallons of nonfat and whole milk. It occurs to Abe this is why he cooks most every meal in Miami—feeding his loved ones makes him feel connected to his family on the Rez.

Everyone takes a seat (the folding chairs from the garage are still cold). Since Budge is distancing himself from Abe during the healing, and the Billings don't want him eating alone, none of that side is here. Aunt Maisy sits at the head of the table, where Tóta sat until she died. There's some bustle over who's giving the Address—mostly protestations from people who don't want to do it, but Adam's pretty insistent that Abe should speak. Aunt Maisy's shrill voice cuts through the chatter.

"Adam's right. Why in hell ain' Abe ever given the Address?" She sounds pissed, but that's how she always sounds. It's only when you look closely at her face that you notice her eyes dance merrily while her lips twist sideways in a sardonic grin. Basically, she's fucking with him. "Seriously, we never hear from you. What're you thankful for?"

"Yeah, Toots." Adam has the same twinkle in his eyes as Aunt Maisy. "Every year you fly all this way, eat, and fly home, like a goddamn mosquito. You owe us an Address."

That's all it takes; the whole table clamors for Abe to speak. He nods, trying to remember the different parts of creation to thank. "We are here at Aunt Maisy's table in celebration of Thanksgiving." While Abe speaks, platters go around the table and people load their plates. "We gather each year as a family. We gather to give thanks. We're thankful because we're lucky to have this." Abe nods.

"Now our minds are one," the family says, voices overlapping.

"We give thanks to Mother Earth, for supporting us," Abe says. "We thank her for providing this amazing meal that Aunt Maisy and Mom and Aunt Ella and Aunt Abby have all worked so hard on."

"Now our minds are one."

"We give thanks to Grandmother Moon, our Eldest Mother. Thanks for watching over the women at this table, as you watch over all women."

"Now our minds are one."

"We give thanks to . . ." With the easy ones out of the way, Abe's mind goes blank. No one expects some long, drawn-out thing—the joke is that when we had Turtle Island to ourselves, the Thanksgiving Address took three days—but he wants to do well. "We give thanks to . . . Brother Sun, who—"

"C'mon." Adam speaks softly. When Abe looks up, he sees a painful little grin on his brother's face. Between the meds and the disorder, it's clear Abe is being whittled away to nothing; Adam must think expressing gratitude is going to help him in some way.

"I come home once a year. I soak this up for a week, sometimes two, and somehow it gets me through another year." As Abe looks around the table at his family, making eye contact with each of them in turn, the words feel thick in his mouth. "I'm thankful for the time we share. I'm thankful for everything you've taught me, for everything I've learned from you. I'm thankful you can make me laugh. Even now. Especially now."

Abe looks at Alex, sitting beside him, holding his hand. Her expression is pained. If he says he's thankful to have her there, will it sound like he's judging her for waiting until the night before to show up?

Via text, he'd tried to get Alex to extend her stay, but she didn't want to take Monday or Tuesday off. She wanted to know what Abe expected her kids to do without her. "I didn't realize they close the school when you take a personal day," he'd texted back, trying to make a joke. The humor was lost via text. Alex's following responses were curt, businesslike. She has a flight back on Sunday morning at eight thirty. There were other Thanksgivings when Alex was barely up, but not when they'd been apart for close to two months, not with Abe waiting for vascular dementia to come knocking.

The night they picked her up, Alex knocked off early, citing her long day of travel. When Abe went to bed after beers and spades, he found Alex in bed scrolling her phone with all the lights off (they were staying at Sis and Robert's, along with Adam and his wife, to maximize their sibling time).

"Hey," Abe said. *I thought you were tired.*

"Hey." One word and Abe could tell Alex actually was exhausted; he assumed she'd meant to sleep but had gotten sucked into scrolling.

He grabbed his pajamas, flannels borrowed from his father, and piled the antibiotic cleanser, bandages, scissors, and tape on top. Abe stopped at the door. "You didn't wait up for me, did you? You said I should stay and have fun."

"When did you start using a cane?" In the light of her phone, Alex's eyes were cold.

There had been an awkward moment with Sis at the airport, when she realized Abe hadn't told Alex about the cane. Abe hadn't been able to bring himself to put it in a text. *Well the thing is*, Abe had thought, *I passed out walking home after our video call—isn't that nutso-bubbuttso?* Now, given the look in her eyes and exhaustion in her voice, Abe had no desire to tell her what had prompted the cane. He said the weird, watery feeling in his legs had gotten worse, so doctors had prescribed a cane. Not a lie, technically, but withholding enough of the truth that it might as well have been.

"I didn't like those grandpa canes at the health service," Abe said, "so I grabbed one from Tóta's collection."

"Cool." Her sarcasm was not the least bit playful. "It makes you look like a pimp."

"What would you have done? Would you have texted me, 'I keep losing my balance, now I need a cane, see you soon'?"

"I mean, something. Something, Abe." She closed her eyes and sighed. "I guess it's too late now. I'm sorry you have to deal with that."

"I'm sorry I didn't tell you."

"Anything else I need to know?"

Just that I passed out the one time, and they don't know why. Plus, my hips and knees feel like they're full of ground glass. Oh, and the lesions shrink one day, then the next they open wide; I bet if you did a time-lapse, they'd look like dozens of hungry little mouths.

After his shower, they cuddled together and slept. In the morning, Alex's probing hand, gripping his hip, had woken Abe. He squinted against the sunlight.

"What's this?" Alex tried shaking his hip. When she couldn't, she pulled his pajama bottoms and underwear down. The fabric caught on his morning erection, making him yelp. Her hands snatched back, like she'd touched a hot stove. When she reached for him again, at first Abe thought she was returning to his arousal.

Instead she ran her fingers over his jutting hip bone, then unbuttoned his top. Bruises from the beating peppered his stomach and ribs, and there was an apple-sized red and purple knot on his chest, courtesy of Yonder's boot. If she could have seen Abe's whole body, she'd know his back, thighs, and forearms had been beaten even worse. Alex frowned, running her fingers over his ribs, brushing the denuded flesh of his chest. "You weren't even this skinny at eighteen." She sounded scared.

At Thanksgiving dinner, Abe looks into Alex's eyes. She squeezes his hand fiercely, her expression rueful. She gives a nod of encouragement for him to continue, but underneath, it looks like she wants to flee. Abe says, "I'm thankful for the time I have left. I'm glad we can see each other, share a meal, share some laughs, and eat some pie."

"Now our minds are one," the family says. Alex doesn't join them.

Aunt Maisy invites everyone to dig in, and it's a lot of prep for maybe forty minutes at the table, talking, laughing, and eating. Then the aunts pack up the food again and the nephews bring the folding furniture back to the garage. Most of the family squeezes onto the living room couches or puts pillows on the carpet to watch (or pass out in front of, really) *Focus*, a con-artist thriller with Will Smith and Margot Robbie. Since dessert can't hit the table until the dishes are washed and the food is stored, there's a contingent of washers, dryers, and storers crowding Aunt Maisy's kitchen (excluding Mom and the aunts, who are taking a much-deserved rest). Once everything is clean again, the dining room table gets covered with desserts—a chocolate Yule log, peanut butter blossom cookies, chocolate fudge (with and without walnuts), angel food cake, and pies—pecan, cherry, strawberry rhubarb, cranberry apple, deep dish apple, Dutch apple, chocolate cream, banana cream, pumpkin, and pumpkin pecan. Abe's dad brews a pot of Starbucks, a pot of Folgers, and a pot of decaf, and everyone has a round of desserts, filling what little room they've made during the dinner cleanup.

Every year, Abe wishes the meal included white wine, and for someone to make fresh whipped cream for dessert instead of putting Cool Whip out. Maybe next year, the last year he'll be himself, he'll whip some heavy cream at someone else's house and hide it on Aunt Maisy's porch, along with a bottle of Chardonnay. The meal will be perfect, and Abe will pass into middle-aged brain rot with a smile.

Brennan Brown brings one of Sis's boys outside to help get the bonfire going. Once it's good and hot, most of the family gathers around. They feed it with yard trimmings and pallets, and carefully selected trash (occasionally, they get to burn something fun, like furniture, but not this year). Aunt Maisy offers to bring out campfire skewers and a pack of Glazier's hot dogs, but everyone is too full to eat anything else. Not too full to drink Bud Light and Labbatt's Blue, of course. There's also a bottle of Southern Comfort sitting on the ground by the beer, in case anyone wants to hit the gas. Alex, for instance, who has more than a few drafts even though she's not much of a drinker. Abe takes a few slugs as well.

"Is that good for you?" Mom asks. His parents are on either side of him, arms laced behind his waist, shoulders bracing him. Normally, his father stays on the couch after dessert; Abe doesn't need to wonder why he's here.

"Not at all," Abe says easily. In fact, he's not supposed to drink any alcohol with Amethopterone hammering his liver, but staring down the barrel of dementia buys him a whole lot of *fuck it*. His father opens his mouth, then closes it again.

It rained hard at the start of the week and the ground is still squelchy, so no one really wants to play Kick the Can. There isn't a bonfire in the world big enough to make wearing wet, muddy clothes in twenty-degree weather sound fun, but Alex won't let it go.

"What if we don't hide that much?" Alex looks around the fire at Abe's family, who are turning like rotisserie chickens to stay warm. "Like, we don't touch the ground, or the bushes?"

"We might as well play without the can." Adam pokes the fire stick into the bonfire, sending up sparks.

"We could play lacrosse; light the ball on fire." Alex grins, her eyes wild in the shadows cast by the bonfire's flames. Abe hasn't been counting her beers but she must've had a few; he can tell she isn't joking.

"Remember the year we built the bonfire too close to the trees?" Robert asks. The Jacobs laugh at the memory of branches singeing overhead, wondering what they'd do if a tree went up. Abe sees Alex's disappointment. Maybe if they had a visitor—a college roommate, or an old friend, say—the Jacobs might have shown off how wild they can be. Told Alex to grab a can of lighter fluid from Aunt Maisy's garage, scrounged up lacrosse sticks for all of them. But with nothing to prove, and the wisdom—or inertia—that comes with age, they'd just as soon drink around the bonfire and play Remember When.

Hey, remember when you backed into Aunt Maisy's garage and pushed the one side back five inches?

Well, at least I'm not the one who knocked the mirror off Aunt Abby's car.

Remember when Cass walked the railing outside of Cricket's?

No, but I remember she fell off the railing, busted her ass, and had to ride home in the truck bed 'cause she was puking.

Remember the time Mom told that cashier to have a happy fucking Thanksgiving?

Watching his nephews talking shit around the bonfire, Abe is struck by the fact that they're old enough to drink. Buy guns. Rent cars. Then he thinks of his Uncle Fritz, who died of liver failure when Abe was nine years old. The boys will be adults when Abe dies, much more aware of what loss means.

Back at Sis's place, even though Alex usually abstains to keep her "instrument" healthy, she smokes weed with the pothead contingent of the family. After, she convinces the boys to fire up the Xbox for karaoke, chomping down bourbon and keeping everyone singing until midnight.

Abe's brother and siblings-in-law head up to bed, leaving Sis and Brennan. With the Widow Jane demolished, Alex switches back to Bud Light and pushes the boys to set up *Rock Band*. She hasn't mixed alcohol and pot since they first moved to Miami, when she'd just gotten the halo removed and had been a little reckless. Alex pushes them into another hour of video games, then exhorts them to drink and talk shit at the kitchen table. It's nearly dawn when they go to bed.

Upstairs, changing into their pajamas, Alex giggle-stumble-slurs a drunken come on. Abe helps her get changed and tucks her in. "C'mon, you know you want this," Alex says, smiling as her eyes drift closed. Abe does his ablutions to keep infection at bay, and by the time he joins her, Alex is snoring contentedly.

Alex's Sunday flight is too early for them to ask for a ride, so Abe is out front heating Sis's car. Alex said her goodbyes to everyone the night before, then showered and packed up everything but her deodorant, toothbrush, and travel clothes so she'd be ready to go as quickly as possible in the morning.

Alex had garnered a dubious honor this Thanksgiving—being so hungover she'd missed not just the following day, but Friday night's dinner as well. Saturday, Abe and Alex went to his parents' house for breakfast. A ravenous Alex scarfed Dad's hash and eggs, then wandered around the Jacobs' house, a look on her face similar to one she wore for museum trips. She picked up photos, ran her hand over quilts, and sat in front of windows to take in the views. When

Abe asked her what was wrong, she claimed embarrassment over her "cocktail flu." The four of them went back to Aunt Maisy's for a lunch and dinner of leftovers and pies, then lit another bonfire, at which Alex abstained from drinking. To Abe, watching her laugh in the firelight with his family, Alex's smile looked genuine for the first time all day.

With the car toasty, Abe returns to Sis's house to collect Alex and her luggage. Alex looks everywhere but his face, hustling past him to the car in her light coat. Abe drops her bag in the back seat and pulls out of the driveway. Turning on the radio, he hears Creedence Clearwater Revival's *Willy and the Poor Boys* album. Their mother is so sick of the local rock stations she's switched to country and gospel, but Sis loves the classics so much she's got the CDs. Just as John Fogerty takes shots at millionaires, Alex clicks the radio off.

"I've been thinking, Abe. I want a divorce."

For the briefest moment, shorter than a second, Abe waits for the punchline. Alex has always joked about divorce, after all. Abe bought the wrong razor? Accidentally used lemon extract instead of vanilla when he made whipped cream? Came too quickly, leaving her wanting? Alex would shake her head and sadly say, "Divorce." Abe would have to go back to the store and exchange the Venus for the Daisy, whip up a batch of lemon ricotta pancakes and convince her they'd be better than chocolate-banana waffles, pull out Alex's favorite toy and sic it on her until she gasped for mercy. "Marriage saved," she'd say, giving him a sly look. "For now." But the hope is the flare of a match head; he knows what Alex sounds like when she's joking.

Alex rubs her jeans like she touched something sticky, trying to warm her hands. "I knew if I said anything before I came up, that you wouldn't be able to act normal around your family. It also gave me a chance to have one last visit with everyone. That meant a lot to me."

Pressure builds in Abe's chest, like his heart is filling with lead. Alex has spent the whole visit waiting to drop this bomb then hop a plane, and she's grateful for one last visit? He glances at the directions on his phone, sitting in the recess of the car door; they'll be there shortly. At Massena International Airport, the person who takes your ticket, the person who walks you to the plane, and the person serving as your steward on the flight are all one and the same; no one ever needs the suggested two hours before takeoff. Yet Alex insisted they be there early. Maybe to give them extra time to talk? If that's the case, then she's out of luck.

"Abe? Say something."

Why? You said it all, he thinks.

"A year and a half," he finally manages, hands tightening on the wheel. What a difference, taking this bridge over the Saint Regis River with Sharon Oaks at the beginning of the month. "Not even. Last month it was a year and a half, now it's down to . . . And you can't even . . ." Abe's jaw keeps working, but no more words come out.

"I've known you for a long time, Abe." Alex sounds sad. More than that, she sounds tired. "Let's call this . . . Systemic . . ."

"Systemic Necrotizing Periarteritis."

"Let's call it what it really is, Abe: the Latest Excuse."

Abe hears the capital letters in her voice. "What's that supposed to mean?"

"C'mon, Abe. You know." Alex turns away from the road, toward him. When she speaks, her voice is flat. She lays out her case like she's giving a math lesson. "You hurt your knee running. Fine. But you didn't even try to work out again for seven years.

"You couldn't write because you didn't have a decent computer. Okay, so we got you a new laptop. And did you write more? Or did you eat shit on Netflix all morning?

"You met that agent. You two were back and forth for a while. But as soon as she wanted to sign you, you 'forgot to answer' her email. For a year.

"You had that blog post go viral, then you stopped blogging because all the new followers were too much pressure. You had a tweet go viral, then you quit the platform because it was toxic. You say you want to be successful. You want people to see your work. But Abe . . . whenever anyone looks your way, you run and hide. Then you get depressed because you're not successful. It's exhausting."

"Is my company so terrible?" His tone is joking, but the words are thick with unshed tears. "I'm talking about sixteen, maybe seventeen months here. You can't put up with me for that long, then go on your merry way? I won't even know the difference."

Alex shakes her head and sits back again. "You think I trust these last few years? Working out, buying new clothes. Tai Chi meditation class." She presses her fingers to her cheeks. He hears a quiver in her voice, but her eyes are dry, her jaw hard. "We've been here before, Abe. This is what you do. Only this time, instead of waiting around for something to happen, you're waiting around to die. No. Just, no. I can't. I'm done."

It's a real no; he hears it in her voice, her face is a closed door. Still, Abe wants to beg. He takes a left, away from the water. They'll be at the airport in a matter of minutes.

"You're a drifter, Abe. That's not going to change because you're sick. I can't handle it anymore."

I'm not "sick," Abe thinks, *I'm fucking dying over here.* Abe pulls into the parking lot, leaves the engine running. He doesn't want to be near Alex any longer. She realizes he's not going to turn the car off. She runs her fingers through her hair, clears her throat.

"Can I please have a hug?" Her voice is small.

Abe wishes he had it in him to curse her out, tell her to shove the hug up her ass. Or at the very least, say no. Where's the steroid rage when he needs it? Instead, Abe gets out, grabs Alex's rolling bag from the back seat, and brings it around to her side. Then he holds Alex. The feeling makes him sick. He also never wants to let go.

HOW TO FLIRT WITH DEATH

by Dominick Deer Woods

Don't make eye contact
with another terminal patient
lest you see your lie reflected.
Smile
determined enough to inspire
desperate enough to illicit
GoFundMe donations.

Don't despise your body for its failings.

You better *fight like hell.*
Show the battle, not the casualties.

Try not to hate this ruse you've been given, your only life.

When you become pain
and thoughts narrow
to a funnel
Be Brave™.

When the time comes, spit in his eye to make Death
    blink first.

Fourteen

e've been here before, Abe opening his eyes in the dark, looking at the slanted roof above his childhood bed, Uncle Ghost gently snoring across the room. It's been three weeks since Alex asked for a divorce. Since the airport hug everything has been playing out by text. Alex packed up Abe's stuff and moved it to the sunroom at the front of the house for when he's ready to claim it. Susa (the divorcée from Alex's birthday dinner party) is moving out of her single-girl condo and into what was Abe's home office. Abe and Alex only have one joint bank account, for shared expenses, and Alex offered to take care of closing it out and sending him a check for his share. She asked if he was also going to take half of her bank account. "That's mostly your dad's money," he texted, "why would I?"

"You supported me while I got my master's, it's in your rights," she wrote back. "And you have to be pissed. You have every right to want some payback."

Abe took a break from texting her at that point, as he usually did when she seemed to be seeking comfort. He's angry, sure, but more than that it feels like his heart is melting, leaving a hollow space in his chest, filling his limbs with lead. He'd take a thousand agonizing autoimmune disorders over the emotional torment he's feeling. It's nothing to text about though, so he faded from the conversation until some new bit of housekeeping came up.

Since they don't have children, the dissolution of their marriage is straightforward. Alex took care of all of that as well, emailing him paperwork. Once Alex files everything, the two of them will need to schedule a court date and appear in front of a judge.

Alex sent him pictures of their CDs, DVDs, and books, and texted him, "Take anything you want. Do you want to send me a list, and I'll box it up for you? Or do you want to do it when you get back?" Court date or no, Abe can't picture returning to Miami. He doesn't want her to have to unbox everything after he's dead, so he texts to leave it for him. In taking over the arrangements, offering him first dibs on not just entertainment but everything—furniture, lamps, kitchen implements, artwork—Abe senses guilt. "I'm sorry, I know this is all happening because of me," she texted one night. He didn't answer.

His family was shocked, almost to a person, and that person was Adam. Everyone else had seen fun, freewheeling Alex having a blast on vacation. Adam had seen the desperation beneath her behavior, noticed all the time she spent alone in her room, or with them and not Abe. He was still sad for Abe—they all were—but Abe's family seemed to be taking a wait and see attitude. There was no shit-talking against Alex, no mention of other fish in the sea.

What else happened in those three weeks? Abe didn't post about the divorce on social media, but he did finally spill about his illness. *I'm sorry to do it like this*, it began, the cliché every Facebook post as memento mori uses, *but I don't have the bandwidth to approach you one on one. I have an autoimmune disorder called Systemic Necrotizing Periarteritis. It's not looking good. I'm back on the Rez for some much-needed family time, so if any of you have anything pressing to say to me, better leave it here in the next year or so. Know that even if I've let weeds grow in the path of our friendship, I still love you.*

He got calls from his oldest friends, and his closest. Three out of four ran into reception issues, so they ended up texting back and forth instead. People responded to his Facebook post, too, and they texted as well. Some days he could barely move—a symptom of the divorce and not the disease, Abe is sure—so he'd lie in bed all day, reading responses and messages.

A friend from his writers' group sent him a selfie. Larissa was an aspiring poet who looked like an Afro-Latina Amélie—impish grin, sad, dangerous black eyes peeking from an oval face surrounded by a bushel of black curls. He was surprised to see fresh, jagged scars running above her jaw from her mouth to her ear on one side. The impish grin was replaced by a wide, winning smile, with several missing teeth on the scarred side of her face. Apparently, she'd swerved to avoid an accident with a guy driving the wrong way on a one-way street and hit a tree going forty.

"The scars I don't mind . . . believe it or not," she texted, "not *so* much . . . but the teeth are . . . hard to live with."

Abe believes it. Romance authors love to give beautiful women one "flaw"—a mole, or a slanted tooth—that serves to underline how beautiful the rest of her face is. The scars on Larissa's face do exactly that, so I guess it's a cliché for a reason. Larissa is also right about the other thing, though—there's nothing cute about missing teeth.

"I stumbled on something in an old journal I thought you might appreciate," she texted. "I wrote it while I was processing the accident." Then she sent another picture, a cropped shot of a lined journal in her distinctive penmanship (Abe always thought she'd make an excellent calligrapher). It read "OBITUARY" across the top, then went on to detail her death as a whimsical newspaper posting. Apparently, the accident happened fourteen months ago and, according to her fictitious obit, she'd "passed away quietly" in the hospital from unnamed complications. She called herself an "aspiring writer, poet, and muse" who left behind "two beloved cats, a hoard of jilted lovers, five hundred unpublished poems, and her much-discussed and cherished Dominican ass." She claimed to spend her days haunting Irish pubs and being an imaginary friend to children around the world.

Then she texted some self-critique, as writers do. "How does one pass away . . . and why did I call it quiet? Perhaps I'd go screaming to my death LOL . . . I think you should write your own little obit . . . it's quite cathartic . . ."

"Oh, that's good," Abe texted back. "I wish I'd thought of it."

And so, after several drafts in Budge's leather notebook, this is what Abe came up with:

Abraham John Jacobs of Ahkwesáhsne, NY (and Miami, FL; and Richmond, VA; and Syracuse, NY), walked on yesterday, May 22, 2018. More specifically, after discovering he'd left his boots in the fridge, Mr. Jacobs took his life, held it down, and made it eat the wrong end of a shotgun. In unwritten novels, stories, plays, and essays (perfect seeds inside his mind), and in dozens of unpublished poems of varying degrees of quality, Mr. Jacobs illuminated the human condition. Or maybe he just talked shit about people, it's tough to tell the difference. Had he finished these works, or published these poems, perhaps any place he'd lived would have fought for the right to parade his body through the streets with a jazz band in tow, rather than forgetting he'd ever been there at all. Mr. Jacobs is survived by every family member he ever knew and loved, apart from Tóta on his mom's side and Uncle Fritz on his dad's, each relationship also of varying degrees of quality. He met his wife of ten years in 1992 and they never stopped loving each other, so at least he did something right. Maybe the important thing.

Except . . . Alex had stopped loving him, right? Her leaving him took the exclamation point off the end of his life, and "He met his wife of ten years in 1992 and she left him when she realized he was going to die" is just a bummer ending for an obit. Although Alex had also texted, "I feel like I've stepped into an alternate reality and can't find my way back" a few days ago, so maybe some part of her still loved him, or loved being with him at least. She had also written that she'd expected him to "put up more of a fight." Abe could sense the expression of a bigger regret coming from her, maybe even a plea to get back together, but the idea appalled him. Apparently, he has more self-respect than I thought he did.

Abe texted Larissa to thank her and share his obituary.

"I love it," she texted back. "What's a 'Tóta'?"

Abe laughed. Reading the text he thought, *The person I'm most looking forward to seeing when I die.* What he wrote was, "I guess you'd say abuela? Only for us there's no gender attached."

Abe thought his obit was funny. I thought it was okay. Woulda been better if he mentioned me, ya' know? Most importantly, writing it made him feel better about his death—who gave a fuck if he'd never published a word? He doesn't know how else to experience the world—or maybe "process" the world is a better word choice—other than by writing about it. He's not sure if he'll really kill himself when he starts losing the plot. When he gets there, he'll just have to see how he feels. His family has plenty of shotguns to choose from. Abe likes the one hanging over the hearth at Sis's place, propped up by a pair of taxidermy deer forelegs. He doubts they'd keep it afterward, but it's old and they won't miss it too much. If he decides to walk that path, of course.

Like I said, we've been here before. Abe lies in the dark of his childhood bed, chronicling his aches and pains, mourning the loss of the time in his life when he wasn't constantly thinking about his body. His joints feel decent this morning, only a dull, distant ache. Abe's not sure what force he's thankful to in moments like this, but he expresses gratitude to whomever may be listening. Since Alex cracked his axis, Abe has been feeling sorry for himself, bumming around his parents' house, waiting for Uncle Budge to call him for the final part of the healing. Although the truth is, Abe's health issues prevent him from even getting a proper wallow going. He can't be all *fuck everything*, not *everything*-everything, because skipping pills causes too much pain to function, and leaving on old bandages ruins his sheets. No, he has to keep popping pills for his immune system and showering twice a day to fight infection. How the hell can you wallow if you're still showering on a daily basis? You can't. In the midst of depression and despair, hygiene is among the first casualties.

Whatever you wanted to call what Abe was doing, I'm sick of looking at it. He's stronger than lying in bed all day implies and I know it. This is the morning I decide to be more than a voice in his head or an image he keeps in his mind on stage; this is the morning I decide to push him.

Abe sees me as a shadow at the edge of his vision, which doesn't surprise him. The only surprise is that the harbingers of death have taken so long to show up. Abe isn't in the mood, so he looks toward me to make me disappear. Instead his vision lands fully on me as I squat by his bed, staring him in the face. I give Abe an upward nod, amused by his shocked expression.

My hair is loosely pulled back in a braid hanging down to my waist. I'm wearing my stage outfit, dad jeans belted low and baggy on the hips, denim jacket with the AIM patch on one shoulder and a red circle-slash over an Atlanta Braves logo on the other, and burgundy Red Wing boots, all items Abe has donated to charity over the years. The only thing he hasn't gotten rid of are the iron feather earrings dangling from my lobes, a gift from his cousin. Abe keeps these boxed up in a desk drawer back home, along with the courage required to vanquish white space on a page. I showed up to give him his courage back.

"I miss that hair," Abe whispers. Abe's currently parts in the middle and falls in curtains to his jaw—where the swelling has gone down, I'm glad to report. The cuts on his lips and face are much less obvious as well. I wonder if we look the same, or if he sees me as he was at nineteen. Maybe we're the same age but living different lives has given us different faces. I bet my nose is ugly-broken; I'm too much of a wise-ass for someone not to have bent it for me at some point. Abe has removed layers of dough from his face, leaving a wrinkle of flesh beneath his chin like a denuded pouch. I've weighed about the same through the years, so I'm probably missing his neck wattle. His skin is unlined but his face has a certain lived-in topography to it; he's no longer a young man.

"Damn right, you miss this hair." I swipe my braid over my shoulder. "It's precontact, precolonial. It's all natural. Women love feeling it brush inside their thighs."

"Is that a fact?" He glances beyond my shoulder, but Uncle Ghost is still snoring away.

"You should know." I push his knee. "Remember how Alex told you she used to look down and pretend you were a woman? Remember how much that turned you on? Then she asked if—"

"Please, please don't reminisce about the times Alex and I had sex. Please."

"You know what? You're absolutely right. Alex is old news. Let's get you a new woman, hey?"

I hold up his phone. Abe opens his mouth to protest, then he falls back with a sigh.

"I downloaded some apps for you. FWB—that stands for Friends with Benefits. It's just what it sounds like; everyone there is looking to hook up. I also downloaded HookUp. Then there's WILD, all caps. WILD is absolute fuckin' Cocoa Puffs. No one has an identity, just a list of sex acts they're looking for. What you do is check off what you want, and everyone in your age range in a fifty-mile radius—I mean, whoever wants to do what you want done—they light up like a sign over a strip club."

"I'm too depressed for this," Abe whispers.

"Speaking of strip clubs, we can go to one. Never seen the appeal myself, but hey—if it gets you outta the house, then let's go get a pile of singles."

"Who do you think you're talking to?"

I laugh at Abe's pearl-clutching tone and scroll furiously through the photos on his phone. "Damn, your pictures are weak." I turn on his camera. "Hey, you finally got your Sonny Landham cheekbones. Too bad they come with a side of Skeletor jaw." I take shots while he ducks, holding his hands up. "Smile."

"I don't want to date."

"Who's talking about dating?" I ask. "I'm trying to get a woman to come over here and ride your dick."

Abe looks appalled.

"What, would you rather have a guy? Then I'd recommend Grindr. Ain't no one looking to date on Grindr."

There's a hitch in Uncle Ghost's breathing. I hold a finger to my smiling lips. Soon, his uncle's breathing smooths out and we hear him snoring again. I stand, motioning for Abe to join me. He throws the covers back, sits up, kicks his feet a few times, then presses his toes against the floorboards. Telling himself they'll hold up just fine, he slides his feet into an old pair of Dad's slippers. I point to the journal on his nightstand like, *Bring it along.*

Abe gives his head a shake, raising his hands like, *What for?*

I frown and mouth, *Just bring it.*

Abe grabs the journal and we make our way out, crouch-walking beneath the low ceiling. In the hallway outside, which is really more of a landing at the top of the stairs, we ease the door shut. Abe rests a hand on the stair railing. Across from us, a cousin is sleeping in Sis's old room. Next to her door, there's a sheet tacked to a beam, covering the entrance to what was Tóta's room before climbing the stairs got too risky for her. Abe's parents sleep there now, a fact Abe doesn't love given that they're not exactly spring chickens, either. But with Abe in town the aunts like to visit, so Aunt Maisy is sleeping in the front room and Aunt Abby is on the couch.

"Damn, Abe." I pitch my voice low. "When did you get so uptight? Didn't you and Alex fuck on South Beach once . . . in the middle of the day?"

"That was Crandon Park on a Tuesday. No one goes to Crandon Park on a Tuesday."

"What about the time you dressed as Lara Croft?" I snort a laugh, less at Abe's newfound prudishness, more from remembering the image. "You wore the harness and everything, only the guns were vibrators."

"Stop talking."

"Abe." I put my hand on his shoulder, ready to tell him hard truth. "If you're going to talk to yourself, you really should keep your voice down."

Abe doesn't look amused; I take some more shots with his phone.

"Jesus, look at you." I hold the screen up to his face. "Anyone sees this picture and you're gonna end up on a watch list."

"I'm fine," he says quietly.

"I get it, you like your mood heavy at the moment." I wrap my arm around his shoulders, leaning close. "Well, picture this, Heavy Heart. You finally publish a poetry collection. It's like John Kennedy Toole and *A Confederacy of Dunces*, or Mary Ann Shaffer and that *Guernsey Potato Pie* book. Your death gets all tangled up in the work, adding to the mystique."

"Or I'm Anna Sewell writing *Black Beauty*"—Abe smirks—"and you're the horse."

"Listen, listen. Touched by the tragic death of an unsung poet, Graywolf snaps it up."

Abe snorts laughter.

"Hey, you don't know." I give him a serious tone for a second. "Don't prereject yourself, Abe. Maybe you're the Mohawk poet laureate, who knows. We'll call your collection *All the Real Indians Died and Twitter Resurrected Them*. Books & Books, in honor of their fallen former coworker, will have copies displayed prominently. One day, Alex will walk by the window. She'll see your poetry collection, go inside, and read the dedication, 'To Cheyenne, whose beauty exists beyond time.'"

Abe frowns, looking at me. "Who's Cheyenne?"

"Who's Cheyenne? She's whoever you want her to be, my friend. Point is, Alex won't be able to ask you, because SNiP will have rotted holes in your brain, or you'll be dead. It'll drive her nuts. She'll be at the grocery store, picking up a grapefruit and wondering if Cheyenne has bigger tits than her, right? She'll play a gig and see a gorgeous woman in the crowd and think, 'Cheyenne, is that you?'

"Then she'll be like, 'Pshh. Cheyenne, what a stupid-ass name. Probably some trashy stripper,' and go on with her day. Until she gets stuck in traffic, and she thinks of Cheyenne, this six-foot, Puerto Rican, Lebanese, Nigerian spin instructor, a biologist saving the Everglades who tutors blind children in her spare time, a tantric-workshop-teaching, double-jointed Savage Fenty model. Cheyenne, who drives a cherry-red rag-top Jeep, keeps your poems in the pockets of her cutoff jeans, and bakes brownies from scratch that have been known to make grown men weep with joy."

Abe looks amused. He keeps his voice low, aware there's only a sheet between him and his sleeping parents (although his father is likely awake; the smell of coffee wafts up from the first floor). "First off, Cheyenne sounds too good for me."

"There you go, prerejecting yourself again." I shake my head.

"Second, is this a revenge fantasy against Alex? Or are we just fantasizing?"

"Can't we do both?" I raise Abe's hand so he's holding the notebook Budge gave him between us. "But you need to get crackin.'"

It's unseasonably warm on the back porch, but Abe's coffee mug still steams in the morning air. He takes one Adirondack chair and I take the other. We sit in silence for a time, waiting for a poem to happen by.

"You think you still got it?" Abe sounds apprehensive. Which is fine. It'll help him later with whittling away excess where he got in the poem's way. My job is to bring the poems to him.

"Don't you worry about me." I ease back into my chair, crossing my legs. "You worry about your end of things."

Abe opens the notebook and rests it over his knee. He holds the pen that was marking the page, dancing it up and down the arm of the chair.

"Damn, I love it here," he says. The sky is lightening from a deep indigo Chagall to the violet of a Van Gogh, revealing the half acre of lawn where Tóta's garden used to be. They'd let it run fallow for a time, then eventually resodded the area. "No one's going to plant there again," he tells me. "Not with the memory of Tóta still lingering."

I grunt in agreement, wondering if the rustling sound in the blackberry brambles is what I think it is.

"Sometimes when I was a kid, I'd hide under the porch and watch Mom and Tóta planting, or walking the rows, pulling weeds. They'd talk, without any idea I was there . . ."

Sure enough, a Poem eases its way out of the blackberry bush. I'm off my chair like a shot. Or what feels like a shot; maybe I'm a little out of shape. The Poem sees me coming and bolts. I give chase across the field, winded almost immediately, but the Poem doesn't count on my long arms. Just before It reaches the tree line, my hands land on Its shoulders. It's soft, slippery, but my touch has startled It into slowing. I get a better grip, drag It toward me, and wrestle It to the ground, feeling the excitement of Its beating heart.

Tóta taught me how to stand and breathe the soil, Abe writes, barely able to see the page by the kitchen light coming through the window. He doesn't think, letting the pen move itself. It's the early stages, where I catch Them and he puts Them down. Soon, too soon, I'm exhausted, and the Poem slips from my grasp.

I stand in the field, hands on my knees, catching my breath. The sky is slate blue; dawn is approaching. Abe listens as the few birds who chirp in winter greet the sunrise. I straighten again, limbered up now, ready to go. Poems are coming to greet the dawn, and I'm here to take down as many as I can. Left and right, I'm tackling, throwing punches, wrestling, grappling. It's me against an army, just how I like it, and I'm determined to go down swinging. Alas, I fail spectacularly, coming up empty. Before too long, I drag myself back to the porch, panting with effort.

"Can you use any of that?" I ask Abe, pointing at the few lines scribbled in his notebook. Sometimes all we get of a Poem is the struggle to capture It, and even if Abe manages to make those remnants work on the page, it's always a pale imitation of the Poem I met. I see these thoughts flicker across Abe's face as he looks at me.

"Nah," he says. He watches me wipe the blood and sweat from my face as I lie back in my chair. "You look worse than I did after Yonder beat me in back of Pyke's." This makes me laugh. Together, Abe and I observe the slow journey of night into day. It's the Golden Hour, and it's filled with poetry. An apology forms on my lips, but Abe cuts me off.

"Get back out there. Maybe don't try so hard this time. You know, just—" Abe gives me *take it easy* hands. "This is supposed to be fun, remember?"

Of course, he's right. I stand up and stretch, then I stroll down the stairs into the field. There are so many of them, wandering in the Golden Hour, where the light is soft and red. Whether they're sad or small, gleeful or giant, all the poems are beautiful. It seems a shame to pick only one, but it's all I can do. I approach with my head bowed, not to spook anything. My hand is in the air, an invitation to dance; let them pick me, hey. Soon, I feel a whisper of gossamer drape over my palm. I might not know how to waltz but I know how to fake it.

"All the Real Natives Died and Tinder Resurrected Them," Abe says, then he writes.

> The dating apps are lousy with Native Americans
> Some women mean they were born here
> in the by-gosh US of A.
> Their profile says Native American and means
> 'Murica, fuck yeah.

> To really be N8V, rent *Frozen River*.
> Listen to Lila Littlewolf's dialogue one thousand times.
> Go to ancestry.com.
> Claim your native identity.
> Misty Upham played Lila Littlewolf.
> Misty Upham was Blackfeet.
> Misty Upham was raped at the Golden Globes.
> The manner of Misty Upham's death
> —whether by foul play, suicide, or accident—
> could not be determined.

> Open your Twitter app.
> Spend one hundred days on the MMIW hashtag.
> Tell me where to find all the Missing and Murdered
>   Indigenous Women.
> Tell me what killed Misty Upham.

Walk a mile in my sister's moccasins* then tell me
how Native you wish you were.

*A Real Indian Poem requires a mention of Native footwear,
eagle feathers, an aphorism, a wolf's howl (preferably
lonely), quilts, and/or the blue corn moon.

Some women mean their great great great grandmother
was a Cherokee Princess.
They don't have a problem with mascots
or massacres.
White-coded women who claim a teenth
while no one claims them
measure their blood in cheekbones,
and old family photographs
check Native American on their dating profile.
They want to be a "sexy" Native
without all the pesky rape, kidnap, and murder.
They want to be exotic
but not to disappear.

I forgive them their ignorance.
I can forgive a lot on Tinder.
It's not life,
not a soul mate.
I'm looking for a woman who will make me forget
for a night
the onrushing rectangle of grave
waiting for me
and who will let me do the same for her.

The French call orgasm the Little Death.
Kenien'kehá:ka call orgasm It Fends Off Death.

They are both correct.

There are two versions of this poem.
One of them is funny,
one of them is angry.
Tell me which one this is.
Good Mind or Bad Mind,
Sky-Holder or Flint,
tell me who wrote this.

These Tinder women
want to know me better.
They want my Longhouse Medicine.
They want the power of my Flint.
They want the wisdom of the Turtle.

Whether I message back
is determined by an algorithm
involving my loneliness
and her attractiveness.

I don't claim to be a good person,
just an actual Indian.

"Weep for the Love You May Have Had?" Abe wonders aloud.
"The Kanien'kéha Word for Hate Sex is Tinder?"

Dad brings the coffeepot out to the porch. He pours Abe a second cup, drops a hand on his son's shoulder for a brief squeeze, then stops short and looks across the lawn. "I swear I can see Tóta in the yard. You see that?"

Dad gestures right at me as I say my goodbyes to the dance partner who offered me company this morning.

"Looks a little too big to be Tóta," Abe says.

Dad grunts and goes back inside. Tired, wrung out, yet invigorated, I approach another Poem. We put the outsides of one foot together, toes facing opposite directions, and clasp hands. We're ready to wrestle, but the air is good-natured rather than violent. Abe's mom comes out, stretches in the sun. She complains about the cold. Abe wishes her a good morning. The Poem and I are testing each other's strength, smiling. Mom squints in the rising sun, looking toward us.

"Friend of yours?" she asks Abe.

"More like a hunting buddy."

"Hey, get your butt inside and sit with your aunts." Mom knows Abe won't be on the Rez forever, one way or another, so he needs to soak up as much family time as he can.

"Okay."

Mom goes back in.

"I've looked in the face of a woman like animals look at the sunrise," Abe says.

"While she's looked at me the same," the Poem answers.

I smile, clapping my free hand to the one gripping mine. We relax our bodies and stand. Abe closes his notebook, hoping the snippet will be enough to find the Poem the next morning. The Poem pulls away, turns, and walks off.

"See you tomorrow?" I yell, before It's out of sight. The Poem gives a finger gun over one shoulder to acknowledge my words, but the gesture could mean anything. Nevertheless, I'm hopeful for tomorrow's work. I walk back toward the porch, stopping ten yards from the steps. In the morning light, Abe looks content. Maybe not happy, but content. That's good enough for me.

"Seeya tomorrow, Abe." I wave, turning around.

"Where you going?" he calls.

"Gonna go run the trails in the Gravel Pit."

"But it's gone."

I turn back and give Abe a smile. "Not if you know where to look."

■ ■ ■

There's a lot more of Abe's day I'd like to walk you through, but I'm worried trying to make you part of the family would be like explaining when something is you-had-to-be-there funny. Plus, it would probably feel like a retread of Thanksgiving. Suffice to say, all this family time, after weeks of family time, has to feel claustrophobic to the younger generation of Jacobs. So when Rè and Rowi . . . these are Sis and Robert's kids, Abe's nephews. Anyway, when Rè and Rowi heard tell of a barn concert, Abe, Brennan, Sis, Robert, and the boys decide to go.

"Just watch yourself." Aunt Abby points at the fading bruises on Abe's face.

"It's not going to be some drunken brawl," Rè says, telling them the band is still in high school.

"Don't worry," Brennan says. "Even Yonder ain't stupid enough to mess with Robert." Sis's husband, Robert, is the Marine Abe was thinking of when Yonder had a knife to his back, the one he once saw drop five men who rushed him at a bar.

The group takes a pair of four-door pickups to get to the party, one smoking, one nonsmoking. They drive the country roads briskly, tree trunks and barbed wire fencing flying past. Abe is always amused when Miami folk complain about driving at night because it's "too dark." Outside the range of their headlights, there's nothing but blackness. How black? Abe's family considers *The Blair Witch Project* a comedy.

After driving far enough that Abe doubts they're still properly on the Rez, their two-vehicle caravan pulls up to a farmhouse surrounded by wooden fencing with the gates open, moving slowly in deference to two large dogs cavorting in the glare of their headlights. The main house is a big freshly painted craftsman, with low gables and thick, tapered porch columns. The barn looks like a new build, everything solid and level, the color of dried blood in the moonlight, the white trim nearly glowing. The doors are rolled wide on either side, the sash windows tilted open. Light pours out, along with some aughts music Abe thinks is Outkast. People mill around outside, smoking, shooting the shit, beer cups in hand. Inside, despite the open doors and windows, the packed bodies make the barn almost balmy. It smells like sawdust and weed. The people in Abe's age bracket wear flannel, baggy dad jeans, and dirty hunting boots, while most of the kids around his nephews' age wear better fits, leather jackets and pea coats, Adidas and Puma sneakers. Abe is somewhere in between.

He finds it ironic he's here to listen to music but Alex isn't. Their years together are longer than the part of his life that came before. Now, without enough time to get over her, there's a very real chance that everything Abe does until he dies will be tainted by her absence. He's angry with her all over again. He welcomes it, so much easier to feel than the crushing sadness.

Scanning the crowd, Abe spots Sharon Oaks standing close to the semicircle around the band. Abe elbows Sis and tilts his chin toward Sharon and her husband, and Sis nods, telling Abe to go ahead. He navigates the crowd slowly, making sure the tip of his cane lands on floorboards instead of feet, trying to keep his cup level. He barely filled it and has no intention of drinking it; he only took it because he doesn't want to answer questions about why he's not drinking.

There's a woman draped over Sharon's shoulders with wavy hair reminiscent of Cheryl Bero née Curly Head. Then the woman laughs, an explosion of sound, like she has something inside she's trying to cough up, and Abe realizes it is her. Abe debates turning around—he doesn't want Cheryl to see him using his cane, let alone sporting the yellow bruises and cuts her brother gave him—but Sharon Oaks spots him before he can hide in the crowd. His cousin crinkles her face in mock distaste like, *this guy*, before breaking into a smile. Cheryl follows Sharon's gaze. When she sees Abe her eyes go wide. Abe makes his way over.

Sharon Oaks raises a hand in greeting but Cheryl cuts her off before she can speak.

"Oh my God, Abe!" Cheryl Curly Head is clearly tipsy, a condition Abe has never seen her in. Her mouth is slack. She slaps her hands to her face hard enough that Abe hears it over the crowd. "Sharon, it's Abe, didja see 'im?"

"He's kinda hard to miss." Sharon grips Abe's hand hard. She's smiling, but there's a warning in her eyes. She gives him an upward nod. "Yonder's handiwork?"

"You should see Yonder . . ." Abe lowers his voice, filling it with grim satisfaction. "Not a scratch on him." This isn't exactly true—Brennan tagged Yonder a pretty good one; "rocked his shit," as they said growing up—but it makes Sharon Oaks laugh.

Cheryl unwraps herself from Sharon Oaks and throws her arms around Abe. Beer slops from his cup onto the back of her jacket and into her mess of wavy hair. His sore ribs groan in protest but he hugs back as hard as he can, holding his cane in one hand, leaning in to her for support. She's pressed against him in full, booze enabling the hug they didn't allow themselves before. Cheryl's hair smells of sweat, smoke, and northern air. Abe feels suddenly dizzy. He tells himself he didn't inhale her scent on purpose, he was just breathing and her hair got in the way. When they pull apart, Abe plants his cane firmly. Cheryl's smile is broad, her eyes buzzy and excited but not glassy.

"Abe Jacobs," Cheryl says. She curls her hand into a fist and bounces it off his chest twice. The gesture puts Abe in mind of someone kicking the tires on a used car they're thinking of buying. "Still skinny."

"Shoulda seen me a couple years ago," Abe says.

"Don' worry about my brother." Cheryl tells him that Yonder is on the Canadian side, trying to get his ex to take him back.

"Where's—?" Abe lets it trail off. He can't remember the name of the good man he's glad Cheryl found.

"Ted?" Sharon Oaks uses the name like a stiff finger poked into Abe's gut. His cousin's voice is flat, her brow arched. "He ain' here."

"Watchin' the kids," Cheryl says.

"How about that?" Sharon eyeballs Abe. *Don't be a dick, okay?*

Abe keeps his face neutral. He catches Cheryl staring at him. Smiling to herself, she quickly looks at the teenage musicians, swigging from the neck of her bottle. Abe tries not to read anything into it; maybe Cheryl is the type to present single when she's not around her family, to reconnect with her prewife, premom self. He looks at the beer he didn't intend to drink and gulps it down.

"So"—Abe gestures at the women—"how do you know each other?"

Sharon and Cheryl's answers overlap, then they chuckle, then they gesture at the same time for the other to go ahead, then they laugh again. Before either woman can explain, the lead singer's voice thunders into the microphone, overwhelming all the chatter, filling the barn. "Thanks for coming out. We're Halcyon."

Abe doesn't know what he expects their first song to be, but it isn't "Ruby, Don't Take Your Love to Town." Their rendition is met with applause and appreciative whoops. Halcyon wastes no time, swinging into "Local God" and following it up with "Cherry Bomb," the drummer screaming into the mic hanging over her kit. The crowd eats it all up, singing along when they can, going wild as each song ends. When they play Cake's "The Distance," Abe realizes that's exactly what he expected their first song to be. He wishes Alex was there to see them. They're good, a group you'd pay money to see. Well, at least a cover charge to see, let's not go nuts. But they're having a great damned time and their young joy is infectious. People will talk about this performance for months, wishing to capture that feeling of being in the barn again. No gig Halcyon plays around here will be as well-received as this one, since the reality of them will always be chasing listeners' memories. But they have tonight, and they play and sing like the world is ending tomorrow.

He feels a tug on his arm, Cheryl pulling his sleeve. "Come with me," she yells in his ear. "I gotta smoke."

Before Cheryl Curly Head pulls Abe away, his cousin catches her. Abe can only hear the edges of their words through the music, but he can guess what they amount to.

You're married, what are you doing?

Having a cigarette in peace for once, without Ted nagging me about it.

Great, I'll come too.

I don't need a chaperone.

Abe wants to tell his cousin not to worry. He wants to tell her he's not that guy. But Abe knows he'll be whatever Cheryl wants, like he's always been.

As Halcyon launches into "Jerry Was a Racecar Driver," Cheryl grabs Abe's hand in both of hers and pulls him through the crowd, too fast for him to spot anyone from his family. The tip of his cane skitters over the floorboards. Abe stumbles and they lurch to the side, but Cheryl manages to keep them both on their feet.

Most of the smokers have moved inside for the music but there are a couple of diehards still outside. Cheryl steers away from them, away from the barn, the chill air refreshing after the heat of the bodies inside. She brings him as far from the barn as possible, practically to the fence at the edge of the property. When she turns around, the shadows from the vehicles cast half of her face in darkness while light from the barn illuminates the other half. A cigarette dangles between her lips. With the threads of Cheryl's gray hair lost to the darkness, the three decades that have passed since they were last together fall away. She removes a lighter from her jacket pocket.

"I felt like being bad," she says, cigarette clamped in her teeth, looking him dead in the eye.

Abe opens his mouth but has no response. Cheryl lights up and takes a long drag. Abe shivers, burying his hands in his pockets, making her laugh. "You're cold? Seriously?"

"Hey, I've been in Miami since ninety-six. Give me a break."

"Yeah." She smirks, looks to the side. "Do you remember, under the bridge that time?"

He knows what she means, still he considers playing coy. *What bridge? I've been under so many bridges with so many people* . . . Instead, he simply nods. She steps closer, raising a hand to his lips. Her touch is light, almost nonexistent.

"Yonder is such an asshole." Cheryl's tone lands between anger and affection. Then she wraps her hand around Abe's neck, pulling him down. He leans into her to keep from falling back. How many times have they kissed before? A thousand? More? It feels like the most natural thing in the world, finding her mouth with his, after all these years. If she'd loved him as much as he'd loved her, then Abe would have waited. He would have returned to her after college. He would have worked at the library or opened a tattoo parlor, brought Cheryl over for dinner with his family every Sunday, moved in, made her Cheryl Jacobs née Curly Head, given his parents more grandchildren. She tastes like the life Abe could have had.

As quickly as she reached for him, Cheryl breaks away from their kiss. She looks at Abe, scoffs, and steps back. Her cigarette has barely grown an inch of ash while she's held it to the side.

"What are we doing?" She looks toward the barn, pulling smoke from her cigarette. The slightly elongated tip falls off.

"Reminiscing?" Abe offers. He looks for guilt over her good husband, what's-his-name, and finds some. Not as much as he'd like— not enough to consider himself a good person, say—but enough to know he's human.

"Ha, right." The barking laugh, like she's punching the world with her sarcasm.

"You save any of my poems?"

"Ha, no." She's still looking toward the barn instead of him.

"Where are they, in your nightstand? Your underwear drawer?" She's trying not to smile.

"No . . . your recipe box."

"Think I used 'em to line the litter box."

Abe claps both hands to his heart like he's been stabbed, and she laughs. The sound is less pained this time. She finally looks back at him.

"You still write?"

"Sure."

"Mohawk poems?"

He shrugs.

"Shit, look at you up here shivering." She raises one foot, steadying herself on his shoulder to do so. The touch has all the intimacy of grabbing a handrail, whatever electricity they'd felt moments ago lost to the night air. Cheryl grinds the butt of her smoke into the sole of her shoe, pocketing it when she's sure it's out, then peers up at him. "What d'you know about being Mohawk, Miami?"

Abe is about to say, *I know enough to know I don't know enough.* But Cheryl walks back toward the barn, not waiting for an answer. It sounds like the drummer is singing again, something by the Alabama Shakes. "Let's get you warmed up, Miami."

"Hey," he calls, "I was tryinna get warm but someone changed her mind."

Several cars away now, Cheryl snorts a laugh. Abe takes a breath and follows. It's easier to maneuver the cane outside, without having to worry about all those people's feet in the barn, but Cheryl doesn't give him a chance to catch her before she's back inside. Abe takes a breath sweet with crisp, winter air. As far as last kisses go, a person could do much worse.

They get home from the barn party at four a.m., just like when they'd return from the dive bars in the old days. The biggest difference is they've managed to do it without any of them puking.

Sis's kids, who prefer weed to alcohol, also managed to avoid getting sick, a rare feat for Abe's generation when they spent a night out in their twenties. I have to think the Jacobs are getting better at life.

Abe wants to get the cigarette smell off himself before going to bed. His bandages also feel grimy, so he decides to shower, change his bandages out, and sleep till the afternoon. Like the flimsy corkboard door, the bathroom's overhead light is a cheap first thought that has never been updated. It lights the bathroom like a surgical suite. Abe strips to the waist. He was thin months ago, when Dr. Weisberg asked him to raise his shirt and spin around (at the time, he'd assumed she was looking for more of the "palpable purpura" or whatever she called his rash); now he looks gaunt.

In the mirror over the sink, Abe examines his torso. The bruising had grown more colorful for a time, even as his pain decreased; now they're a faded yellow-brown, and his ribs barely ache. The apple-sized mark on his chest still looks the worst—a circle of scuffed red around a dusky brownish blur, like Abe's broken heart has been marked. As he eyes it, a flash of black near his waist catches his eye. Abe freezes.

Just scabs, he thinks. *The ones wearing workboots left a lot of marks, that's all.* Except he's been tracking his bruises since the beating at Pyke's, and the friction scuffs had faded after two weeks. Besides, there's no mistaking that wet-tar shine. Abe angles his body sideways, toward the mirror. The lesion dips into the flesh just above his hip. He sees two tell-tale clusters of purple-black punctures near it, soon to become more tarry divots of missing flesh. He takes a shaky breath.

Abe's phone vibrates on the edge of the porcelain sink, startling him. It's an unknown number, area code 518. "Little early for a phone call, Uncle Budge." Abe is surprised by how even his voice is. "You trynna wake the whole house?"

"That house phone rings like damn fire brigade alarm," Budge says. "Ain' no one over there worried about your little electric *bring-bring*."

Abe can't bring himself to reply.

"Heard my daughter bumped into you last night," Budge continues. "Want her to pick you up today? Think it's about time f'that last healin'?"

Abe opens his mouth to agree but there's a catch in his throat. He coughs, trying to kick his mouth into gear. "It's almost five in the morning, Uncle Budge. How'd you hear Sharon saw me?"

"Heard it on the wind." There's a pause, then Budge laughs. "I'm messin' with ya, kid. The drummer is my granddaughter. Sharon called last night to let me know how good she was."

"She was."

"Get some sleep," Budge says. "Be ready in the afternoon."

Abe wants to ask how Budge knew to call, but his great uncle has already hung up.

WHAT I THINK OF WHEN I THINK OF SAVAGE

by Dominick Deer Woods

Here's what happened: Momma spoke Kanien'kéha and English when she started at the Catholic school, but she was too shy to speak in either language. A teacher—white as anybody on *The Lone Ranger* who wasn't Jay Silverheels—came over to where Momma stood against the wall, squatted to face level, and spoke Kanien'kéha. In Momma's mother tongue, this nice white lady encouraged Momma to play with her classmates. Momma smiled, thinking the Catholic school might not be so bad. The nice white lady stood and switched to English for the benefit of another white teacher. "Do you see? They're savages; they don't even teach their children how to talk."

The white women spent years beating the language out of Momma. Momma stopped speaking Kanien'kéha, even at home, and developed a stutter in English.

Here's the poem:

> Teachers pruned scions of my mother's Mother Tongue
> scarring her juvenile skin
> maiming her young mind
>> until curses were all she had left for me.

Here's the truth:
Kanien'kéha has a word for grief and rage mixed together. I don't know what it is, but I feel the emptiness where it was gouged out.

Fifteen

"What happened to your face?" Budge asks Abe, holding the trailer door open for the third and final part of the healing.

"Misunderstanding."

"Misunderstanding how much Yonder Curly Head loves trouble," Sharon Oaks says. She's standing behind Abe, holding two large paper bags that Abe asked her to bring for him.

"Sounds like there's a story there," Budge says. "To do with men and drinking?"

The brass tip of Abe's cane can't find purchase on Budge's metal steps, so Abe moves slowly, holding the cane in front of himself the way an acolyte carries a candle. The pain in his hips and knees is tolerable, and his legs feel weak but not watery. Still, these few steps without the cane feel like walking a rope bridge.

"Good guess," Sharon says, following Abe up the steps. When she reaches Budge's kitchen counter, she squats and sets the paper bags down.

"Thanks for doing the heavy lifting," Abe says.

Sharon points the finger of one big mitt toward him. "Don't be scared."

"I ain' scared, I'm sacred." Abe pronounces it "sacrit," a small joke mocking Native Mystic tropes. Sharon laughs.

On the drive over, in a tone of approval, his cousin said, "Cheryl tells me you were a perfect gentleman."

Abe answered, "It's a lonely life, but it's the only life I know."

"Don't break him, huh, Dad?" Sharon says now. "He's growin' on me."

"He's in good hands, don' worry," Budge says.

Once Sharon leaves, Abe walks toward the kitchen. Budge stops him by resting a hand delicately on his, the one holding the cane. Abe forces a chuckle, embarrassed. "Can't seem to let it go."

Budge plucks the cane from Abe's grip, leaning it against the door jam. "If you still need it, you can pick it up on your way out," his great uncle says.

"You don't think I will?"

"That's the idea." Budge's eyes are merry and inscrutable. At last, he's wearing a t-shirt with an album cover Abe recognizes: Taylor Swift's *1989*.

"Big fan?" Abe gestures.

"Don't knock it 'til you try it."

Abe shuffles to the kitchen, one hand crawling over the counter for support. He removes a green canister from one of the big paper bags and holds it up for Uncle Budge's inspection. Abe points to the logo on the side, the black profile of an Indian in headdress against a yellow circle. "They don't sell this tobacco outside of New Mexico," he says, "but I know a guy."

"Asher."

"Yeah, exactly." It surprises Abe how well Uncle Budge has come to know his family, how the rift between Billings and Jacobs has healed. Abe missed a lot, being so far away. Does Uncle Budge know Asher sold a quilt portrait of one of his guitar-playing, fedora-and-sunglasses-sporting Indians to the CEO of the company? Probably. "But he just supplied the tobacco." Abe pops the lid and runs his fingers through the mixture to show his uncle. "This blend, they don't sell anywhere. Cass worked her magic on it, and it's got all sorts of good stuff for your lungs. You got four cans in here, along with a rolling machine and plenty of papers."

"Y'think I need a rollin' machine? Been rollin' smokes since you were a hiccup in your momma's cycle." Budge hooks a finger into the top of the bag, leaning over to peek inside. His mouth twists into a grin. "Bury me w' whatever I don' smoke, hey?"

"Come on, don't let it go stale." Abe seals the plastic lid on the tobacco can and sets it on Budge's counter. "Freeze it if you can't keep up. Better yet, share the wealth."

Budge grunts noncommittally. *Keep talking, kid, but I'll do what I want,* the grunt says. Or he might be wondering who Abe is, trying to school him on giving excess away. Budge knows more than him that a Mohawk is judged wealthy not by how much they have but by how much they give away. "What's in th'other bag?"

The second is doubled up for the weight. Abe pulls out a giant, wide-mouth jar that once held five gallons of mayonnaise. Mom, Aunt Maisy, and Aunt Abby have been reusing these jars—glass, barrel-shaped, labels long gone—for as long as Abe can remember. The sisters each have one. Since Mom's is filled with beef stew, he asked his aunts to borrow their jars so he could bring more Corn Soup for Uncle Budge.

"Hey, all right." Budge grins.

"I made this on Friday. Sitting around gives the flavors time to mingle. It'll be way better than the first batch I made you." I suppose the timing should surprise Abe, but it doesn't. He made the soup for Budge on Friday because Budge was going to call over the weekend. The fact that Abe couldn't have known Budge was going to call when he made the soup didn't matter; it made Indian sense. He didn't sing into this batch, but he might have let some melancholy seep in—losing Alex has broken the husband part of his identity, and for years—before they were married on paper, in fact—he'd put that number one on his list, above Mohawk, above poet, above brother, or son, or friend. "Aunt Maisy and Aunt Abby will kill me if they don't get these jars back when you're done."

"I'll fill 'em up good, don' worry. I make a mean chili." In the Jacobs family, when you get a full food container, you return a full food container. Returning someone's dishware empty is cursing them to starve, and even though no one would admit to believing such lore, the Jacobs would never return a dish they'd borrowed without putting something in it first.

"Listen . . ." Budge cradles the jar like a baby. "How about you put one of these jars in the fridge, crack the other one open, and heat us up a serving or two?"

"Sounds good."

"Did you bring bread?"

"Ayuh." Abe lost the Northeastern version of "yeah" living in Miami, but now it's back in force.

Budge hands the jar to Abe, walks around the counter, and takes his seat. Abe sets the jar down and opens the utensil drawer. After some digging—there are more kitchen implements than he would have thought—Abe removes the ladle and sets it on the counter.

"So where's your tribute?" Budge asks.

Squatting to grab a medium-sized pot from a floor cabinet, Abe looks up at his great uncle, a questioning expression on his face.

"My soup's not good enough for you?"

"Made it with your own two hands, but it's your Tóta's recipe." Budge spreads his hands and shrugs. "You got Cass and Asher's tobacco. So . . . where's your tribute?"

When Abe stands, closes the cabinet, and sets the pot on the stove, his movements are soft and slow, likes there's a sleeping baby he's trying not to wake. One question, and the air in Budge's trailer grows heavy with the same sensation Abe felt when he saw those odd snails trailing around his feet in Coral Gables. Sounds are distant, yet amplified. Time has left the room, and not in a pleasant way. Decades ago he'd welcomed the idea of stepping on a stage and having all eyes on him, but this goes beyond holding an audience. It feels like he's caught the attention of the universe.

"I made you this soup before." Abe looks at Budge, trying to read his great uncle's expression.

"C'mon, kid. The song was the tribute, you know that."

Abe opens his mouth to protest, but he realizes Budge is right. "How did you know I brought something besides the soup, or the tobacco?" Abe's voice hovers between wonder and exasperation.

"S'how these things work, kid." Budge grins. "You figure it out, be sure to let me know."

"Okay, so I wrote something," Abe says slowly. "For you. Well, with you in mind, anyway. I've been trying to write in that notebook you gave me. I'm rusty as hell, but I'm trying."

Abe and I wrote Budge's poem in bed this morning before passing out. You want to know what it feels like trying to catch a poem? When you get up in the middle of the night to get a glass of water, or use the bathroom, you go through the motions but you're not all there. You're trying not to lose your sleep, so you can fall out when you get back in bed. Catching poems, it feels like trying not to lose your sleep. Sometimes it works, sometimes it doesn't. I think we got a lot of Budge's poem. Maybe even most of it.

Abe twists the lid off the jar of Corn Soup and pours some in the pot to heat. He reseals the jar and rests it on its side in Budge's fridge, beside the full one. "For some reason I tore this poem out of the notebook before I left my parents' house today. It's in my pocket, because I thought I might work up the guts to read it to you. And somehow, you know all about it."

"Not all about it." Budge squints at Abe. "I din't know you wrote a poem, but I knew you'd have somethin'. Somethin' jus' from you. That's what you have, innit?"

"A piece of myself, you mean?"

Uncle Budge shrugs.

"And if I didn't?"

Budge shrugs again. "Then this healing wasn't for you," he says.

A be cleans the dishes quickly, anxious to be done. If you'd told him two months ago that the future him would be in a hurry to take his clothes off and get a massage from an Elder, Abe would have laughed in your face. Yet here we are.

Budge sits on the living room couch with his head bowed, Sis's balm close at hand. This time the sheet laid over the carpet is green-and-white gingham. Something has been nagging at Abe, and cleaning up from their soup gives him the chance to ask. "Uncle Budge?"

Budge lifts his head as though roused from a doze, looks at Abe, and raises his eyebrows.

"What do black shells mean?" Abe feels stupid asking, profoundly un-Mohawk, but if anyone would understand the sign he saw, it's Budge. "Like, what do they symbolize . . . for us?"

"You mean like wampum, in a belt?"

"Maybe." Abe turns back to the sink. He can't look at Budge. This is not like asking him to pronounce a word in Kanien'kéha, this is like admitting colonization succeeded and Abe's mind belongs to the white man. "I'm wondering if there's a legend about them, or if they have a meaning."

"Death."

Abe looks sharply at his great uncle, but the old man's head is already bowed, his eyes closed again. Abe hopes Budge is gathering himself for the final step of the healing rather than nodding off.

"Shit that's what Mom said, too." Abe hoped the Billings might have a different take, being more traditional than the Jacobs. "Really, though? Just death?"

"Yeah." Budge cracks an eye at Abe. "Why?"

"Not like, the end of a journey or something? Or change, some kind of big change?"

"Only you can interpret wampum. Those clamshells only got two colors, white n' purple. Different parts a the same shell. You only got so many ways to put 'em together, so when you use 'em to tell a story, it's what you make outta it. Like dreams. They say dreamin' of losin' teeth is fear of gettin' old, but that's not for everyone. You could be afraid your dick won't work. I'm worried no one's listenin' to me. This one's sad she's wastin' her life on a bad marriage. This other one's scared a dying.

"Wampum works the same." Budge holds one gnarled hand out, palm up, then covers it with the other. "I could put white shells on a purple background and I'm tellin' you times were bad before but now they're okay. You could do the same pattern, only you're tellin' me that bad times have us surrounded." Here, Budge swaps the position of his hands, switching top for bottom. "So it don' matter what black shells mean t'us, it's what they mean t'you." Budge looks intently at Abe, who finally nods. "What shells are we talkin' about, anyway?"

The dishes are done and resting on the drying rack. Abe moves around the counter and takes a stool, wiping his hands on his pants, hoping his impatience doesn't show. "Nothing."

"Not 'nothin', what?"

"Just some shells." When Budge won't drop his gaze, Abe sighs. "Spiral shells that should've been either tan, yellow, or white. Only they were dead black instead."

"If they spoke to you, then they were supposed to be black." Budge raises his brows like, *Tell me I'm wrong.* "And what did these black shells mean to you?"

Abe looks through the window above his great uncle's couch. A front yard that's more dirt than lawn, where gravel that once marked a driveway spread like a rash. Beyond that, a country road like any other, lightly traveled, but ridden like the devil by the few cars using it. Abe rarely considers how different Miami is from where he grew up, until he comes home and sees it everywhere. He turns his attention back to Uncle Budge.

"You come to a stop sign, right?" Abe leans back against the counter, trying to convey what he'd felt. "It's not like you read it. I've seen stop signs in Wynwood—this artsy fartsy section of Miami— covered with graffiti and stickers, but they still did their job. You know what it means, so you do it without even thinking about it. These shells felt just like that. It felt like something I already knew about. I was sure when I came home, someone would be like, 'Oh, yeah, black shells mean your old life died and a new one's being birthed from the husk.' Or they'd pull out a book and I'd remember I read it a long time ago, and it had a scene with black shells."

"Atokén:tshera," Budge says.

"Atokén:tshera, right." The word means knowledge and premonition at the same time.

"Abe, how many Kanien'kéha words do you know?"

That's not something you ask, Abe thinks. Or at least, Abe has never asked anyone, and I've never heard anyone ask someone else. Like asking someone "how much" or "what percentage" they're Native—only non-Natives do that shit. But Budge is an Elder and his great uncle; Abe has to answer.

"I don't know," he says. "A couple dozen, maybe?"

Budge nods like he expected as much. "Why d'yuh think y'know Atokén:tshera?"

Abe shrugs. He'd heard Tóta use it talking about tending her garden. When he asked what it meant, the word stuck in his mind because he found the idea fascinating, that understanding could run so deep it uncovered the future.

"This is your vision," Budge tells him. "If you don' know, then no one's gonna."

There it is, "vision," the word Abe doesn't want to use. It isn't mystical, it just is. Like when a book title he hadn't seen popped into his mind, like coming to a road sign.

"You know what I found out when I tried to look up what black shells mean?" Abe asks. "They don't start out black; pollutants make them that way. That's something you never see in postapocalypse movies, is it? Miles of beaches covered in black shells." Abe drops his eyes. He can feel Uncle Budge looking at him.

"Think you have that Kanien'kéha word, so you'd have a name for what happened to you on the beach when you saw those shells?" Budge asks.

"It wasn't the beach."

"Good. That was my point." Budge sounds irritated for the first time.

"Okay." Abe is irritated, too.

"Look at me."

Abe does. His great uncle is leaning forward, elbows on knees, his normally jovial face lined with intent. "You have a vision, Abe. Not a Mohawk vision, your vision. That's good, because there is nothin' more Mohawk than havin' your own vision. You know why it was so easy to stop most of us speakin' the language? Because no one could agree what to call anythin'. Snow wa'n't jus' snow, it was 'what we pack tight and throw.' It was 'covers where we live in popcorn.' It was 'walking across in special shoes will make you float.' It was 'lay down and swing your arms and legs to draw crows.' How you chose t'describe snow told the listener who you were. And if you could make 'em laugh with how you described snow? Shit, then the two a youse were halfway to bein' brothers.

"From what I heard an' what I know, black, in beadwork, means death. But I ain' the be-all, end-all on bein' Mohawk, kid. No one is, as far as I can tell. So what do those black shells mean to you?"

Abe has been wondering this for months now, but as Uncle Budge walks him through it, the answer comes without hesitation, as if it's been there all along. "They told me to stop. Stop drifting through life, stop letting random storms push my boat. They meant come home and learn to row."

"Okay." Budge nods. "Good. Are you ready to read t'me?"

Abe blinks, surprised at this transition. But also surprised to realize he's more than ready—he wants to read the poem to his uncle. He stands to do it, almost like being back at the coffee house.

RAKENONHÁ:'A (MY UNCLE)

My Uncle has a healer's hands
if you believe the rumors
he's knit broken bones
shrunk tumors
made splintered minds whole

Before the rumors my Uncle
lived barstool to barstool sweeping
remnants of the night before
mopping vomit
hauling trash
he crashed on couches
and in cars slept in
toolsheds and barns

Before he became a pye-dog
he held his sister
in the room they shared where
their stepfather
execrated the world

The Healer hides
that room
behind his smile
his hands speak in riddles
    "When does a gas station become a battleground?

... When my stepfather is standing in line for cigarettes."
My Uncle's hands clench and clamor
   "When will healing be done?
   When will we seek our revenge?"

My Uncle's hands
are his reknown
my Uncle's hands hold
the pain of our Nation
in their cracks and creases

Budge sits on the couch in silence, staring off. His eyes are wet but the tears don't run. While waiting for a reaction, Abe stops himself from speaking more than once. He holds the paper where the poem is written between them like a shield, afraid to move.

"Rakenonhá:'a ain' the right word," Budge finally says. He speaks the Mohawk word for "great uncle," but Abe doesn't catch it.

"That's good, Uncle Budge, because that was my point," Abe says dryly.

"Oh, no—not my own medicine." Budge's face has been shadowed by emotion, but he brightens a bit. He pantomimes spitting. "I hate it, iotskâ:ra, it's bitter, bitter." He clears his throat and swipes at his eyes, sniffling. "You must like watchin' old men cry, kid. Jesus, why would you read me that?"

Abe doesn't know how to answer, so he keeps silent.

"Damn. You just wrote it all out, didn't you? My whole life."

"I'm sorry, Uncle Budge. It came to me, that's all. It's not like I'm publishing it."

"Go ahead, if you think anyone's gonna wanna read it. Shit, no'n knows me off the Rez, whatta I care?" Budge rubs his palms across his forehead. "Damn it. Isn't poetry supposed to be made-up?"

"Depends on the poet, I guess. Emily Dickinson says you tell the truth but you do it slant."

"Shit, that makes me a poet already then." This time Budge laughs. "Jesus." He shakes his head and stands. Then he thinks better of it and sits back down. He looks at his hands, lying palm up in his lap. Softly, Uncle Budge thanks Abe. Or the Creator, depending on how you want to interpret it. "Niawen'kó:wa. Read it again, would you, Abe?"

Stripped to his boxer briefs, Abe lies back on the gingham sheet covering Budge's living room rug. He watches dust dance in the sunlight, then Budge pulls the living room curtains closed. When Budge kneels beside him, Abe feels it again, that stillness like stepping outside the flow of time, plus a wave of warmth. Lying next to Budge is like being near an open oven door.

Budge starts by working Sis's balm into the places where he mapped Abe's pain during his second healing. Prior to that his throbbing joints and sore muscles changed day to day, hour to hour. Since the mapping, Abe can't decide if the suffering has remained in the same places, or if he's fooling himself. Feeling Budge's touch now clarifies his affliction. Tendrils of pain have seeped around since his last visit, the way a drop of dye bleeds through fabric, but for the most part it's been pinned. Abe imagines a monster, all thrashing tentacles and snapping teeth, clamped to the earth with metal bands.

"Don't worry about that," Budge gestures toward Abe's side, at the new square of gauze taped to his ribs. "That's just desperation. We got it on the run."

"Do we?"

Budge grunts an affirmative. He continues to dip his fingers into the tin of Sis's balm, working the flesh and skin around Abe's joints. Budge also uses ointment on the remaining bruises Yonder and the boys gave him. "Hold still," he says, wiping at the fading wounds on

Abe's face. "Your sister's ointment makes her a part of this healing. Do you believe that?"

Abe nods; he does.

"Good. Your uncle gave tobacco so he could be part of this healing; do you believe that?"

Abe says yes.

"Adam pointin' you toward gratitude on Thanksgiving makes him part of this healin.' Do you believe that?"

"I do," Abe says.

Budge tells Abe riding to the doctor in Malone with his Uncle Dan, Aunt Maisy, and Aunt Abby makes them part of his healing; that sharing a room with Uncle Ghost makes him a part of the healing; that Tóta's recipe in the glass jars makes her part of his healing; that his parents sheltering Abe while he's here makes them part of his healing; that their blood in his veins and stories in his heart are why Abe is here. Budge throws the stories of their ancestors into the healing for good measure. Abe agrees with his great uncle on all counts.

"You see that, Abe?" Budge nods toward a large wooden mask, hanging to the right of the hall, above the record player. Abe's not sure how he missed it before. The mask has to be more than two feet long. Half of the features are warped, the product of a skilled carving job. The whole mask is painted maroon and the eye sockets are lined with shimmery metal. Shaggy hair frames it on both sides.

"Yes, I see it."

"One night I dreamed about it." Budge shakes his head. "'Cept it wa'n't a mask yet. It was a two-hundred-year-old basswood tree, back in the woods a hunnert yards or so." While Budge speaks, he continues to massage Abe. "It was the year I quit drinkin.' I was white-knucklin' my sobriety, diggin' in like a bat grabs a wall in the daytime. One morning, I'd had it. It was still dark out but I didn't care. I got dressed to go to the liquor store. I'd wait on the stoop, and when Curtis Bond opened, I'd slap a twenty in his hand and get back a pint of Bulleit Bourbon for my trouble. Only when I opened the front door, instead of goin' up the driveway, my feet took me around back, into the woods. I decided to walk the cravin' off with th' trees. Right when dawn hit, I looked up an' saw that old basswood tree, five feet across, eighty high, all knotted up the trunk. I took out my pocketknife an' started carvin' on it. After that first time, I took my good carvin' knife out there. Every day I'd carve on that tree.

"It took a couple weeks to understand I was makin' a mask. Once I did, I cut it off the tree and brought it home. I took my time carvin' it. The day I added horsehair, I wa'n't diggin' into sobriety so hard. By the time I put copper around the eyes, I stopped bein' an alcoholic who don't drink an' became an ex-drinker. That was a long time ago. Nowadays, I see myself as more of a nondrinker."

"What's the difference?"

"You ain' never been an addict." Budge rests a hand on Abe's bandages. "Start doin' what God put you here to do and you'll learn all about addiction. Only you're lucky, Abe—your addiction feeds you. Might suck the life outta people close to you, but it feeds you."

"You don't make it sound all that great, Uncle Budge."

"Not everythin' we're put here to do feels great." Budge stands, balls his hands into fists, pushes them into his spine, and leans back. His vertebrae pop like knots in a fireplace. "You ran from what God put you here to do. You know it, so you made yourself suffer. This is your body tryin' to wake you up, innit.

"Take your bandages off, stay a while. I'll be back."

Abe does as he's told, peeling the bandages from his shins, calves, and torso, and laying them on Budge's couch. Budge returns carrying a rattle made from a turtle shell in one hand and something cool and scary in the other—something Abe recognizes but didn't know existed in Mohawk culture.

"Is that what I think it is?" Abe can't keep the surprise from his voice.

Budge sets his turtle rattle on the couch, then walks toward the kitchen, lightly tossing his weaponized objet d'art—an antique tomahawk pipe—from one hand to the other. Budge peels the lid back on Sis and Asher's tobacco mix. A sweet, heady wave of aromas hits Abe's nose. Budge tamps a serious pinch into the bowl of the pipe, which is also the butt of an axe head.

"Could you hurt someone with that?" Abe asks.

Budge holds the pipe sideways toward Abe so he can get a good look. A filigreed steel blade and bowl atop a foot and a half of polished hard maple. There are two additional, decorative steel bands across the length, and a matching mouthpiece on the end of the shaft.

"Whether you wanna smoke or chop, this'll do the job. But we didn't fight with these. We made 'em to symbolize peace n' togetherness." Budge is running his fingers through the tobacco and letting it fall back into the can, inhaling the scent. "Really, it stands for how hard it is to keep th' peace. We'd settle our differences, then make one a these n' share a smoke. We'd agree to fight for peace."

"Where'd you get this one?"

"Family heirloom." Budge drops a wink. Abe wonders if his great uncle lifted it from the wall of a museum. Good for him if he did.

"And you need it now because . . . ?"

"If this don' work, then we chop the bottom half a your legs off."

"Uncle Budge, you are painfully unfunny."

"Says you." Budge hooks a thumb over his shoulder, toward the kitchen. "We've eaten corn. That's the first part. Tobacco is another." Budge strikes a match and puffs on the pipe, seasoning the air with sweet smoke. He tucks the blade of the tomahawk pipe between the cushions of his couch to keep the bowl from spilling. "This story is the next part."

"How many parts are there?"

"Five hunnert, somethin' like that."

Abe laughs.

"Do y'now Raweno?"

Abe shakes his head. Budge dips his fingers into the Magic Mend balm. Abe sighs, anticipating his touch.

"Raweno means 'big voice.' It's our name for the Creator. One a th'names, I should say." Budge rubs his hands together to soften the balm and warm it up. He works Sis's herbs into Abe's lower legs and feet, into his ribs with the new lesions, then he starts to massage Abe again.

"This was before the time when dogs could talk," Budge says, "because nothin' even was yet. Then Raweno, Big Voice, came along. Like any artist when they finish somethin' they're proud of, Raweno took some time to bask in Their handiwork. They wandered the earth, checkin' out everythin' They'd made. They was pretty darned pleased with the job They did. All Their creation needed was an audience, so They decided to make people. Just then, Raweno saw an old man wobblin' toward Them.

"Raweno couldn't believe what They was seein'. 'Who are you?' They asked.

"'I am Ónhka,' the old man said. 'I am wanderin' the earth, enjoyin' everything I made.'"

Abe giggles, he can't help it. His eyes are closed but he hears the smile in Budge's voice as his uncle continues the story.

"Now Raweno didn't wanna disrespect Their elders, but They put a lot of time and effort into buildin' the earth. They wasn't about to let some old stranger who shouldn't even be there hog all the credit.

"'Pardon me,' said Raweno, 'but *I* just finished makin' the earth and *I* am enjoyin' *my* creation and everythin' *I* made.'

"'If you say so,' Ónhka said, yawning. 'All that creation wore me out. I'm too tired to argue with you.'

"'I'll tell you what, Ónhka,' said Big Voice, 'ya see that big mountain in th' distance? Let's have us a contest to see who can move it farther. Whoever moves the mountain farther is stronger, which means they've gotta be the one who made all this.'

"That sounded good to Ónhka, so he volunteered to go first. The two a them turned away from the mountain and closed their eyes. Ónhka grunted with effort. When the two a them turned back, Raweno was shocked all over again. The mountain had moved. You or me wouldn't have noticed it, but Raweno knew every blade of grass on Earth, so They could tell. The both of 'em turned away again so Raweno could take Their turn.

"The commotion was so loud that Ónhka whipped around to see what was goin' on. Too bad for him, because Raweno was pretty riled up. When Ónhka turned around, the mountain smacked him dead in the face. The old dude looked at Raweno with his nose bent to the side, one eye knocked half out, an' his jaw all crooked.

"'You're stronger than me,' Ónhka said.

"'Okay,' said Raweno, 'I'm makin' people now, so you gotta go.' They'd seen that Ónhka had a little power, and They din't want him messin' with people.

"But Ónhka begged Raweno to let him live. If he was allowed to stay on Earth, Ónhka promised t' use his powers to make sick people better.

"'I will travel in dreams and speak t' the people you create while they're sleepin',' said Ónhka. 'I will ask them t' carve a mask in my image from dying trees. When they wear the mask, it will bring me forth, and I will help sick people get better.'

"Raweno liked the idea, so They agreed. With one catch: Raweno made Ónhka promise to never heal his face so that everyone would recognize him and he couldn't try anything tricky. That's where my mask came from. I carved it t' keep my hands away from a bottle, an' my mind off a drink. I din't know it at the time, but I also carved it t' call on Ónhka when I need him."

With Budge's hands working on him, Abe can almost believe a supernatural being is about to appear and make him well. He starts giggling again, wondering if herbs were all Sis put in the tobacco. "Uncle Budge, I cannot wait for you to put that thing on."

"No need, kid," Budge says. "Think a' that mask like the door Ónhka uses t' get in."

"If you say so." Abe can't stop smiling. He feels drunk, or doped.

Budge gives Abe's ankle a friendly pat and rises to his feet, knees popping. He grabs the pipe from between the couch cushions, and fires it back up, making little grunts of satisfaction with every puff. The smell of the pipe is richer than Sis's home-rolled cigarettes, a musk that's almost floral.

Budge goes back to the kitchen counter and returns with the American Spirit canister tucked in the crook of his elbow. Cradling the tobacco pipe in the same arm, Budge walks to the mask hanging on his wall. He pulls out a handful of tobacco and herbs and stuffs it into Ónhka's distorted mouth, where it hangs like grass from a cow's jaw. Budge takes a huge pull from the pipe and expels it back toward Abe, more smoke than should come from a single exhale. Walking back, Budge continues to puff on the pipe until the room becomes hazy. By the time he reaches Abe, the pipe is kicked. Budge adds more tobacco. His chest heaves with the strength of his pull, and he blows smoke across Abe's shoulders, arms, and face, over his torso and legs.

Kanien'kehá:ka don't have sweats, but the air in Budge's trailer grows so thick with smoke it's what Abe imagines a sweat must feel like. The furniture has become suggestions, silhouettes that could be anything—rock formations or mounds of earth. His great uncle is a shadow in an impenetrable cloud of grayish white. No way this much smoke came from one pipe. Ónhka's mask is still visible in the haze, like it's hanging in midair. There might even be a fig-ure behind it. Abe thinks of Tóta's last dinner, surrounded by the shadow-men she greeted like old friends. One of them could be wearing the mask now, still invisible to Abe's eyes. Or it might just be the edge of the wall leading back to the hallway, obscured by the smoke. Or maybe it's an open Longhouse door, leading back to the ancestors.

The turtle rattle goes off in a burst over Abe's forehead. Budge's guttural voice fills the air with a song that would be limited by words. A shiver runs through Abe's body, twisting him on the floor even though he's not cold. Every hair stands on end, like his pores are drinking in the smoke. The tobacco is for Ónhka, the sound of the rattle is to frighten the sickness from Abe's body, the song is to heal his soul, and together all of it has him stuck fast, like a swaddled newborn. He feels awestruck and humbled as some unknowable Power trains Their dread regard on him. Abe's family is in this smoke, the Turtle Clan is in this rattle, his ancestors are in Budge's song, and Abe is overwhelmed by it all. For a moment, he resists, feeling like it's more than he deserves; then he embraces it at last.

Abe shakes all over. He sees the pain inside his body—pointed and black like those snail shells—rattled by Budge's song. The sensation reminds him of a loose tooth wiggling back and forth, except it's everywhere, in his joints, inside his muscles, embedded in his torso, behind his eyes. The happy accidents and painful struggles that brought him into existence flash through Abe's mind. Tears leak from his eyes and tickle across his face. Budge's song is beautiful. The only missing piece is the drum.

Then Abe hears it, thudding in his ears: it's his heart, beating, keeping time with Budge's song.

Budge waves his rattle and swings his pipe over the dim outline of the couch. The bandages Abe left there rise. Only it's not actually the bandages; Abe can't make sense of what he's seeing, so his mind has coughed up something familiar. If the bandages were made of soft white light threaded with sickly red and putrid yellow, then they would look something like this gossamer jellyfish, swimming in the smoke. Budge uses the flat side of the tomahawk pipe to sweep the mass of light toward Abe. Fear makes his heart pound faster, and Budge's song speeds up in time. When the shining jellyfish hangs above him, the rattling in Abe's body steadies, becoming an upward pull.

Standing over Abe, Budge swings his arms, herding the light in a circle. He starts slowly. Abe feels a tugging inside. Budge moves his arms faster. His song keeps rhythm and Abe's heart pounds like a horse at gallop. With each pass of his uncle's arms, the pull inside Abe's body grows stronger. Budge increases his speed, voice high, yipping fast and loud. The ball of light pulses, timed to Budge's yelps, to Abe's sprinting heartbeat. Foreboding grips Abe, along with a manic energy, something like when a roller coaster reaches a peak before rushing downward.

His great uncle's arms are twin cyclones, dark blurs in the smoke. The rattle is constant, the song reaching a feverish crescendo. A ripping starts inside Abe's toes and fingertips. He sobs, a noise he can't hold in. The rending travels up his limbs, tearing at his flesh as Budge voices a string of high cries. Abe's torso feels like it's being torn in pieces, his head ripped in two. Abe wails. The agony is mercifully brief. Ahead of the blur of Budge's circling arms, the gauzy light has morphed into a wet, fetid, purple-black mass.

Budge's voice stops, leaving only the turtle rattle, the drumbeat of Abe's heart. The thing above him no longer pulses in time; instead it crackles, like a bulb that's about to blow. Budge steps away from Abe, his swings taking the noxious mass with him. The walls and ceiling are gone. A light breeze carries the billows of smoke from where Budge's trailer once stood, shrouding the tree trunks like fog. Abe catches a glimpse of sky as Budge drives the mass before him. Then, his great uncle slows, coiling like a spring, and the repellant light grows brighter. Budge hops into a final turn, whipping his arms in an arc, leaning over like a batter who's getting all of a pitch. The dripping shape soars through the air, its passing staining the smoke. It sails toward the outline of the trees behind Budge's trailer, starting to dissipate as it goes. By the time it reaches the woods, whatever Budge tore loose from Abe is gone. Relief floods his body even as his consciousness fades. He's been hollowed out— gnarled roots ripped from brackish depths inside him, and filled instead with sweetgrass and flowers, crisp river water and dappled sunlight. Abe wonders if he's really passing out or just merging with the smoke for a while.

One of them is laughing, delirious with joy, but I can't tell who.

be and Budge lean against the outside wall of the trailer, watching the road for Sis's car. Abe's eyes feel heavy. He may have been born on this patch of cold dirt, leaning against a trailer, Elder by his side. He doesn't remember putting his clothes back on, doesn't remember walking outside . . . Doesn't remember calling Sis, now that he thinks about it. Abe knows she's on her way to collect him the way he knows what people are thinking in dreams. The body whose imminent passing he's been mourning has come back to him. Weak, to be sure. Not what it once was. But he senses he can trust it, finally. His brain is foggy, but the relief is so great his eyes are wet with tears. Now that the feeling is gone, he realizes how claustrophobic he'd felt in his own skin.

"How you doin', Abe?" Budge smokes a cigarette rolled from Sis's tobacco and herb mix. True to his words, Budge's creation is perfectly even from tip to tip, like it was factory-made. Abe wishes he could express how staggered he is.

"Woozy," he answers, after a time. He smacks the brass head of the cane between his palms, the movement like a metronome. It's Tóta's cane again, no longer his. "Wrung out. Great. Like I ran a marathon."

"Make sure you drink plenty of water the next few days." Budge blows smoke out, saying what Abe assumes is a prayer. Abe watches the smoke bring Budge's prayer to heaven. The old man holds the cigarette sideways, looking at it. "Man, this is good."

"Water. Got it."

"Lots of water."

"A lot of water, okay." Now that the healing's done, Abe's sure he can coax his great uncle back to the house for dinner. Since he's already asked everyone on the Jacobs side of the family, Abe goes for it. "Uncle Budge? Can I ask you a stupid question?"

Budge arches a brow. *I'm listening*, the brow says.

"Did Mohawks used to eat people?"

I've mentioned this in passing before, but the full story is this: in third grade, Abe read a history book that said Mohawks sliced open the chests of their conquered foes on the battlefield, cut out their hearts, and ate them raw. This was a thick book from the school library with boards worn thin at the edges and a beleaguered binding embossed with the author's name and *History of the North American Indians Native to New York State*. If capital-T Truth didn't come from such a boring, weighty tome, then where would you ever find it? But when Abe got home and bragged to his father about their fierce ancestry, Dad had scoffed. "Abe, don't believe everything you read."

In all the reading Abe has done since, and all the pestering of his relatives, he's never gotten a straight answer. Now here's his great uncle, one of his oldest living relatives, and Abe wants to know the answer to the question he never had the guts to ask Tóta.

"We didn't eat people." Budge rolls his eyes.

Abe nods. He knew it—just bullshit settler propaganda, feeding the stereotype of the savage to make it okay to "cleanse" the valley by killing us all. Or maybe when other Nations tried to explain what we were like to white dudes, it got lost in translation. Either way, bunk.

"Not much, I mean."

Abe slowly turns to look at his great uncle. Budge's expression is inscrutable.

"A fella would have to be real special for us to make him into a meal, innit. The Algonquin say we ate them, but they were pissed over gettin' their asses kicked. Why would we want to eat an enemy? Gettin' eaten was an honor. Say you've got a fast runner. We might take a little from behind the knee, or a nibble on her toe. A strong guy, we fry up a piece a his bicep. When someone wise dies, we go *Dawn of the Dead*. It's why we keep gettin' better with each generation."

"Thanks, Uncle Budge," Abe sighs, "thank you so much for sharing your Elder wisdom."

"Anytime, kid." He flashes the gaps in his smile. "I'm here for you."

Sis's truck appears in the distance. Abe waves, knowing she's too far away to see but too excited to stop himself. He feels goofy, giddy. Life had been narrowed to pain, to accommodation, to anxiety and fear. Now, even though it's decades after he expected it to happen, Abe feels like the world is opening up to him at last.

"Uncle Budge . . ." Abe rests a hand on the old man's shoulder. "You're very special to me. When you die, what piece of you should I eat?"

"I'm a funny son of gun, kid," Budge says. "Even if you don appreciate it. Go on an' eat my tongue. Help you with them poems, anyway."

Abe would love to know if Mohawks really ate people. So would I, come to that. But Budge's telling is about as straight of an answer as an Indian will give you.

A POETRY INTERLUDE WITH
DOMINICK DEER WOODS

I know what you're wondering: Did Budge's healing really cure
Abe? Before we answer that and tie up some other loose ends, it's
time for me to make a confession. When I first introduced myself,
I told you I could write a single poem in which I paralleled eighties
action movies with anti-Native US laws, linked Elizabethan stage
racism to Hollywood racism, and married deuterocanonical stories
with colonial genocidal practices. Well don't hate me, but that poem
didn't exist. I'm sorry, I just wanted to sound smart and cool, innit.
I wanted you to like me.

As we've rolled on, I started to feel guilty for lying to you. So I've
risen to the challenge. Or rather, Abe and I have. This feels different
from our usual efforts, more like setting a trap with very specific bait
in the hope that a particular poem would wander through. It doesn't
have a name. Give it one, if you want. Write it down, burn it, and let
it rise to heaven like a prayer.

    Hanif Abdurraqib told me
    to ask a Black friend
    about The Dozens
    (or rather, he said it at a reading
    but like a joke it's better in first person).
    I knew the concept, as it happens;
    "Your momma so ugly she's got

to sneak up on a glass to get
a drink of water," etc., etc.

Every culture save the contrived one
America teaches like a bedtime story
uses denigration as a love language.

The culture we breathe like toxicants
uses denigration to degrade.

Lethal Weapon 2 gave us villains
trafficking drugs and women
killing people on US soil,
shielded by Diplomatic Immunity.

Sergeant Murtaugh splattered
the villain's brain and
the sold-out theater cheered.
In 1989 schadenfreude looked like gore
dripping down a cistern and
sounded like clapping hands.

But I knew the atrocities of war were
ongoing and legally inviolate.
I stood and told the sold-out crowd
your people so white, they
beat
rob
rape
murder
and bring their valor home
heroes all.

Andrew Jackson told Congress,
"The continent belongs
to the Glorious White Race."
He legitimized Manifest Destiny as
of the Whites, by the Whites, and for the Whites.
Since Savages could not control their many
    shortcomings
(you could say I'm paraphrasing; I say I'm removing
    euphemism),
"They must necessarily yield to our Moral Superiority
and ere long breathe their last."

Andrew Jackson's father
moved from County Antrim.
There, at Carrickfergus Castle,
hung *Judith Beheading Holofernes*,
one of thousands of renderings of the act
    by the Old Masters
        —Judith Slays—Judith Beheads—Judith Kills—
        Judith Murders.

They didn't have Art-O-Ramas in those days.
Painters mixed lead white with iron oxide,
scumbled with yellow earth and mercury sulfate,
shaded with red ochre, yellow ochre, and manganese,
for their warm Renaissance tones.
To capture the tendons popping at her wrists.
The tension in his throat.
His terrified, agonized expression
as her blood-soaked blade saws
his head from his shoulders.

Not a culture of violence
but of
Destiny.

When colonizers took
Manhattan they played
soccer with the Natives'
severed heads
a school fact learned in past-tense.

The Lenape did not give their heads willingly.
The Dutch decapitated the Lenape
to play a civil game of football.
Dutch navigator David Pieterszoon de Vries recorded:
    "Sucklings ripped from their mother's Breasts
    and Hacked to Paces, [sic] in front of their own families
    etc. etc."

During the Dakota War
the 1863 *Daily Republican*
let readers know,
"The State of Minnesota increased the Reward for Dead Indians
to $200 for Every Redskin Sent to Purgatory"

Dozens more scalp bounties
where that came from.
Pick a state.

New York State offered $60 for Kanien'kehá:ka scalps
also known as a year's wages
minus room and board.
($20 for children because nits make lice.)
(I'm supposed to write that slant but I can't.)

Your history so white
it hangs Native bodies on museum walls.
Your history so white
it smelts brass unto statues
clutching Native scalps by the fistful.
Your history so white
it uses Native scrotums
for tobacco pouches.

White Men too tender to listen
to any of this, too fragile
to contemplate the Other.
White men so fragile, they
dressed as women at the Globe.

The woman playing a man in *As You Like It*
was a man playing a woman playing a man.
A gentile wore curls and a caricatured nose
for *The Merchant of Venice*.
A white man painted his face with soot
to play Othello.

Your culture so white
it claims every narrative.
From the stage
to minstrel and movie shows,
white culture fabricates its own rainbow
    reflecting, "This is you."
        "This is you."
        "This is you."

"Iron Eyes" Cody cried
over roadside trash in 1971

and America wept with him.
"Iron Eyes" Cody was Italian.
Italians became white in '76
when *Rocky* won an Oscar.

White man so white
he can't take a joke
but it's fine
We never found white men
all that funny either.

Sixteen

t's a fine spring evening, hot enough to steam your sinuses, and the sun is going down. Abe's walking from his bachelor pad in Little Haiti to open mic night at the Villain Theater. His pace is vigorous—no cane required—and will get him there in twenty minutes, enough time to catch you up with what's been going on with Abe since he returned to Miami four months ago.

Budge's healing cured Abe. In the weeks afterward, the rash retreated and disappeared. Abe's lesions dried into fibrous scabs, like his legs were covered with dry moss or fungus, and then shed in layers, forever altering the topography of his shins and calves. There are bumpy coronas of purple-brown skin where the inflamed edges of the lesions once were. Where rotten flesh fell away, white indentations remain. *Trouble surrounded us but it's fading into the distance*, this skin-wampum says. Pain still randomly travels around Abe's joints. Most days, he can tune it out. Many days, there's no pain at all.

Dr. Weisberg wouldn't say "cured," of course, rather "remission." Her faith lies in IMDH inhibitors, DMARDs, and targeted approaches. She'd had Abe on Amethopterone since November, but switched him from pills to weekly injections when he returned to

Miami. To hear her tell it, the fluctuating milligrams caused by taking a medication orally explained why his lesions hadn't improved previously. Abe is happy to give her the win, because in his heart he knows better.

Abe flew back to Miami after Christmas. He found an apartment in Little Haiti, a new build on the alley behind Edison High, modern bones fleshed out by things that bring Abe joy—artwork, bookshelves, and a full-size Saatva Classic mattress his family pitched in to buy him for Christmas. He doesn't have a TV or Wi-Fi. Instead, he opens all the windows and writes like a man obsessed. Not to be published, or because of the Sword of Damocles SNiP is hanging over him. Not even to make sure Alex is filled with regret. Abe writes because it brings him joy.

To finalize their divorce, Abe and Alex only had to appear in front of a judge once. "No cane?" she'd asked. Abe had shaken his head. Afterward, she'd talked him into breakfast. Abe hadn't wanted to go, but he'd thought he owed her that much after all the time they'd shared. They hit a Latin café around the corner from the courthouse.

"Where are you living now?" Alex said, once they'd ordered.

Abe found it hard to believe she'd asked. He didn't know how to express it without snapping at her—*Why'd you split us up, if you're so interested in where I spend my time?* or something along those lines—so he sipped his coffee and let the silence draw out.

"I guess I don't need to know." She looked down at her coffee mug. "You're so different." She made it sound like a miracle and an accusation.

"Am I?" Abe swallowed past the thickening in his throat. "Well, you would know."

They made small talk, getting over the awkwardness long enough for inside jokes and callbacks to better days to emerge. She lectured him on society's obsession with fidelity, told him artists hate conventional relationships because monogamy only works on paper.

She said they should stay friends, with an emphasis that implied more. Abe's good cheer immediately dried up.

"Maybe," he said weakly. She didn't seem to understand how badly she'd broken his heart. They split the check, hugged, and he hasn't seen her since.

Abe strolls down Fifty-Ninth. People laugh and talk shit on their porches and in chairs on the front lawn. Abe soaks up their energy as he passes. He stops at North Miami Avenue, looking across at Lemon City Park. Little Haiti isn't called Lemon City anymore, but the soil here still gives especially sweet fruit to folks lucky enough to have backyard mango, avocado, and lemon trees.

You can't see him like I can, but he's walking tall in his Doc Martens, wearing rust-colored jeans and an Ahkwesáhsne-flag-purple t-shirt with white block letters that reads, "Corn, Beans, and Squash the Patriarchy." He's talking under his breath, repeating his lines for the umpteenth time. Knowing them so well they're second nature is paramount to giving a good reading.

He crosses the street, passing in front of Toussaint L'Ouverture Elementary School—named for Haiti's answer to George Washington, if Washington had been born enslaved rather than enslaving people. A slight breeze chills him. He recently got a "mohawk" haircut that suits him down to the ground, but he had no idea shaving his head would make him so susceptible to wind, no matter how hot and humid the air. With the silver shaved from the sides of his head, and more weight on his bones, his age is impossible to guess. The stripe on top is a Pawnee hairdo rather than the scalplock Mohawks actually wore, but sometimes to get the point across you have to show people what they expect to see, even if it's wrong. If you're feeling generous, you could call the haircut an external commitment to his internal self.

Abe comes to the intersection of Sixty-Ninth and Northeast Second, looking across the street at the Villain Theater. His heart, already beating fast with nervous anticipation, double-pounds when he sees it. The corner building is lit for the event, illuminating the red walls and blue awnings, all of it trimmed in gold. In the smattering of people outside, vaping, holding drinks, and talking, Abe sees Valentina, the Brazilian American you met briefly at Benny's pig roast. No longer a bookseller but a successful pharmaceutical rep with a condo on Key Biscayne, Val's been taking Abe out on weekends, trying to get him laid. He's not at all interested in a one-night stand, and not ready for anything like a Cheyenne, but he appreciates the company (and that she always foots the bill). Having been partnered since he was a teenager, Abe finds himself content being alone.

When Abe walks up, Val kisses him on the cheek and gives him a hug. "Everyone's inside," she says, flicking her cigarette away. More people drink and mingle in the lobby. Apart from Valentina, you don't know the half dozen folks who've come to see Abe. Caught up in his own shit, Abe has been a piss-poor friend, but he's done turning down invites and hiding in his head. His old friends love the new haircut. They're excited to hear him read.

The theater has rows of cushioned folding chairs and a dozen tables in front of the stage. It seats maybe sixty, maybe eighty. There's a waitlist to read but Abe signed up the week before to reserve a spot. He gave the host his own name instead of mine. Kind of broke my heart, you know? But it also makes me proud.

He sits in the third row, not hearing a word of anyone else's performance because he's still running lines in his head. When the host calls his name, Abe forgoes the stairs on either side and steps dead center onto the stage. He perfected the move during his musical theater days; it makes him seem outsized and grabs the audience's attention. With the haircut and patented one-step ascension, Abe knows he better bring something special to the stage. It's been a while, but he believes he can make good use of the time he's been given.

My mother was born and raised in Akwesasne, and I'm an enrolled member of the Saint Regis Mohawk Tribe (the white name for the American side of Akwesasne). I've used the spelling "Ahkwesáhsne" in this text, a spelling I've encountered online and on some maps but have rarely seen in person, because visiting the reservation can't offer the same perspective as someone who was born and raised there. Likewise, "Hotinonshón:ni" for Haudenosaunee, as a bit of distance because *Old School Indian* is primarily a work of fiction. This is the Akwesasne of my imagination. For anything I got right, thank my family—both those who came from there and those who still live there. For everything I got wrong, blame me.

Including Akwesasne, six reservations speak Kanien'kéha. The Kanien'kéha used here comes from a language course taught at SUNY Potsdam, which originated with the Mohawk Language Standardization Project of 1993, wherein hundreds of Elders, teachers, and parents (and one linguist) worked to ensure dialectical and spelling differences among the various Mohawk Nations would not contribute to language loss.

When Budge Billings (based on my Great Uncle Louis Burning Sky "Butch" Conners, who was never a drunk but an avid softball player) begins to tell a story, he refers to a time "when dogs could talk." I learned the phrase from Kiowa author N. Scott Momaday, the first Native American to win a Pulitzer, while he was working on his play *The Indolent Boys* at Syracuse University in 1994. When a Kiowa said, "This was a long time ago, when dogs could talk," it alerted the listener that they were about to hear the sort of story a non-Native might call a fable, myth, or legend. I couldn't find the Mohawk equivalent. Probably because we start every gathering with the Words We Say Before All Else, the Thanksgiving Address. I loved the way "when dogs could talk" walked and talked on the page, and every phrase I tried instead felt like a pale substitute. I don't think N. Scott Momaday would mind but the pan-Indianism bothers me, so I'm pointing it out.

Systemic Necrotizing Periarteritis (SNiP) is not real, nor are any of the specific conditions Abe mentions, or the drugs which treated him. Polyarteritis Nodosa (PAN) is. As of this writing, I'm in remission.

The Missing and Murdered Indigenous Women movie Abe thinks of when looking at his family—*Wind River*—came out in 2017, so Abe couldn't have heard of it in 2016. Now we have *Rutherford Falls* and *Reservation Dogs* and *Echo* and *Dark Winds* and *Resident Alien* and a cartoon for children called *Spirit Rangers* and a whole damn episode of Disney's *What If... ?* spoken in Kanien'kéha, so Abe would be gratified to see representation moving in the right direction. I know I am.

While we're on Taylor Sheridan, contrary to his remarks in June 2023, *Wind River* did not change any laws. Native activists and advocates—primarily women—have been pushing the Violence Against Women Act (VAWA) since 1994. In 2022, a database was created for Missing and Murdered Indigenous Women, and it's finally possible for Natives to prosecute US citizens for committing rapes (and other crimes) in Indian Country.

When Dominick introduces himself, he admonishes the reader, "Stop amusing yourself to death." *Amusing Ourselves to Death: Public Discourse in the Age of Show Business* is a 1985 book by Neil Postman. I name-dropped it because it's worth your time.

Tori Amos's *Under the Pink* tour took place in '94, not '96.

"Consulting Dr. Google" is a phrase taken from Roxane Gay's essay "Feel Me. See Me. Hear Me. Reach Me."

While the number of court-ordered involuntary sterilizations pales compared to the number committed by average doctors who believed they were performing a public good, government-sponsored involuntary sterilization is ongoing. Thirty-two states started eugenics panels in the early twentieth century, focused on people with disabilities, with immigrants and people of color getting sucked into the government machine as well. In the 1970s, these panels replaced the word "eugenics" with euphemisms like "social protection." As of this writing, forced sterilization is still legal in thirty-one of those thirty-two states, committed in state prisons and Immigration and Customs Enforcement (ICE) facilities under every presidential administration since George W. Bush.

Mary Ann Shaffer's epistolary novel that Dominick struggles to name is *The Guernsey Literary and Potato Peel Pie Society*, which was finished by Annie Barrows—Shaffer's niece—after Shaffer died.

If you're in the market for a "Corn, Beans, and Squash the Patriarchy" t-shirt, please be sure to order one from the original designer, MOHAWKEMOTIONS, on Spring.

In the seventies, stand-up comedian Charlie Hill of the Oneida had a joke. He said he struggled doing stand-up because whites thought Indians didn't have a sense of humor. Then he deadpanned, "We never thought you were too funny, either." The last line of the unnamed poem comes from this joke.

ACKNOWLEDGMENTS

The epic journey from solipsism, self-doubt, insecurity, distraction, procrastination, and general laziness to published author is not a trek made alone. Apologies to anyone I forgot.

Thanks to Mrs. Temple, my seventh grade English teacher, who taught me that the right editor could make my writing into something infinitely better than I could create on my own.

Thanks to Andi, who said I'd get everything I wanted out of life through my writing. Your support was almost enough to silence my inner critic.

Thanks to Becky, who changed the name of my backup drive from "writing" to "BRILLIANCE!" at a time when I was doubting myself.

Thanks to JC, who gifted me the hyperbole a budding writer needs to stick with it by calling me "the most talented writer in Miami" when I was getting started, and who also arranged for me to read my stories in front of his students. Nothing will teach you humility about your work faster than trying to keep the attention of dozens of teenagers.

Thanks to Carl Lennertz; an industry insider enjoying my work made me want to keep at it. Thanks to Eric Svenson for putting us in touch.

Thanks to Debra Linn, who pushed me to sell myself and went out of her way to make industry connections for me (on which I never followed up). Your enthusiasm for my writing helped keep me going.

Thanks to Mitchell Kaplan, who once said, "You've got the gift, kiddo" after reading some early stories—high praise from a literary titan. I appreciate you letting me set my own hours; sometimes the muse grabs hold, and a 9:00 a.m. start time just won't do (thanks as well to Noah and Joanna for covering for me).

Thanks to La Nosti, who has—in ways great and small—treated my debut novel as an inevitability. Your faith remained unshakeable when mine was not.

Thanks to Elena and Alistair, steadfast fans of my blogging days who made me feel like my voice would find an audience.

Thanks to Paola Mendez, Liz Tracy, and Marta Viciedo for publishing my words about books. You made me feel like the book world needed me, and that readers might dig what I have to say.

Thanks to Andrea Askowitz and Allison Langer. Writing Class Radio opened up a world of nonfiction and helped keep my writing muscles in shape. Thanks for the breaks.

Thanks to P. Scott Cunningham, who took me to lunch and pointed out that other than Connie Ogle at *The Herald*, there weren't any Miami-based book reviews besides mine. You called it "important," and that gave me hope, even as it terrified me.

Thanks to my O.G. writers' group, Evelyn Infante, Jeffrey Slone, and the rotating cast of characters who passed through to fulfill that all-important fourth slot—Amanda, Carlos, George, Jose, Larissa (thanks for sharing your obituary and encouraging me to write my own), Rebecca, Vic, and likely others I've forgotten. We got nothing published, doubled Fox's vodka order, and I have no regrets.

Thanks to the writers' group who took *Old School Indian* from a short story to a novella to a novel: Diana Abu-Jaber, Jake Cline, Scott Eason, Andrea Gollin, Elizabeth Hanly (who suggested adding a healer), David Hayes, and Ana Veciana-Suarez, with special guests Ana Menendez and Cristina Nosti (who encouraged me to go full autofiction). A group with better snacks does not exist, and the feedback isn't half bad either.

Thanks to Lis Mesa, Michelle Massanet, Leah Messing, Leandro Pereda, Nilsa Rivera, and Daniela Ustariz, the writers' group who helped me find Dominick Deer Woods.

Thanks to Melissa Danaczko. There's a worse version of this book—and frankly, a worse version of my life—which never met you. To quote Rod Tidwell in *Jerry Maguire*, you are my Ambassador of Quan.

Thanks to Erin Wicks. Working with you was a joy which sometimes hurt, in the best possible way. Your insights made me push myself further than I thought I could go, and made the book so much richer. Thanks in particular for your work on the poem "Solatium." You found a stick-it-in-and-break-it-off ending which elevated the whole thing.

Thanks to Rachel Kowal, who knows all the rules and when to break them.

Thanks to Caolinn Douglas, Emily Morris, Sarah Schneider, Chloe Texier-Rose, and the rest of the fine folks at Zando for all of your hard work and support.

Thanks to the good folks at Hillman Grad—Naomi Funabashi, Rishi Rajani, and Lena Waithe—for taking a chance on a middle-aged debut author.

Thanks to Emily Mahon for a gorgeous cover.

Thanks to current and former booksellers Alexa, Alexander, Allison, Alyssa, Ana, Bella, Betsy, Brandon, Caroline, Chris A., Chris P., CN, Cristina L., Cristina R., Dan, Dana, Debra, Doni, Ed, Eden, Elena, Elizabeth, Emily, ES, Gael, Gail, Geoff, George Henry, Hillary, Jeanne, JoJo, Joy, Katherine, Laura, Linda, Lissette, Marquietta, Marsha, Michelle N., MK, Nicole, NLW, Raquel, Robert, Sean, Stephanie, Steve, Viv, and Wendy, for marketing advice.

Thanks to Alex Jacobs (aka Karoniaktatie, aka Dr. Mohawk, aka Uncle Alex) for the use of "Santa Fe Dude" for the cover art, and working with Emily to re-create it. Your artistic life is a poem that has inspired me over the years.

Thanks to Aunt Jeri, Aunt Val, Aunt Elly, Uncle Mark, and Uncle Nicky. How lucky was I, growing up with so many moms and dads? You had bigger parts before the editing process, I swear.

Thanks to Shane, Shawn, and Shannon. Growing up with you as sometimes siblings was the best. Some of our fabric doesn't match but together we make a beautiful quilt.

Thanks to Cass and AJ. I don't have the words to capture what it meant—and means—to have the two of you to look up to, so I'll just say I love you both.

Thanks to Mom and Dad. You always accepted whatever craziness I came up with. It was a long road but we're here. I love you both so much.

Thanks to Tóta. I wish I remembered more of what you taught me. I wish I'd asked more questions. I wish you were still here.

Thanks to the writing of Akwesasne Notes and Ted C. Williams for de-colonizing my thoughts as best you could before I sat down to revise.

I've had all sorts of writers groups but I've never managed to pin down any poets on a regular basis, so thanks to Hanif Abdurraqib, Jericho Brown, Franny Choi, Natalie Diaz, Joy Harjo, Terrance Hayes, Eugenia Leigh, Layli Long Soldier, O, Miami!, Warsan Shire, and Ocean Vuong. I could not have found any of the poems in this book if you hadn't beaten the path before me.

Thanks to Ani DiFranco, Carole King, Florence & The Machine, G. Love & Special Sauce, King Crimson, Lana Del Rey, Luscious Jackson, the Magnetic Fields, Nina Simone, Prince, Tori Amos, and especially Johnny Cash for setting the writing mood. Thanks to Beyoncé and Thelonious Monk for providing the proper editing tone.

And finally, thanks to Michi, who sees all that I am and doesn't shy away, and all that I could be and helps get me there. Before you, I'd forgotten what love felt like. Alex's birthday poem would not exist without you. Let's keep creating an amazing life together.

AARON JOHN CURTIS is an enrolled member of the Saint Regis Mohawk Tribe, which he'll tell you is the white name for the American side of Akwesasne. Aaron has judged for the Center for Fiction First Novel Prize, the Southern Independent Booksellers Alliance Prizes, the 2019 Kirkus Prize for Nonfiction, and the 2021 National Book Award for Nonfiction. Since 2004, Aaron has been quartermaster at Books & Books, Miami's largest independent bookstore. He lives in Miami.